PAST THIS
POINT

NICOLE MABRY

Past This Point

Red Adept Publishing, LLC

104 Bugenfield Court

Garner, NC 27529

http://RedAdeptPublishing.com/

First Print Edition: August 2019

Cover Art by Streetlight Graphics

This is a work of fiction. Names, characters, places, and incidents either are the product of the author's imagination or are used fictitiously, and any resemblance to locales, events, business establishments, or actual persons—living or dead—is entirely coincidental.

For Zeke

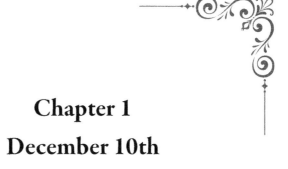

Chapter 1
December 10th

Charlotte from accounting was patient zero at my office. She had come in just after Thanksgiving with a bright-red nose and spent half the day coughing into a tissue before her boss told her to go home. The next day, three others coughed and sneezed until they, too, were sent home. Within a week, half of my coworkers were gone, and many of those who remained were sick.

My medicine cabinet was full of immune-system supplements because I'd always been a slight hypochondriac. But news reports on the virus were coming in from all across the Eastern states, saying it was a vicious flu strain they hadn't seen before and that it was resistant to all medications and vaccinations. People were just going to have to ride this one out, they said.

As a project manager at Burke & Davis, a big graphic design firm in Midtown, I was one of the lucky few to have my own office, so I barricaded myself behind its glass walls. I kept my door closed to discourage drop-ins and frequently used the hand sanitizer stations outside of every elevator bank and bathroom. Instead of ordering lunch, I brought food from home so I wouldn't have to venture outside my disinfected sanctuary. Every time I heard someone cough, I squirted sanitizer into my hands from the jumbo-sized bottle on my desk.

I tracked my remaining coworkers' movements throughout the day, tensing any time someone came near my door. As I was finishing up a few loose ends before heading home, my boss wandered over to chat with my team, and I feared a breach was imminent. He glanced at me through the glass while talking to Lance, my coordinator. My fingers shook over the keyboard as I distractedly responded to an email, one eye still on my boss. He turned and walked toward my door. My body stiffened. I silently prayed he would hang a left back to his own office. Instead, he walked straight to mine and opened the door.

I tried to calm my nerves as he spent twenty minutes pacing the room, complaining about a client and scattering his germs all over. Every time he came near my desk, I leaned away from him, trying to make it look casual.

"Do you agree, Karis?"

Frantically, I reviewed what he'd just said. *Something about adjusting the estimate to accommodate the client's demands?*

"Well?" he asked impatiently.

"Sorry. Yes, I completely agree. I'll send you a new estimate to approve by tomorrow. Doug, I wanted to ask—with this flu outbreak, maybe it's better if I work from home? I really can't afford to get sick right now."

His face scrunched into a frown. "If you aren't sick, we need you in the office."

My hopes dashed, I replied, "Of course."

He nodded then sneezed twice into his hand as he turned to leave. I watched in horror as he turned my doorknob with that same hand and walked out, not bothering to close the door. I jumped up and cleaned the handle with Lysol, sprayed some in the air for good measure, then quickly shut the door. On the other side of the glass, Lance gave me an odd look. Ignoring him, I reached into my top drawer for an Airborne lozenge, imagining invisible flu molecules flying through the air. My mind was already buzzing with which supplements I'd take when I got home.

I waited an extra fifteen minutes for the cluster of coworkers around the elevator to thin out before I left. In my twenties, I'd found crowds exhilarating and fed off the collective energy. It was a large part of why I moved to New York City. But lately, I'd come to hate crowds and avoided them as much as I possibly could. It was no easy task in the city. We were on top of each other in the streets, elevators, and stores. We breathed in the exhalations of those around us on the subway, passing germs around like rumors. One was never truly alone in the city, and I'd begun to feel anger that bordered on rage if someone even slightly encroached on the ten inches of space I'd staked claim on in the train. I felt my anticipatory irritation pressing up from my stomach the moment I pushed the down button on the elevator.

My office building housed countless other companies, and as I rode the elevator down to the lobby, the small carpeted space filled up with men in suits and women in high heels. They towered over me since I was only five foot one and had given up on wearing heels in my first month. I felt claustrophobically hemmed in. The urge to scream was overwhelming. When the doors opened, I joined the short line of people at the exit door, each holding it open for the person behind them to catch as they walked through. I tucked my shoulder-length brown hair behind my ears and pulled on a cream-colored wool beanie. A cold snap from the north had swept in the night before and made my eyes water and my nose run that morning on my way to work. When the man in front of me got to the door, he rushed through the opening before it closed and didn't bother holding the edge for me. The glass door slammed shut in my face. My simmering annoyance turned into full-fledged, boiling fury.

I yelled through the glass, "Seriously?!"

The man glanced back and shrugged as he merged into traffic. I wrenched the door open and marched to the sidewalk. My hands were shaking. The man was just three feet away, moving in the opposite direction from where I was headed. I feared if I did nothing, I would be seething all night.

I waited until he again stole another look in my direction. His eyes met mine, and I screamed, "Asshole!"

It came out louder than I'd intended, and everyone in the area flashed a confused look at me. The man raised his arm in the air and flipped me off before the undertow of the crowd swallowed him. I shook my head and clenched my hands over and over in an effort to curtail my anger. After taking several deep breaths, I adopted my long-perfected linebacker stance, clasping my handbag under my chest with each arm rigidly forming a V on either side of my body. Being adjacent to Times Square meant that the short distance from my office to the train was packed with oblivious tourists who hadn't bothered to learn the common courtesy rule—stay to the right—that seasoned New Yorkers knew was imperative for smooth flow of traffic on the sidewalks. I plowed through the crowd, knocking several bodies with my stubborn elbows along the way. They turned to me with shocked faces and outraged comebacks that died on their lips. I'd never had a resting bitch face, but over the last few months, I was sure one had set up residence in my eyes and on my mouth, obviously causing most to rethink challenging me. I'd made a conscious effort to appear pleasant to my coworkers, but I no longer garnered that perfunctory closed-lip half smile and nod from the strangers I passed in the hallways.

As I waited on the subway platform, more E-train straphangers gathered around me, but not as many as I'd come to expect. Usually, the platform was jam-packed during rush hour, but the crowd was only three people deep. When the train finally came, the doors opened, revealing a large woman with a stroller blocking the entrance to the car. The people around me grumbled and walked to another set of doors to board the train. On any other day, I might have followed suit. But not today. With my hackles already up, I felt emboldened.

I looked at the woman and said curtly, "Could you move your stroller? This is an entrance."

The woman shot me a dirty look, rolled her eyes, and sighed loudly before angling the stroller slightly to the right, creating only a few inches of space. I stepped onto the train and, using my knee, scooted the stroller several more inches. The woman whispered, "Bitch," as I walked by. I decided to let that one go, which proved incredibly difficult. In my mind, I came up with several good retorts. The desire to snap back at her was strong, but I'd already had one confrontation since leaving my office, so I tried to rein it in.

After finding a spacious spot against the opposite doors, I noticed that some people had surgical masks over their faces. I pulled my thick wool scarf up over my mouth and nose in an effort to join that bandwagon. No one in my car seemed to be sick, but the first symptom was a fever, so I couldn't be certain.

At the next stop a man got on and coughed as he sat down two rows away. I moved farther down the car, grabbing the poles with my gloved hands as I went. When I got to the end, I turned and saw several others had followed me. We glanced at each other in understanding. The guy coughed again, and two more people joined us. The mass exodus left the man alone on the other side. His chin dropped to his chest, and his shoulders slumped in dejection. *I know how you feel.*

While the train muscled through the tunnel from Manhattan to Queens, I unintentionally locked eyes with a woman standing across from me, and I saw familiar heartbreak and solitude on her face. In that moment of shared scrutiny, we passed miserable details of our lives to each other. I held her gaze in a momentary game of chicken, wondering whose life was more depressing. As I suspected, she looked away first.

My last boyfriend, Brian, had dumped me three months before. A solid eight years of looking for love in the city, online and otherwise, had completely dashed any hopes of finding the right guy, and I had stopped bothering altogether when Brian entered the scene. He sent me a message on a dating site I hardly checked anymore, and something about his sincere tone—as opposed to the mindless "Hey, Sexy Lady!" messages I usually received—made me want to meet him.

On our first date, he took me to Menkui Tei, his favorite ramen place, and we talked over glasses of sake and bowls of pork noodle soup. Even though the date went well, he didn't move in for a kiss at the end. To my surprise, he texted me the next day to set up another date. Six months later, we were still going strong, and when he told me he was falling in love with me, I said it back, surprised that I actually meant it. I hadn't realized how strong my feelings were until that moment.

When he'd invited me to a picnic in Central Park, a gesture that was unlike him, I'd been hopeful that our relationship was moving forward. I had to admit that part of my happiness with Brian was the intense relief I felt at finally being in a solid relationship. But the minute I saw him waiting for me at the Sixty-Sixth Street east-side entrance to the park, I knew something had gone terribly wrong. He had no basket of food, no wine, and no blanket, just a worried look on his face. I stood rooted to the concrete, causing people to bump past me, lost in their own dramas while I contemplated running in the other direction. I watched Brian force one foot in front of the other, my eyes never leaving his guilty face. I could have warmed my expression, smiled, or looked away, but I didn't. It was too late for that.

I was no stranger to the ending of a relationship. For men, dating in New York City seemed like a veritable paradise with endless available options. For women, however, it was a nightmare, at least if the goal was a real relationship. At thirty-eight, I'd been on too many dates to count, most ending with one or both of us not interested. Worse was the guy pretending to be interested. That usually began with him telling me how much he liked me, how *we* should go do this or that together, or how he was going to lend me his favorite book, and it ended with the stock "I had a great time. Let's do this again. I'll text you." Spoiler: he wouldn't.

When Brian stopped in front of me, it was written all over his face that it was over. His hands were thrust deeply into his pockets, and he kept nodding to people as they walked by as if grateful for any reason not to look at me.

I squared my shoulders in an effort to brace myself for what was about to come. "Someone steal your basket?" I asked, my eyes narrowed.

"Listen, Karis," he said nervously, "you're an amazing woman, better than I deserve, actually. You should be the perfect woman for me, but..." He paused, his eyes straying from mine.

I vaguely heard him move on to some variation of "it's not you, it's me," and it was as if he was reciting a poem that we both already knew by heart, "Ode to Dissolution."

"I don't know what I want or who I am right now. I don't even know what I'm doing with my life."

"But what about everything you said about this being the best relationship you've ever been in? About how you could really see us going the distance? You said you were in love with me. You're forty years old, never been married, no kids. Shouldn't you have some of this figured out by now?"

"You're right. I should. But I haven't, and that worries me. I need to go figure out my life before committing to a relationship, and I need to do that alone. I did mean all of those things at the time, but... I guess I don't anymore," he finished lamely, his eyes pleading with me to act like a good dumpee and feign understanding.

I just stared and watched him squirm in my silence. He'd clearly run out of words, so I turned and walked away, pushing past a group of teenagers arguing about who was the best dancer. I heard him call my name once, but I didn't look back. I ran to the train and hopped onto the first car that came. I felt the burden of despair wash over me, its force pulling me down as though it carried a few extra ounces of gravity. Another promising relationship was down the drain. As I bitterly eyed all the happy couples, part of a private club whose ranks now excluded me, I made a resolution. Past this point, I was done dating, done hoping for someone who was never going to come. That was the first day of the rest of my officially single life.

I snapped out of my reverie when the automated tone sounded with the train's opening doors. I stopped at the grocery store on my way home. Over the past two days, while the outbreak progressed, I'd been stockpiling supplies and dog food. I couldn't really say if it was irrational or not but figured there was no harm if it was, and no one would ever know anyway. My dog, Zeke, was overjoyed by all this added food. He seemed to be wondering when he'd be able to get his paws on it and did an occasional drive-by, sniffing the bags of food and looking longingly in my direction, though that look could've also been worry that his once semi-sane owner had officially gone nuts. He might have had a point.

First, I headed to the pasta-and-rice aisle to stock up on dry goods. With my basket half full, I walked over to the snack aisle, veering around a man picking out soup from an endcap display of sale items. After I passed him, he sniffed. He didn't appear sick, but I watched him for a minute anyway.

I was so lost in my suspicious stalking that I didn't notice a woman coming up behind me until she said, "Excuse me!"

Startled, I glanced back and mumbled, "Sorry."

I moved to the side, and when she squeezed by me, I got a look into her basket. Hers was filled with dry goods, too, almost all the way to the top. She looked in my basket, then her eyes traveled up to mine. The annoyance was replaced with a look of understanding and a quick smile as if we were in on something together.

The man pushed his cart past our aisle and sneezed into a tissue, interrupting our silent conversation. Our heads whipped toward him. I gave the woman a quick nod and followed her farther down the aisle, distancing myself from the man. We tossed crackers, chips, and Little Debbie snacks into our baskets then hurried to the checkout area.

While the cashier loaded my groceries into doubled plastic bags, she cleared her throat. When she was done, she held out the receipt. Her nails had been bitten down to the quick, the skin around them red and inflamed. I stared at the receipt, my eyes conjuring up glowing germs flickering around the paper.

"Ma'am?" she asked, thrusting the strip of paper at me impatiently.

"Can you just throw it away?" I asked.

She frowned before dropping the receipt into the trash. I scowled back and strode toward the exit. Before I walked through the sliding doors, I glanced back while adjusting the bags in my hands. The woman from the aisle was watching me. We smiled at each other, and I turned to go home.

The second I walked through my front door, I smelled chili verde simmering in the crockpot, a recipe handed down from my mom. After dropping the bags near the rapidly growing pile in my spare room, I changed into jeans and harnessed Zeke for his evening walk.

Downstairs, we stopped at a tree so he could sniff out the scents of other dogs. The thin coat I'd foolishly thrown on wasn't thick enough to combat the cold, and I shivered when a strong gust of wind blew down my street. Zeke, however, was enjoying the air flowing through his soft white fur. His head was high, and he was panting as he paused to enjoy the breeze. He was half American Eskimo and half cocker spaniel—they called it a Cockamo. His Eskimo coat was so thick that he almost always ran hot.

An old woman wearing a surgical mask passed us, pushing a utility cart full of bottled water. She shot me an intense grimace, warning me with her eyes of some imminent calamity. Shaken, I turned away as Zeke pulled me to the next tree. I was probably reading too much into that look.

At the end of the street, we crossed and made our way back up the block. Zeke ventured into the cement planter bordering a lofty oak tree and squatted in a patch of dirt to do his business, and a man coughed violently in the house nearest to us. The wet hacking followed by spitting made the hairs rise on my neck, and my skin felt clammy. I rushed Zeke through the rest of the walk, tugging him away from poles and shrubs while he looked up at me, annoyed.

I ran up the stairs. Zeke, an unwilling participant in my hasty retreat, dragged his feet as I pulled him up each flight. When we got to our floor, I leaned against the wall and tried to catch my breath. I was anxious and ill at ease, feeling as if I couldn't escape the flu no matter how careful I was. It was everywhere.

In an effort to calm myself down, I put Damien Rice on my iPod, poured myself a glass of wine, and started slicing and sautéing onions for the cilantro rice to accompany the tender pork stew. My commitment to an unsocial life had allowed me the time to get back into cooking, something that comforted me in a way that nothing else could. I'd learned from my mother how to make everything from scratch, and I heard my mom's words in my ear, correcting my dicing and measuring, making me feel less alone. My kitchen, while a bit outdated with its fifties-style stove and black-and-white-checkerboard tiles, was spacious and had a big window that overlooked a small park.

I felt that certain foods went with different moods. When I was sad, I wanted pasta, grilled cheese sandwiches, or fried chicken with mashed potatoes and buttery corn on the cob. When I was happy, I craved steak, fresh vegetables, and chocolate. When I was angry, I could kill a Halloween-sized bag of Reese's Peanut Butter Cups in under ten minutes. But in my current state, bored and lonely, I wanted slow-roasted pork that fell off the bone, my aunt's chicken mole that took two days to make, and homemade sweet pastries. Perfecting my peanut butter cookies helped keep the apathy at bay.

Since the breakup, I'd learned to wear my hardened personality like a coat of armor. While I ate dinner, I wondered if that was why I still hadn't gotten sick. Others were out socializing and busy being part of society, sharing their lives, experiences, and the flu. I didn't want any part of that society or their germs. The loneliness was easier to take than the continual line of commitment-phobic, always-looking-for-something-better men who had sucked the soul right out of me. I felt better about my self-imposed exile, heavyhearted but realistic about my future.

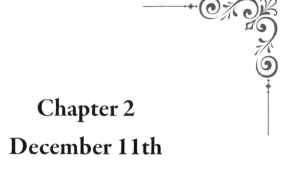

Chapter 2
December 11th

I tossed and turned all night, intermittently dreaming about the man in the grocery store following me down aisle after aisle. I finally gave up around six thirty and crawled out of bed. I put water and grounds in the coffee maker and hit the start button, but my refrigerator revealed that I was out of cream, and the grocery store didn't open for another hour. I sighed and switched off the appliance.

I slipped on my sneakers, leashed Zeke, and headed down to The Burly Bean, coffee's answer to Jamba Juice. Everything was organic with fancy names and even fancier price tags. I usually avoided shops like that, favoring small, family-run bodegas. But it was the only place in my neighborhood open so early. The anticipation of The Bean's long line made me even crankier than usual.

I clipped Zeke's leash to the bike rack outside. As I turned to walk into the cafe, a man looking at his phone exited and almost plowed right into me. I took a step back to avoid running into him, but he didn't even look up.

"Excuse me!" I said loudly.

Startled, he finally glanced at me. "Oh, I'm sorry! I didn't see you there," he said with a hint of an accent before going back to tapping the keys on his phone.

"I'm sure you didn't with your nose buried in your phone."

With his eyes still on the phone, he nodded and smiled as if I'd just given him a compliment. But he did reach over with one arm and pull the door open for me. For some reason, it irritated me. *How can I be annoyed with him when he's doing something nice?* I felt cheated of the opportunity to be angry. I gave him a tight smile and walked through the door. I was surprised to find the café virtually empty. Only two people sat in front of the big-screen TV tuned to the *Today Show*, and one employee worked behind the counter.

When I stepped up, the perky cashier looked my way, and I could almost hear the ding from her wide smile. "Good morning. What can I get for you today?"

"Can I get a small coffee with cream and sugar?"

"Of course you can! What kind of coffee would you like?"

"Just coffee, regular coffee."

Her smile faltered for a second but quickly returned. "For here or to go?"

"To go."

"All right. That'll be four fifty-three."

I begrudgingly swiped my card, thinking I could have bought three coffees for that price at Kwan's deli, and mumbled my thanks.

I stood at the counter and watched Zeke through the window while she poured my coffee.

A few minutes later, she handed over a paper cup with a protective sleeve. Just as I was about to take a much-needed sip, she said, "Have a wonderful day. Just remember, every day is full of new possibilities!"

I scowled. "You see this coffee in my hand, right?"

Her smile didn't crack, but fear rose in her eyes. "Yes, I do. But it's not just coffee. It's great coffee!" She was really committed to the chipper act.

"So clearly, I haven't had my coffee yet. Do you really think I'm ready for your overly optimistic slogans right now?" I knew I was being surly, but for some reason, I felt the need to put the girl in her place.

Her face fell, and she muttered, "I'm sorry, ma'am. I'm just trying to be nice."

I felt like an ogre. "Look, it's not you. It's me. I'm sorry. Have a good day," I said as I walked away, embarrassed. I had no idea why I thought going off on that barista would make me feel better. It was exactly why I wasn't fit to be in society anymore.

As I was about to push through the door, one of the other customers, a wiry man with glasses, said, "Hey, can you turn this up?"

I looked over at the TV while the cashier raised the volume. The screen had changed to say "Breaking News" with a ticker at the bottom slowly inching across the screen: *Ten people confirmed dead from recent flu outbreak.*

That got my attention. *Dead?* That was unsettling. My hand fell from the door, and I walked closer to the television. I took a sip of my coffee—and I had to admit, it *was* great coffee—as the cashier came around the counter to join us.

The image changed to a newswoman staring intensely at the camera. "Doctors are baffled by this rare strain of the flu. We go now to Dr. Herbert Schiffer with the Center for Disease Control."

A big man with thick glasses and a lab coat appeared on the screen. "We've never seen anything like it. We've tried every medication, every vaccine, and they do nothing to this mutation. We have designated it as NOS-9 because of its non-specific properties and symptoms. This is a deadly virus, and we are working day and night to find some way to diminish its effects."

The anchorwoman came back on and announced a press conference before the scene shifted again. The mayor of New York stood on a small platform in front of a crowd of reporters.

He walked over to the podium, shuffled some papers, and cleared his throat a few times. When he looked up, he seemed worried and unsure of himself. "As of last night, the virus that has been sweeping across the eastern half of the United States has become deadly. Reports have come in from several states, some as far as Louisiana, confirming ten deaths from this virus, including five deaths here in New York City. We have not been able to ascertain whether the virus is airborne, but we should all proceed as if it is.

"Because of the recent deaths and widespread infection, I am declaring a state of emergency and advising everyone to stay home. Do not go to work and only go outside if absolutely necessary. Subways and buses will be operating on a limited schedule and will be shut down after ten p.m. tonight. Non-emergency vehicles will be banned after eleven p.m. on city streets. Those who choose to ignore this directive will be fined.

"If you are not at home, make your way there as soon as possible and stay there. Please exercise extreme caution. At the end of this broadcast, we will provide a list of hospitals in all five boroughs that have units dedicated to providing care for this virus. If you are experiencing any symptoms, go immediately to a participating hospital or call the number below, and we will send an ambulance for you. We will update you as soon as new information becomes available. Thank you all for your cooperation."

The scene shifted back to the set of the *Today Show* with the ticker at the bottom reiterating what the mayor had just said. I stared at the screen, my muscles tense and my stomach fluttering with anxiety. I kept reading the ticker as it scrolled continuously, waiting for it to sink in. Al Roker looked as though he wanted to sprint off the set.

"Oh my god!" the cashier exclaimed, breaking me out of my trance. "I can't believe people are dying from the flu!" She put her hand to her forehead and ran it around her face as if testing for fever.

"That's because it's not the flu," the man in glasses said, jabbing a finger at the TV. "They aren't telling us everything. That many people don't die from the flu. Go home." He grabbed his coffee and half-eaten bagel and walked out.

I shivered. If he was right and it wasn't the flu, then it could be even worse than I'd been thinking. The three of us stared at his retreating back, dumbfounded. The other customer, a woman with a baby in a stroller, took a cue from the cashier and felt her baby's forehead then her own. She hurriedly grabbed her purse and rushed out of the shop, leaving her latte and muffin behind.

The cashier's hand fluttered to her chest. "But I'm not off until three."

"I think your manager will understand," I replied. "I'd close up if I were you." I walked out the door.

Hearing a noise, I looked back over my shoulder. The cashier had taken my advice and turned the sign to Closed.

My mind was racing as Zeke and I rushed home. They'd shut the subways down when storms made them unsafe, but they'd never done it for health reasons. Even though I'd been acting on my suspicions, I'd assumed it was my paranoid side rearing its annoying head. My hoard of food would soon come in very handy.

When I entered my apartment, I locked the door behind me. I looked down at my dog. "Zeke, buddy, you were wrong."

He huffed in response and shuffled his paws, which had an overabundance of fur sprouting from between each toe. I'd nicknamed them his bedroom slippers.

I ran to the bathroom and took my temperature. After an agonizing minute, I was relieved to see the digital window read ninety-eight-point-four. I relaxed against the sink while I thought about what to do next. *I should knock on my neighbors' doors to see if anyone else is home.* We weren't the most sociable neighbors, but my recent hermit-hood had caused me to ignore them more than usual.

I racked my brain, trying to remember if I had seen any of them in the past month. The last time I saw Kelly from the second floor and her son, Isaac, was about two weeks ago. Isaac loved Zeke and always screamed when he saw him. She had said her mom was sick, and they were going to take care of her. That was the last contact I'd had with anyone in my building.

My building was a block-C shape, the middle section thinner because it only housed the stairs. The east and west sides were almost mirror images, holding all two-bedroom apartments with the same layout. But on the first floor, the bodega took over the west side, leaving only seven apartments.

I started at Kirk's apartment since it was across the hall from mine. In spite of the proximity of our apartments, I rarely saw Kirk. He was a quiet man who usually just nodded to me and only became garrulous when talking about renovations to his apartment. I pulled the collar of my sweatshirt up over my face and knocked softly. After a few seconds, I knocked again, louder. I pressed my ear to the door, but all I heard was a vehicle racing down our street.

I walked down one flight and knocked on the door of apartment four, which was directly beneath mine. I often speculated about the resident, middle-aged Tom, who had an impressive handlebar mustache, and his mysterious movements. I only saw him once every other month or so, and a few times, he had been with younger women. He always wore a suit, so I imagined he was a travelling salesman. But I also thought he could be married and using the small apartment as his love nest. I knocked and listened. No answer. I wondered if he was away on a sales trip and had managed to avoid the whole debacle.

I walked the few feet to apartment five, where a gay couple lived. Out of everyone, I'd chatted with Terrence and Eric the most over the years, but I hadn't seen either of them in at least a month because they had a condo in Florida where they spent most of the winter months. I knocked four separate times, waiting for an answer and hoping I wasn't completely alone. But my knocks went unanswered.

I ran down to the second floor and knocked at apartment two, where a single woman named Barb lived. When there was no answer, I put my ear against the door. The low sounds of a TV resonated through the door. Barb coughed, and I jumped back quickly, my back hitting the door of apartment three. My heart was beating as quickly as a bird caged in my chest. I closed my eyes and breathed deeply.

Turning around, I knocked loudly on Kelly's door, not expecting an answer. After my expectations proved correct, I went down to the solitary first-floor apartment, which belonged to Mr. Tablock. He was over eighty years old and had lived in the building for forty years. I'd seen his live-in Haitian nurse, Regine, in the hallway from time to time, taking out the trash. I used to ask her how he was doing, but her response was always the same: "He's getting old, but he's got spunk." I stopped asking and just said hello.

I pounded on the door, praying Regine and Mr. Tablock were still there and not sick. But all was quiet. Besides infected Barb, I was alone.

Back in my apartment, I saw that it was nearing eight a.m., which meant the store on the corner would be open in a few minutes. I threw on my coat and wrapped my scarf around my face before running downstairs.

When I reached the shop, there was a note on the door, stating that the store would be closing at six p.m. due to the quarantine. The place was already packed with people frantically grabbing food. The line for the single checkout stand disappeared down an aisle.

There wasn't much left in the canned goods section, and the dry-goods section had been almost cleaned out too. Since I had a stockpile of both, I decided to buck the trend and grab some fresh produce and a large pork shoulder, both of which were still in healthy supply. I could make a stew that would last a week or two if I froze half of it. I doubted the quarantine would last that long. I added four bags of dog food, a combo pack of batteries, and two cartons of much-needed half-and-half to my cart.

Joining the line, I noticed that everyone had something covering their faces, making us all look as if we were about to rob the place as our eyes darted around suspiciously. It took thirty minutes to finally make it to the front and check out.

Back at my apartment, I thought about calling my mom, but I procrastinated by washing my hands and face. Mom was overprotective with everyone, but where I was concerned, she took it to another level. I had been born four weeks premature and exhibited signs of what doctors called "failure to thrive." In school, I was much smaller than the other kids, and when we moved to a new town during my third-grade year, none of the kids would talk to me. After my many failed attempts at friendship, I cornered a girl named Sarah, who happened to live across the street from me. She told me all the kids thought I was a five-year-old prodigy, and they didn't want to play with a five-year-old. Once I persuaded her that I was eight, she launched a campaign on my behalf, pulling kids aside and convincing them of my age. Eventually, they were swayed, and Sarah and I became best friends. But it didn't help when my mom called me Peewee in front of all my classmates one day as she dropped off my forgotten lunch box. My face had turned bright red as everyone snickered.

I wasn't allowed to go on roller coasters until I was fifteen because Mom was afraid I would fall out of the harness. I begrudgingly granted her that because, at the time, I only weighed eighty-five pounds. Her concerns were probably justified. All of that would have been enough fuel for my mom's vigilant worrying, but then I did the unthinkable.

My entire family was still living in California, where I grew up. My mom's large Mexican side had each other's backs, no questions asked. My dad came from a group of fun-loving Norwegians, and even though he had a brother and two sisters, his extended family couldn't compare to the size of my mom's. He had no idea what he was getting himself into by marrying into my mom's loud, intrusive clan. He used humor to deflect their invasive questions, but at gatherings, I often found him alone outside, taking a much-needed breather from the chaos.

When I decided to move to New York without knowing a soul in the city, none of them understood. I could never tell them that it was their protection that I wanted to escape. My two sides were polar opposites, and my identity was spread between both but not firmly planted in either. Even my appearance was ambiguous: I had brown eyes and olive skin but a slightly upturned nose and a small, bow-shaped mouth. People usually had a hard time placing my ethnicity. I'd always felt as though I was in the middle of nowhere, perpetually in between. I had needed to go in search of a version of myself that was true and not just who I was with them.

Most of my friends chose to stay near home, marrying into comfortable, safe lives. Part of me still longed for that life: marriage, kids, a job that I sleepwalked through, and my eyes closed to other possibilities, or perhaps daydreaming of another life. Instead, I chose the path of most resistance, giving up my college boyfriend and all I'd ever known for a chance at bigger dreams.

When I had first moved to New York, I'd constantly heard about the three hardest things to accomplish in the city: find an apartment, find a job, and find a boyfriend. I got lucky and secured a room in a rent-stabilized apartment on a designated historic block in Long Island City, right over the Queensboro Bridge from

Midtown. The long block was lined with towering oak trees surrounded by large cement planters in front of rows of brick Brownstones. The first time I saw it, I thought I'd landed smack dab in the middle of Sesame Street. Because of the street's landmark status, it was more maintained than the surrounding ones and, therefore, a highly sought-after avenue to live on. I considered myself lucky that a room had even been available. I moved in with another California transplant, who later moved back home, leaving the apartment in my sole possession. But trying to start a career in New York City was like trying to be popular on the first day at a new school. No one knew me, and they were all just waiting for me to give them a reason to be interested. When it really counted, I proved myself by pulling confidence from some foreign place inside me.

I never told my mom that she was partly responsible for my departure because she'd shown me at every step what it meant to be strong, to persevere, and to be better than I thought I was. She was the oldest of five siblings and was just thirteen years old when my grandmother died of ovarian cancer. The heavy burden of caring for the family fell onto my mom's unprepared shoulders. She never had the money for a college education, so she got a job in the mailroom at a large corporation and worked her way up to senior management before she retired.

Even after fifteen years, when I went back home to visit at Christmas, my aunts still asked, "*Mija*, when are you moving home?" Mom had given up. In some way that she would never voice, she understood. However, she still insisted on calling me when the weather was bad and telling me not to go outside. She'd been worried about the flu outbreak since it started, calling and texting me to be careful. Unfortunately, I'd been flippant with her about it, so I knew our conversation would contain an "I told you so."

I bit the bullet and called anyway. "Hi, it's me."

"Oh my god! I just saw the news. Are you okay? Are you feeling sick? Are you at home? Do you have enough food to eat? Don't go outside!"

"I'm fine. I'm at home, and I have plenty to eat. You know just as much as I do, but don't worry. I'm not sick, and I'm not going outside, except to walk Zeke."

"What? Don't do that! Take him up on the roof of your building. I knew this would happen. I knew you should never have moved there. How can I help you when you're so far away?"

"I know. I'm sorry I'm not home too. But I'm not sick at all, and I'm going to follow the mayor's instructions. I promise."

"Can you come home? You're coming home in a few weeks anyway. Maybe you can change your flight. I'll give you my credit card. Spend whatever you have to. Just come home!"

Her idea was tempting. "Hold on. Let me see if I can change it. Give me a second."

I grabbed my laptop and pulled up the airline page. My body went cold when I saw the banner across the top of the site: "All flights cancelled until further notice." That was it. No links to click, no number to call, nothing. I even tried clicking the link in the email confirmation from when I had booked the flight a month before, but it took me to the same sparsely worded page.

"Mom, the page says no flights are leaving until further notice."

"Oh god. Your dad just told me there was breaking news that all flights going into or out of any state east of Texas are grounded. What do we do?"

I let out a deep breath. "I don't know, but for now, let's not panic. We'll sit tight and see what happens over the next couple of days. I'm sorry. I hate to put you through this."

"Oh, stop it. It's not your fault! Let's just try to think positive. I'll keep the news on, and you let me know if anything happens on your end. If they do open up flights, we'll make sure you and Zeke are on the first one. Okay?"

I said I would keep her posted. When I hung up, a feeling of dread came over me. I walked over and looked out the window at the street. I was completely alone.

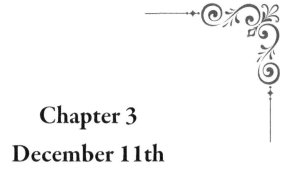

Chapter 3

December 11th

I chopped all the produce and added it to my slow cooker along with a box of chicken broth and the pork shoulder. While the stew simmered, I took Zeke up to the roof to go to the bathroom, starting a pile of his poop bags in a distant corner. I felt an odd obligation to follow my mom's instructions even though she would never know.

Honking horns from stalled traffic on the Queensboro Bridge called out like a cautionary alarm. I rubbed the back of my neck, feeling the frustration of the drivers as they made their painstakingly slow treks to the safety of their homes. People on the street pushed shopping carts full of food like squirrels storing up for winter. I contemplated making another run to the store for more supplies, but my fear of being around the infected kept me home. I had quite a bit, and the grocery store was probably low on stock anyway. It was recycling day, but I could only assume the big truck wouldn't be around to do its job. Usually, the sidewalk was lined with piles of translucent recycling bags that everyone put out the night before, but only a handful of buildings had bags in front of them. Our super, Tony, lived in the building next to mine and was in charge of sorting and putting the bags in front of both buildings for pickup. There were no bags.

At five o'clock, Mrs. Kim closed the twenty-four-hour convenience store that sold lottery tickets and late-night snacks on the corner across the street. After she pulled down the metal gate and locked it, she hunched over and coughed into a handkerchief. When she straightened, I saw blood on the cloth. As if she could sense my presence, she looked directly up at my window. Her mouth sagged as she panted to catch her breath. We stared at each other until she finally turned and walked toward the subway. With a sense of despair, I watched her silhouette disappear down the steps.

By the end of the day, the sounds and movements from the streets had dwindled. The quiet was foreign to me, and I raced to the window every time a small noise cut through the silence. A car honked outside just after sunset, and it sounded louder than a horn should. I rushed to the window and spotted Barb, bundled up in a thick blanket, climbing into a black car. The door closed with a bang that echoed down the street. When the vehicle drove away, I realized I was probably the only one left in my building. I wondered if Kirk and Mr. Tablock had gone to the hospital. I hoped so. The thought of dead bodies nearby made my stomach clench.

The evening news reported on the dwindling stock at local grocery stores while the screen showed empty shelves and toppled displays. Some stores had closed their doors early, only to have looters break the windows and steal the food they could no longer buy. The camera panned across several storefronts with smashed windows.

The death count from the virus had risen to forty-nine. They didn't give any new information on how the virus had started, which made me wonder if the government did know but didn't want to share the information with the public. If the reason was to keep us from panicking, I agreed with that decision. The last thing we needed was hysterical people taking even more drastic measures.

I took a few extra vitamin supplements, just to be on the safe side, and scrubbed my hands three times.

When I returned to the couch, they had switched to a story about the oak trees having a "boom" year, which resulted in double or triple the amount of acorns falling from the trees. It was odd to see such a mundane story capping off the more serious headline, but I watched anyway, thinking I would see an increase in the parks department's employees in their telltale green outfits, cleaning out the planters in a few months. The story was interrupted when the screen changed and the mayor appeared on my TV, stationed in front of the podium. I grabbed the remote and quickly turned up the volume.

"Good evening. If you've been watching the news, you know the death count is rapidly rising. The CDC is working on finding a cure, and you will be notified as soon as that happens. We are doing everything in our power to care for those who are sick.

"The federal government has issued a standing order for the Eastern states to comply with a set of guidelines designed to help those who are not affected by the NOS-9 virus. We will need everyone to log onto the website shown at the bottom of the screen and fill out the questionnaire. In order to get a grasp of how widespread this is, we need to know who is exhibiting symptoms and who is not.

"If you are symptomatic, we will send an ambulance and a medical team to your house and transport you to a medical center. If you are not, we will send a team to your house to take a blood sample to be absolutely certain you are clear of the virus. If your test comes back negative, you will be given a wristband that is not removable by anyone other than a representative from the CDC.

"This process will help us determine how we proceed. We hope to have teams out to the public by tomorrow morning, so please fill out the questionnaire as soon as possible. If you do not have access to a computer, call the number below, and we will take down your information manually. Thank you all for your cooperation."

A wristband? It was suspicious how quickly they'd organized their response. I immediately went to the website and filled out the half page of questions. I wanted to be first in line for one of those wristbands.

Next, I logged on to Facebook. I hadn't been on in months because I'd feared my friends' happy lives would make me feel even worse about my own. But I figured it might be a good place to see if anyone had heard anything more than what they were saying on the news. There were countless posts on my timeline asking if I was okay. I posted that I was fine in my apartment, awaiting further instructions. Immediately, a friend from California commented on my post. "Check this out!" She included a link to another Facebook page.

When I clicked the link, my browser opened a public forum called "What's Really Going On." I read through hundreds of posts by others also in quarantine, and I began to believe that the government had known how deadly the virus was for much longer than they were letting on. Some posts were weeks old. While some people were allowed to travel, others had been detained at the airport and not allowed to fly. Those who were detained had been stuck for almost a month, sequestered at a hotel with armed guards who refused to answer their questions.

After reading all of the posts, I feared they were correct. I was usually skeptical when it came to conspiracy theories, but they couldn't all be exaggerating.

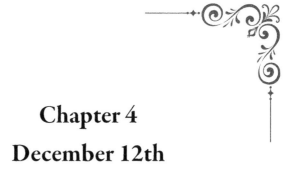

Chapter 4
December 12th

After my morning trip to the roof with Zeke, I got a call from my boss. The company had decided that everything would be placed on hold, and we wouldn't be working during the quarantine. Relieved not to have to go to that hotbox of contagion, I turned on a movie. I kept a running commentary for Zeke. He was a great listener.

At noon, I poured a glass of my favorite Sancerre and turned on the news. I sat through reports about rising death counts, Red Cross efforts, and interviews with city officials. When the screen changed to a static image stating "Breaking News," I turned up the volume and leaned forward.

A male newscaster came on the screen with his finger to his earpiece as if he were receiving instructions. His eyes darted to the camera. "This is Dave Abrams from CNBC News. We come to you live now from the financial district in lower Manhattan, where our own anchor Lindsay Ballard is currently quarantined. Lindsay, what are you seeing?"

The screen switched to a shaky cell phone video. The camera showed the outside of a building with people looking down to the street from the balconies. Car alarms, the sound of breaking glass, and distant screams and chants told the story of the obvious chaos coming from below.

"Dave, I've been in my apartment since yesterday morning without incident." Lindsay had raised her tremulous voice to be heard over the din. "But half an hour ago, that changed. A small group of people left their homes and began protesting the quarantine. Their chants drew others out to join them. The group has now risen to as many as fifteen or twenty."

Lindsay was breathing heavily as the camera moved forward a couple of feet then tilted downward over a railing, probably on the fifth or sixth floor of her building. People darted back and forth on the street. A man was smashing a lock on a metal gate covering a storefront. The lock broke, and he pulled the gate up. He picked up a metal trashcan and threw it through the large front window, causing an alarm to blare loudly.

Lindsay's cell phone jumped, then she got the storefront centered on the screen again. People climbed through the new opening, heedless of the glass shards. Seconds later, some ran out with their arms full of electronics, clothing, and household items. A few yards away, two men were trying to pull a woman's grocery cart away from her. They managed to rip it out of her hands, and she fell backward onto the asphalt as they ran off.

Several men were walking down the street, wielding bats, yelling, and smashing cars as they went. Something exploded nearby, and the cell phone wobbled. Lindsay let out a small scream. The video feed blurred for a second then cleared to a view of a brick wall. The wall receded as the camera was picked up, then it only showed the floor.

"Oh god. What was that?" Lindsay whispered.

"Lindsay, can you hear me? Are you okay?" Dave asked.

"I'm okay. Dave, it appears that a car has been set on fire."

As the camera crept over the balcony railing again, Lindsay zoomed in, and the burning car filled the screen. A group of men were standing in front of the car, pumping their fists in the air while chanting, "We will not be caged!"

Dave said, "Lindsay, I've been told that police have been deployed and should be there shortly. Can you tell me what sparked this protest?"

"Unfortunately, I don't know. But I do know that it quickly turned into looting and rioting. We are seeing a mix of that now." A faint horn sounded, and Lindsay added, "I think the police are here."

She leaned farther over the railing and tilted the camera to get a view up the street. A barricade of police vehicles blocked the path. A pack of officers in full riot gear began marching forward. The rioters threw bottles and rocks at the police shields, but the officers were undeterred. The crowd was slowly being pushed back. Lindsay and Dave had stopped reporting, allowing the video to speak for itself. The chanting got louder as the rioters were forced to retreat. Some of the men had scarves tied over their faces, but others did not. If they weren't already sick, they were possibly being exposed to the virus.

A loud voice on a bullhorn called, "Everyone, go back to your homes, and you will not be harmed. Get back into your homes!"

A few people broke off from the group of rioters and ran. The camera moved back to the right, showing a fire truck dousing the flames surrounding the car. Within minutes, the fire was dead.

The bullhorn voice shouted, "This is your last warning! Go back inside your homes!"

More people separated from the group and scurried into buildings. The fire hose was turned toward the rapidly diminishing group of protesters. A forceful stream of water blasted the rioters, knocking the first line to the ground. As the police continued to move forward, the group finally broke apart and dispersed, except for a few men who stood their ground and continued their chant. The police put down their shields and aimed their guns at the men.

"Go back inside, or we will shoot!"

I couldn't believe they might actually shoot unarmed people. The men pumped their fists in the air and chanted louder. A gunshot rang out, and the camera jerked.

Lindsay gasped and whispered, "Oh my god, oh my god."

"Lindsay, are you okay? What are you seeing?"

"I can't see anything, I—" The camera seemed to be clenched to her chest, showing only the frantic movement of her chest heaving up and down.

"Lindsay, can you move closer and show us what's happening?"

"Uh, I don't... Dave, I don't know." With the cell phone up against her clothing, her voice and the other sounds were muffled. She panted as if struggling to get enough oxygen.

I was on the edge of my seat. My breath felt like hers, pumping too fast through my lungs.

"That was a warning!" Bullhorn Voice yelled. "Go inside, or we *will* shoot."

"Lindsay, be careful, but if you can, show us what's happening."

After an agonizing ten seconds, the camera went back to the railing. Lindsay must have been on the balcony floor because the camera moved through the railing instead of over. Lindsay's hand trembled, but the image finally stilled enough that I could see the men backing away with their arms raised. All but one of them turned and ran into adjacent buildings.

The solitary man doubled over and began coughing. When he straightened, he looked at the police, who were still screaming at him to go back to his home. Suddenly, he sprinted toward the officers. The sound of rapid gunfire rang out, and the man's body jerked several times before dropping to the ground. Lindsay screamed, and the camera fell again. The screen cracked, and a spidery web appeared on my TV just before it went black.

We could still hear Lindsay's frantic cries. "They shot him! Dave, they shot the man. Oh my god! He was just—" She started coughing.

The TV screen changed to an image of Dave sitting behind the news desk. His stunned expression was replaced by a startled one. Then he stared into the camera. "For those of you who have just joined us, Lindsay Ballard has just reported from lower Manhattan, where rioters were protesting the quarantine. The police have managed to force the group back into their homes. One man was shot when he rushed the police." Dave's finger went to his ear. "I'm being told that police are breaking up similar protests in several other places around Manhattan."

The image switched to a live helicopter feed. The sky view showed streets littered with trash and debris and some fires. People dashed from building to building as police marched and rode through the areas.

Dave came back on the screen. "What we've just seen are the effects of multiple riots around the city. We know that at least one person has been shot, but it is unclear how many people may have been injured. We urge residents to stay inside their homes. We will update you throughout the day with any new developments."

The station abruptly flipped to a commercial. Zeke whined, and I realized I was clutching him too tightly. I relaxed my grip and leaned toward the window to look outside. Several helicopters hovered overhead, and three separate plumes of smoke sprouted up from buildings on the other side of the Queensborough bridge. Scanning the street below, I felt grateful that the people in my neighborhood had remained civil. I gulped down my wine then poured another glass.

For the next two hours, I flipped through the channels and watched various reports from different parts of the city, but all feeds were from helicopters, making it hard to see the action. By the time the rioting seemed to have been contained, four people were confirmed dead and countless others injured. Only two days into the quarantine, society had already begun to break down.

When the reporters began repeating the same stories, I flipped over to Netflix and settled on *The Walking Dead*. Maybe I could pick up a few pointers about surviving our pseudo-apocalypse. After several episodes and a few more glasses of wine, I turned off the TV and put on some music. Since no one was around to complain, I cranked up the volume and sang at the top of my lungs while dancing around the apartment. Zeke ran around and tried to jump on me.

An hour later, I was fully spent, so I took Zeke up to the roof with my wine and a throw blanket for warmth. Down on the street, no one was out except the occasional police car or ambulance. The streets were never that empty, even late at night or during horrible weather. The piles of recycling bags still dotted the sidewalk, where they would most likely remain. Picking up recycling would be low on the city's list of priorities. The sounds of coughing from various buildings around me sent a shudder of fear up my spine.

But I felt confident that New Yorkers could survive. We had a unique brand of common sense. We'd trained our ears to the subtleties of subway noises, so we knew when to run for it. We had an inherent ability to look at a cramped space and comfortably pile in ten pieces of furniture. We'd learned how to carry six heavy bags of groceries up five flights of stairs by balancing them in a certain way. We'd all earned our place in the city, and we were tough and loyal.

Out of the corner of my eye, I noticed two blond girls, about eight and twelve, making faces at me from an apartment window across the courtyard. My roof was bordered by a wide half wall, except for the narrower middle section, where there was a three-foot-high wrought-iron fence. I walked over to the fenced section to make faces back and have Zeke do some tricks for them.

The younger one was wearing a frilly yellow dress over jeans, and perched on top of her mountain of curls was a pink plastic tiara with fake rhinestones. The older one was jumping up and down while she pulled her face into various shapes. They were laughing and having a great time. I realized that I was, too, and that it was the most fun I'd had in months. I held up my finger to say "one minute" and ran downstairs to grab my iPod and portable speaker.

Back up on the roof, I blasted Prince's "Let's Go Crazy" and started dancing. When I looked over, I saw that they had found some throw blankets to wave around while they danced. They'd also opened the window to hear the music better.

When the song ended, I turned the music down a little so I could talk to them. "What are your names?"

The older one said, "I'm Julia." She hooked her thumb over to her sister. "That's Emma, princess of Long Island City." Emma's shoulders came up to her ears as she giggled.

"I'm Karis, and this is Zeke. Are there other people in your building?"

"Mr. Standhope is in the apartment below us, but he doesn't go out much. He's really old, so my mom brings him food sometimes. I think she just wants to check on him. We haven't seen him in a while, but we hear him moving around down there sometimes. Yesterday, we heard him yelling the F-word a lot." That made them giggle with their hands over their mouths. When they recovered, Julia asked, "Is there anyone else in your building?"

"I don't think so. I've knocked on all the doors, and no one's answered. There was a woman on the second floor, but she left yesterday."

"It must be lonely with no one there," Emma said.

"It was, but now I'm talking to you." When they smiled, I pointed down at my dog. "Plus, I've got Zeke. He's great at keeping me company."

"I wish we could have a dog. My mom says they're too much work. When I'm older, I want to have a lot of dogs," Julia said.

Then they both turned around to talk to someone. I assumed it was their mom telling them to stop talking to strangers.

Julia spun back around and said, "Same time tomorrow?"

I gave her a thumbs-up.

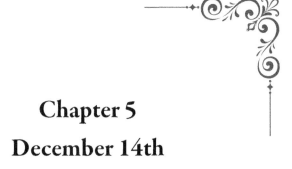

Chapter 5
December 14th

I'd spent two days waking up late, compulsively watching news reports about the virus, and talking to the girls. It felt like I was playing hooky from school, and I had to admit, it was kind of fun. But the emptiness in my building was putting me on edge. The sudden intrusion of my buzzer made both Zeke and me jump.

I walked over to the intercom. "Who is it?" I asked then pressed the listen button.

"The Center for Disease Control, Ms. Hylen."

A suspicious voice in my head, which sounded a lot like my mom's, wanted to question them further and to make sure they were who they said they were. Instead, I buzzed them up. Zeke was barking with excitement and an innate desire to protect our home. When I opened the door, two women wearing HAZMAT masks stood in the hall. Zeke gave them both a thorough sniffing. I led them to my living room, and we all sat down on my sofa.

"I'm Ms. Thompson," the taller one said, "and this is my colleague, Mrs. Camden. Ms. Hylen, have you had any symptoms? Sore throat, fever, congestion?"

"No, I feel fine. I took my temperature this morning, and it was normal."

"Thank you," she said, writing down my response. "Have you come into direct contact with anyone who is infected? Saliva or blood contact?"

"Nope, just my dog, and he seems fine," I said, smiling.

They looked down at Zeke but didn't smile back. While they took out their supplies and started drawing my blood, I asked a bunch of questions. The only thing they would say was that they didn't have any new information, and I should remain inside my apartment.

"How long have you known about this?" I asked.

They kept their heads down, but I caught the look that passed between them. I could feel unsaid words floating in the air.

Finally, Ms. Thompson looked at me and said, "This won't take long."

When they moved to the kitchen table to run their tests, Zeke hopped onto the couch next to me. I almost asked if they wanted a drink, the mom inside of me bringing out incessant hosting instincts. But with those masks on, they wouldn't be able to drink, and I knew they wouldn't take them off. Ten minutes later, they came back and told me I was clear.

Ms. Thompson measured my wrist then said to Mrs. Camden, "We'll need the child-sized one."

Yes, I have the wrists of a child. I suppressed an eye roll. Mrs. Camden pulled a thin bright-orange metal wristband out of her bag. She scanned the barcode on the underside with a wand, and it produced a loud beep, followed by a few smaller beeps.

Thompson snapped the band on my wrist with a device that reminded me of the ones retailers used to put security tags on high-priced merchandise. She held up her strange-looking tool. "Ms. Hylen, this is the only device that can remove your wristband. If it's removed in any other way, it becomes deactivated and will no longer signify non-infection." She handed me a flyer with a website

address on it. "You can go to this site to get information. It's updated every few hours."

They packed up all their supplies and rose to leave. I knew it
was useless to ask more questions, so I thanked them and showed
them to the door. After they left, I grabbed my laptop and went
to the website. I clicked on a link that led to a page about airline
flights. The announcement said they had several outbound flights
scheduled over the next two weeks. The flights would only be available to those with a wristband.

My hopes soared at the possibility of going home. The first one
available was in four days. I checked the small print and verified
that they were allowing service animals on the flights. When Zeke
was younger, we were a therapy dog team that visited hospitals. He
loved it because he got tons of attention and treats. I'd had him reg-
istered as a service dog, so we could take the train to get to the hospitals and do our good deeds.

I started reading through the instructions about the wristband
and verification processes at the airport, but it all seemed standard.
I called my mom and told her the good news.

"I feel so much better," she said.

"I know. Me too. If all goes well, we'll be seeing you in four
days. I can't believe it. I thought this was going to be so much harder."

"So did I. But let's not jinx it. They're asking everyone to go in
to get tested here, too, free of charge. Your dad and I went in last
night. We're fine."

"Really? Well, I'm glad they're being thorough. Have you heard
of any positive results yet?"

"No, not yet. Hopefully, it will stay in the east. I'll let you know
if I hear anything." She paused, and then her voice softened. "Honey, how are you doing? Don't spare my feelings. I need to know."

"I'm good, Mom, really. I can do this."

"Just be careful. I'm here if you need me."

"I'm going to start going through my things and getting my apartment ready. I don't know when or if I'll be back, so I need to make sure I take anything that's really important. I'll call you tomorrow."

"I love you. Think positive!"

"Me too. I will. Bye."

I hauled my suitcase out of the closet and opened it on the bed. I went through all my drawers to see what I wanted to take with me. While sorting my jewelry, I found the sapphire ring Brian had given me on our six-month anniversary. The memory of that night was so sharp, I almost flinched. That was the night he'd told me he loved me for the first time.

After Brian had broken up with me, I'd gone home and cried into Zeke's fur. My dog had been there for me through every good and bad time in the past eight years, so he knew the drill. When my tears slowed, my gaze landed on a photo of Brian and me grinning at an outdoor film festival. Anger quickly replaced the sadness. I yanked the picture from the matting and tore it into tiny pieces. Turning to drop the remains in the garbage can, I spotted the Bob Dylan poster my ex-boyfriend Jack had bought me after the concert six years ago. I ripped it from the wall and shredded it. I looked around for more and found the collectible Pinhead talking action figure from my favorite horror movie, *Hellraiser*, which my ex-fling Christian had given me on my thirty-sixth birthday. I grabbed the figure, got my hammer, and smashed its head over and over, causing its automated voice to protest, telling me it would tear my soul apart. I glared at the crushed plastic and thought, "Too late. Someone beat you to it." I'd torn through my apartment and given every ex-lover's memento similar treatment. Somehow, the ring had survived my purge.

I wondered why I'd lied to my mom—I wasn't okay. I usually told her everything. She was my touchstone. It wasn't that I didn't think she could handle the reality of my depression. I knew she could. But I could, too, and I needed to shoulder it on my own. I wanted to prove to myself that I could be alone and that I didn't need anyone else. I just didn't know if that was true.

I thought about texting my New York friends to see who else had gotten a flight, but I hadn't spoken to most of them in months. I wondered if they would even respond. The first few weeks after the breakup with Brian had been pretty restless, and I had gone out with friends occasionally. But many of them were in relationships, and being around them made me feel like a third wheel. I felt like I was underwater, unable to surface, while everyone else was waving at me from dry land. I would sit in my living room in the dark and think about the emptiness in my house, in my heart. I feared my sadness was so strong that it floated up the walls, seeped into the cracks, and poured over people in other apartments, infecting them too.

Socializing became a chore, an unnecessary exercise I performed to appear emotionally normal to the masses—*if I'm going to be alone, why not just be alone?* Only one of my friends had noticed my withdrawal: Lori, who I frequently met up with at the dog park. She'd texted me to ask if I was avoiding her.

I'd replied, *No, I'm just hibernating. See you in the spring! :-)*

I pulled out my phone and started texting my friends anyway. I was anxious to know how others were faring. A few responded, saying their flights were booked, but a lot of my messages went unanswered. I couldn't reach Lori or my ex-boyfriend Jack, though I called them both several times and left messages.

I contemplated calling Brian but settled on a text instead. He replied that his test result had come back positive. He was at his parents' house in New Jersey, and they were sick too. I didn't know how to respond. My anger toward him seemed ridiculous compared to the situation, and I certainly didn't want him to die.

A few minutes later, I texted, *I'm sorry.*

He replied, *Me too. For everything. :-(*

My emotions were all over the place, up one minute because someone confirmed he had a flight then crashing because another friend replied that she was sick.

When my friend Axel group texted, *Can't believe I'm going out like this. I love you all, it's been a blast. See you in the next life,* I broke down and sobbed.

After reading the responses of our mutual friends, I texted, *I'll miss you.* I wished I could think of something better, something that conveyed everything I was feeling. But my nerves were shot, and my mind was blocked by grief.

Zeke must have sensed my emotional turmoil because he crawled under the blanket with me. He rested his chin on my leg and licked my hand in support.

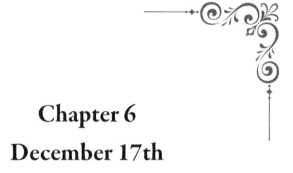

Chapter 6
December 17th

My apartment was filled with tempting aromas from the homemade flour tortillas and stuffed Mexican cornbread I'd made with all my stockpiled food. Since it only needed to last me one more day, I figured I might as well enjoy it. My mom had made the cornbread every Christmas morning since I could remember. The tantalizing smells lured me out of bed more effectively than the promise of presents under the tree.

I dug into the chorizo-filled cheesy cornbread while continuing to send messages to those who hadn't responded, but they felt like words lost in a void. The responses trickled in until late afternoon then stopped altogether, leaving me feeling detached from all I'd known in the city.

I went up at four o'clock for my standing playdate with the girls, hoping to reconnect with humanity. I hadn't told them yet that I was leaving. Our relationship was based on fun and distraction, not reality. Julia had colorful splotches all over her face and hands, and Emma was wearing a gray leotard and mouse ears.

I laughed and asked, "What's going on with you two? Is that paint?"

Julia giggled. "I love to paint, and Emma likes to dress up. So I paint her in different costumes."

"How fun! Can I see the painting?"

"Sure." She reached over to the coffee table and held up a piece of cardboard. "She's smelling lasagna. It's our favorite dinner. My mom makes it all the time."

I squinted at the painting of Emma as a mouse on all fours, sniffing a plate of food. "It's really good." I meant it. For a twelve-year-old, Julia was pretty talented.

"Thanks! I love art class. My teacher said I'm the best in the class, so Mom bought me all kinds of art supplies."

"And I get to dress up," Emma said happily. She sniffled and veered behind the curtain quickly, but I thought I heard her cough.

When she came back, I looked her up and down before saying, "It's great that you found something you can both enjoy in different ways. Does your mom have any makeup? You could use eyeliner to draw whiskers and some pink lipstick to make a nose."

Emma stuck out her lower lip. "My mom doesn't wear makeup, and she won't buy us any. She says we're beautiful just the way we are and don't need makeup."

"Oh. Well, she's right. You are both beautiful."

Julia mumbled, "Thanks," and looked away, but Emma beamed.

"You have the prettiest hair. I wish mine was like yours. And, Emma, look at your dimples! They're adorable."

Julia frowned at her sister. "Emma, say thank you!"

Emma sighed and rolled her eyes. "I will. I'm waiting for her to finish!"

I laughed. "I'm done for now."

Emma smiled widely, showing two missing teeth and the afore-mentioned dimples. "Thank you."

I was reluctant to spoil our jovial mood, but I couldn't delay any longer. "I have a flight out tomorrow, so I wanted to say good-bye."

They exchanged a sad glance. Emma asked, "Zeke too?"

"Yep, Zeke too." I glanced down and saw that neither of them wore wristbands. "You didn't get a flight, did you?"

"No, we didn't get bracelets like yours. Momma's been sick, but she didn't want to go to the hospital, so she didn't fill out the questionnaire. We've been taking care of her," Julia said.

"How are you guys feeling?"

"I'm okay, but Emma started coughing last night. It woke me up."

I noticed that Emma was a little flushed and kept sniffing. Tears stung the corners of my eyes. Even in such a short time, I'd come to care for the girls. It was incredible what a person could overlook just because the heart wanted to.

"I'm sorry. I wish I could help."

Emma said, "You *are* helping."

Her words lifted my heart. "Let me know if you need anything. I have some food here. In fact, hold on one second."

I ran downstairs and grabbed a bag of gummy bears I'd been saving for the flight. Back up on the roof, I told them to step away from the window. Leaning over the railing, I took aim and threw the bag through.

Julia picked it up, squealed, and ripped it open. "Oh my god! Thank you. These are my favorite!"

"Sure," I said. "If you need anything, make sure to tell me when I come up tomorrow. That'll be my last day."

Their smiles fell. "Maybe we can have all your candy before you go?" Emma said hopefully, brightening some.

"Of course. I'll bring whatever I have up here tomorrow. But I'll come up at two instead. I'm leaving for the airport at three."

Julia nodded then glanced behind her. "My mom is calling us. See you tomorrow."

I waved. "Feel better, Emma. Bye."

Once they were out of sight, I wandered over to the far ledge and sat down. I was starting to shiver from the cold, but it was a good distraction to keep the sadness at bay. I wasn't ready to deal with what I'd just heard. My body felt sharp with hard, raw edges. The streets were completely empty, but a helicopter flew over every ten or fifteen minutes. Our apartments had become tombs. Life was taking place above us now.

When I made it back downstairs, heartache overwhelmed me. The girls were probably going to watch their mom die, then they would die slowly, and there was nothing I could do. Sitting on my couch, I cried for them and for all the other people I had known who had died or would die soon. I thought about praying, but since I wasn't sure if I believed in God, I didn't know who to pray to.

An hour later, my eyes had no tears left. I washed my puffy face and started going through the piles of stuff to sort out what was important enough to take and what wasn't. We were only allowed one large suitcase to check and two small carry-ons. The task was easier than I thought it would be. In a time of death and disease, material things no longer seemed important.

The next morning, I made sure I had all my important documents and my old Rolleiflex twin-lens box camera, a gift from my dad. In my carry-ons, I packed food for Zeke and his chamomile calming drops. At two o'clock, I went up to the roof. When the girls saw me, they jumped up and down happily. Emma wasn't in costume, but she had her hair in braids with bows at the ends and was wearing a rainbow-colored dress.

I pointed to the left of their window. "Julia, see that old clothesline out there?"

She stuck her head out and peeked over the sill. "Yes, I see it."

"Can you reach the bottom line?"

She stretched her arm up and touched the line. "I can reach it."

"I'm going to run downstairs. I'll clip the bags to the line and send them over. Don't lean out. Just wait for them to come to you."

The corresponding pulley was on the outside wall next to the top of my narrow hall window. I stepped up onto the sill and pulled the top window down. With clothespins I'd used for sealing half-eaten bags of chips, I secured two bags to the bottom line. When I tried to pull the top line, the pulley didn't spin—it was rusted from years of neglect. But I yanked harder, and with a squeaking noise, the pulley finally started moving.

The girls clapped their hands excitedly. Once Julia had re-trieved the bags, I sent two more. As the wheels loosened, I picked up the pace. Zeke was barking like crazy, apparently thinking it was some kind of game. I managed to get seven bags into their apart-ment. One bag slipped out of its clothespin and dropped to the ground, but it only contained pretzels and trail mix, so the girls weren't too sad.

I ran back up to the roof. The girls were emptying the bags onto the floor while they danced around the pile of junk food. They opened a bag of M&M's and started munching.

I leaned on the fence. "How's your mom doing?"

Julia shrugged one shoulder. "I don't know. She's still got a fever and coughs a lot. But she told us she's okay. She just sleeps most of the time. I took her temperature this morning, and it was one-oh-two."

I winced. Their mom might not have much time left, and I wouldn't be there when she died. Sadness overcame me at the thought of them going through that alone. "Where's the rest of your family?"

"We don't have any other family. My mom is an only child, and both her parents died before we were born."

"Oh, I'm sorry. What about your dad?"

Julia stopped chewing and glanced warily at Emma. "He's not here anymore." Emma seemed oblivious, intent on plowing through all the candy.

I waited for Julia to explain, but she didn't say anything else. "Did he die too?"

Julia hung her head. "He's not dead. He just left a long time ago when Emma was little. It's just us now."

"Do you remember him?"

She thought for a second. "There's one thing I remember really well. He used to love the *Huckleberry Hound Show,* so I'd watch it with him. Sometimes he would do Yogi Bear's voice and say, 'Hey, Boo Boo, how's about getting us a pic-a-nic basket!' And then I'd say, 'But, Yogi, the ranger wouldn't like that.' We used to think it was so funny. I don't know why. Now it seems kinda dumb."

I laughed. "I remember that cartoon. I used to watch it when I was little too. It's nice that you have at least one memory of him."

"Yeah, I guess. I still don't know why he left. My mom doesn't like to talk about it. She just says, 'Some people aren't meant for this kind of life.' I don't even know what that means. I thought he was happy with us." She looked down at her hands. "He was an artist too. He taught me how to draw cartoons and stuff. I think I'm good at art because of him." She raised her head again. "What's your family like?"

"They're great. Really supportive and fun. I have a big family, and everyone is always in your business. My mom cooks a lot and takes care of everyone. My dad is funny. Kids love him. He's like a big teddy bear, and when I was little, I spent hours climbing all over him. He used to take me fishing at a few rivers near where I grew up. We hiked then sat side by side." Talking about my family made me miss them even more.

"We've never been to California," Emma said. "What's it like?"

"It's beautiful. Lots of mountains, beaches, farms. I miss it a lot. I grew up in a really small town where everyone knew everyone else. You could walk the perimeter of the town in less than an hour."

That prompted a game of "when you get there, do this for me."

"Go to Disneyland and ride the teacups for me!" Emma said. "I've seen them on TV. They look fun."

"I've always wanted to learn how to surf," Julia said. "You should do that for me. And get more dogs and some cats. You could name one of them Piper. I've always wanted a pet named Piper."

Emma clapped excitedly. "Oh, and name one of them Miko! My friend gave me this Japanese comic book, and the hero was named Miko. I wish my name was Miko."

"And go on a hot air balloon! I wish I could do that."

"And eat as much candy as you can!" Emma yelled.

I had to blink back tears as I listened. "I promise I'll do all of it, except maybe the candy. But every time I do eat candy, I'll think of you two."

Emma asked, "Don't you have any kids?"

The void in my heart yawned wider. Trying to mask my sadness, I gave her a little smile. "No, I don't."

"Why not?"

"Well, I never met my Prince Charming, and you kind of need a Prince Charming to have kids."

Julia rolled her eyes. "No, you don't. Prince Charming is a fairy tale. My mom didn't meet Prince Charming, either, and she's got us." Her eyebrows were raised, wrinkling her forehead.

I stifled a surprised laugh. "I guess you're right. But I've never met anyone I wanted to have kids with. And now, it might be too late."

"My friend Katie never had a dad," Emma said through a mouthful of chocolate. "She has two moms, and they bought an invisible dad from some bank. Couldn't you do that? Don't you want kids?"

"Yes, I do. But we don't always get what we want. I thought about going to a bank. But I decided I didn't want to do it alone, that I wanted to share that with someone. Being a parent is tough, even when there are two of you. So I just kept waiting, thinking I would eventually meet someone. But I didn't. Life has a way of derailing your plans sometimes."

Julia said, "When you get home, there's one more thing I want you to do. You should have a kid. Even if you have to adopt one, just do it. You'd be a great mom. It would be sad if you didn't."

I didn't know if I could do that, and I took promises very seriously. I stared at her, and she stared right back. She seemed much older than twelve. She was right though. I *would* be a great mom.

"I promise." I checked my watch and saw that it was a quarter to three. I had to get Zeke ready to go. I looked at them sadly. "I brought my camera. Can I take a picture of you two? Just to remember you by?"

"Sure!"

They both leaned against the sill on their elbows and smiled broadly. I snapped the photo and peered at the small digital image. They looked so happy. It was hard to believe their world was crumbling around them.

"Got it! I gotta go now. I'm sorry."

"It's all right. Give Zeke a big hug from us. We'll miss you."

"I'll miss you too. Take care of each other."

Tears started rolling down my cheeks, and I had to fight to hold it together. We waved at each other, then I turned toward the door. Before I walked through, I glanced back. They both smiled and gave me a thumbs-up.

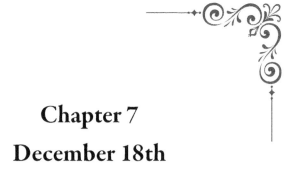

Chapter 7
December 18th

The curved roof of the JFK departures terminal appeared like a beacon of hope as our van rounded the bend to the airport entrance. The drop-off area was crowded with vehicles delivering other uninfected survivors. Most people still wore surgical masks. As we approached the curb, a quiver of nerves spiked through me. I yanked my scarf up over my face before climbing out with Zeke. The check-in line was incredibly long, snaking around numerous stanchions, and it took over an hour to reach the front. The ticketing agents were frantically trying to get through the line as quickly as possible, but many appeared run-down as if they'd been at it all night. Their hair was unkempt, strands escaping from chignons and sticking out haphazardly. I could feel the frustration in their red-rimmed eyes over the white paper of their surgical masks.

I stepped up to the counter and handed my ID to the agent. Her nametag said her name was Donna, and her kind eyes were more bloodshot than the others, which could have been from exhaustion or from tearing up over having to turn away needy people.

Donna pointed at Zeke. "Do you have documentation for the service animal, Ms. Hylen?"

I pulled out Zeke's ID card and set it on the counter. He had on his official therapy vest and an attachment on his leash that confirmed him as a service animal, but I guessed they were being thorough.

She glanced down at it. "Well, this is good, but where are *your* documents?"

"What do you mean?"

"We need a note from your doctor, stating that he is *your* service animal providing a medical service for you."

"What? No one said anything about that. He's a trained and certified service animal." I tapped his ID card. "That's his official serial number. Isn't that enough?"

"Unfortunately, ma'am, no. They are only allowing service animals for people who medically need them. No exceptions. The flights are fully booked, and space is limited."

"But I can't leave him behind! He's like my child. My family. You don't know what you're asking..." I felt the first pinpricks of panic rise in my throat. They weren't going to let me bring him. I could feel it deep in my gut. Tears gathered in my eyes. "Isn't there anything we can do?"

"I'm sorry, but the protocol is very strict." She pointed behind me. "There's a van station for passengers needing a ride back home. You'll have to go wait in that line. Now please, step aside."

Tentacles of anxiety reached up into my brain. I yanked my scarf down. "No, no. Please. You have to let us on the flight! Please, you have to understand. I can't leave him. There's got to be something you can do." I stomped my foot. "I won't leave until we're on a flight!"

Donna pursed her lips and glanced around. My hopes soared. Maybe they would make an exception. He wasn't a large dog. We could make room.

She pushed our ID cards across the counter, leaned forward, and whispered, "Listen to me carefully. Go home. Do not make a scene, or they *will* arrest you."

I looked at two police officers stationed behind her, their guns hanging at their sides. They were watching us with interest.

My face crumpled, and a sob broke loose as I tried to gulp in air. "Please, just let us through. He's not big. I'll hold him on my lap if I need to. It'll be fine, please!"

She placed her left hand over mine. "Listen to me! You need to pull yourself together." She looked to the left and the right then put my hand over the cards. "Take these, go home, and find a doctor to write you a note. Even if I let you through here, they'll check again at the gate. This is your only option. Once you have a note, you can book another flight. You have a week before they close flights. Do you understand me?" Her eyes were pleading.

"I understand. Thank you." I sobbed.

She gave my hand a quick squeeze before straightening and motioning for another passenger to step forward. My feet felt cemented to the floor, and I continued to stare at her in a daze. She caught my eye again and flicked her head in the direction of the door. I looked at those still in line with envy, tears sliding down my cheeks. Their freedom was still in their grasp. Mine had been denied. I'd been turned away. There was no exception to be made. No miracle would get us on that flight.

I forced myself to move toward the exit while I shuffled ideas for obtaining a note from a doctor. When I reached the sliding doors, I stopped, my shoes squeaking on the rubber mat below my feet. Just outside the doors, a line of other rejects with slumped shoulders zigzagged in front of the exit. I didn't belong in that line. I looked over my shoulder at the people in line for flight check-in, their bags sitting idly on the ground next to them. The look of hope in their eyes was hard to resist, and I felt a renewed sense of determination. Even if another agent denied me, I would be in no worse shape than I already was.

I turned around and walked slowly back to the line. My eyes darted to the policemen. *Are they still watching me?* It was hard to tell behind the thick plastic of their helmet masks. I watched them out of the corner of my eye, a bead of sweat trickling down the groove in my back. The policemen stepped away from their post and moved purposefully in my direction. My steps faltered, and my heart rate jumped erratically. The men walked faster, their hands on the guns dangling at their sides. I sucked in a breath and took a step back. As they closed the distance between us, I became more convinced that they were coming for me. Their eyes seemed to bore holes into mine. I averted my eyes in an effort to look nonchalant, but my chest heaved and my hands were shaking. I kept my eyes on Zeke, who sat next to my feet, looking up at me anxiously. In my periphery I saw their boots close in. *This is it. I'm about to be escorted outside.*

I raised my eyes and opened my mouth to concede defeat when suddenly a man in a green jacket was thrown to the ground next to me. I jumped and watched as the policemen fought to subdue him. I hadn't even noticed the man standing there just a foot away. Another policeman rushed over to help haul the man to his feet and drag him outside, the tips of his sneakers dragging across the floor.

He screamed, "This is illegal! I have a wristband!"

When his shouts faded and the doors closed, I exhaled in relief. They hadn't been coming for me. But then it dawned on me that they would just drag me out too. I had no new arguments to support my case. Feeling defeated, I turned and walked through the sliding doors. While I stood in line for the van ride home, I pulled out my phone and called my mom.

"Mom? I'm at the airport, but they won't let me bring Zeke because he's not *my* service animal. They said I need a doctor's note stating my medical condition."

"Oh no! Oh my god! Karis, you have to leave him!" she said frantically.

"Mom! I can't leave him! You know I can't!"

"Karis, I know this is hard, but listen to me. Take him home and leave out a bunch of food. Then go back to the airport and get on a flight," she pleaded.

Tears streamed down my face while masked faces watched me. My voice was thick with anguish as I stared at Zeke's brown eyes and floppy ears, both raised in concern. "I'm sorry, Mom. I can't. I can't do it. I'm looking at him right now, and I don't have it in me. It would kill me. He'd be all alone for who knows how long!" My mind was filled with images of him alone in my apartment, emaciated, dehydrated, and lonely, his glorious fluffy white fur falling out in patches due to malnutrition.

"Karis, you can't stay there! You don't know what will happen—we could lose you!" Her voice was shrill, and I felt her desperation.

It broke my heart, but it didn't sway me. "I'm so sorry, but I can't leave him. Please forgive me, Mom. I don't know what else to do! I won't be able to live with myself if I leave him behind. I just can't do it."

I pulled the phone away from my ear, and as I was about to hang up, I heard her screaming, "Karis! Karis, leave him behind! *Go back to the airport!*"

I was still crying when the van came, and I hadn't stopped by the time the man put my bags on the sidewalk. I watched in a daze as he stepped back into the van and drove away. I walked Zeke and my bags back into the building. Zeke was looking at me, confused—he didn't understand what had just happened or what I'd given up for him. But I knew I'd made the right decision.

My mom had been calling constantly since I hung up, but I'd turned off the ringer. I picked up my phone and saw ten missed calls. There was nothing she could have said to change my mind, and I knew that she knew as much. She knew exactly who I was, she knew how much I loved animals, and she knew how important Zeke was to me.

I'd fallen in love the minute I laid eyes on him. He was six weeks old and the cutest thing I'd ever seen, a small white puffball of fur with two little dark eyes peeking out. Zeke and I ate together, slept together, and even watched TV together—he preferred horror movies too. He was my other half, my support system, my closest friend. There was never a possibility of leaving him behind.

But knowing this didn't diminish the fear of what lay ahead. I catalogued my options, anxious to start calling people for a doctor's note, but I had to call my mom back. I'd never hung up on her before, and it made me uncomfortable. I waited half an hour, texting some acquaintances to ask if they knew a doctor, and finally called my mom back.

"Hi," I said quietly, taking a bottle of Woodford whiskey out of my liquor cabinet and adding a healthy pour into a glass tumbler.

"You aren't calling me from the airport, are you?"

"No."

"Dammit, Karis! It's just a dog! You could have just given yourself a death sentence. Do you understand what you've done?"

She was crying, and I felt unbelievably guilty but resolute at the same time. I took a big gulp from my glass. "I'm sorry, but you know there wasn't another option. You know I could never have left him. He's not just a dog, and you know it." I said this with such resolve that it left no room for misunderstanding.

She sighed, and I heard her sniffling as she cried. I gave her the space. "Well, there's no use in arguing about it now. What can we do?" she asked.

"I really don't know. I'm going to call the number on the website and beg. I don't think it'll do any good, but I've got to try. Do we know any doctors who could write me a note? That's all I need."

After a pause she said, "I don't think so, but I'll start calling around." She took a deep breath. "I need a drink."

I looked at the whiskey in my hand. "I'm way ahead of you there."

Chapter 8

December 20th

"We went through classes and certification. I have all his vaccine paperwork and his ID card. That's all I've ever needed when I've flown with him before. I don't understand why he's not allowed this time. Can't you make a note on my boarding pass or something?"

"Ms. Hylen, if it were up to me, I'd allow him on the flight. I have a dog too. I completely understand. But our hands are tied right now. You need a doctor's note for a service animal to be allowed on these flights. They've even been calling and confirming some of the doctor's notes. If this were any other time, it wouldn't be an issue. But these aren't normal circumstances. The process is stricter than usual. I'm sorry."

She was the fourth person I'd talked to from the TSA over the past three days, and by far the nicest. While they all sympathized with my situation, they'd said the same thing. The protocol was very strict and was double- and triple-checked along the way. There were no exceptions.

"Thank you for your help. I appreciate it."

The service agent paused before dropping her voice into a whisper. "Just get a note from a doctor however you can, okay? Don't wait too long. There are still plenty of seats available on the last two days of the evacuation."

When I hung up the phone, I took the last bite of my lunch and checked my texts. I hadn't gotten replies to the numerous messages I'd sent asking if anyone knew a doctor. I tried calling, but none of them answered. I left pleading voice messages and anxiously waited for someone to call me back, but no one did. My mom continued to call everyone in her phone book, too, and we were hopeful when my uncle remembered he had a pharmacist friend. He'd passed along my info. My phone's ringtone jolted me awake around midnight after I'd passed out on the sofa.

"Hi, Karis. This is Aaron. Sorry it took so long to call you. We've been swamped at the pharmacy with the testing stations. Your uncle gave me your number. I understand you need a doctor's note?"

"Yes, I need one for my service dog stating he is providing me with a medical service. Is that something you could do?"

"Unfortunately, no. I wish I could help, but a note like that needs to be signed by an MD. My stationery has RPh in my title, and that would be a huge red flag. I know a doctor, but he's a by-the-book kind of guy. I don't think he'd write a note without seeing your medical records."

Defeated, I thanked him and crawled into bed. The next morning, I called Mom to let her know about the pharmacist. With our last hope gone, we decided I should take things into my own hands. I only had a few more days left to make it out of here. I googled "doctor's notes" and found one from a doctor here in NY that I could work with. Luckily, working in graphic design gave me a thorough knowledge of Photoshop. I manipulated the document and changed it to my name and today's date, giving epilepsy as my medical condition. My perfectionism made me zoom in and check every letter and number for signs that it'd been Photoshopped. I printed it out and looked again for any flaws, but I didn't think anyone would be able to tell it was a fake. They'd only know if they made that call to the doctor, which was a risk I was willing to take at this point. I just hoped the agents would be too busy and stressed out to bother making that call. By the time I was finished, it was two o'clock, and I went back online to book another flight. But when the page came up, it said there were no more flights available. Fear raced through me. *Dammit, she said I had a week!* I quickly called the customer service number.

After listening to hold music, nineties lite rock, for thirty minutes, I was finally connected to an agent. "Hi, I tried to book a flight with my barcode, but it says there are no more flights available. How can that be? I was told just yesterday that there were open flights on the last two days of the evacuation."

"I'm so sorry about that, ma'am. We've been forced to close flights early because the virus is spreading faster than they'd anticipated. Late last night, the timeline was moved up a few days, and the final flight is leaving tonight. They announced it on the news this morning."

I'd been too focused on the doctor's note to watch TV. "Oh my god. Is there any way you can get me on that flight?" My hands started shaking.

"Last time I checked, there were no seats, but let me check again. What's your name and phone number?"

After giving her the necessary info, I said, "I'll have my service dog with me too. I have the required doctor's note and his ID card."

The sound of her nails tapping on the keys came through the line. Then she exhaled and said, "I'm sorry to say this, but the flight is already overbooked. They had to move some passengers from the later flights onto today's flights. I can put you on the waitlist, but you'd be number thirty-two on the list. Chances aren't good."

"Oh, come on! Clearly, they need more flights if there's a waitlist," I argued.

"That's not up to us, Ms. Hylen. These are the only flights I can book for you."

"Is there anything you can do to get us on a flight today? Please. I'm begging."

"I'm sorry, but there's nothing I can do. I've placed you on the waitlist. You'll be notified if a seat opens up."

"But what if—"

The click of her hanging up interrupted my pleas. I threw the phone on the table and dropped to the floor, hugging my knees. I was angry at myself, at the TSA, at the woman who'd told me I had a few days left, and at whoever had started the epidemic in the first place. My body shook as I cried and pounded my fist on the hardwood floor. I thought about every opportunity I'd missed, everything I should have done differently.

But after the shock wore off, I knew it was pointless to go down that road. I was stuck for the time being, so I had to come to terms with that. I called my mom to tell her the bad news. She cried and cursed my decision to wait. I let her rage for a few minutes before she finally calmed down.

"So what's your plan now?" she asked, her voice raw and rough.

"I guess I'm going to stay in my apartment until something changes."

I hung up, feeling beaten. I put on my thick down coat and went up to the roof to clear my head. My thoughts were starting to jumble. I sat on the wide ledge with my legs out straight and laid my head against the old chimney that led to my living room. A few minutes passed before I heard a woman crying. Her moans and wails pierced the air, and it was quiet enough that I heard her struggle to catch her breath, shouting "no!" every few seconds. I pulled my head up and listened. I couldn't tell where she was, and I didn't know why she was crying, but it didn't matter. I was suddenly a part of her suffering. There was so much emotion in her sobbing that I felt it pulse through my veins.

At some point, my breath caught in my throat. Tears slid down my cheeks, and I whispered, "I'm so sorry," over and over. When the woman quieted and my cheeks were dry again, a dim light clicked on in a window across the street. I looked closer and noticed it wasn't a light but the faint glow of a television. I pulled my legs from the ledge and went back downstairs.

The next couple of days passed in a blur, and it was pretty rough trying to keep myself occupied without going crazier than I already was. One morning, I looked through an old photo album and found a picture of my college soccer team, the Ladyhawks, at Disneyland after a tournament in LA. We were huddled around a smiling Mickey Mouse, grinning as one teammate slyly grabbed Mickey's crotch. I chuckled at the photo, remembering what a great time we'd had on the rides and stuffing ourselves with junk food. *What was the crotch-grabber's name? Sarah? Samantha? No, it was Stephanie!* I looked back at the photo and tried to remember every name. I wrote their names next to their faces on the photo. I recalled all but two, who I'd guessed were Kayla and Marie, though I knew that wasn't right. They'd been freshmen when I was a senior, so I hadn't known them well.

After I put the photo back in the album, I sat back and looked around for something else to do. The *Hellraiser* DVD on the bottom of the stack in my TV stand sparked a clear memory of watching it huddled up with Christian under blankets on my couch. I shook my head and pushed all the disappointing men in my life to the background. I had more troubling things to worry about, but I had to imagine I was a lot better off than those who *hadn't* been in a self-imposed isolation when the virus hit. I laughed at the notion that the past few months had conditioned me perfectly.

It also helped that I loved my apartment. My parents' house had white walls everywhere. I called it "the house of no color." I'd begged them every year to let me paint my bedroom or any room—even the garage would do. Finally, during my sophomore year, they allowed me to paint my room an equally boring beige.

In direct response to my upbringing, the minute my roommate had moved out, I'd painted each room a different bold color. My living room was a loud yellow, bordering on neon. The dining room was an intense shade of red, called "Sashay," that I'd found in the discount pile at Home Depot. My kitchen was a bright, warm gold. I'd painted the hallway dove gray in an attempt to lead guests into the color show beyond. My bedroom and bathroom were varying shades of blue, which I'd read produced a feeling of tranquility. It was liberating to finally have color in my life. And by New York standards, my apartment was pretty big. In the old buildings, not many people had a separate living room and dining room, but I did. And even though the bedrooms and bathroom were a bit small, the rest of the place was spacious, giving me plenty of room to roam around. It was one of the perks to living in an outer borough.

With pen and paper in hand, I mapped out a daily routine. It made the empty days much more bearable if I had a purpose. I took my temperature first thing every morning before taking Zeke to the roof. Then I had coffee while he had his breakfast. Since I had no idea what obstacles might stand in my way at some point, I thought it would be good to keep in shape. If I had to run for any reason, I needed to be able to do it. I hadn't worked out in over a year, and the ten pounds I'd put on over the past three months made it slow going at first. I spent fifteen minutes running and, as I petered out, walking up and down the four flights of stairs in my building. Then I moved on to crunches, push-ups, and squats, finishing with several plank positions I remembered from the Pilates class Lori and

I used to take on Sundays before long, boozy brunches at our favorite French place, Café Henri.

I staked out two hours every day to watch the news and scour
the internet for more information. I was also trying to find out if
there were others like me, who weren't sick but for some reason
decided to stay—I couldn't be the only one. Recent searches confirmed there were others, more than I would have thought. There
was no laundry in my building, so on Tuesdays, I washed my underwear for the week in the sink, and Thursdays were for a large
wash of everything else in the tub. I used the old clothesline outside
to dry my clothes. I usually got bored by two o'clock. The rest of
my day was consumed with trying to find some way to fill the time
and attempting to drown out the sounds of glass breaking, screams,
and thumps from outside. Most of the time, I could place what the
sounds were, but sometimes it was an ambiguous creak or vibration.

At four o'clock, I went up to the roof and hung out with the
girls. While they were sad for me because I didn't get out, they were
ecstatic that I was still around to play with them. They thought I'd
made the right decision to stay in the city with Zeke. After that,
I would make dinner and read or watch TV with Zeke curled up
next to me on the couch.

Luckily, I had bought all those extra bags of dog food. There
was enough for a few months if I cut each meal down a quarter
cup. Zeke's pot belly made me think I'd been feeding him too much
anyway. I also knew that I needed to ration my own food. I didn't
know how long my stash would have to last, but I assumed it could
be quite a while. I cursed the days I'd spent rashly eating more
than I needed because I'd assumed I would be in California soon.
I worked out how much food I had left, stacking the cans, bags of
rice, and pasta in rows and dividing the total by days. I only had
enough for a month at most, even after strictly rationing. Then a

thought popped into my head. I could go into the other apartments and take all my neighbors' food, which could potentially keep me going for a while longer. If anything, I was sure I would run out of alcohol before food—what a sad day that would be.

On Christmas Eve as I watched the news, there was a breaking news conference. The president was about to speak. This was the first time he'd addressed the nation on the outbreak. He walked to the podium and looked gravely into the camera.

"Good afternoon. The NOS-9 virus that has devastated the Eastern states over these past few months is at epidemic level. We have formed a special committee to organize medical care, supplies, and evacuation of uninfected survivors. Our first order of business is to set up a border, spanning north to south, from western Minnesota to eastern Texas, essentially cutting the United States in half. We've sent teams to the public to test every resident and are confident that there are no infected cases past this point. This border will be staffed with armed forces, a medical team from the CDC, and temporary housing. Because we don't know how long it will take to find a cure or vaccine, our first priority is to stop the spread of the virus.

"We have arranged a number of flights to transfer those who are not infected out of the Eastern states and into the Western states. In the coming weeks, government officials and police forces will also be evacuating. For those of you who did not make it onto one of these flights or have chosen to stay, be aware that there will now be a state of martial law in these regions. While a small military team will set up patrolling stations in each state, there will be no police presence. Because of how deadly this virus has become, we cannot offer protection or help to anyone who has chosen to stay within the infected border. We urge everyone to be civil and to not engage in acts of looting or violence. However, we understand that without a police presence, these instances may occur. Your best course of action is to remain inside your home. If you are in need of food or supplies, log onto the website before the end of the week and register your address. We will be sending supplies to as many people as possible before the final evacuation. We are allowing a small group of workers to reside in each state in order to maintain electricity and water supplies for the time being.

"We are working on a cure and a plan for the country to move forward during this crisis. Our hope is to devise a system that allows uninfected survivors who can make it to the border into the Western states safely. While we understand how dangerous this prospect is, it is the only salvation we can offer at this time.

"There has been increased speculation about the government's involvement and knowledge of the virus. I would like to put all questions to rest by being completely transparent. On November fifteenth, we received an anonymous message threatening to attack New York City with a biological weapon in the form of a virus. Our government receives anonymous threats on a regular basis, and it's our job to determine which are credible and which are not. Because of the nature of this message and the details involved, it was determined that this message was at an elevated threat level. We can't be certain if any threat is real or a hoax. We can only decide which threats to take seriously, and about ninety-five percent of those turn out to be fraudulent. Any message of an elevated threat level or less automatically goes into a monitoring mode. A message deemed high threat or higher goes into an action or evacuation mode. While we do our best to accurately determine the validity of these claims, at best we are only guessing.

"On the night of November fifteenth, the body scanners at airport security checkpoints were activated to begin temperature testing everyone flying out of New York City and Newark as a part of the monitoring process. About a quarter of those flying out tested positive for a fever higher than ninety-nine degrees. As a precaution, we then quarantined these people until we could be certain that they were not infected with this so-called virus. Unfortunately, that did not turn out to be the case, as these people have all tested positive for the virus. Reports began coming in from other states of the virus beginning to spread. It is our belief that the virus was released sometime shortly before the threat was delivered to our government, allowing a small number of infected travelers to make it out of New York undetected. These people have all been identified and quarantined. We then broadened our testing and were able to ascertain that the virus had in fact started in New York and was slowly spreading across the country. At that point, we were able to increase the emergency to a high threat level and inform the country of the outbreak. We regret that we were unable to accomplish this sooner and save more lives.

"But we must move forward now with hope and determination. We are working around the clock to find a cure and to help those infected and uninfected. I have great confidence in our medical teams and our people to come together and fight this virus. While we are in a time of crisis and uncertainty, I look to our community to remain strong, to help one another, and never to give up hope."

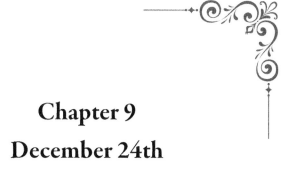

Chapter 9
December 24th

The speech made me feel as if I was in my own dystopian drama and left me pondering my options. *Is there any way we could make it halfway across the country alone and without any form of transportation?* I didn't think so, but it was my only hope of getting to my family. I could walk to the border, but that would be extremely dangerous. Maybe I could find a bike, and Zeke could run next to me. That was less dangerous but not by much. And I wasn't sure Zeke, at eight years old, could handle that level of activity. The last time I'd taken him for a run, he'd lasted only ten minutes before putting on the brakes and refusing to go any farther. Maybe a car still parked on my block had keys in it. There were only six or seven cars left on my block, and I didn't want to venture beyond my street. It was unlikely that anyone would have left the keys, but it was the best idea yet. I walked to the window and looked outside, considering the idea. A door slammed somewhere in the distance, making me jump and drawing my eyes across the park. I wasn't sure if I had the courage to go outside.

I logged on to the website to register my address for supplies. The page loaded, and there was a long paragraph stressing that supplies were limited, so only those with extremely low food supplies should request a care package. I wasn't extremely low, but I would be in a month, so I decided to register anyway. My mom called to discuss the speech. I didn't plan on mentioning my idea to try cars. I was sure she would tell me not to do it.

"Oh, Karis, this is great news. We have hope!"

"Yeah, but I have no way of getting to the border."

"I know. But maybe the government will provide transportation at some point. We shouldn't dwell on that part yet. Let's give it some time, okay?"

"All right. Call me after dinner, and we'll talk more. I'm gonna go work out."

"I love you, honey."

"Love you too."

I didn't say it because I couldn't bear to crush her spirits, but I wasn't confident that transportation would be provided. I needed a backup plan. I put it on hold for the time being because the next day was Christmas, and I wanted to try to make it special for the girls. After my workout, I made them gingerbread cookies and found corn syrup in the back of my cupboard to make caramels. For Emma, I wrapped up a gold necklace with emeralds and diamonds forming a clover that my college ex-boyfriend had given me. I hadn't worn it in years. After rummaging around, I found a hodgepodge of craft supplies and markers in random drawers for Julia. I also found my favorite childhood book, *The Boxcar Children,* and wrapped that up for them too. It was about four orphaned kids who made a home in an abandoned boxcar in the forest. They spent their days finding supplies in a dump to make a fireplace and even a swimming pool. It seemed appropriate, given what we were going through.

When I was done, I opened a book I'd found when searching for gifts for the girls. It was wedged behind a shelf in my makeshift closet. It must have belonged to my old roommate because I didn't recognize the cover. Since it was the only book in the house I hadn't read, I was grateful for the distraction. By bedtime, I was three quarters of the way through the book and threw it down in frustration. The main character was a bitter forty-year-old woman who turned her back on everyone after a nasty divorce and the death of her daughter, blaming everyone else for both tragedies. She eventually became agoraphobic and spent the next ten years alone in her house, battling her inner demons. It made me uncomfortable to read about the descent of my proverbial Ghost of Christmas Future, so I filed it away in my bookshelf and went to bed without finding out if she redeemed herself in the end.

Before I went up to the roof the next afternoon, I clipped a large bag to the pulley and sent it over. A few minutes later the girls came to the window, wearing red velvet dresses. Emma had on reindeer antlers made out of pipe cleaners. Julia's Christmas-themed drawings, featuring Emma the Reindeer, were taped up all over the windows.

"Wow, you two look great! Merry Christmas!"

"Thanks. My mom wanted us to dress up for her. We opened our presents already. I got some books, some pastels, and an easel to paint!" Julia exclaimed.

"I got three new dresses and a bunch of glitter hair ties. Julia made me the antlers," Emma said happily.

Julia pointed to a drawing on top of the others. "This is for you." She had used the new pastels on the drawing, and it was really good, better than the rest. In it, Zeke was on my lap, smiling at me with his tongue hanging out the side of his mouth.

"Aw, thanks! I love it. You really captured Zeke's personality," I said. "I have something for you guys too. It's on the line already."

Julia looked up, and a big smile appeared on her face. She reached up and unclipped the bag. They squealed in excitement and ripped open the wrapping paper I'd made out of paper bags. I'd taken my time carefully drawing snowflakes and bows on the bags, hoping it would resemble real wrapping paper.

"Awesome! I can make some cool stuff with all this. Thanks!" Julia said, plowing through the box of crafts.

"You're welcome."

Emma was holding up the necklace but not saying anything. "Emma, do you like it?"

She looked at me. "It's so beautiful. Is this real gold and diamonds?" She was handling it as though it was worth a million dollars.

"Yep. You'll get more use out of it than I will. I'm glad you like it."

Julia stuffed a cookie and a caramel into her mouth at the same time.

"Don't eat the candy and cookies all at one time! You'll get a stomachache," I said, some maternal instinct taking over.

She paused. "Um, okay, but they taste really good together," she said through a mouthful of crumbs.

I laughed and realized my warning was ridiculous. They should stuff their faces if they wanted. "Eat whatever you want. That's why I made them, right?" I said, throwing up my hands. "I hope you like the book. I've read it about a billion times. It's one of my favorites."

"Really? I bet it's good. I'll read it to Emma."

"How's your mom's fever?"

Her smile fell, and she looked down at the cookie in her hand. "It's at one-oh-three. It jumped to one-oh-four last night for a little while. But I put a cold washcloth on her forehead for a few hours and gave her some medicine. This morning, it was back down to one-oh-three. I think she's okay for now."

"That's good. You're doing all the right things, so keep it up." I looked at Emma, but she was fumbling with the necklace and wasn't paying attention to our conversation. Julia followed my eyes and reached over to help Emma put the necklace on.

"You know what I was thinking last night? Isn't it funny that we live this close and never met before?" I asked.

They looked at each other then back at me. "We've seen you around a few times. Well, we've seen Zeke. He's so white and fluffy that he's hard to miss. We petted him one time outside our apartment building when you were walking by. Do you remember?" Emma asked.

I thought about it. "I'm not sure. I stop to let everyone pet him when they want to, but I do remember stopping in front of that building. It's too bad we didn't talk and get to know each other more."

"Yeah, I wish we knew you longer. We could have hung out," Julia said.

"That would have been fun. But we know each other now. At least we have that."

We chatted about their Christmas gifts. Emma modeled each new hair tie and talked about their individual virtues. It was getting darker and colder, so I said goodnight and sat on the ground with my back against the roof door, watching them run around their apartment playing. Zeke climbed up onto my lap and watched them too. After another hour, it was completely dark, and I walked over to the far ledge. The city was a black hole dotted by scattered lights here and there around the boroughs I could see from my rooftop. I couldn't see the shapes of the buildings. There was no iconic skyline anymore. Even the Empire State building melted into the void. Without the usual glaring ambient light, I could see a sky full of stars. They faded into the blackness of the earth, and the lights of stranded survivors blended into the star-filled sky. They'd become stars too. Looking across the endless darkness, I thought about the people behind those lights, wondering how they were surviving and whether they were sick or just willing prisoners like I was. When my legs became numb with cold, we went back downstairs. I fed Zeke and had a glass of wine while talking to my parents. I was sad not to be there with them on Christmas, but I was glad I could be in the city for the girls. The thought comforted me.

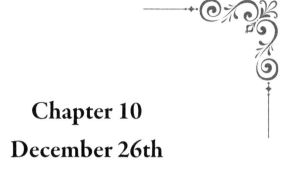

Chapter 10
December 26th

W hile my coffee brewed, I heard a truck pull up downstairs. A man got out and grabbed a medium-sized box from the back and entered my vestibule. After he drove away, I ran down and pulled the box in. Upstairs, I ripped it open and found about three or four days' worth of food in blank packaging with black bold letters telling me what was inside. I wondered if they assumed everyone left was sick and were only giving us enough food to last until we died.

I sighed and turned on the TV, absentmindedly flipping through the channels while I drank my coffee and thought about my limited food. When I looked at the screen, I bolted upright. The channels were filled with static, the jumbled specks screaming "it's gone" at me repeatedly. I stared at the screen, dumbfounded, futilely hitting the channel button repeatedly.

It was the first sign of the government turning off our services. My thoughts immediately went to other amenities they would eventually shut down: electricity, water, gas. And the internet—without that, I also wouldn't be able to access Netflix or Facebook, which had been my mental lifeline. If I didn't have them, it might tip me over the edge. I shuddered at the thought. My knees buckled, and I dropped back to the couch. Quickly, I picked up my laptop and checked the internet. Breathing a sigh of relief that it was still working, I snapped the computer closed. My body felt as if it was dissolving into a mass of wandering black-and-white dots.

I searched for any channel still in service and discovered a few were still operating. I stopped on a news report and learned that they'd turned off cable except for the most basic channels so those still within the border could still access news on the outbreak and information on the quarantine.

I turned the TV off and finished my coffee in silence. Zeke finished his food and sidled up next to me on the couch. The loss of cable was pushing the idea of checking cars to the forefront of my mind. I looked outside again, and fear trembled through my body, but I couldn't dismiss it because it might be my only chance. I decided I would venture out sometime that week. I would watch the street for any threats and gather courage.

The first day I saw a person in my periphery darting across the park, but otherwise there was no movement. I saw a few stray cats and the wind blowing plastic bottles and paper bags down the street from the now-open bags of recycling. Every day that I didn't see a person on the street gave me more confidence that I could do this. The only things that gave me pause were the sounds I'd heard: some heavy thumps and crashing clanks, a loud, muffled argument, and once an eerie braying laugh. Nighttime was more alive with sounds, shadows and movement just out of my line of sight. My mind filled in the blanks in a horrifying way. I'd have to pull myself away from the window, my eyes squeezed shut tightly, and remind myself that I was safe inside my apartment. But today I'd heard very little.

I did more research, mostly Facebook and news articles, looking for any morsel of information on a possible way home. I found a page called *The Salvation Railroad,* which was dedicated to people posting ideas and tips for making it safely to the border. The posters on the forum had abandoned NOS-9 and were now calling it the

Comeback Virus because of how resilient it was. The main pinned thread on the page caught my eye. It was an open forum where people could chime in and discuss escape plans. Some people in the states closer to the border had started making the trek. It was a day's drive at most for them, and many had posted their successes. Others had encountered rogue survivors who'd been violent, attacking them and stealing their supplies. So far, no one had been killed, but it had only been a few days since the president's speech, and I suspected that would change. There were no posts from people farther away.

I started taking notes about how I would go about my journey. I was a lot farther away than those who had made it, so there was much greater danger. Even if I had a car, I would have to travel for three to four days at minimum. Some people, seeking safety in numbers, were arranging caravans with others who wanted to make an escape.

Unfortunately, there were no caravans leaving from New York City. The closest I found was in Ohio. After two more days of scouring the internet, I concluded that I had to sit back and wait. Given the danger, I needed to allow others to make mistakes so I didn't make the same ones. I was also hoping a caravan closer to me would arrange itself and I could get to it somehow. If I didn't find a car with keys, it was my only chance of getting out. Feeling better about having a shred of a plan, I turned in.

The ding from a news alert on my phone woke me up the next morning. I rubbed my eyes then picked up my cell. The Red Cross had announced a death toll of approximately a hundred thousand and posted a list of those who were confirmed dead and a list of the missing and unaccounted for. I bolted out of bed and ran to my laptop. After reading the article and glancing at the endless list of names, I read some of the comments posted below. People were calling it the Death List.

It was sorted by state and then by county. I scoured the New York list page by page. It was massive—ten pages of names made up the confirmed dead list, and even more were missing. I found names of co-workers, neighbors, and friends—most of the people I knew in New York were gone. Barb and Kelly's names were on the confirmed list, but no one else from the building. *Maybe they made it out,* I thought hopefully. My breath caught in my throat when I found my friend Lori on the dead list, and I wondered about her dog, Cody. *Where is he?* Even though I hadn't seen her since my self-imposed exile, I missed Lori with a palpable, deep, dull pain. I squeezed my eyes shut and choked out a sob, a burning ache twisting in my stomach. I found a few guys I'd dated on the confirmed list, including Brian, and my ex Jack's name was on the missing list. I texted him again, hoping for a response to prove the list wrong. But no reply came.

After a few hours of searching and crying over each name I knew and all the ones I didn't, I slumped over in my chair. I was overwhelmed by so much loss, each name shredding my heart into sharp shards that continuously pierced my nerves. My own survival seemed wrong in the face of so much death. The only reason I was alive was because I'd turned my back on people because I'd done something I probably shouldn't have. My mind was vomiting images of everyone I'd lost, playing like a recap reel at the beginning of a depressing television drama. I cried until my eyes dried up, I raged until I had no energy left, and then I sat in numb silence. I fell asleep, my head and arms resting on the dining table. When I woke up an hour later, my brain and body felt wilted, unable to jump back to life. But I forced myself to push the never-ending list of names to the bottom of my emotional pile and focus on my own struggle. The list helped put things in perspective. I'd taken for granted all those people in my life, hiding from them for months, assuming they would be there when I decided to emerge. I vowed to appreciate the ones I had left and immediately sent a text to my mom and dad, telling them how much I loved them.

The list was the final encouragement I needed to go outside and check the cars. I couldn't let my name be added to that record. I'd waited too long to forge that doctor's note, and look where that had gotten me. I had to do something *immediately*. I did a video search of how to hotwire a car in case I found one that was unlocked but had no keys. Several videos made it look complicated, especially since I wasn't very mechanically inclined. But I took notes and hoped for the best. I pulled on my short puffer jacket and running shoes. I put my cell phone in the jacket pocket along with a box cutter, which could double as a weapon, to strip the wires. I wasn't sure who I would call if I got into a jam, but it was better to be on the safe side. I zipped the pocket shut. Before I headed out, I grabbed an empty backpack in case I found something I wanted to bring back. Zeke looked at me, concerned, when I walked to the front door.

I crouched and cupped his face in my hands. "I'll be back soon, buddy. Don't worry. I promise I'll be careful." I kissed his nose then grabbed my keys from the rack and walked out.

At the vestibule door downstairs, my hand trembled when I reached for the knob. I pulled my hand back and shook it. A loud bang outside made me jump. My courage waned, and I contemplated scrapping my plan. It had been two and a half weeks since I'd left my building, but it was time, and the bang sounded far away. Taking a deep breath, I reached out again and opened the door. The next door had a small window in it, but I had to stand on my tiptoes to see through it. I watched for a long time, willing my limbs to be still, but they continued to quiver. After pulling the backpack straps onto my shoulders, I patted the box cutter in my pocket then pulled the door open slowly. Holding the door open with my foot, I listened for any suspicious sounds. The air was so still it felt dead.

There was a small car a few feet to the left and three more down along the block. Another two were parked across the street, toward the end. I darted outside and over to the first car. Crouching down, I eased my eyes up to the window. The ignition was empty. When I pulled the door handle, it remained locked, and I saw that the driver's side was pushed to the locked position too. I stayed low as I ran down the street and repeated my actions at two more cars. Both were locked and had no visible keys.

As I ran to the fourth car, I heard a noise and looked up the street, then my foot hit the cement planter for the oak tree in front of the car. I launched forward and slammed into the tree, landing in a crumpled mess at its roots. My knee throbbed from colliding with the tree. My hands had scratches and stung from catching myself on the trunk. After giving myself a minute to rebound, I inched toward the car. The doors were unlocked, and I felt my hopes soar. The car was an old Audi that I remembered being popular in the late nineties. The glove compartment creaked as it opened, revealing only the owner's manual and a handful of ketchup packets from McDonalds. I pulled down the visors but found nothing of value there either. When my foot slid back, it collided with something solid. I reached under the seat, and my fingers curled around a box. Inside was a set of high-tech binoculars encased in foam, which would come in handy when scanning the streets, so I threw them into the backpack and tightened the straps on my shoulders. The plastic cover underneath the steering wheel popped off easily, and I inspected the wires. Finding what I hoped were the right two wires, I stripped them both and quickly touched them together. The dashboard should have lit up, according to the tutorials, but nothing happened. I twisted them together, hoping that would do the trick, but still nothing. Thinking maybe I was mistaken about the wires, I tried a few others, but nothing worked. Maybe the battery was dead. My shoulders slumped as I sat back on the passenger seat, feeling discouraged.

I crawled out the door and shut it as quietly as possible. But it still made a loud click that echoed off the buildings. My body froze. Expecting to hear the sound of running feet, I dropped to the ground behind the tree the car was parked next to. But all I heard was my heart pounding in my ears, my breath puffing in and out, and birds chirping. I moved around the rear bumper of the car, scanned the sidewalks one last time and then dashed across the street. Ducking behind the next car, I noticed a Baby on Board sign hanging in the back window. The front door handle was locked. The back seat held a pink-and-gray car seat, and toys littered the floor. The back window was open just a crack. As I tried the handle to the back door, a baby cried in an apartment across the street.

A door slammed, and a woman wailed, "Tommy, you have to go get it! We need it!"

The baby cried louder, and it seemed closer than before. My stomach clenched, and my limbs shook uncontrollably. I looked back at my building. *Should I run back or try the last car?*

I jumped when another door slammed, followed by the woman screeching something I couldn't understand. She was sobbing, and I heard a man yell viciously, "Damn it, Amber!" A raucous bang followed, making me jump again.

I looked at the last car and was just about to dash toward it when a front door opened and closed across the street. When I looked across through the backseat window, a man with scraggly blond hair was standing on the stoop, looking left and right. That brownstone belonged to Mr. and Mrs. Eckstein, a retired couple with a yappy Lhasa apso named Schatzi. They had a son, but I knew that wasn't him. He lived in Texas with his boyfriend. They didn't have any other kids. *Who are these people?*

The man brought his hand to his face and took a long drag from a cigarette. He dropped his hand to his side and slowly exhaled a thick plume of smoke. His eyes darted back and forth for a few seconds before coming to rest on the car I was behind. I dropped down to a pushup position and eased myself down. Under the car, I could see the sidewalk across the street. The dull sound of his footsteps thudded down the stairs. His combat boots hit the sidewalk, and he paused again.

My heartbeat thundered rapidly in my ears. I watched his feet walk toward the car and heard the key slide in the lock. He pulled the door open, and I heard him rifling around in the front seat. *Oh my god, can he see me?* I turned my body over onto one elbow and up into a side plank position, flattening myself against the car. The man got out and slammed the door before opening the back door. I heard toys being tossed around and the automated voice of a stuffed animal giggling creepily. The man swore, and after several long seconds, he began talking to someone, presumably on a phone, since I hadn't seen anyone else come out of the house.

The man said, "I found the bag, but it's not in there. I'm coming back." I could barely hear the voice on the other end of the line but couldn't make out what she was saying. A few seconds later, he raised his voice. "I looked in the back seat! It's not here!" The voice on the other end began to scream. Finally, the man cut in, "It's not in the trunk! Fine. Okay! But after that, I'm coming back. Amber, stop it now!" He sounded angry as he swore under his breath.

My stomach muscles were vibrating. I wasn't sure how much longer I could hold the pose. Sweat dripped down my forehead and chilled my skin in the cold air. He swore again, and then the back door closed. Anxiety surged through me. He might have been able to see me from the trunk. I slowly pulled my body down and crawled on all fours to the front of the car. I heard his boots move around to the back, and I crouched as low as I could. I peeked over the hood and saw the trunk pop open. It was my chance. I ran in a hunched position as fast as I could back up the street. There were no other cars to hide behind on my side.

I made it six houses down before I heard the trunk slam shut and the man say, "What the...?"

Fear sank its claws deeper into my gut. I straightened and broke into a full run. I didn't look back.

Then he growled, "Hey! Hey! Come back! Dammit!"

My feet slammed into the pavement as I accelerated to my top speed. My muscles were remembering how to sprint from soccer. Only the tips of my shoes were hitting the ground, and sometimes it felt like my feet didn't touch the ground at all. The binocular box was banging up and down on my back. I couldn't go back to my apartment. The man would know where I lived.

When I made it to the large apartment building on the corner across the street from mine, I made a wide left. Then I cut back to the building and crept up to the edge. I didn't hear his footsteps running after me. I peeked around the corner and spotted him in the middle of the street by the car, his arms full of bags. He was looking right in my direction. I jumped back. My chest was huffing up and down. I couldn't catch my breath. I unzipped my pocket and pulled out my phone. Turning on the camera, I slid it over to video. I eased it past the corner of the building and hit Record. My hand was shaking so badly that I almost couldn't see anything. I looked at the image and tilted the phone back and forth, searching for the man. I found his shape and zoomed in on him. He was still standing there, watching, his figure bouncing in my quivering hand.

I jumped when I heard what sounded like a glass bottle kicked down the street to the left of where I was standing. My head buzzed with adrenaline, and my skin was slick with sweat under my jacket. I pulled my eyes away from my phone and furtively looked around.

The street and sidewalks were empty, but I saw a clear bottle rolling into the intersection. I turned back to my phone and willed the man to go back inside his apartment. I whispered, "Come on, come on, go back inside." The baby's cries rang out again and screeched to a higher level. His head turned toward the apartment then back in my direction. He watched for another minute then turned and walked back into the brownstone.

When I heard the door slam, I took three deep breaths then sprinted across the street and up my steps. My body slammed into the front door. I rushed through the door and let it slam shut behind me. I pulled out my keys and tried to unlock the vestibule door, but my hand was trembling too much. I tried gripping one hand with the other in an effort to control the shaking. The key made a scraping noise as it bounced around the lock before finally sliding in. The door banged shut behind me, and I leaned back onto it, sliding down until I sat on the ground. My eyelids drifted down as I tried to slow my breathing. My hands were shaking, so I clasped them tightly in my lap to still them. *What am I going to do now?* I wasn't sure I could go back out there again. I would have to think of another way.

When my breathing returned to normal, I ran upstairs and practically bathed in Purell. I tore off my jacket and pulled the binoculars out of the box. I searched the street, hoping I didn't see the man looking for me. A faint, childlike giggling sprouted up in the air around me, similar to the toy I'd heard in the car. Anxiously, I scanned the area. The giggling was getting louder, but it seemed to be coming from everywhere—I couldn't find which direction. The maniacal snickering filled my ears so completely that I couldn't hear anything else. *This isn't real. It must be in my head.*

Suddenly, the air in my lungs felt thicker, as though fluid was flowing in. I gasped, trying to force it through my windpipe. The binoculars fell from my hands and clattered to the ground. The world wobbled. I grabbed the edge of the windowsill and eased my-self down to the ground, sitting with my back to the wall. My skin was cold with goosebumps, but I also felt feverish and clammy. My ears were hot and began ringing so loudly that I couldn't hear the giggling anymore. *Am I possibly getting sick? Am I hyperventilating? Or maybe this is a panic attack?* I'd never had one before. I wasn't sure of the symptoms. I looked up and saw Zeke's worried face wavering near me, and it looked like he'd grown another set of eyes. Black dots danced in my vision.

I closed my eyes and tried to slow my breathing, focusing on moving air in through my nose and out through my mouth. After several minutes of deep breathing, my shaking body calmed, and the air began to thin. When the ringing in my ears tapered off, I opened my eyes and saw Zeke still standing there, his eyebrows and ears arched. My world was steady again, but my shirt was drenched with sweat and sticking to my skin. I pulled Zeke into my arms and hugged him, probably too tightly, but he didn't protest.

What is happening to me? I had rarely been without the sounds of laughter and voices in the city. Even in my apartment, I constant-ly heard conversations and arguments from the streets. *Is my mind making up the giggling in the absence of sound, filling an unfamiliar void?* Zeke followed me over to the couch, and we both lay down. "I'm okay," I whispered repeatedly into Zeke's ear as he nestled in the crook of my body. My words lulled us both to sleep.

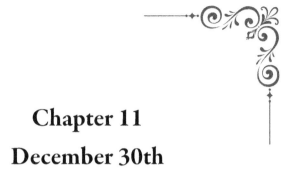

Chapter 11
December 30th

The next morning, I printed out an online company directory and scoured the Death List again, searching for the names of the people I used to work with. I found my coordinator, Lance, Sheila from marketing, whom I'd sometimes had lunch with, and just about every person in my department, including the executive director. I counted all the names that were left uncrossed on the list. More than three quarters of our company was gone or missing. The only ones left were a handful of designers, several accountants, a few IT guys, the CFO, and me. We were no longer a company, a team, coworkers, or friends. There would be no more strategizing and creating with them. I felt even more adrift. All my ties to the city were gone. I had no job. I had no friends. All I had left was my apartment and my dog. Zeke laid his head on my leg, and I told him his mom was now unemployed.

We'd been having some very interesting one-sided conversations, Zeke and I. While he couldn't answer me, I felt confident in my abilities to translate his head nods and eyebrow raises into actual responses. He thought we should stay put too. His mental clock has synced with our four o'clock play date with the girls. Every day around three-thirty, he would get antsy, tip-tapping the hardwood floor with his nails to get my attention. As an additional treat to our time together, Julia had been taping her daily drawings on the window for me to see. Each day, she rotated the oldest one out and replaced it with her new one.

Unfortunately, the visit that day wasn't a happy one. The girls were visibly upset, and Emma was coughing a lot more, her little alien-antennae headband shaking back and forth each time.

"Mom's not doing good. It's hard for her to breathe sometimes, and she says she's in pain. She coughed up blood this morning, and it got all over the bedspread. I don't know what else to do," Julia told me.

"Do you have any cold medicine? It would have pain relievers in it and something to help her breathe. Or even some aspirin or ibuprofen?" I asked.

"We did, but we ran out yesterday. We've been making her tea and chicken broth so she eats. But today she won't eat or drink anything because her throat hurts too much," Julia explained, and I noticed the glint of small tears rolling down her cheeks.

"Let me see if I have anything. Be right back."

Downstairs, I found some Theraflu packets at the bottom of my utensil drawer. *Those should help.* In the bathroom cabinet, I found a bottle of Chloraseptic from when I had sinus surgery four years before. The intubation had really hurt my throat, and I could barely swallow. I didn't know if it was still good, but it was worth a try. I grabbed a plastic bag and added ibuprofen and Sudafed to the lot. I found some Zicam melts for the immune system at the back of the drawer and threw those in too. I sent the bag over before running back upstairs. Julia unclipped the bag and ran off to make the Theraflu for her mom. I yelled at her to try the Chloraseptic first so she could drink it. Emma remained at the window.

"Is it hard to breathe?" I asked.

"Not really. I just cough a lot, and it hurts here and here." She put her hands to her ribs then to her throat. "It's hard to eat be-cause it burns my throat, but I do it anyways cause I'm hungry. Julia makes me soups and slushies. The slushies are just ice blended up with fruit juice, but they taste really good. You should try it. Do you have a blender?"

"Yes, I do. I'll definitely make one. Is there anything I can do? Do you guys need anything else?"

"I don't think so. We've been eating the candy slowly so it lasts. Kind of like Halloween when you know that the end of your stash is the end of the candy."

I smiled. "Good idea. When I was a kid, I could make that candy last for a few months if I was really stingy with myself."

"Wow, a few months?" she asked, her eyebrows raised and forehead crinkled. "We've never made it that long. But that's probably because we both steal from each other's bags."

I laughed. "So who are you today?"

She smiled broadly, putting her hands on her hips and puffing her chest out in a superhero stance. "I'm Bugsy the Bug! I have wings Julia made me, but they scratch my back." She held up what looked like hangers shaped into wings with plastic wrap stretched around them and glitter sprinkled over the surface. They weren't bad, given the girls' limited supplies.

Julia came back and sat on the sill. "She used the Chloraseptic and said it's helping. She's sipping the Theraflu now. She told me to say thank you."

"No problem. Let me know if you need anything else. If I don't have it, I can try another apartment. I put some Zicam tablets in there. They melt on your tongue and taste good. Both of you should start taking those. Maybe they'll help."

"You're going into other apartments?" Julia asked incredulously, her eyes widening.

"No, but I can if I need to." I wiggled my eyebrows conspiratorially at her. "The super keeps the keys in the basement. That door is locked, but I have a crowbar, and I'm sure I could pry it open."

"Do you think any other apartments have candy?" Emma asked hopefully.

The corners of my mouth quirked up. "Maybe the second floor. One of my neighbors has a son, and I'm sure there are some sweet snacks in there. If I need to go in, I'll see if she has any. Did you see the cloth bag in the plastic bag?"

Julia reached over to the table and pulled it up. "This one?"

"Yeah, Emma, that's for you."

Emma grabbed the bag and unzipped it, her eyes widening when she saw what was inside.

"I know your mom said no makeup, but it can be used for fun, like for your costumes. There's some bunny ears in there too." I'd used them once on Zeke to make an Easter card for my mom. He was not happy about it. Once I had them tucked in front of his ears, he froze and would not move until I took them off. Apparently, he didn't like things on his head, but he was fine with other costumes. He pranced around at a Halloween party as Zeke-a-saurus Rex one year, loving the attention.

"Oh my god, makeup!" she squealed as she pulled out makeup brushes and eye shadows, examining each one thoroughly.

"We really liked that book," Julia said. "We finished it last night. Violet is my favorite."

"She's mine too!" I said, excited they enjoyed it as much as I did.

Emma smiled and was about to say something but broke into a minute-long coughing fit.

"You should have some of the Theraflu, too, but maybe only half a cup. The full cup is an adult dosage."

Julia jumped off the sill and said, "I'll make her some now. Talk to you tomorrow?"

"Yep! But wait, let me take your photo before you go."

I'd made it a daily occurrence, like a photo diary of my time with them. Emma grabbed her wings and put them on. Then she looked over her shoulder at me and smiled with her hands on her hips. Julia put her hand on Emma's shoulder and smiled at the camera.

"That's a good one. Okay, take care of each other!"

Julia turned back to look at me. "Who's taking care of you?"

Immediately, I felt a sharp sting in my heart that shot up my throat and caused my breath to catch. The question made me sad in so many ways. I could see every failed relationship pass through my mind in a depressing rundown. But I pushed it all into a deep, dark corner of my brain, wrapping the memories in protective layers. "I can take care of myself, but Zeke and I look after each other," I finally replied.

She nodded her head then looked at Zeke. "Zeke, take care of your mom."

He responded with a whine and a glance in my direction. I smiled and waved goodbye.

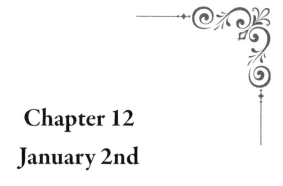

Chapter 12
January 2nd

A few days later, as I was running up and down the stairs, I saw something in a window across the courtyard directly below the girls' apartment. *What is that?* I remembered they'd said an old man named Mr. Standhope lived there. I opened the hallway window and pulled up the screen. Resting my hands on the sill, I leaned forward over the child guard and focused on the window. A chill surged through me, and my eyes widened in horror when I realized what it was. A hand with long, bony, tapered fingers reached from behind the curtain and rested on the window. Condensation surrounded the appendage. It wasn't moving—it was as if it had been placed there in a plea for help. I watched it for a few minutes, hoping to see some kind of movement, but it remained still. I turned and sat on the sill, closing my eyes. Either Mr. Standhope had died or he was dying. My breath was heavy and solid, full of anguish that felt tangible.

After a few deep breaths, I turned away to resume my workout and kept my eyes down when I passed that floor. A few hours later, I went back and checked again. The hand was still there but had slipped slightly, leaving finger trails through the condensation. I was sure that he was dead, and I knew that hand would be a macabre souvenir of Mr. Standhope's death every time I looked over there. *Oh god, can I handle that? Should I cover the window with something? Maybe a blanket or a sheet?* I looked back at the hand and felt tears on my lashes at the thought. I couldn't deny his existence. It didn't feel right.

I ran upstairs and searched my bottom kitchen drawer for some small tealight candles that I knew I had. I found them near the back then put them by the window and lit them in remembrance. I hadn't known the man, but someone must have loved him. He probably had friends or maybe even children. Surely, he'd had an impact on others. He was impacting me, and the least I could do was pay my respects and let the hand lie. I didn't tell the girls about it, but I did look over there occasionally, expecting it to have fallen. The hand remained, so I took a moment each time to pay homage.

MY BODY WAS RESPONDING well to my daily workout. I'd lost the extra weight that had filled out my butt and thighs. My arms and legs were starting to show faint lines of definition, and I didn't need to walk any portion of the stairs anymore. I could do a solid fifteen minutes of running up and down as long as I paced myself. My muscles felt firm and unrelenting, becoming stronger every day. Physically, I was on solid ground. Mentally, I wasn't so sure.

Something had happened the day before. I was cleaning the blinds in my living room, wiping each slat with bleach, when I felt the apartment shake, and a loud boom filled the silence. My eyes darted instantly to the street, where a huge pothole had been for years, right outside the window. That side of my apartment was on a main truck route, and when the trucks drove quickly over the pothole, it created a forceful thud, and the whole apartment vibrated, exactly like what I'd just felt. I quickly pulled the window and screen up and leaned out. Scanning the street, I searched for a truck, but the streets were empty. I pulled the window and screen closed again and sat down on the couch.

Is it possible that a truck went past and turned a corner before I saw it? I peered out the window again, scrutinizing the streets. I didn't see any vehicles, and I would have heard an engine or squealing tires if it'd been going fast enough to get around the corner without me spotting it. *Did I imagine it? Is this some sort of sensory memory coming back to haunt me?*

My mind was starting to slip. The situation with the girls wasn't helping either. It had been a rough week, despite starting out well. I'd found a pack of bottle rockets left by my ex-boyfriend in a box of old vitamins and long-dead batteries way in the back of my junk cupboard. On New Year's Eve, I lit them off my roof with the girls. They screamed and clapped while Zeke ran around, barking at the sparkly lights and loud bangs.

But soon, our visits became strained again. I didn't think their mom would last much longer. I could faintly hear her pained moans in the background when we talked. The girls told me her fever was up to one-oh-four and was gradually increasing. It was the last phase, according to the CDC. We'd been told that a low-grade fever would persist for the first few weeks, accompanying the other flu-like symptoms. Then the fever would start to rise as the virus began attacking the body more aggressively. The elevated fever was the immune system's response as it attempted to gain an advantage over the virus, but the virus would win, and the spike in temperature was really just the body's last-ditch effort to survive. It usually took only a few days at that point. A fever over one-oh-six meant brain damage and eventually organ failure. What a painful way to die.

I talked to the girls about what they should do. They tried everything, including ice baths and cold washcloths, yet the fever continued its march upward. We didn't talk about what to do when she died.

After only ten minutes one day, Emma told us she was tired and was going to take a nap. Her eyes seemed drained of life, and her cheeks were bright pink, but she'd still managed to put on the bunny ears and apply whiskers and a nose with the makeup I'd sent over. I snapped her photo before she left, but she could only manage a weak closed-lip smile. Julia was sad, though she was trying not to let it show. I could see it in the slump of her shoulders and in the way her eyes flicked down between each sentence as if she could dismiss her heartache with that one small move. I wished there was more I could do.

She looked at me and said quietly, "My throat started hurting last night. I took my temperature, and it's ninety-nine-point-five. I haven't told Emma yet. I don't want to scare her."

My heartbeat jumped erratically, and I took a step back as if to distance myself from her words. I knew it was coming, but I wasn't prepared. I put my head down for a second to rein in my emotions. I had to be strong for her. It took extreme effort to swallow the lump in my throat.

I pulled my head back up and said, "I'm sorry. The Zicam tablets aren't helping?"

"I don't know, maybe. I've been around my mom this whole time, and I felt okay until last night."

"How is Emma doing?"

"Not good. It's going quicker for her than it has for my mom. She's okay for now, I think. I've been making her tea and giving her the Theraflu in little bits to sip. I think that's helping slow it down." She shrugged one shoulder. "Maybe not," she said, crying quietly. The sight of her crying made tears escape my lashes too. I didn't know what to say. Words were completely inadequate.

Finally, I said the only thing I could think of. "You're doing a good job. You are a great big sister and daughter."

"Thanks," she said as tears slid down her cheeks. "You're doing a good job too."

I knew she meant that I was helping them, and they saw that. But what she didn't realize was that the visits helped me just as much, if not more. If I didn't have that basic human contact every day, my slow decline into madness would certainly accelerate. I talked to my parents once a day, but it wasn't the same. Being able to see the girls just forty feet away while we talked was keeping my mind in check. We talked for a while longer about inconsequential things just to pass the time and to avoid all the sad energy surrounding us. As the sun went down, we said goodnight, and I walked over to the far ledge by the main street. I heard a click and the faint hum of the streetlights turning on. The bags of recycling were wide open and rustling slightly in the wind, the plastic, paper and glass drifting around aimlessly as if searching for someplace to land. I felt like those abandoned bags, forgotten and discarded. The helicopters were long gone, and it felt like the loss of another life.

I didn't tell my mom any of it when I talked to her that night. She had enough to worry about without adding the idea of her daughter going cuckoo. It seemed as though she was reluctant to tell me things too. I sometimes had to drag details out of her.

"Hi, Mom. What's going on over there?"

"Do you remember when you were five and we went to Indiana? You met a second cousin of your dad's named Alan?"

"I have a vague memory of our trip, but it's hazy."

"He and his wife needed someone to host them until a place opened up for them in New Mexico. That's where her family lives. So they'll be here tomorrow night and will stay a few weeks."

"That's nice that you can help out."

"Yeah, it feels good to finally be able to do something to help someone since we can't really help you. Last night on the news, there was a report on all the flights that are coming in. They showed the Sacramento airport, and it was packed! They were interviewing people, and the stories these people told…"

I waited for her to finish her sentence, but she remained quiet. "What were they saying?"

"Just… just about what they've seen and how grateful they are to be safe."

"And what have they seen?"

"Oh, you don't want to hear about that!"

"Mom, yes, I do. What did they say?"

She sighed and said, "I don't know. One man was talking about people being attacked on his street, the violence, the abandonment of morals and kindness. One woman said several houses on her street had been broken into, and she'd heard the people inside screaming. It was just so overwhelming to hear, and I kept thinking of you and how dangerous it is there for you." I noticed the change in her voice, rounding out like a bubble was in her throat. She was crying, and I felt guilt pushing down on my chest. "When they were showing the lines of people, I swore I saw you. She looked so much like you. But then I noticed she was wearing a hot-pink hoodie, and I know you'd never wear hot pink."

Tears ran down my face, but I laughed at her comment. "No, you're right. I wouldn't be caught dead in pink."

She chuckled softly.

"Mom, I haven't seen much violence here. It's scary because I know that could change, but I'm safe here in my apartment. The doors are locked and bolted." I was trying to reassure her but knew that was probably impossible. I changed the subject. "Was there anything in the report about a cure?"

"Not really. They just said the CDC is still working on it and have had some success with some medications temporarily knocking the virus out in test animals. But it always comes back."

"That's not encouraging. I've seen people on *The Salvation Railroad* forum calling it the Comeback Virus instead of NOS-9, and it seems to be catching on. Appropriate, I guess." I heard glass breaking somewhere, followed by dogs barking. The sun had gone down, so the sounds were picking up. My heart pounded faster, and Zeke's ears perked up as he lifted his head off the floor and gave a short, muffled bark. "Mom, I'm gonna go. I'm tired. I'll call you tomorrow."

"Love you, honey. Take care of yourself."

"Love you too."

I walked to the window and looked out, searching for the source of the noise. I felt jittery and nervous about what I might see. Near the park on the sidewalk was a pile of broken glass illuminated by the streetlights. I grabbed my new binoculars from the box and looked again. It was a pile of green bottles, but I didn't see anyone around. Maybe someone had thrown them out a window, but I couldn't figure out why or how they had all landed in the same spot.

It was quiet again, so I tried to put it out of my mind, which was easier said than done. I jumped at every noise I heard the rest of the night, my nerves vibrating like a rubber band stretched too tightly with every movement. My brain was on high alert. While I knew there were people out there who might try to break in, I also knew my building was fairly secure, and I hadn't actually seen anyone. But my years of horror-movie bingeing wouldn't allow me the comfort of relaxing. My paranoid subconscious had taken over.

Right before I went to bed, I heard a click and the whir of an air conditioner. *Who would have their air conditioner on in the winter?* I scoured the apartments across the street in the direction of the noise. In an apartment directly across from mine, I saw the curtains flutter, and then they moved aside slightly as though someone was peeking out. I stared at the window, trying to get a glimpse of who was behind it, but the curtains snapped shut again as if they knew I was watching. I chewed on my lip and squinted, trying to figure out why they'd turned on the air conditioner. Maybe there was someone sick inside and they were trying to keep the fever down. But another, more gruesome thought snuck in. *What if someone had died, and another person was keeping the body cold so it wouldn't smell? Would that even work?* I looked back at the windows and wondered if the people behind them were watching me too.

I stepped away from the window and crawled into bed. I was getting paranoid about all the sounds I heard outside, and the escalation at night was frightening, but the noises inside the building were worse. In reality, the building was probably just settling, but my mind could quickly spin any small noise into something sinister. A day earlier, I'd heard a floorboard creak and imagined it was someone walking up the stairs to steal all of my supplies and kill me. I'd looked around, frantically trying to find a weapon. I settled on a hammer and stood in the bathroom doorway adjacent to the front door. I held the hammer above my head, poised to strike for ten minutes until my arms began to shake and I couldn't hold them up any longer. In the morning, I'd heard a bang followed by a clink downstairs. I was sure someone was trying to break down the locked vestibule door. That one kept me cowering silently in the bathtub for twenty minutes, clutching a large kitchen knife and conjuring up all kinds of escape routes. Zeke pushed his head through the shower curtain, and I pulled him in with me. He had watched me for a few minutes then lay down with a big resigned sigh.

Moments like those made me question my sanity. It was as if my mind wasn't my own anymore and instead was being controlled by some outside force that was out to get me. I would drag my hands down my face and shake my head, trying to win control. Sometimes, I would let out a long scream until there was no air left in my lungs, hoping to clear out the noises and jumpstart rational thinking. The small noises were also making it impossible to sleep. I'd been waking up every ten minutes, convinced someone was in my building. I would jump out of bed and check all the rooms for intruders, a knife shaking in my hand. Then I would check the front door lock again and make sure all the windows were closed firmly.

One night, I did it so many times that I lost count. I had to fix it somehow. In my bedroom, I set up a fan and my old sound machine that I'd bought when my ex-boyfriend moved in and promptly developed a snoring problem. The fan and the machine set on "rain" drowned out all the small noises, and restful sleep returned.

But it had become harder to know how much time had passed. I checked the date on my computer every day, expecting the onward march of the calendar. But most of the time, it was the same day as when I'd checked the last time. I started making ticks on the wall in my living room with a black sharpie. It became part of my morning routine. I would make six straight ticks then the seventh across them for a week. I circled four batches of seven ticks. I'd been stuck for a month.

I made coffee and turned on the news just as my mom called. "Honey, are you watching the news?"

"I just turned it on, what's happening?" I saw the headline stating that a group of the infected had taken three military officers captive. My breath caught in my throat. "Wait, I see it."

"Yeah, it's bad. They are demanding to be allowed across the border even though they are sick. They've threatened to remove the men's HAZMAT masks soon if the government doesn't comply."

"Oh god, that's horrible! I'm gonna watch the report. I'll call you after."

I hung up the phone and turned the volume up. From a helicopter feed, I could see police and military trucks surrounding a two-story Victorian house. The reporter said they'd been in a standoff for over an hour, and snipers were being called in. I could hear other helicopters buzzing around. I watched for an hour on the edge of my seat, my heart thumping wildly in my chest. The reporter said they'd made a deal with the captors and would be emerging from the house soon.

The helicopter swooped lower as the front door opened and three people came out, each holding a gun to a military officer's head. They still had their masks on, and I exhaled a sigh of relief. All of a sudden, all three captors' heads snapped back simultaneously, and blood sprayed across the masks of the officers. They all fell to the ground, and police rushed in. I gasped and jumped up from my seat, my stomach suddenly queasy. *They never had any intention of letting those men go.* The newsfeed switched to an anchor sitting at a desk, reporting that all three captors had been shot, while the officers were seemingly unharmed. I watched for ten more minutes, but my legs had gone weak. I turned off the TV and sat back down, feeling conflicted about what I'd just seen. The safest option was to take the men out since they were going to die from the virus anyway—they couldn't allow them across the border. But seeing them shot like that was horrifying.

My limbs were shaking, so I made myself a cup of chamomile tea to calm down. My brain kept flashing to the image of the men's heads snapping back. An hour later, I changed and worked out, trying my best to delete those images from my mind, but they were still lingering while I made my lunch. As I was about to eat the last bite of a sandwich made from my last piece of bread, I heard scraping and banging outside my living room window near the fire escape.

I froze. *Is someone coming up the fire escape? Oh my god, I have to get out of here! I can go downstairs with my crowbar and bust open the basement door. I can grab keys and hide in someone else's apartment. Can I do all of that before they make it inside?* I looked at Zeke, who was standing near the window and gazing out intently. *Why isn't he barking?* I whispered his name as forcefully as I could so he would come to me. He looked over at me and whined but didn't move.

Then it dawned on me that if Zeke didn't perceive the sound as a threat, maybe it wasn't. It hadn't occurred to me to use Zeke as a danger barometer, but now I thought I should. His instincts were probably more accurate than my own. I crawled over to the window and cautiously pulled the curtain back. A tree branch had partially broken off in the wind and was resting on my fire escape, the branches eerily scratching against the window. I let out a deep breath as my body sagged against the wall in relief.

A winter storm was on the way, and the wind was already picking up. The trees swayed, and my bird feeder was swinging around the railing from the increasing wind gusts. We'd had a relatively mild winter so far and hadn't seen any snow yet, but the night before, the weather app on my phone had started buzzing. They were predicting a storm that would hit soon, producing over a foot of snow. If nothing else, it could add something new to my monotonous routine.

The sound of a rattling cough interrupted my thoughts. I moved to the dining room window and waited for it again. When I heard it, my eyes fell to the apartment building across the way. I squinted, trying to see into all the windows. Then I saw a movement in the third-floor window as my eyes adjusted. I could barely make out a woman lying on a bed. The bedding was crumpled up around her body, and she was coughing and gasping for air. My eyes were glued to the scene, unable to look away. Eventually, she stopped coughing and took a sip from a cup on the windowsill. I swallowed unconsciously when she did. She looked out the window for a long moment then reached up and pulled the curtain across, blocking my view. All I could see was the cup.

I looked at the surrounding windows and felt them all looking back at me. I shuddered and walked away, squeezing my eyes shut for a few moments, the image of the woman still a ghost in my vision. When I opened them, I noticed that it was after four o'clock, so I pushed the woman out of my head. Thinking the girls might be low on supplies, I gathered up the last of my cold medications and some tea bags and tossed them in a bag. When I pulled the hallway window down, the girls were already waiting at their window, and Emma was again in the bunny costume. She seemed more animated, and I grinned when I saw her.

"I found an old bottle of Nyquil and some cough syrup in my bathroom cabinet," I said as I attached the bag and sent it over before running upstairs with Zeke.

"Thanks," Julia said, opening the bag.

"How's your mom doing?" I asked, the wind whipping my hair around.

"Her fever hasn't gone up any. I got her to eat some soup last night."

"That's good. How are you two?"

Julia replied, "Our fevers haven't gone up much either. The Theraflu is helping Emma and my mom with their cough. I'm not taking anything yet. We only have one packet left, and I don't really need it."

"We're getting a snowstorm tonight. Are your radiators working?"

"Yeah, we're good."

"More than twelve inches of snow!" I exclaimed, trying to drum up some excitement. "Tomorrow, maybe we can have a snowball fight? Me and Zeke on the roof against you guys in the window. What do you think?" I asked hopefully.

They brightened. "Yeah! Us against you and Zeke!" yelled Emma.

"Sounds like a plan! There are packets of hot chocolate in there with the tea. After we're covered in snow, we can drink hot chocolate to warm up."

Emma was excited and jumped up and down. "Yummy! Hot chocolate!"

I laughed and took a moment to savor that morsel of happiness. "Both of you, go get some rest. We'll have fun tomorrow, okay?"

"Bye, Karis," they said in unison.

The wind was picking up, and the clouds were getting dark. It was better to be inside. The rest of the night got progressively colder, and it started snowing by eight o'clock. My radiators were pumping full blast and clanking loudly, so it was nice and warm. I made a hot toddy and

watched an apocalyptic movie about a global power outage. The movie was terrible, but like *The Walking Dead*, it had useful survival tips.

One interesting idea was how the lead character made a candle by melting crayons and using a string from a mop for the wick. I kept it in mind in case they turned off the electricity and I ran out of candles. It reminded me of something my dad would have done. He was a real modern-day MacGyver. Once, he created a makeshift shower in the woods when we were camping in a remote area. From a tree, he hung a thick plastic water bag with a spout at the opening that could be opened and closed. He then made a shower curtain by using a tarp, some wire suspended from the tree, and some paper clips. My mom wasn't too thrilled with his solution, but I looked at him like he was the coolest man alive. No one else could have thought of something like that.

The drink and the movie made me tired, so I turned in, feeling strangely content—all bad thoughts were hiding out of sight, and I didn't go looking for them. But that night, I dreamt that I found some loose boards in my bedroom floor. I pried them up and saw ladder rungs leading down a long, dark vertical passageway that was so dark that I couldn't see the bottom. I grabbed my phone, turned on the flashlight app and made my way down, feeling as though it wasn't going to end. Finally, my feet hit the ground. I turned around, and my phone lit up a door. I pushed against it, and to my surprise, I found myself in a subway tunnel. The only movement came from rats scurrying around. There wasn't much light, but I could see the concrete ledge bordering the tracks, so I walked in the direction of Manhattan. After only ten steps, I saw graffiti on the wall that read "This is not a dream." I felt the walls and ledge slowly start to vibrate. Suddenly, I was blinded by train headlights speeding toward me. I covered my face with my arm and hugged the ledge. I woke up breathless and shaking.

I climbed out of bed and peered out the kitchen window. We'd been blanketed by a foot of snow, and all I could see were faint outlines covered in white. The tree limbs right outside my window bowed under the weight. I still got a jolt of snow-day glee at the sight of it. I knew it would be cold even though the sun was out, so I bundled up and took Zeke upstairs. He was ecstatic when he saw the snow and forgot his need to pee as he darted back and forth, burrowing into snowdrifts. I let him run around excitedly for a while, watching his head pump up and down as he ran. His joy was infectious, and I hadn't gotten much of that lately. It was nice to let his delight distract me for a minute.

Back downstairs, Zeke ate his breakfast, and I nursed my cold coffee. My mind kept wandering to a thousand different scenarios, varying between our safe escape to different ways we eventually died, when the TV began emitting a low buzz. I looked up and saw the usual screen of looped updates had changed to simply say "Stay tuned for presidential announcement." A minute later, the president came on, sitting at his desk in a stately office somewhere, certainly not in the White House. His face was grim. *Uh oh*. I turned up the volume.

"Good morning. As of today, we have successfully evacuated the majority of uninfected residents, government officials, and police out of the Eastern states affected by the virus. However, there are those of you who remain. Our government has done its best to provide supplies and aid in every way we can during this difficult time. But we are entering a time of extremely low resources. Our international allies have offered financial aid, which we've gratefully accepted. But even with this aid, we are currently stretched beyond our means. The Western states have been flooded with survivors, and we are now without available housing. We've set up programs with homeowners to allow survivors to stay in their unused bedrooms, living rooms, and even garages. To supplement this, the Red Cross has set up temporary housing in auditoriums, churches, and gymnasiums, and has provided a large number of trailers for families of three or more. I regret to say that all of this housing is now at full capacity, and we are officially without additional space. We can no longer provide housing or entry into the uninfected border to anyone without a family member or friend willing to host them.

"In addition to the housing shortage we are now facing, our ability to keep electricity and water on for those who have decided to stay within the infected border is limited. Groups of utility workers in each state have generously offered to stay for the next three months. At that time, they will be evacuated, and electricity, gas, and water will be turned off as it is too dangerous to leave them on without monitoring and maintenance.

"We have estimated that nearly five thousand uninfected survivors remain within the infected border. If you have a place to stay, I strongly urge you to make your way to the border as soon as possible. The danger of living without electricity, water, and police support is far too great to remain inside your homes. Thoughts and prayers from around the world are with you. To those of you who cannot or choose not to make your way to the border, may God be with you."

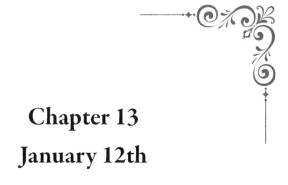

Chapter 13
January 12th

After watching the broadcast, I felt numb. We were being called survivors, but I didn't feel like one. Maybe if I made it home, I would, but not yet. I sat back on the couch and went over the speech again, but the words held no weight. The idea that the government would abandon us had definitely crossed my mind. I knew they couldn't leave the electricity and water on indefinitely. I'd assumed a cutoff date would cause me to panic, but instead, it just felt as though the inevitable had happened. I had a deadline, three months to make my escape. I called my parents to see if they'd watched the speech.

"We saw it," my mom said as a hello. "For you that's good, right? You have us to host you, so that's one problem down." I could hear the hope in her voice.

"Yes, that's true, but I still don't know how I'm going to get there."

My mom sighed. "Yeah, I know."

"I've been looking for caravans leaving somewhere close to New York, but so far, there are none. A guy from New Jersey is offering to take as many people as he can fit in his van, but he's also posting paranoid, crazy rants. I don't think he's a safe bet."

"No, that doesn't sound good. Besides all that, how are you doing?" I was startled by her question. I worried that she could sense that mentally, I was barely hanging on.

My lower lip quivered. I was trying to push my emotions back, but it was my mom. "I'm restless most of the time. I don't know if I can do this, Mom."

"Honey, you've done so well this far. You can do this. I know you. You are stronger than you think." She paused, allowing me to cry. "I know you think it's silly, but you know those self-affirmation stickers I use from time to time?"

I snorted a laugh, smiling through my tears. "Yeah."

"Don't laugh. They help. I know you don't believe in that stuff, but it can't hurt."

"I'll try just about anything right now." My tears were unstoppable. Something about my mom's voice was causing all my emotions to force their way out, and for once, I let them. "Mom?"

"Yes, honey?"

"How do you know I can do this?"

Her voice softened. "Because you're the best of your dad and me. I don't know how you managed that, but you did. I admire you, you know? I fought you when you wanted to move so far away, but that came from the weakest part of me, a part you don't seem to have. And I'm sorry I didn't encourage you more. I was scared, but I shouldn't have put that on you. It was selfish. You had the strength to know what was right for you then to go out and get it. Not many people have that kind of courage. No one helped you. You did it all on your own. That's how I know. You just have to know it yourself. It's there inside you. Go and find it."

Her words were rebuilding my weakened confidence. "Okay, you're right. I can do this. I will do this."

"Good. That's my girl."

My tears slowed, and I felt determination sprout inside me. I sat up straight on the couch and took a deep breath. "I'm glad I called you."

"I'm always here for you. You know that. So how are you spending your time?"

"Exercising, catching up on my movie watching, and reading."

I could hear the smile in her voice. "This would be a great time to read *War and Peace*."

I groaned. "No, thanks!"

I was supposed to have read the book in high school. I tried and tried, and even though I was an avid reader, I just couldn't get into it. I made it about a third of the way through before I gave up and ended up taking a D on the book report. My teacher said it read like the CliffsNotes version of a paper, which was probably because I'd only skimmed the CliffsNotes version of the book. I'd never gotten anything less than a B before, so I told my mom the truth. As punishment for not doing the assignment, I had to read the book. I faked it for a month before finally confessing that I'd barely read two chapters in that time. At that point, she admitted defeat and told me I had to do the dinner dishes for a week instead. I was happy to accept the punishment if it meant I no longer had to look at that book.

Later, I went up to the roof with my winter gear on and a thermos of hot chocolate in hand. Zeke ran around again—being half American Eskimo meant he loved the snow and adorably mushed through it. The girls came to the window, no doubt having been alerted by Zeke's excited barking. They were laughing and cheering him on.

Emma was wearing white-nubby footy pajamas with ears on the hood. She'd drawn black circles around her eyes and nose with eyeliner. "I'm Amanda the Panda!"

They'd brought a bucket with them and began piling the snow from the windowsill into it.

Julia told me, "We've already added the snow from the other windowsills. We almost have a full bucket!"

"Oh no! I better watch out, then!" I started making my arsenal of snowballs. Once I had a pretty good batch, I looked over and saw they were poised to start hurling. I shouted, "Ready! Set! Go!" and let one fly.

It hit the window next to them, and the girls screamed excitedly. They both started throwing some back at me. I let half of them hit me, and Zeke ran around trying to catch the other half. He was barking and having more fun than all of us. I didn't want to hit the girls, considering they were sick, but I did land a few right at the edge of the window and sprayed some snow onto them, which they loved. They were ducking and swerving around their apartment to avoid any snowballs they anticipated coming through the window. I threw a couple through when they weren't nearby. The whole game was fun for all. When our snowball stash was completely depleted, we sat and drank our hot chocolate. While they drank, I took a few more candid photos.

"That was fun!" said Emma.

"Yeah, it was. I think we all needed that."

Julia was nodding while she sipped her hot chocolate, and I noticed her wince as she swallowed. "Are you using the Chloraseptic and cough syrup?"

She looked down. "I don't need it as much as they do."

"Julia, you need to use it. It will help. If you run out, I'll go into another apartment and find more."

She looked up at me. "Okay, but I'm really fine."

"I know you are trying to be strong, but you have to take care of yourself too. Promise me you'll take some tonight."

Reluctantly, she said, "I promise."

"How is your mom?" I didn't want to ask, but I needed to know.

Emma looked at Julia, who was looking toward their mom's bedroom. Julia finally responded, "She hasn't woken up today. Her fever is up to one-oh-five, but we checked, and she's still breathing."

Emma started crying, causing the black makeup to run like fingers down her cheeks.

Julia pulled her into a hug and cried too. "What are we going to do if she dies?"

I noticed that she said "if," even though we all knew it was inevitable. "I'm sorry. I'll help you as much as I can." I pointed downstairs to some windows. "See those two windows there and the one next to the pulley?"

They both nodded.

"If something happens and you need help, throw something at it. Nothing big or heavy but maybe buttons or something like that, okay? That one's my bedroom, and the other is the hallway."

"Okay," they said in unison.

"You are not alone. I'll be here with you no matter what happens," I told them.

They seemed relieved.

Emma began coughing, and when she stopped, she looked up at Julia, alarmed. She brought her hand up, and blood was sprayed all over it. I winced at the sight.

Julia looked at me and said, "Oh my god!"

I swallowed, trying to force back the lump that was stopping me from talking. "It's okay, Emma. Just wash your hands and rinse your mouth."

Emma began to whimper while Julia cleaned her hand with a towel. I told Julia to give her some Theraflu, and we adjourned for the day. Emma was coughing a lot more, and her breathing was a bit ragged. It scared me. Plus, I only had maybe two days of food left, so I decided it was time to try to get into the basement.

I grabbed the crowbar, which was still in my apartment from when the landlord had new hardwood floors installed a few years back. My building was pre-war and had a lot of issues, mainly that the whole place tilted slightly to the left. It didn't offer laundry, garbage disposals, or even closets. There were fireplaces in the living room and dining room, but they had been bricked up, and only the mantels remained.

Over time, I'd grown to love all my apartment's quirks. I didn't mind the lopsided doorframes, the TV stand that needed to be propped up on one side to make it level, or the creaky hallway floorboards. The character of the building was one of the things I loved most about it. But the floors had been by far the worst. They didn't have character. They were just badly deteriorated. I actually got splinters in my feet from walking on them.

After years of my complaining, the landlord finally broke down and said he'd have them redone. Once the contractor saw the state of the wood, he advised the landlord to rip most of it up and put in new wood. The landlord had almost blown a gasket at that one, but the contractor said the condition of the wood was unsafe, and he was required by law to replace it. Score one for tenants!

Once I got to the basement door, I realized I had no idea how to pry it open. I stuck the slanted edge into the space between the door and the frame and pulled back with as much strength as I could muster. The door creaked a little but didn't budge. It wasn't going to work. I pulled out my phone and dialed my dad's number.

"Hi. How do you open a locked door with a crowbar?"

"Ask it nicely?" he replied with a chuckle. *My dad, I swear.* He was a man of very few words that almost always fell into one of two categories: useful or funny.

"Always joking. Can you walk me through it? I need to get into the basement of the building. Don't ask why."

"Well, what kind of lock are we talking about here? Is there just one lock?"

I inspected the lock before saying, "Only one lock. I think it's a standard lock. It doesn't look heavy duty."

"In that case, wedge the crowbar into a spot where it will push the lock out toward you. Then push as hard as you can toward the door. That should put enough pressure on the lock to break it."

"So I'm pushing against the lock, not the door?"

"Yes, correct."

I'd been doing it all wrong. "I'll try it now. Hold on."

I set the phone on the windowsill and faced the door. I wedged the crowbar into the crevice and pushed with all my might. The doorframe groaned, and the lock buckled slightly but held. I let go and took a few deep breaths. Trying again, I pushed so hard that I yelled along with it. Slowly, the frame splintered, then the lock snapped, and pieces went flying across the lobby area as I stumbled toward the vestibule door. I looked back, and the basement door was wide open.

I grabbed my phone, feeling triumphant. "It worked!" One less obstacle was in my way. "Thanks. I'll call you guys in a little bit."

"Glad to help! Don't do anything stupid!"

A rush of love for my dad filled my heart. "I won't. Bye."

With the door open, I could smell a musty odor coming from below. I covered my mouth and nose with my shirt and walked down. I pulled the string to turn on the light and saw tools, buckets, and a box full of pieces of wood. Along the wall was the key rack. I grabbed all the keys and ran out of there.

I started with Mr. Tablock's solitary first-floor apartment. I found the key and unlocked the door. I pulled my shirt up over my mouth and nose again to avoid taking any chances. I reached for the knob but pulled my hand back. I was nervous about going in-to the apartments. *What if someone is sick in there? Or worse, dead?* The thought of seeing a dead body forced me to take a step back. I rubbed my sweaty palms over my pants and pressed my lips togeth-er. I pulled my shoulders back, took a step forward, and turned the knob. The door squeaked open, and I paused, listening for move-ment. The apartment smelled stale but clean with a slight antiseptic odor. I walked slowly down the hall, peeking into the empty bed-room along the way, then spotted a hospital bed facing the televi-sion in the living room. I checked the bedroom off the living room. The apartment was empty.

Exhaling, I went back down the hall to the kitchen and searched under the sink for cleaning supplies. I found Clorox Wipes and rubbed down the cabinets and drawers in all the rooms, then took the wipes with me. I went back to the bathroom and scoured the seventies-style medicine cabinet. Since he was elderly, Mr. Tablock had prescriptions for just about everything. *Jackpot!* I threw them all in a trash bag and contemplated taking his tooth-paste too. I'd run out and had been using baking soda. But if he'd been sick... I wasn't sure I wanted to take that chance. I left the toothpaste behind but took his pack of toilet paper from under the sink since I'd run out the day before and was using my last roll of paper towels instead. Then I headed to the kitchen. I found cookies and a box of Nips caramels that I took for the girls. I threw all his canned and dry goods into the bag. The fridge was bare, containing only a spoiled carton of milk and two moldy tomatoes.

I climbed the steps to the second floor and opened Barb's door first since I knew she was no longer there. But I also knew she'd been sick. I wiped everything down, including the windowsills and doorknobs, twice. After filling a bag with more supplies and food, I closed the door and walked to the apartment across from hers. I opened the door and crept in slowly, my heartbeat fluttering. After checking all the rooms, I began to loosen up, feeling more confident there was no one else in the building. I paused between floors to store the goods in my extra room and use hand sanitizer. I repeated the process at the other three apartments and found they were all clear of dead bodies.

There wasn't as much food as I'd hoped for—New Yorkers usually bought food on a daily basis rather than weekly. But I scored some DVDs of movies I hadn't seen and a good supply of toilet paper. Tom had a bike on a rack in his second bedroom, and I thought about my idea to ride a bike to the border. If I gathered up enough courage, the bike could work, although I doubted I would be able to reach the pedals while seated. Tom was over six feet tall.

From Barb's apartment, I took an unopened bottle of wine and a really nice leather-bound journal. I flipped through the first few pages, and it appeared to be empty, so I took it to make notes—it would be handy to have. *I should have done this long ago.* I wasn't sure what had stopped me. Maybe some misguided notion of respecting privacy.

I heard a loud, piercing scream when I was in apartment seven, directly across from mine. I'd just started loading up my loot. I froze. It was definitely a woman. I waited a few seconds and heard it again, followed by a few cracks that sounded like gunshots. It seemed to be coming from outside and maybe down the street. The bangs escalated the horror in my head tenfold, and my thoughts darted to the couple with the baby in the Ecksteins' house. Fear crept up my spine as the screaming went on, and my muscles tightened and trembled when I heard her yell something like "Please!" Fear overcame me, so I grabbed the bag and ran to my apartment.

Once in, I locked the door and tried to slow my breathing. I peeked out the window in the hall at the girls' window and saw them looking in the direction of the scream. I waved my arms to get their attention, and they looked down at me, their eyes wide and unblinking. I put my finger up to my lips and pointed to the far side of their apartment. They nodded their heads and walked away from the window. *That was a close one* kept repeating in my head as I leaned against the wall, shaking. The screaming went on for another minute, and then it was quiet again. I could only imagine what that woman was going through. *Was she raped? Beaten? Or was that a wail of grief?*

Chapter 14
January13th

When I took Zeke to the roof in the morning, the sun was shining brightly and had started to melt the snow. The roof was covered in a slushy mess, annoying Zeke— he loved the snow but hated water. When it rained, it was like pulling teeth to get him to go to the bathroom. The slush after a big snowstorm was his biggest source of irritation. He reacted as if we'd just turned his favorite pastime into a chore. If the sunny weather held, I hoped most of the slush would be gone in a day or two.

After I finished my coffee, I sorted all the food I'd found in the other apartments and realized that there was only enough for about another month. And maybe less because I'd have to start sending some of it over to the girls. Julia told me they didn't have much left. In Kelly's apartment, I'd found a bag of green apples in a basket on her counter. The skin had started to pucker slightly, telling me they would go bad soon. My mom had dried her own fruit whenever it hadn't been eaten in good time. I called my mom and got her method for drying apple slices. After peeling, slicing and sprinkling them with cinnamon and sugar, I placed the apple slices in the oven on a low setting and let them bake slowly. I checked them after five hours and kept testing them for moisture. Finally, after seven hours of baking, the apples were ready. I separated them into two baggies to keep them fresh and sent one over to the girls along with some cans of soup. It would help, but it wouldn't be enough.

I'd had an idea when talking to my mom. When I was little, every Sunday, my mom and I would make a large batch of flour tortillas for the week. She would let me knead the dough, and then she would stand behind me and help me roll them out. All I needed was flour, salt, water and lard. I'd kept the fat from any pork I'd cooked in the last few months in the freezer to use for stock and stews. I spent the next two hours rendering the fat in my Crockpot. When it was done, I had three cups of melted fat that I put in the refrigerator to solidify, and a good portion of pork cracklings at the bottom. I could eat those too. I had Julia send me over all the flour she had in her cupboards, and I gathered the flour from the other apartments. I guessed I had enough for about four dozen full-sized tortillas, which would be a big addition to my dwindling food supply. I made the dough, using all of my flour, and rolled it into plum-sized balls. I set twelve aside and put the rest into a bag, which I placed in the freezer for future use.

I made my first batch, rolling out the dough and cooking each one on a skillet. I could ration to only one tortilla a day by breaking it into three parts, one for each meal. I sent half of them over to the girls. I also had a bag of cornmeal, and I remembered my mom making corn cakes for breakfast, but she'd used flour in hers. I figured they could be made without the flour. I mixed together cornmeal, hot water, baking powder, lard, and sugar, adding more of each along the way for consistency. I didn't want to use more of my lard to fry them as my mom had, so I decided to try baking them. Fifteen minutes later, the cakes had puffed up slightly and were browned at the edges. After letting them cool down, I took a bite. I made a face at the bland flavor, but I couldn't be picky. They were edible and would help keep me going. I decided that next time, I would try adding cumin and a little coriander for more flavor.

Feeling better about my food supply, I returned to finding a way out. From all my online research, I'd only found one other person from New York who'd posted about trying to make the trip. It seemed promising—a woman who had a small car was looking for others to join her. The post was from a day ago, and as I scrolled down, I saw she'd posted an update. She said that she had a wristband but was bringing her mother, who did not. Her mother was showing no signs of the sickness, but the CDC had found irregularities in her blood work. It sounded fishy to me, so I moved on.

A link was posted in the comments to a story on the *What's Really Going On* page about a group of infected people who'd tried to sneak across the border. Witnesses said the military spotted them and told them to turn around and go back, but the group moved forward anyway, trying to squeeze through a hole they'd created in the fence. When they didn't stop, the military shot them. I touched my fingers to my lips, my eyes glued to the screen while I searched for any news articles to corroborate the story. I didn't find any. *Is the government covering it up, or are these people making up a story? What would be the point in that?*

An alert came up saying a new video had been posted on *Salvation Railroad* by a woman named Anna Clement. I clicked the play button, and she began talking frantically. Her eyes were opened too wide, her hair wildly sticking out in different places. She stopped several times in the video, and her eyes went to the side as if she'd heard something. She spoke of military trucks driving down her street and soldiers threatening to shoot anyone who came out of their houses. She turned her phone toward the window, and I heard a loud voice but couldn't make out what it was saying. I didn't see a truck but heard a pop and a scream. She turned her phone back to herself and said her test results had been negative for the virus, but they still wouldn't give her a wristband. They'd told her that even though she'd tested negative, there were irregularities in her blood work, so they needed a second sample. After the second test, they told her they couldn't clear her. She'd argued with them but was left without a wristband. She was convinced that instead of simply taking her blood the second time, the CDC had injected her with the virus because she was sick. She started crying, and the video ended, her crying face frozen on my screen.

There were numerous responses below her post, accusing the government of starting the epidemic and speculating about population control. A few others posted that they'd had a similar experience with the CDC, but only one of them was sick. I considered everything I'd read. There were similar conspiracy theories about AIDS and other infectious diseases. Even if I took everything posted as truth, I had to wonder why so many tested negative and had been evacuated. *How did they choose who to infect and who to save? What else had they tested when they'd drawn our blood? And why had they saved me?* I shook my head and sighed heavily. I didn't know if I could trust the post or the people responding, but I also wasn't sure that I could trust the government. I just didn't know.

As I continued to read, I heard a light, scattered tapping on the window down the hall. I ran down and pulled the window open.

Julia was in her window, sobbing uncontrollably. "My mom, she won't wake up. She's barely breathing. I don't know what to do!"

"Where's Emma?"

"She's in bed with her. I can't get her to leave."

"Does her bedframe have wheels? Is there any way it would fit through the doorway so you can push the bed into the living room near this window?"

She stopped crying for a second while she thought about it. "I think so. Her room has double doors. It's not a big bed, but let me go check if it has wheels."

The hall window was very narrow, and I could barely squeeze onto the sill. About five minutes later, I saw a bed with a woman lying on it slowly edging around the corner. I could only see the top half of her from my angle, but she didn't look alive. Then I saw both Julia and Emma behind the bed, pushing as hard as they could, their faces red with exertion. They got the bed right next to the window then climbed onto it. They were both crying loudly.

"Is she still breathing?" I asked.

Julia put a finger under her mother's nose and nodded. "She is, but just barely."

"Girls, look at me. This is the bad part."

They both looked frightened and cried even harder.

"I want you to sit on the bed, hold your mom's hands, then hold each other's hands. Does your mom have a favorite song? Or a favorite type of music?"

Julia looked up and said, "Yes! She loves Joan Baez. She makes us listen to her all the time. She says she has the voice of an angel."

I ran over to my iPod and plugged it into my computer. I quickly downloaded Joan Baez's greatest hits. Back at the window, I pulled up the screen. I sat down, straddling the sill with one leg dangling outside and the other in my hallway. I put the iPod and speaker on the sill in front of me. "Do you know the words to the songs?"

"Yeah, we've heard them a thousand times," Julia sniffled.

"I'm gonna press Play, and we're all going to sing to your mom. She doesn't have long. I'm sorry, but the best we can do is be here with her, okay?"

They were crying so hard that they could barely nod.

When I pushed Play, "Diamonds and Rust" came on. I didn't know a lot of the words, but I could fake it. The girls looked at me, and I started singing along. They followed suit while watching their mother. We sang for an hour. Emma fell asleep on the bed next to her mom. Finally, the playlist was over, and I looked at Julia resting her head on the window frame, still clutching her mother's hand.

"Julia, you need to check to see if your mom is breathing."

She looked at me, and a fresh batch of tears poured out of her eyes as she shook her head. "No," she said over and over.

I gave her a second to come to grips. "Julia, listen to me."

She looked back at me.

"I need you to be strong right now. I know this is hard, but I need you to check your mom's breathing."

She looked at her mom and reluctantly placed a finger under her nose. Slowly she shook her head and cried.

"Put your head on her chest and tell me if you can hear her heartbeat."

She put her ear to her breast and a few seconds later pulled up. Her face was completely distorted with grief. "She's dead! Oh my god, she's dead!"

I put my head down for a second when my throat constricted. Even though I was trying to be strong for the girls, a sob escaped loudly. I pulled my head back up. "I'm so sorry."

Emma woke up and saw us both crying. She looked at her mom then back at Julia. "Is she dead?"

Julia nodded and pulled her into a hug. They cried together, locked in each other's arms for a good twenty minutes before they pulled apart. All I could do was sit with them.

Julia looked over at me, her face red and splotchy. "What should we do now?"

I took a deep breath and let it out. "I think you should cover her up in the top sheet. Do you think you and Emma could carry her?"

Julia looked scared by that prospect but nodded. "Yeah, I think so. She's not very heavy."

They worked together to wrap their mom like a burrito in the sheet. They stopped when they got to her face and looked at her for a few seconds. They took turns kissing her on the forehead. Then Julia slowly pulled the sheet over her face and tucked the corner in. They hadn't stopped crying the whole time.

Julia looked at me and asked, "What now?"

"Do you have a room you could put her in? A room you aren't using?"

"We could put her in her bedroom."

"Okay, after you have her in the room, close the doors, and roll up a towel lengthwise. Put the towel at the bottom of the doorway to cover the gap between the doors and the floor. Go slowly. Julia, see the fitted sheet underneath her? Pull it away from the bed and use that to carry her."

Julia pulled the sheet out from under the mattress on all four corners. She picked up the two top corners of the fitted sheet, and Emma did the same with the bottom. They lifted her off the bed and slowly carried her to the bedroom. Once they were back, I could see they weren't sobbing anymore, but tears continued to spill down their faces. They sat on the bed next to the window.

Emma broke the silence. "Is that going to happen to me?"

How can I tell her yes? "Honey, I don't know, but it might. I went into the other apartments and found all kinds of medicines. The painkillers will help, so if it does happen, you won't feel it. I promise."

She nodded, surprisingly calm. "When that happens to me, I don't want music. I just want to watch *The Little Mermaid*. When I was little, my mom used to put that movie on for me when I couldn't sleep. It always worked."

Julia responded, "We'll be together. We'll watch it together."

Emma smiled. "I know."

We sat in silence until it grew dark. Emma fell asleep, so Julia grabbed a comforter off their bed to drape over her. I told Julia to leave the bed there in case we needed it again. She knew what I meant and nodded sadly. We said goodnight, and I saw her turn on the TV and crawl under the covers with Emma.

I watched them, completely envious. I knew I shouldn't have been—their mom had just died, and they were both sick. But their closeness, the fact that they had each other to hold and count on, was something I couldn't deny I wanted.

Chapter 15
January17th

I was starting to smell death in the air. It was so faint at first that I almost convinced myself that it wasn't the odor of rotting corpses. But over the next few days, it got more intense, and I knew that was what it had to be. It was kind of like rancid meat but slightly sweet as if someone had sprinkled sugar on the bodies. The girls hadn't mentioned it yet, but they'd wrinkle their noses sometimes in an unconscious twinge. It had to be worse in their apartment with Mr. Standhope downstairs and their mom in the other room. There might have been even more that we weren't aware of.

I made sure to check in on them more frequently since their mom was gone. I'd sent over more tortillas and cold medicine, and Julia sent back a half-empty can of coffee her mom had on hand that I quickly wiped down. I held onto the prescription medications for the time being. Emma was slowly getting worse, coughing up more blood from time to time, but her fever remained at one-oh-three. Julia was progressing more slowly—her fever hadn't gone above one hundred, and it was still just her throat that was giving her problems.

I did a google search to see if there was any way to combat the smell. Things were bad enough for us without that sweet-and-sour stench surrounding us, reminding us constantly of the dead. There were many posts by others trying to tackle the same problem. The most popular remedies were cups of vinegar or ammonia placed in various spots around the house and cinnamon incense. One woman had cut the heads off of cloves of garlic and hung them all around the house, and she posted that it was helping. All sounded doable, so I went through all the apartments to search for supplies.

I found five bottles of vinegar, two bottles of ammonia, and nine heads of garlic. I had a combo box of incense, and I was certain there were a few cinnamon ones in there. I would keep those and a bottle each of vinegar and ammonia for myself.

I went to the hall window with my supplies and used a carabiner to secure the bag since it was much heavier than usual. I moved the bag across the line then went upstairs early. Julia was on the couch, fiddling with some red tissue paper, and I flagged her down. "Hey, I need to talk to you guys. Where's Emma?"

"She's in the other room. I'll go get her."

A minute later, they were both at the window, Emma in a short blond wig and lots of makeup plus a black beauty mark above her lip. My lips twitched, and I broke out laughing at her getup. "Who are you today?"

Julia pointed to one of her pictures taped to the window. "She's Marilyn Monroe from *Monkey Business*. It was on Netflix, and I thought it was a kids' movie, but it wasn't. We liked it, so we watched it anyway. My mom had the wig from her old mermaid costume."

I looked at the drawing, which was a depiction of Emma Monroe holding a monkey's hand. "I love the monkey's expression, and Emma looks so glamorous! Let me take your photo. Julia, stand next to her."

Emma thrust a hip out and put her hands behind her head. Julia laughed and mimicked her while I took the photo.

"That was great!" After a pause, I set my camera down. "So I'm not sure how to bring this up. Do you guys smell that weird smell?"

They both wrinkled their noses. "Yeah, we've been trying to ignore it, but it's getting worse," Julia said, folding and shaping the paper into something.

"Do you know what it is?"

Emma looked down, not able to put it into words, but I could tell she knew.

"Yeah, it's all the people who have died, right?" Julia responded.

"Yeah, that's it. I know this isn't something we want to talk about, but I think it's just going to get worse." I didn't bring up their mom in the other room, but I was sure they were both thinking it too. "I looked it up online, and there are things we can do to cover the smell. I sent over a few things. There are some heavy glass bottles, but I wrapped them up."

Julia put down her craft project, unclipped the bag, pulled out the bottles, and placed them one by one on the coffee table.

"You'll need to get cups and pour the vinegar in them, then put them all around the house. Once the vinegar's gone, use the ammonia. It's stronger though, so let's use that last. There's also garlic in there. I've cut the tops off, and you should hang it around the house. Do you have string?"

"Yeah, I have some in my friendship-bracelet kit," Julia said, picking up the red paper again.

"That's good. You don't have to do it right away, but you should do it soon."

"Are you going to do it too?" Emma asked.

"Yep. I have some vinegar I can use. Julia, what are you making?"

She didn't stop what she was doing or even look at me. "I'm making some flowers to put in front of my mom's door."

"Oh, that's nice. Can I see them?"

She picked up the few she'd already completed, showing me a bouquet of red roses.

"Those are beautiful. I'm sure your mom would love them."

She nodded distractedly, her face downcast. We chatted for a little while longer, but they were both tired so we said goodbye sooner than usual. I walked to the east side of my roof and looked out over Queens. I spotted the sign for the Korean day spa that my roommate and I used to laugh at. It read, "Loose Yourself. Recover Piece of Mind." We'd contemplated going over and pointing out the spelling mistakes but thought better of it because they probably weren't going to spend the extra money for a new sign, and we would just have looked like condescending jerks. *Yeah, I'd love to recover pieces of my mind right now.*

Zeke and I continued our normal routine, except Zeke had taken to lounging near the window by the street for hours. I wasn't sure why. Maybe he was hearing the ominous sounds, too, and wanted to monitor them. Every now and then, he would perk up and bark. His diligent supervision was comforting me, so occasionally I sat on the floor next to him, stroked his fur, and told him he was doing a good job. Sometimes, I would throw his ball against the wall opposite us, and it would bounce back for Zeke to catch. He would drop it in my hand, and I would repeat the throw. I could waste an hour or two on the game, and it gave me something to explain away any external thumps I heard.

The next afternoon, after watching the news for the fifth time, I was bored. I'd already watched two movies, scoured the Death List again, and read several chapters of a book. I frowned at my TV, my bookshelf, and my computer, frustrated and angry with them for no longer holding my interest. I stood in the living room, searching for something to do. But besides the objects that had already failed me, there was only furniture.

I rearranged my living room. I tried my Ikea couch in two different places before I got my Allen wrenches from the toolbox and took the couch apart. I separated it into two pieces, one loveseat and one chair. I shoved them into different spots until I found a good configuration. They looked better separated, the loveseat along one wall and the chair next to the bricked-up fireplace. I glanced at the clock and saw that three hours had passed. Satisfied with myself, I went to grab a couple of crackers for a snack and promptly banged my knee on the coffee table, not used to the new arrangement yet.

Just as I was about to take a bite, I heard muffled footsteps on the roof. The thuds coming from above were rapidly going across my living room as if someone was running back and forth. Sweat broke out on my upper lip, and my pulse beat a fast tempo. Zeke stood below me, shuffling his feet and whining. I rose slowly but froze when I heard it again. *Did someone climb up the fire escape to the roof? I can't remember if I locked the door to the roof after Zeke's morning visit. What if they come down?* My brain felt like a tornado was whipping through, my thoughts coming all at once as if they were jockeying for a better position in my consciousness. I shook my head to clear them and ran to the kitchen, where I grabbed the largest knife I could find. Once I shut the drawer, I heard it again. I really didn't want to go up there, but my only other option was to sit there all day, waiting for someone to break in and kill me or allowing my mind to play tricks on me again. I had to start taking control. I had to see for myself.

I went up to the roof door and waited to hear something, anything. But my heartbeat filled my ears in pounding thumps, and I heard nothing else. I turned the knob, but it slipped in my sweaty hand. I wiped my hand on my pants and creaked the door open an inch. I scanned the small area, expecting to see a figure run past. After a minute with no movement or sounds, I pushed the door open wider and crept out onto the roof. I looked from side to side, but it was empty. I eased my way over to check the side of the doorway and peeked around the corner. No one was there. I inched back to the other side. If someone was up there, they had to be on that side because it was the only hiding place left. I held the knife out in front of me. As I crept to the edge, I sliced the knife through the air, but it only hit the wall and vibrated in my hands. My roof was clear.

I let out my breath and looked toward the girls' apartment. Their building was about half a story taller than mine, but standing on the ledge surrounding the roof brought me almost to eye level with their roof if I stood on my tiptoes. I hoisted myself up, my fingers tightly clutching their roof as I peeked over the edge. Their roof was empty too. I jumped down and checked the ladder that led down to the fire escape on the east side. All seemed untouched.

My shoulders slumped, and I shook my head. I locked the roof door and went back downstairs but was no longer hungry. The noises were driving me crazy, and I didn't know if they were real or imagined. The ones coming from inside the building were worse. The rational side of my brain was slowly losing its footing, and although I could feel it happening, I couldn't do anything about it. I would sit for hours, coming up with excuses for sounds I'd heard. I told myself it was the building settling, the wind, or an echo from my own steps. Sometimes, I was successful, but other times, the terror won, and I would be in its grip for hours.

But the silence was even worse. When the air was completely empty of any tone or vibration, my ears would start ringing. At first, I thought it was a low buzzing coming from some appliance, and I went around the house, pulling plugs out of the wall. I finally figured out that it was coming from inside my head when the noise got so loud that I put my hands over my ears, which made it worse. I turned on my stereo to drown it out. After five minutes, I turned the stereo off, and the ringing was gone. My ears could only take so much inactivity.

I'd been chatting with a group of people from *The Salvation Railroad* page. Five of us were frequent posters. One guy who'd stayed behind to protect his massive, priceless action-figure collection from looters created a Google Hangout, and we spent hours coming up with different plans to make it to the border. I trusted those people as much as I could trust anyone, but they were spread out from Georgia to West Virginia. Unfortunately, we were all too far away to organize our own caravan. One woman, who'd stayed to take care of the animals on her farm, said she'd heard reports of traps set up to ambush the caravans and steal their supplies. I'd been making little red dots to mark the reported locations of these traps in the big atlas I'd bought when I drove cross-country to New York. Each state had five pages dedicated to it, so it was a good resource for planning my route.

I pulled out the leather journal I'd found and started making notes. But as I was writing, I spotted something just barely peeking out from the journal. I found a four-by-six glossy photo tucked inside. I recognized the woman as Barb from apartment two, but she was much younger. A handsome, dark-haired man had his arms around her, kissing her cheek. They looked incredibly happy, the smiles on their faces infectious, and I felt myself smiling in return. I turned it over and saw an inscription that read, "Barb and David. July, 1998." Staring at their enamored faces, I wondered what had happened. She'd always lived there alone, and I'd never seen a man with her. I didn't know her well. She mostly kept to herself except for the polite hellos we'd exchanged when passing one another in the stairwell. I noticed writing on the page the photo was marking, and my heart dropped.

November 25th

Michael and Johnny are both in the hospital now, both sick from this flu. I haven't seen them in a week, and they are my only real friends left, my last connection to David. What's happening? I've never heard of a healthy young man being in the hospital for a week from the flu. I know a lot of other people are sick, too, and no one's recovered yet. What is this? I'm scared. I think I have it too. I woke up with a sore throat, and I have a fever.

November 30th

Michael and Johnny are still in the hospital, and when I called to check on their status, the nurse said it's not looking good. What does that mean? Are they going to die? Who dies from the flu? My head hurts so badly. It's so hard to go through this without them. They've been my lifeline since David. I'm alone now, and I don't want to be. Like when David died. I feel it all over again.

December 3rd

Today, I said goodbye to Michael and Johnny. I visited them in the hospital. I had to see for myself. Part of me also wanted to see what I'm in for. I don't think they'll make it, which means neither will I. They were both unconscious and on respirators. The doctor said they haven't been able to keep their fevers down, and none of the medicines they've tried are working. They looked so fragile, lying on those beds and hooked up to all those machines. I know I have this flu, too, and seeing them like that is terrifying.

December 8th

Everyone I know is sick. This fever is killing me. I take medicine, but it only works for a short time. I can barely get out of bed. My whole body aches, and I haven't eaten any real food in a few days. How long can a person live on liquids alone? That's all I can manage to swallow now. I don't think I'll get better, but I don't know if I want to.

December 10th

This is not a flu, it is a death sentence. Today, people died. I can't stay here any longer waiting for that to happen to me. I'm giving up and going to the hospital. I don't think I'm going to make it through this. There is no fight left in me, and I hope this will all be over soon. I've called a car, and it should be here soon. This is the last thing I'll write. All I can think about is David. I pray we'll be together soon. God knows I'd give anything to see him again. That's my only consolation. My David, my sweet David. I'm coming home.

When I finished reading, tears were running down my face. I rushed to the sink and washed my hands before spraying the inside pages with Lysol. I thought about what I'd read. It was amazing how one could see someone almost weekly for five years and have no idea what they were going through. She hid her sorrow well behind a mask of pleasantries, but I guess I did too. Our loneliness could have bonded us together if either of us had broken through that cordial barrier. I wondered if we might have been friends.

Chapter 16
January 19th

The next day, I pulled together all the fresh food I'd found in the apartments, throwing anything mushy or moldy into a bag that I added to Zeke's poop corner on the roof. I knew I needed to cook whatever was still usable before it went bad. I made a pile of wilted carrots, potatoes, and cabbage then started chopping and adding everything to my slow cooker with a variety of spices and the last of my chicken broth. I contemplated a few slices of salami I'd found in Kirk's apartment. They smelled okay, but I didn't know how long they'd been there. I took a chance and ate them for lunch since I didn't have any meat left. My rows of cans were all gone. I'd sent the girls my last cans of soup the day before because that was all they could manage to eat now. All I had left was rice, some pasta, a few bags of chips, and my tortillas and corn cakes. The stew would last me a few days if I ate only small portions.

I set the cooker on low and turned toward the window. I noticed movement from the roof of the building across from mine, a flutter of white. A woman with long dark hair was climbing up onto the ledge of the roof. *What is she doing?* She was crouched down, holding the ledge and staring at the street. Slowly, she let go of the ledge and straightened her body. She was wearing only her underwear and a white T-shirt. *She must be freezing.* She held her arms out to her side limply, creating a vision of Christ on the cross. Her head fell back, and her mouth moved as though she was whispering a prayer. *Oh my god, she's going to jump!* My heart pounded wildly as my breathing picked up pace. My head felt light, as if it might float off my body.

I pulled the window and screen up and screamed, "Hey!"

She didn't move, so I yelled more loudly. Her head snapped up, making her wobble slightly as her eyes focused on me. "Don't do it! Don't jump!"

She shook her head and looked down at the street for a few seconds.

"You don't have to do this!" I screamed.

My limbs were trembling with fear. She was looking directly at me. Her eyes were sad and dazed, and I swore I saw the glistening of tears before she smiled. She looked to be in her twenties. Her face was so pale that the redness around her mouth and nose was glaring against her white skin, stained by the blood she must have coughed or sneezed out. I shook my head and leaned out farther. I reached a shaky hand out to her to let her know she wasn't alone.

She smiled wider, her eyes locked onto mine as her upper body fell forward. I screamed, "NO!" and watched as she flew through the air. Everything moved in slow motion until her body hit the ground with a loud thump.

I winced and pulled myself back inside, my hand over my mouth. I tripped over my stepstool and landed on my butt on the kitchen floor. I sobbed, hugging my knees, and didn't realize that Zeke had curled up next to me. When I noticed him, I put a hand on his head and let myself cry, my chest convulsing with each sob. There was a buzzing just under my skin that made me shiver. *I just watched someone commit suicide.* I understood why she did it, but the image of her flying through the air, her body limp, accepting her fate, wouldn't leave my mind.

I felt another panic attack coming on. The air slowly got thicker, and I struggled to fill my lungs, making a loud wheezing sound with each breath. The ceiling seemed to be sinking, and the walls were slowly inching closer. My skin was crawling, so I began rubbing my arms to calm it down. I closed my eyes and held my breath for the count of ten then exhaled. I continued to do that until I had my nerves back under control, which took about ten minutes.

Finally, I pulled myself up and looked out the window. The woman's body was splayed out on the ground, blood seeping around her in a dark-red pool. My breath caught again, and I squeezed my eyes shut. I'd never seen a dead body in real life. Horror movies hadn't prepared me for the reality. I'd been to my cousin Quina's funeral, but since she'd died in an accident, it'd been a closed casket. I walked away from the window and went to get a glass of whiskey.

An hour later, I felt calmer, and I closed the curtain in the kitchen so I wouldn't see her body every time I walked by the window. My stomach began rumbling in a nauseating way, and I thought about that salami I'd eaten. Maybe it hadn't been a good idea, no matter how much I needed the protein. I sat on my couch, breathing slowly in an effort to calm the nausea, but it overcame me, and I ran to the bathroom, barely making it to the toilet when the first heaves pushed through my esophagus.

The rest of my night was spent intermittently throwing up and sleeping on the bathroom floor. When I woke up in the morning, my stomach had calmed, but my limbs were shaky. I drank a large glass of water and ate a whole tortilla, making a mental note to be more careful with what I was eating. Food poisoning wasn't worth the risk.

OVER THE NEXT FEW DAYS, Emma went downhill quickly. Every time I saw her, it broke my heart. She carried a bloodied towel with her wherever she went, pausing to cough up blood from time to time. I was able to keep it together while we talked, but as soon as I was alone, I broke down. She'd been pushing through and continuing with her daily costumes. It was probably helping her to have something to look forward to. I'd seen her as a dog, a frog, and a fairy. But one day when I went up to the roof for our play date, it was just Julia by the window. My blood ran cold. Julia appeared to be lost in a daydream. I let the door bang shut, and she looked up at me. I could tell by her downcast eyes and mouth that something was very wrong. Her face was splotchy and puffy.

"Hi, what's going on? Where's Emma?"

"She's sleeping on the couch. I didn't want to wake her up. Her fever is going back and forth between one-oh-three and one-oh-four now. She barely eats anything. Karis, I'm scared."

I saw a new painting of Emma wearing cat ears on the window. She was sleeping with little z's coming out of her mouth. Julia's lower lip quivered, and her tears burst forth again.

"I know, sweetheart. I'm sorry. Is she in much pain?"

"Sometimes, but I give her the cold medicine when she starts complaining, and that seems to help a little."

"Okay. Hang tight. I'll send something over." I ran downstairs and rifled through all the prescription medications until I found a bottle of Tylenol with codeine. I grabbed a red sharpie and drew a heart on the label then tossed it in a bag along with a few stronger bottles. I clipped the bag to the line and sent it over before running back upstairs. Julia had already unclipped the bag. "See the bottle with a red heart on the front?"

She searched the bag and came up with it. "Yes, this is it," she said, holding up the bottle.

"That's a pain reliever, but it's for adults. Only give her half of one at a time. That should help with the pain. If it's not enough, give her the whole tablet. The other bottles are stronger, so don't use them unless you run out of these, or—" I stopped myself before I said, "toward the end."

Julia nodded. She knew what I was going to say, and she whimpered again.

"Tonight, have her sleep here near the window so I can check in on you guys."

She looked at me, her blue eyes wide with fear. "Karis, I don't know if I can do this."

I sighed, and my shoulders sagged. I was coming up empty for any words that would make this a little more bearable. "I know this is really scary, but all we can do is our best. You have to try to be as strong as you can for Emma, and so will I. We'll do this together."

We were quiet for a minute, lost in our own bleak thoughts.

"Do you believe in heaven?" Julia asked, breaking the silence.

"I'm not sure. I believe in an afterlife though," I answered.

"What do you mean? Isn't heaven the afterlife?"

"Yes, but it's just one version. A lot of people believe in heaven, but no one really knows for sure until it happens. Buddhists believe in something called nirvana. It's similar to the concept of heaven, except you only get there if you release all your desires. And some people believe we are reincarnated as someone or something else."

She wrinkled her nose. "So, like, they think we can come back as a frog or a butterfly?"

"Yep, and some people believe you can come back as a tree or flowers too."

That made her laugh, a sound I hadn't heard in a while. She arched her eyebrows high on her forehead. "You're kidding me! I don't think I believe that. I believe in heaven."

"Well, if you are right, then you'll be able to see your mom again in heaven."

"What do you believe?"

"I don't know, really. I believe something happens after death. I don't think it's an empty space and you just stop existing. I believe there is someplace we go after we die. Whether that's heaven or not, I don't know."

"Do you think my mom can see us? From heaven?"

I thought about it for a second. "Yeah, probably. My cousin died a long time ago, but when I'm alone, sometimes I can feel her around me. I believe we have spirits around us all the time, guiding us and protecting us when they can."

"And that's not heaven?" she asked with an eyebrow raise and a smirk.

I laughed at her logic. "Maybe it is. I'm just not sure. I guess I need more evidence."

She thought for a few seconds, looking up toward the sky. "So if my mom can see us, maybe she can hear us too. Should I talk to her?"

"Sure, why not? What harm can it do? Maybe you'll feel closer to her."

"Emma was talking to her the other day. I thought she was dreaming or talking crazy because of the fever. But maybe she really was talking to her."

"Maybe. You should try it. It'll probably feel silly at first, but it also might help you through this."

"Okay." She closed her eyes and said out loud, "Mom, if you can hear me, I'm taking care of Emma. She's not doing so good, but I'm trying. If you can, can you help her? Take care of her when she gets to you?" She started crying a little. "I miss you so much, Momma. I'm scared, and I wish you were here. I'll do my best, but I hope we'll all be together again soon. I love you." She kept her eyes closed for another minute then opened them and looked at me. "It did feel silly, but I think maybe she heard me. I could see her face when I was talking."

"That's good. You should talk to her whenever you need to. I think it will help both of you." I paused. "How's your fever?"

"It's okay. It's only up to one-oh-one. My head started hurting last night, but I took some cough medicine and some baby aspirin, and it went away. Every time it starts hurting, I take an aspirin."

"Make sure not to take more than the bottle says."

"I won't. I'm going to go make Emma some soup for when she wakes up. She didn't eat the oatmeal I made for breakfast because her throat hurt too much."

"Whatever you have to do, she needs to eat. Is there more Chloraseptic?"

"Yeah, but she doesn't like to use it because she said it tastes bad."

"I'll talk to her about it. I'll check in on you guys later through my hallway window."

We waved goodbye, and she closed the window.

When I turned toward the door, I saw something down the street out of the corner of my eye. I crouched down and slowly walked over to that edge. Two men were trying the front doors along my block. I sucked in a breath. *Oh my god, what if they come to my door? Or the girls' door?* I watched as they banged as hard as they could against one door, but it held. They gave up and walked to the next building. My mind frantically searched for ideas, and I remembered the wood from the basement.

I ran downstairs and grabbed a few pieces of wood that I thought were slightly longer than the width of the door, a hammer, and nails. I tested out a few boards to see which would work. After I found two, I started nailing the boards across the locked vestibule door. The door was solid metal, but I still wasn't convinced it would hold. After I managed to get both pieces hammered in, I felt better.

I ran Zeke upstairs and shut him in. Then I ran up to the roof again to check the men's progress. They were only two houses away from my building, and I could feel adrenaline coursing through my veins, causing my limbs to shake. I knew I would go crazy in my apartment, so I ran down to grab my crowbar and to put Zeke in my bedroom in case he barked. I sat on the steps near the first-floor apartment and waited.

Five minutes later, they were in the unlocked area where our mailboxes were. I could hear them talking, and it sounded like they were saying something about the door being metal. I hoped that would deter them, but it was an apartment building with seven apartments as opposed to a brownstone with, at most, three or four. Getting in would yield a more bountiful score of supplies. They must've agreed, because a minute later, they threw their bodies against the door. I jumped and squeezed my eyes shut. I ventured a look at the door, and it was holding well. Each time they banged against it, the wood groaned, but it didn't budge. One of them swore, and it sounded like he'd hurt himself. For several seconds, there was silence.

Then a rough male voice said, "Anyone home?" I held my breath, fearing they could hear even that. But finally, I heard the outer door open and close. I exhaled and tried to slow my heartbeat. *Now that was close.*

I ran back up to the roof to see if I could spot them. As I peeked over the ledge, I found them at the larger apartment building across the main street. That door had a small, square, double-paned-glass window. The larger of the two men picked up a rock from the ground and started smashing it against the window. After a few tries, the glass broke, and he reached inside and opened the door.

I heard Zeke barking and rushed downstairs, not wanting him to give us away.

Once inside, I sat on the floor by the window with Zeke in my lap and looked out across the way. I pulled the window up and waited a few minutes but saw nothing. I jumped when screams suddenly rang through the air. I heard both male and female voices. I ran to the hallway to see if Julia and Emma were there. Julia was lying on the bed near the window with headphones on, but I didn't see Emma. *Is she still sleeping? Or in the kitchen eating the soup Julia made?* I waved at Julia frantically until she noticed me and took off the headphones. She opened the window and instantly heard the screams. I put my finger to my lips again. I motioned for her to turn off the lights and TV. She slowly moved around the house, following my instructions, then settled back on the bed and looked at me. The commotion was still going on, and it sounded horrible. I put my finger up to let her know I would be right back.

I peered out the window near the street again. The sounds had finally stopped. Then both men walked out of the building with a large bag thrown over the smaller man's shoulder. Their hands and clothing were bloody, and the larger man rubbed his wrist like it hurt. They walked toward the girls' building, and my heart jumped into my throat. I couldn't see the girls' front door from my window, but I could hear the muffled sounds of the men's conversation. A few minutes later, the sound of glass breaking made me jump—that building had double glass doors in the front, and then one locked door of either wood or metal behind it. Panic pulsed through my veins, pounding in my eardrums and shooting through the synapses in my brain. I was in shock, frozen with fear for the girls.

Loud thumps shook me out of it, and I ran back to the hallway. Immediately, I heard Julia and Emma crying and yelping at each bang they heard. They were holding each other and looking toward their front door.

"Julia!" I screamed.

They both looked at me.

"Someone's trying to break in. I'm going to come help. Be as quiet as you can. Don't scream. Move something heavy in front of the door, whatever you can manage. Then hide somewhere, in a closet or under a bed, anywhere."

"Karis, I'm scared!" Julia cried.

"I know, honey. I'm coming to help you. I'm not going to let anything happen to you, I promise. Just do what I said, okay?" I crossed my fingers, hoping I wouldn't let them down.

They nodded then moved around the apartment. I ran back to my dining room, looking for anything I could use as a weapon. I considered kitchen knives or the hammer from my toolbox. If they got their hands on me, I would be done—my only advantage was that I was small and fast. I needed something I could use from some distance. My eyes fell to the crowbar, the only thing that remotely fit the bill. I snatched it up and ran to the stairs. Before I went up, I looked out the hallway window again. I couldn't see the girls anymore, but I saw movement through the first-floor window of their building. *Dammit, they're inside!* I had to go. I ran up to the roof and hopped up onto the ledge. Hoisting myself up, I threw the crowbar over then followed it.

I heard glass breaking and more dull thumps. I ran to the door and turned the knob. Mercifully, it was unlocked, and I pulled the door open slowly, trying not to make any noise. I tiptoed slowly down the stairs, trying to discern what floor they were on. The stairs were marble, and the railing was wrought iron, so there was no creaking wood as I made my way down.

There were probably more than twenty apartments in the building, and it was likely that they were still working their way through the first floor. The girls were up on five, so I had some time. As I neared the landing for the second floor, the faint sounds of the men conversing floated up. I peeked around the corner but only saw empty apartments through open doors on the first floor. I stood flat against the wall near the entrance to the stairs, clutching the crowbar. As I turned my head to check the other direction, I caught my reflection in a large oval mirror. I jumped at my wide eyes looking back at me. *This isn't going to work. They'll be able to see me.*

I watched the mirror, monitoring their movements. Time crept by as they moved from apartment to apartment, and my heart raced. Sharp clinks of cans echoed off the walls as they dropped their stolen goods on the ground near the vestibule doors. I caught a glimpse of them as they walked to the stairs. Immediately, I dropped down into a crouch, holding the crowbar like a baseball bat. Their steps neared as they guffawed to one another, making jokes about the people they were stealing from. Adrenaline shot through me, and my arm started shaking uncontrollably. *Dammit! I have to get hold of myself.* I took two deep breaths and saw a booted foot land on the top step next to me. Without thinking, I let my last breath go and swung as hard as I could. But I didn't stop. I pulled back and struck two more times. I heard a man scream, and his body fell against the stairwell wall.

I stood up, and in the mirror, locked eyes with the second, skinnier man. In that look, I saw shock that quickly turned into rage. My adrenaline was an asset as I turned and ran down the hall, trying doors. The first few were locked, but the third knob turned, and I rushed into a dark kitchen.

"Charlie, dammit, stop helping me and go get her!" the injured man barked.

"Tony, you're hurt! Let me just pull you up to the next floor. Don't worry. I'll find her. She's trapped in here."

I turned toward the front door and saw it creeping open. *Oh god, I didn't close it all the way!* Then I noticed a closet door on

the opposite wall, slightly ajar. I could just make out two eyes looking at me and the faint planes of a face. *There's someone else here!*
The closet door closed with a light click. *Think, Karis!* The men
were still arguing, so I peeked out the door. Charlie was trying to
drag Tony up the stairs against his will. They were too close. If I
closed and locked the front door, they would hear it and know
where I was. I looked around the kitchen until I saw an old-fash-
ioned round kitchen timer.

"Charlie, you fucking moron, go get that girl! Now!"

I set the alarm for twenty seconds and threw it out the door
and down the hall. It clanked to the ground. It didn't go as far as I'd
hoped, but I would make do.

"Did you hear that?"

"Leave me alone. Go!"

I kept watching through the slit in the door. Charlie finally
gave up and climbed up the last steps to the second floor. His eyes
immediately went to the cracked door, and he started walking toward it. *Why hasn't the timer gone off? It feels like minutes have
passed!* Sweat slid down my back, and the tension in my body was
almost painful. He was about to push the door open when the
alarm sounded. His head jerked to the side as he obviously tried
to decide what it was and what to do. He turned and walked toward the timer. When he bent down to pick it up, I took my chance
and darted out the door. I was already around him and close to the
stairs when he saw me.

I rushed up the stairs and made it almost to the third floor
when I felt a tug on the crowbar still in my hand. I tightened my
grip, determined to hang on to my only weapon. But he tugged
harder and spun me around, pulling the crowbar from my hand. It
hit the marble stairs and clattered down. I saw his fist flying toward
my face right before he punched me, throwing me into the metal
railing. I saw stars, and my vision blurred while my head thumped

in pain. I heard a snap and felt the old railing give as my body sagged over the edge. The top bar of the railing came loose, and the exposed rods dug into my back. Charlie clamped his hands around my throat and squeezed, pushing me forcefully onto the broken railing rods. I breathed in spurts as I choked. Drops of Charlie's spit fell onto my cheeks.

"You think you can beat us, bitch? Huh? You made a big mistake fucking with Tony like that. He's gonna make you suffer now," he threatened through cigarette-stained teeth. His hair was so greasy it was sticking to his forehead.

I could barely breathe, and I saw dark, fuzzy edges in my vision. I pulled futilely at his arms, trying to lessen the pressure on my throat, sure that my eyes were bulging out of their sockets. Then everything began moving slowly, and I thought about my dad teaching me self-defense in preparation for my move to the big, bad city. He told me always go for the groin first, throat second. *That's all I need to get away.* I pulled my foot off the floor, bent my knee, and slid my leg back. I focused all my energy on the leg then let it fly. My knee caught him right in his testicles, and I felt his hands release me. His red face came down to my level as he stumbled back, bending down to grab his groin. His bloodshot blue eyes widened in shock. I didn't even take in a much-needed breath before I pulled my arm back and punched him in the throat. He fell to the ground, gasping, with one hand on his groin and the other on his throat.

My throat burned as I finally choked in several gulps of air. I ran up the last step onto the third floor and saw the door ajar at apartment 3B. I raced through it and straight to the kitchen, looking for a knife, but I couldn't find a knife rack or butcher block. Charlie coughed and yelled that he was coming for me. There was a bottle of vegetable oil on the counter, and my wheels started spinning. I could hear him grunting up the last two steps. I didn't have time to search for something better without making noise, so I grabbed the bottle and tiptoed behind the slightly open front door. Quietly I opened the bottle of oil and put the cap in my pocket. My heartbeat was so loud in my ears that I was afraid he would hear it too. I filled my lungs with air and held my breath. The door opened wider as his body came into view.

"Oh, girl, you are in for it now. I was gonna let Tony have the pleasure, but now? Now you're gonna get us both." He laughed evilly as he moved farther into the living room, hunched over and limping slightly.

I heard Tony staggering up the stairs. "Charlie, did you get her? Tell me you got her!"

"Not yet, but I will. She's here. I can smell her."

I didn't have much time. Once Tony arrived, I would be outnumbered. When Charlie was looking behind the couch, I slid silently around the door, my eyes never leaving his shape. Just as I reached the open doorway, I couldn't hold my breath any longer, so I let it out. Charlie turned and sneered at me. I made a dash for the stairs, dropped my arm, and let the oil flow behind me. It sounded like he was right on top of me. I grabbed the railing leading to the fourth floor as I heard him slip and scream, "Fuck!" I turned just in time to see him slide forward on the oil. He waved his arms, attempting to regain his balance, his feet desperately trying to gain purchase. He looked at me, his eyes wide and frantic. His arms shot toward me as he tried to steady himself. But I took a step back, and his feet lost the battle as he fell down onto the broken railing. His face landed directly onto an exposed rod, and I heard a squishing sound as the rod came out the other side of his head.

I gasped and put my hands over my mouth to stifle a scream. Horror jolted through me—my body felt electrified and rigid. I took another step back, trying to distance myself from the scene, my eyes wide open in shock and my breath coming out in hard puffs. Tony rounded the corner and appeared at the bottom of the steps. When he saw Charlie, his face turned bright red, and he looked up at me.

"You fucking bitch, what did you do? I'll kill you!" His fists were clenched, and I'd never seen anything like his eyes. They looked demonic.

I shook my head, trying to deny what I had done, but Tony started pulling himself up the stairs. I was frozen in place, my feet unable to move. When Tony was halfway up, an inner voiced screamed *run!* I regained my wits and dashed up the stairs. Even though he was limping, I heard him not far behind me. I ran all the way up to the roof and threw the door open. I looked toward my apartment, debating about what to do. *I could run back to my apartment to lure him away from the girls. But I have no weapons, and he's much bigger and stronger.* I imagined him cornering me in an apartment, beating me, choking me the way Charlie had, or worse. I touched my neck. *Best case scenario, he'll kill me quickly. No, I can't take him one-on-one.* I looked to the right. The next building over was the grocery store. *Can I survive a two-story drop?* I searched the roof, hoping to spot the ladder that led down to the fire escape, but it wasn't there.

I jumped when Tony called to me from the landing below. He was too close and climbing the stairs quickly. I was out of time. I acted on instinct and sprinted toward the grocery store. I knew there was about an eight-foot gap between the buildings, so when my foot hit the edge, I launched myself. I flew through the air, terrified. When I hit the roof, my knees came to my chest, my right foot wobbled to the side, and pain shot up my ankle, but I managed to push my legs up straight to counter the impact. I pitched forward and landed on my shoulder as I tucked and rolled. My shoulder exploded in pain, and I heard a pop.

When my body stopped rolling, I turned to look behind me. A second later, Tony jumped off the building, but he didn't launch as I had. *Oh no, he didn't know about the gap!* He screamed as he fell through the air. His knees weren't tucked, and he landed straight-legged. His left leg landed solidly on the roof, but his right leg, the one I'd smashed with the crowbar, landed on the edge, half on, and half off. His legs buckled, and his body wobbled to the right, his arms pinwheeling as he tried to pull his body back up. He looked at me, and there was a moment of surrender in his eyes. His body relaxed, giving up the fight, and he fell over the edge. I screamed and heard a loud thump followed by a thwap. I pulled myself up and ran to the edge, holding my arm to my side, my ankle throbbing. I looked over the edge. His body was lying facedown on the cement next to a large garbage bin, his legs bent at a sickening angle. He must have bounced off the bin. I watched to see if he moved, but I didn't know whether I wanted him to be dead or alive. Then I saw movement, but it wasn't from Tony. A pool of dark blood was fanning around his head. I squeezed my eyes shut and sat back on my heels, crying in anger and frustration.

I stood up and noticed that my tingling arm was dangling. I must have dislocated my shoulder. I couldn't move it at all. I lay down on the roof, closed my eyes, and tried to calm down, attempting to block out what I'd just seen and what I'd just done. I thought about the girls laughing and playing, about the dance they performed for me one night to some Disney song. I thought about my mom and dad, about the time they took me to Mexico for my college graduation present. We'd gone on a boat cruise and danced on the upper deck to a live mariachi band.

A few minutes later, I opened my eyes and pulled myself up, still feeling shaky. I walked over to the edge where Tony was, where the metal railing from the ladder curved down over the edge. The ladder didn't go all the way to the ground, so I would have to drop the last several feet on one arm and a probably sprained ankle. But that wasn't what was bothering me. The pool of blood was making its way directly under the ladder. I climbed down with my one good arm, using my chin to hold the rungs intermittently. When I got to the bottom, I looked down, and I knew there was no way around it. I was going to land in the blood. I took a deep breath, relaxed my body, and jumped off the ladder. When I hit the ground, I heard a wet smack as my ankle screamed in protest. My breath pushed out of me, and I felt nauseous from the pain. My vision blurred while I tried to pull in air as I leaned against the wall.

After a minute, I walked around Tony's body and noticed a bloody bubble pushing in and out of his mouth. I heard a strange wheezing and realized he wasn't dead yet. His eyes were open, watching the blood seep from his body. Fear spiked through me, and I remembered every horror movie scene where the attacker suddenly comes back to life and grabs the main character, who'd wrongly assumed he was dead. I quickly jumped back and leaned against the opposite wall, watching that bubble fill and deflate until it finally stopped.

I limped toward the street, leaving bloody footprints in my wake. Suddenly I heard coughing, followed by a voice that I would have known anywhere. I stopped in my tracks and listened. The voice belonged to Albie, the very large, very loud Dominican super for the building that the men had just ransacked. He lived in the basement apartment, so they must have missed him. He was a neighborhood staple because he would sit in a rocking chair outside his building, greeting people as they walked by, offering up swag others had left on the street to his neighbors. Everyone knew Albie. He was slowly singing a song between coughing fits.

"Papa was a rolling stone. Wherever he hung his hat was his home." He coughed and spit. "And when he died." More coughing, more spitting. I peered around the corner across the street. He was sitting in that rocking chair like it was any other day, rocking back and forth with a baseball bat in one hand, dragging on the ground. "All he left us was alone. Papa was a rolling stone..."

He stopped singing when he spotted me behind the wall. He put his foot down and stopped rocking as our eyes locked. He slowly looked to the left and right, scanning the terrain, then back at me. He gave me a thumbs-up then resumed rocking and singing. My heart was hammering, and my hands were convulsing again. I gathered up my courage and sprinted around the wall and into the girls' building, holding my arm to my side. I pulled the door shut and jimmied it to stay closed through the broken lock. I ran up the stairs, skirting Charlie and averting my eyes as I walked around him. I wasn't ready to deal with that yet.

I went to the girls' door and knocked three times. "Girls, it's me. It's Karis. Don't open the door."

I heard scrambling and then Julia's shaky voice. "Oh my god! Are you okay?"

"Yeah, I'm okay. They're gone now."

"They left? What if they come back?" she cried.

"They won't come back. Trust me. But I'm going to barricade you guys in. I'll find some wood and nail it across your door so no one can get in. Okay? Do you trust me?"

"I trust you," she replied. I heard Emma whimpering.

"I'll be back with some wood."

"No, don't leave us!" Emma yelled.

"It's okay. She's going to take care of us. It'll be okay," Julia said.

"Emma? You're okay. I'll be right back. I promise."

I ran up the stairs, over to my roof, and back to my apartment. Zeke rushed up to me and whined. I patted his head with my one good arm. My ankle was tingling as it swelled, but oddly enough it had stopped hurting and was just throbbing in a rapid tempo. But my shoulder hurt so badly that I was gritting my teeth. After removing my bloody shoes, I called my dad.

"Dad? I need your help. I fell, and I think I dislocated my shoulder."

"Oh, sweetheart, are you okay?" he asked.

I started crying at the sound of his voice. My nerves were shot from what had just happened, and I felt like a little kid again, asking my dad to bandage a scraped knee. "I think so. But my shoulder hurts so much, Dad."

"Can you move your arm at all?"

"No, it's just dangling."

He exhaled long and slow. "Honey, you're gonna have to pop it back into place. It's gonna hurt like hell, but you can't leave it like that. Don't worry. I'll walk you through it. I dislocated mine in football. Do you have tequila or something? Best to numb you up a bit if you can."

"I have some whiskey. Hold on." I went to the kitchen and gulped down two hefty shots. My body grew warm and tingly. "Okay, I'm ready. I think."

"Lie down flat on the floor and use your good arm to slowly pull your other arm out to the side, bent at the elbow and over your head. Once it's over your head, it should naturally pop back into the socket. If it hurts, stop and wait before pulling it farther. I'll stay on the line with you. Just put the phone on the ground next to you."

I did as he asked. Zeke lay down next to me, licking my nose and offering encouragement. "Here goes."

Slowly, I pulled my arm up to the side. At first, it didn't hurt much, and I began to relax. But as I pulled my hand up past my shoulder, a sharp slice of pain shot through my shoulder and up my neck. I screamed and began crying again. I could hear my dad asking if I was okay and telling me I could do it. It hurt so badly that I couldn't even respond. I was sweating and breathing quickly through clenched teeth. I inhaled deeply, and as I let it out, I yelled and forced my arm above my head. I felt a pop, and the pain immediately lessened. Relief coursed through me while I wiggled my sore jaw back and forth to relieve the tension then sat up and tested my arm. I could move it, but it ached painfully with every move.

I picked up the phone. "Dad, that worked. I can move it now. It still hurts though."

"Yeah, it's gonna hurt for a few days, maybe a week. You need to make a sling so it doesn't move much and can heal. Are you okay?"

"Yeah. Thanks, Dad. I love you."

"Love you, too, kiddo. Take it easy for the next few days. It'll be okay."

We said goodbye, and I fashioned a sling out of a scarf after I downed three ibuprofens. Then I ran down to the basement, grabbed some wood out of the box, and put it in a pile on the floor. In the rusty cabinet, I found a box of really long nails. I had to make two trips back and forth with all my supplies because of my shoulder. I was sweating and panting, but I didn't stop, intent on completing my mission.

Back at the girls' door, I yelled, "You'll hear some banging, but it's just me. Go to the living room and put on a movie. This will take me a while. When I'm done, I'll go to the window and let you know, okay?"

"Okay," they said in unison.

I put my hand on the door, wishing I could be in there taking care of them. I waited until I heard the sounds of a movie playing then started my work. Starting at the bottom, I began nailing boards across the door, using my bad arm to hold the nail in place. My shoulder was throbbing, but I ignored it. Thirty minutes later, it looked pretty good, covered halfway up in wooden planks. I couldn't reach higher than that with my bad shoulder, so it would have to do. I walked downstairs, passing Charlie again on my way down. Blood was still dripping from his head and down to the main floor, where a puddle had formed. The rod coming out the back of his head looked like an accusatory finger. I edged around him and kept walking. When I got to the door where I knew a person was still living, I hesitated. *Should I check to see if she's okay, if she needs anything?* The person began coughing on the other side, and instinctively I took a step back. I knew I'd already possibly been exposed to the virus—Charlie didn't have a wristband, and I'd been face-to-face with him. But neither man had appeared sick. I couldn't take any more risks, so I walked away from the door and made a mental note not to touch my face with my hands until I'd had a chance to scrub them.

I ran down to the bottom floor and pulled Charlie and Tony's loot bag open. Inside, there were cell phones, laptops, and other gadgets. I'd assumed they were stealing food. But as I pushed a large laptop aside, I found five cans at the bottom along with a smashed loaf of moldy bread. I removed all the electronics and took the food with me. I could cut around the mold. On my way back up the stairs, I found the crowbar and took that with me too. I walked to the apartment with the open door and scoured the kitchen for food. Either someone had already taken most of the food, or the person didn't have much to begin with. But I found more flour and sugar along with a jar of coconut oil. I could make more tortillas. I made my way back over the roof to my apartment and stripped off my clothes. The bottle cap from the oil fell out and tapped on the ground. I looked at it and laughed at the *Home Alone*–style attack I'd staged. With a trace of a smile on my lips, I stepped into the shower and let the hot water run over me. I reached for my loofah and scrubbed my skin raw. All I could think about was removing any trace of the virus. Zeke poked his head through the shower curtains to see why I was taking so long. He barked once.

"Be done in a minute, buddy," I said, giving him a reassuring smile before his face disappeared.

When I was dry, I grabbed my bottle of hand sanitizer and rubbed it all over my body and face. I filled my mouth with Listerine and gargled deeply into my throat a few times. I took two more ibuprofen then checked my shoulder in the mirror. It was swollen and bruised, and I winced when I touched it. I could also see red finger shapes on my neck. My right eye was swollen and had an inch-long cut next to it. I dabbed it with alcohol, sucking in a gasp at the sharp sting, and placed a small Band-Aid over it. Zeke was watching me, his head tilting with each movement, trying to figure out if he should be concerned. I put my foot on the toilet and inspected my ankle. It was swollen and purplish-red. I'd had just about every injury possible from soccer, so I found an old ankle brace and pulled it slowly over my foot. Pain shot up my leg as I tugged it into place, but it would provide compression. Next, ice. But first, I needed to check on the girls. I put on my robe, gingerly pulling it around my shoulder before attaching the sling again. At the window, I called Julia's name. In seconds, they both ran to the window.

"Are you guys okay?"

"Yeah," Julia said. "I put on *Finding Nemo*."

I looked at Emma, and she was sniffing but looked calm.

"I boarded up your door. I think it'll do the trick. No one else can break in, okay?"

"Are you sure?" Emma asked, looking down at me with scared eyes.

"Yes, I'm sure." I wasn't, but there was no point in telling them that.

"What happened?" Julia asked, looking with concern at my face and arm.

"I'm fine. I hurt myself when I fell, but I'm okay. The men are gone. I promise. Do you believe me?"

They hesitated, staring at me. Julia said, "I believe you." She looked at Emma and gently nudged her. "You trust her, right? She protected us. She won't let anything bad happen."

Emma trained her worried eyes on me. She looked at me for a second, then her face relaxed. "I trust you."

Looking at them, I knew I did the right thing. I didn't want to think about the fact that two men had just died. Instead, I focused on the girls. "How are you feeling, Emma?" Her face was a little red, and her eyes were puffy, but she still had the cat ears on over her tousled hair.

"I'm okay. Julia gave me some of the Tylenol you gave her. I feel better now," she said while rubbing her eyes.

"Use the Chloraseptic if it hurts too much to eat."

"I know. Julia said you were going to talk to me. It's so gross!" she whined.

"But it helps, right?"

"Yeah," she conceded.

"Do you guys have enough food? Is there anything you need?"

"We have enough food. Are you sure we have all the candy?" Emma asked hopefully.

"I gave you all the candy and cookies I could find in the apartments, I swear." I held up two fingers in a mock salute, and they both laughed. "Let me take your photo. Hold on." I limped over and grabbed my camera. Once back at the window, I aimed my lens at them, and Julia put her arm around Emma. Emma tilted her head onto Julia's shoulder, and they both smiled at me. I snapped the photo. "You guys should make some dinner then get some rest. I'll check on you later."

I watched them move around the apartment for a little while, convincing myself again that I'd done the right thing. It made me feel less alone, like I was a part of their lives, however long that might be. Finally, I limped into the kitchen and asked Zeke, "Who's hungry?" Zeke danced across the kitchen floor, licking his lips. I fed us both then snuggled on the couch with my leg elevated and ice packs on my ankle and shoulder. In a moment of clarity, I thought how lucky I was to have my dog and to be alive. I was grateful for the thought, even though it was fleeting.

Chapter 17
January 31st

Loneliness was a different kind of claustrophobia. Knowing there were people on the other side of my walls going about their business had made it much more bearable as though only my world had stopped. But it had started suffocating me, closing in more every day. I missed the intrusive hum of traffic, voices from the street below, and even my vibrating building, which no longer shook because the trucks had all gone. Those signs of life that I had often cursed for invading my seclusion had grounded me and kept me sane. Without them, I found myself getting stuck on irrelevant conversations I'd had with friends, with co-workers, or with Jack, my mind spinning around them until I had to shake my head and return to the present. I did a lot of sighing as I tried to fill my space with fictitious companions.

I knew it was important to find other ways to keep myself in check. I had a few pairs of lace panties that had grown brittle and abrasive with age. I'd contemplated throwing them out a few times, but something always held me back. Since I had so much time to reflect on minor details, I could see what my hesitation had been. Going through breakup after breakup can make a person emotionally numb as the heart attempts to anesthetize itself against further damage. When I found myself in one of these desensitized states, I reached for the lace panties and wore them. I did it because if I was numb, I wouldn't feel pain, but I couldn't feel happiness either. By forcing myself to feel something, no matter how superficial, I was pushing myself to feel again, and maybe it would open my heart up to feel happiness too.

I felt as if the panties had been waiting, biding their time until I'd need them again. Their time had come, but for an entirely new purpose. I hand-washed them in the sink and wore them every day. When I felt my mind start to spiral out of control, I focused on the feel of the rough lace against my skin because it was real, it was there, it was present. They became my talisman, mooring me in reality.

I was focused on that feeling when I heard tapping on my hallway window. My stomach dropped as I ran over. Emma was sleeping on the bed, and Julia was crying uncontrollably in the window.

"She won't wake up!" Julia managed, choking on her sobs.

"And you've checked her breathing?"

"Yes, it's just like Mom. She's breathing, but it's ragged. I've tried everything to wake her up. She's been asleep since last night."

I looked at my watch. It was two o'clock in the afternoon. *This is not good.* "What's her temperature?"

"It's between one-oh-four and one-oh-five." She sobbed. "I gave her a full pill last night because she was in a lot of pain. Then she asked to watch *The Little Mermaid*. This is it, isn't it? She's going to die soon, isn't she? She knew it too!" She was crying so hard I could barely understand her.

I couldn't lie to her—that wouldn't help anything. "Honey, I think so. I don't know for sure, but we need to prepare for it. Put *The Little Mermaid* on again. I'll sit here with you and watch. I'm sorry. I wish I could be over there with you to help."

She jumped up and put the movie on. I could hear it. She sat on the bed with Emma and put Emma's head in her lap.

"Hold her hand, and put your other hand on her heart," I said.

She did that and looked at me, tears streaming down her face. "Can you feel her heartbeat?"

"Yes, I can feel it. It's going really fast."

"Good, keep it there. I'm going to stay here with you, okay?"

She nodded, hiccupping while she cried, her face swollen and red. We watched the movie for about an hour before I saw Julia put her head down and her body start shaking. Alarmed, I said, "Julia, what's happened?"

"Her heart stopped. I can't feel it anymore!"

"Check her breathing," I said with dread. Tears were pricking my eyelids, but I wiped them away, gulping back a lump in my throat.

She put her finger under Emma's nose and waited a few moments then shook her head. I couldn't hold it in any longer. My face dissolved in anguish, and I cried. I wished so badly that I could be strong for her, but that wasn't who I was. I was a person who sobbed along with a twelve-year-old girl who'd just lost her baby sister. We looked at each other and cried for a few minutes.

"I'm so sorry. I'm here with you. Do you want to say a little prayer? Or try to talk to your mom?"

She nodded in response.

"I'll close my eyes and listen."

She closed her eyes and through her sobs said, "Momma, can you hear me? Emma's not with me anymore. I hope that means she's with you. Are you taking care of her, Momma? I miss you so much, and I miss Emma already. I want to be with you both now. I don't want to wait." The TV went off and on again a few times, the sound jolting us from the prayer. We opened our eyes and saw the lights were flickering too. "What's happening, Karis?" She looked scared.

"I don't know, but it's okay. Just keep looking at me." After a few seconds, it finally stopped. "There must be something going on with the electricity."

She looked around then smiled. "No. That was Emma. I know it. When she was younger, if I was doing homework or reading, she would get really upset that I wasn't paying attention to her. She'd drive me crazy flicking the lights on and off. If I told her to stop, she'd say, 'This is how you know I'm here.' She's telling me she's here now with me." Her crying had slowed, and she seemed thoughtful. Finally, she looked at me. "Are you okay?"

Tears were still sliding down my face uncontrollably. "Yes. I'm sorry. I'm just so sad."

"Me too. But I'm also kind of relieved. I know she's okay now. She's better with my mom."

We lapsed into silence while watching the rest of the movie, Julia still cradling Emma. She'd stopped crying and was just hiccupping every few minutes. I was still crying. It was too overwhelming. I didn't know if I would make it through the sadness. When the movie ended, I told Julia that she should wrap Emma up and put her with their mom. When she was done, she came back and sat near the window, and we sat together for the rest of the night, talking some but sometimes just in silence.

"Now, it's just you and me. What about when I'm gone too? What will you do?" she asked.

"Probably go crazy," I said with a short laugh. "I'm already halfway there."

"Are you going to try to make it to the border?" she asked in an obvious effort to shift the subject away from the reality of her own impending demise.

"I don't know. I don't have a car. I've been chatting online with people, trying to find someone who does, but I haven't found anyone near New York yet."

"I hope you make it home."

"Me too," I replied, smiling sadly at her.

"My mom says hope is stronger than sin. You shouldn't give up hope," she said firmly before her voice faded. "I miss Emma so much. I've never missed her before. Sometimes I'll go to my friend Missy's house for a sleepover. Emma gets so sad when I leave and tells me she'll miss me. I never really understood that until now. I'd come home, and she would hand me a bunch of 'I Miss You' cards she'd made out of construction paper and crayons. I still have them," she said, smiling at the memory.

"That's sweet. What else did Emma do?"

"She could make really funny noises with her mouth, ones I couldn't make," she said with a laugh. "She was always trying to find new noises and would spend hours squishing her mouth around to see what she could do. She was funny that way, like she was collecting sounds." She looked at me with a wistful grin. "Last year, I had to get my tonsils out. After the surgery, I was asleep for a long time, but Emma stayed with me the whole time. My mom tried to take her to get something to eat, but she wouldn't go. My mom had to get some snacks out of the vending machine down the hall and eat those instead. When I opened my eyes, Emma told me, 'You're going to be okay. I'm going to take care of you.' And she did. She made me milkshakes and combed my hair. She was a great sister." She was crying softly at the fond memories. So was I.

"You were lucky to have each other."

She nodded sadly. "I'm lucky to have you too." She looked at me. "I'm glad you're here. I don't know if I could have done this without you."

"Don't worry. I'm not going anywhere."

When it grew dark, she took a Tylenol with codeine pill and fell asleep. I stayed there a bit longer watching her. I felt like she was mine all of a sudden, and all I could think about was that soon, she would be gone too. I went up to the roof to get some air and clear my head of all the doom and gloom camping out there. The sky was thick with dense fog. I couldn't see anything, no lights or buildings, no bridges or rivers. It was just me in the night. I felt completely alone, surrounded only by the impenetrable mist blanketing my skin like feral whispers. I closed my eyes and let every hidden emotion flow through me. I didn't hold anything back. It was overwhelming but necessary. I wrapped my arms around my waist and hugged myself, trying to squeeze out every last drop. My body shook from the cold.

I let a strangled scream out into the night. "I'm still here!" I cried until I had no air left in my lungs. I didn't care if anyone heard. I wasn't sure how long I stayed there, letting despair, anger, hurt, and fear cycle through my heart. When I finally headed downstairs, my hair was wet, and I was freezing. I bundled up and went to bed with a heavy heart, and Zeke curled up next to me.

When I awoke the next morning, it was raining. I made a seventh tick on my wall and circled the second month. *Two months down.* I only had one month left before they turned off the electricity. That nerve-wracking line of thinking was interrupted by the sudden, faint aroma of Frito Frito Fried Chicken, the fast food place on the corner by the subway. My mouth filled with saliva, and a strong craving pulled at me. Often, the smell of their chicken would fill my apartment. As much as I resisted, it sometimes provoked me to order my favorite buffalo wings. *There can't be someone in there making chicken, right?* I checked the sky for the usual smoke coming from the building, but the sky was clear. *Is this another sensory memory screwing with me?*

I shook my head and looked out the window again. A faint metal clanking noise was coming from outside. I looked around, and because the trees were bare, I caught sight of a person reaching up toward a fire escape down the block. I grabbed the binoculars and looked out again. It was a man with a long umbrella, and he had hooked the umbrella handle on the last rung of the drop ladder. He yanked hard, but the ladder stayed in place. He walked to the next three buildings and tried each one. At the third building, the ladder creaked as he yanked. I heard scraping as the ladder dropped down and hit the concrete with an annoying clink that hurt my ears.

The man climbed the ladder to the first landing. He used the umbrella to break the window and climb in. My pulse was racing. *What if he tries to climb up here?* I went out and climbed down the fire escape to the second-floor landing. I inspected the hook that held the ladder in place. Rust had eroded the hook, and a small piece broke off in my hand when I touched it. I didn't trust that it would hold. I ran back to my apartment and searched my toolbox for something to hold the ladder in place. I considered duct tape, but I only had a little bit left and didn't think it was enough to hold. I found a roll of thick clear fishing line that I'd used to hang framed photos and had an idea.

My dad had taught me a fishing knot to attach the hook to the line. It was designed to cinch tighter if a fish tugged on it. This line was thicker than what we'd used, but I hoped it would still work. I ran back down and started twisting the line around the top rung of the ladder and the bottom of the fire escape. Pulling the line through the hole and yanking up tightly to secure it in place, I tested it out. It seemed solid. I repeated this until I had no more line left and there were maybe fifteen knots holding the ladder up. I used the last of my duct tape to secure the hook to the railing. I pushed down on the ladder with all my strength, but it held.

I watched the street for another twenty minutes, waiting for the man. Zeke barked, and I hugged him, quieting him down. I went to the window near the fire escape and quietly opened it and pulled up the screen. I heard metal scraping metal. I peeked and spotted the man pulling on the bottom rung of the ladder. The rain was battering him, but it didn't deter him. He yanked several more times, swearing as his umbrella slipped out of his hands, and he lost his balance, his butt landing on the concrete. He stared at the ladder for a few seconds before giving up, unhooking his umbrella and walking away. I laughed. The knots worked!

Feeling triumphant, I cleaned the entire apartment so thoroughly that not a single speck of dirt could be found. I even bathed an unhappy Zeke. Once I was done, I watched *The Shawshank Redemption*. I'd found the DVD under the bed in the spare room during my cleaning spree, and I was grateful for any minor distraction to keep my mind busy. I watched it several times over the next few days since it was newer to me than all my other movies. The third night, I realized I'd watched it so many times that I knew almost all the words, which was quite a feat, given its considerable length. When I'd watched it the night before, I only stumbled over two or three scenes. I decided to challenge myself to see if I could memorize all the words, thinking about that Tootsie Roll lollipop commercial with the owl: *how many views does it take to get to the center of* Shawshank? I watched it over and over, rewinding the parts I had trouble with and saying the words until they seeped in. For the record, it took twenty-three views to recite all the words by heart.

The next morning, after I'd eaten my breakfast tortilla and bowl of rice, I noticed my hand shaking. The past few days, lethargy had pulled at my body. I was barely able to make it through my workout, and I could see my ribs pushing against my skin when I changed. I was sure it was from a lack of protein. All I'd been eating were carbs. My stomach constantly screamed for more than the few morsels I fed it then cramped in on itself. My body needed more, especially if I was going to continue working out, but I had no idea where to find protein. I had no meat or dairy, not even in canned form. The cans I'd found in the loot bag ended up being a can of

SpaghettiOs, beets, and various other vegetables. There was no protein to be found. I'd eaten the last of the pork cracklins weeks ago. I looked outside, wondering if I should try one of the apartments in the girls' building. *What kind of protein might I find in there that hasn't already gone bad? Maybe some canned tuna?* But I didn't know if there were still people in there, sick people, and I was reluctant to take that risk again.

I noticed something in the cement planter surrounding the oak tree right outside my building. I grabbed the binoculars and looked down again. *Bingo!* They were acorns, and acorns were a good source of protein. I scanned the rest of the street and saw other oak trees on my side that would no doubt have piles of nuts congregating in their planters too. Anywhere else, acorns would have already been gobbled up by squirrels. But in the city, other than in big parks like Central Park, there aren't enough squirrels around to take care of all the acorns. Luckily, with the evacuation, the parks department hadn't yet cleared the planters. And with the boom year, there would be more than usual.

When I was at sixth-grade camp, we spent a full day foraging for food. Our counselors gave us a long talk with pictures about what was safe to eat and how to prepare the food we found. My team found a large batch of acorns, and our counselor taught us how to leach out the tannins by boiling them repeatedly to make them not only edible but also quite tasty with salt and sugar. I was pretty sure I remembered the boiling method.

I bundled up and took two large plastic bags with me. I went up to the roof and scanned the streets. Finding them empty, I made my way down the fire escape on the east side, leading to the alleyway behind my building. When I got to the first floor, I slid the hook off the ladder and slowly dropped it to the ground. I made my way down, and when my feet hit the concrete, a whoosh of wind rustled the bare branches. I shivered as I ran to the first oak tree and scooped the acorns into my bag. I crouched and ran to the other trees, scoring a large batch at the third tree, where the acorns had piled up in the gutter because the sidewalk slanted downward. When both bags were full, I sprinted back to my building. I was halfway up the fire escape when a thought sprang up. I'd forgotten about the bag of pretzels and trail mix that had fallen to the ground when I was sending food to the girls.

When I made it to the roof, I rushed back downstairs and into the basement. I cracked the outer door to the courtyard, and it groaned loudly. I peeked through the slit and surveyed the empty concrete courtyard. I slid my body out of the crack and darted to the bag. The pretzels had fallen out, so I piled the bag back into the plastic bag and ran back in. Back upstairs, I portioned the trail mix into fourteen small baggies. Then I sorted through the acorns, tossing any with holes into another bag as they would have been eaten away by worms. I had one full bag of acorns left. I filled a pot with water and left it to warm while I used my hammer to shell the acorns. I dropped them into the simmering water and watched as the water slowly turned dark from the tannins. I drained the water and repeated the process four times until the water stayed clear.

I spread them out on a cookie sheet, sprinkled them with salt and sugar, and baked them in the oven for an hour as our counselor had shown us. When they were done, I popped one warm nut into my mouth. Alone, the nuts were bland, but with the salt and sugar, they tasted like heaven. The nuts would give me the protein and fiber that I would need to keep up my workouts. I would ration them down to a handful a day, and if I ran out, I could venture out for more. I rewarded myself with my first handful, savoring the salty-sweet nuttiness. Over the next few days, I felt more energetic, and my workout became easier.

I spent most of those days seated in the hall window with Julia. Sometimes we watched movies together, and other times we just talked. My shoulder and ankle were still tender, but I'd been using the stationary bike in Kelly's apartment to keep my cardio up. My body was growing used to the cramped position in the window, and it wasn't uncomfortable anymore. Julia told me endless stories about Emma and her mom, and she wasn't sad anymore when she talked about them. She told me that she wanted to be a veterinarian, and Emma wanted to be an actress when they grew up.

Then she started asking me uncomfortable questions, ones I didn't want to think about.

"What's it like being a woman? Having boyfriends, making your own money, staying up late?" she asked, an excited smile on her face.

"It's not all it's cracked up to be. Don't get me wrong—I love that I can live wherever I want and do whatever I want without anyone's permission. And the first five years after I moved here, I went out a lot and had a really good time. It was amazing. I felt like I could be whoever I wanted to be... a whole new person if I felt like it. But once you start focusing on your career, it gets old pretty quickly, and you end up doing the same things every day anyway. As for guys, well, I never met Prince Charming."

"But you had boyfriends, right?"

"Yes," I said, fearful of where the conversation was heading. It felt like a bullet was aimed straight at my locked vault of emotional baggage.

"Why didn't you marry one of them?"

"None of them were right for me."

"How do you know?" she pushed.

"I don't know. I guess you just know."

She looked at me dubiously, unwilling to let my lazy answers pass. "Tell me about them. Let me be the judge of that," she said with a sly smirk.

I bit my lip. "Are you sure you want to hear about this? It's depressing, and we have enough depressing things going on right now."

Julia's smile faded. "I've never had a boyfriend, and I guess I just want to know what it's like."

My heart clenched, and a lump formed in my throat. "Why don't we talk about something else? Something happier?"

"Like what?"

"Like..." I glanced around for ideas. But with all the chats we'd had, I couldn't think of a topic we hadn't covered. I looked back at her expectant face and felt bad denying a dying girl. At the same time, I'd been running away for too long. If I truly wanted to move on from those relationships, I needed to take them out and examine them. "Let's see. Ryan was my college boyfriend."

Julia's eyes lit up, and she clapped her hands.

"We were both in design programs, me for graphic design and him for architectural design. We were together for three years. Everyone thought we'd get married. He's still the nicest guy I've ever met."

"Then what happened?"

"Me and my big dreams. I wanted to move to New York. I needed to see for myself what the world had to offer. He wanted to stay in the Bay Area, get married, and start having kids. He'd just landed a great job as a junior designer at an architectural firm in San Francisco. The world he wanted seemed too small for me, back then at least."

"So you just left? It was that easy?"

"No, not at all." I shook my head. "We talked about him maybe coming out here at some point to join me. We looked up all the architectural jobs in the city and convinced ourselves that we could do it. About a month after I moved, he came to visit, and the minute I saw him, I knew I didn't love him anymore. It was devastating. This new life I was trying had taken over, and I wanted to be free to roam around in it. He knew something was different too. The last night of his visit, he turned to me and said, 'So I guess this is it, huh?' I started crying, and then he did too."

"That's so sad."

"It was, but it was for the best. He met his wife six months later, and now they have three adorable boys. I couldn't have given him that back then. It would have been selfish to try."

"Okay, so Ryan is out. Who's next?"

"Jack. We had a friend in common, and when my roommate moved out, our mutual friend put us in touch because Jack was looking for a roommate too. We met up to discuss the living arrangements and spent the entire time flirting instead. The day he moved in, we basically became a couple. Not a good way to start a relationship, and I think deep down, we both knew it. But we dated on and off for seven years."

"Seven years! Why didn't you just get married?"

"We kept waiting for our problems to be resolved, but they never were. There was nothing specific. No one cheated or lied. It was just a million little things that caused stupid fights. After a few months of therapy, I realized that we just weren't right for one another, no matter how much we wanted to be. I finally broke things off for good even though it hurt like crazy for both of us. But I know it was the right thing to do."

"That sounds complicated."

I gave a short laugh. "Yes, relationships usually are."

"Were there any others?"

"I was single for four years after Jack. I went on a ton of dates, some good, some awful. A couple of guys lasted a few months here and there, but no one stuck around. I was starting to get impatient, and I did something really reckless. I was on our company's soccer team and met Christian, who worked in the finance department.

He was ten years younger than me. I'd heard him in the break room occasionally talking with other guys in his department about all the women he dated, and I could tell he wasn't looking for a serious relationship. We started hanging out, and I knew we were attracted to each other, but I kept him at bay because of the age difference. But he wooed me big time, calling me to hang out, posting on my Facebook page, dropping by my desk and leaving little treats when I wasn't there. He finally wore me down, and even though I knew I'd regret it, I couldn't stop myself. Something happened to both of us. It's hard to explain, but it was almost like the hormones in my body reacted with his, and we couldn't stay away from each other. It was really intense. I think it's what they mean when they say you 'have chemistry.'"

"What does that feel like?" she asked excitedly, pulling herself into a sitting position.

I remembered her comment about wanting to know what it was like because she would never experience it and had to blink back tears. "It feels wonderful and scary at the same time. It consumes you, like your brain can only think about him. You know things are somehow out of your control, and all you can do is hang on. It's kind of like riding a roller coaster. Once you're on, there's nothing you can do except go along for the ride and enjoy the rush. And that's what I did, knowing the whole time I could fall out of the car and go splat. A few times, I tried to break it off. I told him he was going to hurt me. He'd deny it with pretty words. I fell in deeper all while trying not to. It lasted almost a year. Then one day, I asked him what he did the night before, and he got uncomfortable. I knew something was up. He hemmed and hawed until I spotted some hickies under his collar."

"Oh my god, what a jerk!"

"Yeah, but not for that. I mean that was a horrible thing to do, sure. But he was really a jerk for not letting me go when I tried to leave. He was being selfish by keeping me around when he knew he didn't see a future for us, but he didn't care. I should have been smarter though. I wanted to believe him, and I think *he* wanted to believe him. I ignored all my instincts. All along, I knew it would happen, but I stayed. He was like a magnet for me."

"What did you do?"

"I screamed at him and cried. He felt bad but not bad enough. His logic was that he'd always been honest about not wanting to be in a relationship, so he thought that absolved him of any wrongdoing. It was an escape clause he kept in his back pocket. We were in a relationship whether he wanted to describe it that way or not. The truth was he was okay with hurting me. He was young and hadn't experienced that kind of pain, so he had no appreciation for it. I blocked his email, phone, Facebook, everything. I wanted no contact with him, which was probably the best decision I made in the whole relationship. That one really damaged me."

"What do you mean 'damaged'?"

"The emotional and physical connection I felt with him, I'd never felt before. I was thirty-six years old and feeling this for the first time. It was hard to let go because I was afraid I'd never find that strong connection again. I lost faith. I thought I'd missed out on all the good men. I thought there was something wrong with me. I didn't date for a year until I met Brian."

"You didn't give up?" she asked, her eyebrows arched.

"I almost did. But eventually, I realized that those strong feelings for Christian also included the fear of losing him, and I deserved that chemistry without the fear. So I started looking again and met Brian. We only dated for six months before he broke up with me, just for typical guy reasons. He said he was looking for a serious relationship, but in the end, he wasn't ready to settle down. Or maybe he was but not with me. That one finally did me in. I was already pretty beaten down, and it was just the final straw. That was back in October. I'm making myself be content with being alone."

"You can do that?"

"I don't know. I'm still in the process," I said with a smirk.

"And you don't want to try at all anymore? You're okay with just being content?" she asked skeptically.

I thought about that for a moment. It was hard to explain to a twelve-year-old. But I realized that I was trying to explain it to myself, too, to test out my theories and see if they held water.

"When we feel physical pain, we learn to stay away from it in the future. Shouldn't emotional pain serve the same purpose? Isn't it natural to withdraw in the way I have when subjected to chronic emotional pain? It's my heart's way of telling me to avoid what's been hurting me. Dating doesn't make me happy. It's painful and makes me feel flawed. All these people can find their partner, but here I am, barely able to get to a second date with a guy because they all want something better."

"Better than what?"

"Better than me, I guess."

We sat in silence while she thought about what I'd said. It felt pretty good to get it all out on the table, and I was glad I'd given in. Even though that part of my life didn't compare to the real-life struggle I was going through, maybe if I talked it through, I could move past it all. I was feeling somewhat validated in my choices. But something was poking me in the back of my brain, something telling me my logic wasn't as sound as I thought it was. I couldn't put my finger on it.

Then she looked at me and said, "When I was six, these three girls bullied me because I won an award for an essay I wrote, and I guess they were jealous. They said I was the teacher's pet, that I was poor, that I was snotty, and a whole bunch of other things. I told my mom about it, and she said, 'You should never let anyone else define you. You define yourself.' You said all these guys made you feel like there was something wrong with you. But what did you think about *them?*"

Without a beat, I said, "I think they were selfish, dishonest, and callous, among other things. Not all of them, but most."

"Then why are you letting them define you? My mom would tell you to define yourself."

Her words were like a lightning rod, pushing that poker in my head deeper. *Is that what I'd done? I blamed all these guys for the person I've become, but shouldn't I share the blame for welcoming the depression and loneliness in the first place?* "Your mom was very wise, and so are you. Maybe you should have thought about being a psychiatrist instead of a veterinarian."

She chuckled. "That would have been fun too. I'd get to hear all kinds of dirty secrets. So no more Brian, but don't you ever meet anyone nice when you go out with friends?"

I paused. "These past few months, I haven't been going out. I think the whole thing depressed me, so I've been hibernating with Zeke. I just didn't feel like socializing anymore. It felt pointless." I raised one eyebrow. "And besides, no one has been going out for a while now. It's kind of a moot point, isn't it?"

She shook her head, unwilling to let me make a joke of it. "But don't you want to be happy? And be a part of the world? Isn't that why you came here, to see what the world had to offer?"

I looked at her and immediately wanted to end the conversation. She was staring at me, her eyes stern and pointed, telling me she wouldn't back down. The more I let her words sink in, the more I knew she was right. I needed to scrape away years of blame and resentment to uncover what was underneath, but I was terrified that I wouldn't like what I found. "It's good talking to you. You're right. I just haven't wanted to admit that I've let this happen to me. I have to take accountability and not blame other people for how my life turned out. This whole mess is teaching me that I can't be angry at life just because it didn't give me what I wanted when I wanted it."

She smiled. "Is your life that bad?"

"It was, yeah, but only because I chose to see it that way." As soon as I said the words, I felt a queasy shiver of fear flow through my body. I saw things clearly for the first time. *If I'd chosen to nurture this unhappiness, how sound was my judgment?*

She seemed to sense that I was starting to spin out. She interrupted my thoughts. "My fever is at one-oh-two now, but I've been taking the aspirin and cough drops to help."

"Take half of one Percocet when the pain gets bad, okay?"

"Do you smell that?" she asked, sniffing the air.

I lifted my face up and took a few deep sniffs. "It smells like smoke. I'm gonna go up to the roof and see if I can see anything. Hang on." I ran up to the roof with the binoculars and looked around. Then I saw it. I couldn't tell how far away it was, but it seemed to be across the river in Greenpoint. A building was on fire, and flames were billowing out of the windows.

"Can you see if anyone is there?" Julia asked.

"No, it's too far away, and I can only see the top few floors."

"What if it comes over to where we are?" she asked, worried.

"I don't think it will. It's across the river. It can't come across the bridge. It's made of cement and steel, I think, but I'll keep an eye on it."

We chatted for an hour until, coughing, she said she needed to take a pill. "My chest is starting to hurt," she told me.

"Does the pill help with the chest pain?"

"Yeah, mostly."

"If it gets worse, take one of the Demerols. Those are stronger but will knock you out faster."

"Okay."

She took a pill and told me a story as she grew drowsy. "We read this story once in school that reminds me of what's happening now. It's the story of an evil man in a cape who swore revenge on all of the townspeople. He puts poison in the well from where everyone drinks, and it makes everyone go mad. Then they all die, and the evil man is alone in the town and realizes his mistake. He wishes he could go back and undo it because now he's lonely and has no purpose. I wonder if the people who did this to us regret what they did too."

As she finished her story, she could barely keep her eyes open, and she curled up on the bed. I watched her for a little while then watched the fire burning in the distance, thinking about the story. *The people who did this were full of hate.* I didn't think they regretted what they'd done because they'd only taken out part of our population so they could still direct their anger at a large portion of us. I wondered if that was why they did it the way they did. Given how effective the virus was, they could have spread it more widely—they didn't have to warn us. I guess keeping some of us around was accomplishing what they wanted, to spread the message of hatred. There were plenty of us still around to witness that message.

Chapter 18
February 10th

Four nights later, I was headed to bed, getting ready to brush my teeth, when I heard a woman talking to me. I couldn't see her. I could only hear her echoing voice bouncing around the walls of my skull. She was telling me it was my turn, that I hadn't escaped. I asked what she meant, but she just said, "You'll see. Think about Charlie."

I started to panic—*I must be sick!* My throat felt itchy, and I started coughing. It was mild at first, but after a few seconds it got much worse, and at one point, I was coughing so hard I could barely breathe. I felt something making its way up my esophagus, and I thought I might throw up. My throat felt thick and full. I tasted copper as blood gushed up my throat. I tried to hold it back, but I coughed up blood, spraying it all over the walls and my hands. My head pounded, and I scratched at my throat. My vision was swimming. The blood was choking me, and I couldn't breathe at all. I started to lose consciousness.

A loud boom pierced through my dream. I woke up with a jolt, damp with sweat as my whole apartment shook like it did when the trucks bounced past the pothole. As the blackness receded, I turned on my bedside light. I looked at my shaking hands, expecting to see blood all over them, but they were clean. I'd been dreaming. My hands fell to my chest, and I felt it heaving up and down.

175

Closing my eyes, I placed my palms on the bed in an effort to steady my shaking limbs. I pulled in a deep breath and counted to five then exhaled and counted again. Zeke was jumping all over me, licking my face, trying to calm me down. Three sharp cracks rang out in the distance like lightning but not quite.

The light flickered for a minute before stabilizing. My heart pounded a fast rhythm while I tried to decide what to do. *What was that?* It sounded like an explosion. I put on my boots and coat and ran up to the roof. I looked in all directions, but in the dark, I couldn't see much. I inhaled deeply and smelled a faint metallic burning odor. Thinking it was probably the fire in Greenpoint, I sighed and went back downstairs. There wasn't much I could do about it anyway, so I went back to bed, but I couldn't sleep. I was too shaken, the dream still flittering in my consciousness. It was becoming harder to discern my dreams from reality, and instead, I was merely hopping from one dream to another. I was alive in my dreams and sleepwalking in my real life. *Or is it the other way around?*

I'd also been having horrible dreams about Tony, Charlie, and the girls. Each dream forced me to relive the whole debacle in different ways. Sometimes, it just replayed as it happened, over and over in a sickening loop. Other times, I was the one impaled on the railing rod, my one undamaged eye watching the blood drip from my skull and form a puddle three floors below. Once, I was even Tony, jumping off the roof and bouncing off the garbage bin before hitting the ground. I could see the blood seeping from my head around me. I couldn't move, but I could see and feel.

The last dream was the worst though. It featured Emma landing on the railing and Julia falling from the roof as I watched, unable to help. I woke from that one crying and screaming their names. Each time, I had to close my eyes and say over and over, "It's not your fault." I didn't believe it though. I'd branded myself a murderer. I'd been raised with a healthy respect for all life—my parents even moved spiders outside instead of squashing them. Killing someone was completely foreign to me. But that was what I'd done. I'd inadvertently killed two people.

I looked over at the clock and, in shock, saw that it was not on. It was still plugged in but not working. I walked around the house, checking other appliances, but they were all out. I inspected my breaker box only to find them all in the correct ON position. My stomach dropped, and panic raced around my head. My worst fear was realized: no power.

I sat down on the couch in the darkness and tried to remember what to do during a power outage. I went down the checklist: batteries, candles, and water. *Water! Oh god, this is worse than I thought.* I could live without power, but I couldn't live without water. I knew it would pump for a short time, but without electricity, that would end. I ran to each apartment and filled the tubs and sinks. I grabbed bottles and pitchers and filled those too. The water pressure was progressively getting lower as I filled more bottles in my apartment. With my frantic running around, I hadn't noticed that the temperature had begun to drop. I placed a hand on my radiator. It was slightly warm but clearly not working any longer because I could see my breath.

I layered thermal leggings, sweatshirts, and a warm beanie. The electricity shouldn't affect the gas supply, so I hoped I would still be able to light the burners. I grabbed my long butane lighter and turned on one of my burners. I heard and smelled gas flowing. I breathed a sigh of relief and put my teakettle, which still had water in it, on the burner. Two minutes later, I took my cup of chamomile tea back to my room and huddled under the blankets with Zeke. He'd never crawled under the bed covers with me before. With his thick coat, he'd never needed to. The sun was just beginning to lighten the sky. The tea managed to calm me down, and I dozed off.

I awoke a few hours later, shivering, and walked over to the hall window to check on Julia. She'd been sleeping in the bed by the window since Emma died. She was still asleep, but Zeke barked at her, and she slowly rose. She waved at us with one hand, rubbed her eyes with the other, then opened the window. Immediately, she started coughing, and I could tell it was racking her whole body. Her coughs were coming out in white puffs, leading me to believe that it wasn't just my building that was without power. She coughed into a towel, and when she stopped, the towel had blood on it. It was getting worse, and it terrified me. When she saw the blood, she looked at me sadly.

"How are you feeling?"

"Not so good. I started coughing up blood last night," she croaked. "My head and throat hurt really bad. Why's it so cold?"

"We lost electricity last night. I don't know why. You need to take your temperature and get something to eat so you can take a pill."

She got up and wobbled slightly but put a hand out on the bed to steady herself. She reached for the Chloraseptic and sprayed it into her throat before pulling on a sweatshirt. I watched as she slowly made her way to the kitchen. I went to my own kitchen and pulled out the French press I'd won in a raffle at our company Christmas party. I had no idea how to use it, but I would need it to make coffee without power. After fiddling with all the parts and using day-old grounds, I managed to make a decent cup of coffee. I grabbed my hand sanitizer and obsessively rubbed it all over my hands and arms. I knew I was paranoid about getting sick after the attack, but wasn't that understandable? Every sneeze, cough, or headache prompted a panicked run to the bathroom to take my temperature and gargle with Listerine.

I took my coffee back to the window to wait for her. She came back with a rolled-up tortilla and the thermometer on her forehead. Her face was a mask of pain. It was so hard to sit and watch her like that. I was incapable of helping.

Finally she looked at the thermometer and then at me, alarmed. "It's one-oh-three-point-five."

I put my head down for a second to collect myself. "Maybe you should go get food to bring near the bed in case you are too sick to get up. Make sure to keep the pain pills near you too. I'll send over some bottles of water. You won't have water without electricity. And I'm not sure we can talk as much. It's too cold to leave the window open."

Her eyes widened. "But I need to talk to you." She looked as though she was about to cry.

"I know." I looked around, trying to think of some solution. Did those tin-can telephones actually work?

"Wait!" she interrupted my thoughts. "Emma has walkie-talkies. She got them for her birthday this year!"

She slowly got back up and went in search of the walkie-talkies while I put three bottles of water in a bag and wheeled it over. Julia came back and replaced the water with one of the walkie-talkies. Once I had it in hand, I sprayed it thoroughly with Lysol and told her to close her window. We tested them out and were able to hear each other clearly.

"You should layer up and grab another blanket. It's going to keep getting colder. After you eat, grab any candles and flashlights you have too. I'll sit here with you. Eat your food and then take some Tylenol for your fever. Then if you need to, you can take a Percocet."

While she ate, she asked, "What were you like when you were younger?"

"I was always outside, playing in creeks and in the dirt. I was a tomboy, and most of my friends were boys and other tomboys. My mom used to sing this song about a cockroach but would put my name in it. She'd go 'Karisita, Karisanta scurries up and scurries down.'" I smiled at the memory.

Julia giggled then raised her eyebrows. "Your mom called you a cockroach?"

I laughed. "Not really. She was just singing that I scampered around like one. I was always underfoot, and she'd get really frustrated with my energy. I'd bring in worms and snakes, and she'd scream, '*Mija*, get out of the house with those critters!'"

Julia burst out laughing, and so did I.

"But I started playing competitive soccer when I was nine, and most of my energy went to that, much to my mom's relief. I loved it, except I was terrified to hit a head ball. I managed to make it all the way to college soccer without hitting one."

"What was college like?"

"I really liked college. It's very different from grade school or high school. There's much more freedom. You're more in control of what you study and how you study it. I took classes in just about every major to try to find out what I wanted to do with my life. Then I found graphic design, and I knew that was it. I was good at it and enjoyed it. But even though I felt like I was finally on the right path, I still felt insecure and constantly wrote in my journal about who I hoped to become. When I read those passages now, I can see that she was there all along though."

"I feel that way too. Like I know who I want to be when I grow up, but I'm just not there yet. But when I think about who that girl is, I realize I'm already her sometimes. I just want to know how to be her all the time."

"I'm sorry to say this, but I don't know if that ever goes away," I said wryly. "In fact, for me, I think it's just gotten worse. Dating all those guys turned me into someone I didn't like very much. Lately, I've become a bitter, angry person. Other people got what they wanted, why not me? I felt cheated, and I've been taking it out on every person I come into contact with. After all the talks we've had, I feel so foolish for letting that happen to me. I think I even encouraged it to happen."

We sat in silence for a while, both absorbing my thoughts. Uncertainty was a sneaky disease. It lurked beneath the surface and hid around corners in my mind, and I'd allowed it to change me from the confident woman I knew I could be into someone I didn't recognize.

"You know what? I'm going to stop *wanting* to be that person and just *be* her. With all this happening," I said, looking all around me, "I feel more like that person than ever before. I think I *can* be her if I try. It feels possible now. Julia, you've really talked some sense into me."

"That's really cool," she said, smiling.

"Right now, I feel confident about it, but it's easier said than done," I said with a short laugh.

I could see Julia was in pain, so I told her to go grab some more food and blankets and to take a Percocet. I walked up to the roof to check the progress of the fire. It had somehow moved across the street and taken out several other buildings, but I couldn't see flames anymore, just a thick layer of smoke blocking my view of Brooklyn. It looked like all the buildings down to the water were piles of ash. I pulled the binoculars down. I felt I'd been reduced to ash, too, but maybe I could rebuild. I'd been seriously depressed for a long time, not just the past few months. I'd chosen to be alone, but the choice had been taken away from me, and I knew that what I'd become was not the answer. I resolved to walk ahead on more confident feet and to rebuild who I was from that pile of destroyed ash. For the time being, all I could do was hang on. *If I ever get out of this, I will be different.*

I CALLED MY MOM THE next morning, but I wanted to conserve the battery power on my cell phone, so I cut the call short without telling her about the electricity. I knew she would have a lot of questions and suggestions, but I was anxious to check on Julia, and I could tell her the next time we talked. The rest of the day, I monitored Julia's fever, which hovered between one-oh-three and one-oh-four. Zeke and I spent most of the day at the window. By the next morning, Julia couldn't get up at all, and I knew we were close to the end.

"Julia, we need to talk. You know that you don't have much time left, right?"

"I know, but I'm not scared," she said in a hoarse voice, trying to reassure me. "I want it to happen. I'm in so much pain, and I miss my mom and Emma so much. I just want to be with them now. But I don't want to leave you here all alone." She was crying a little, and I was too. She amazed me with her bravery and selflessness.

"Honey, don't worry about me. I'll be okay. Just worry about yourself." I paused. "How do you want this to be? We had music for your mom and a movie for Emma. What do you want?"

She looked up, thinking for a second, then said, "I just want you. I don't need anything else. I just want you to talk to me and be here with me."

I was crying in earnest. "I can do that. Is there anything else I can do for you now?"

"I was wondering, what if I took more pain pills? Like right now, I'm only taking one pill two times a day, and it's helping, but I'm still in pain sometimes. What if I took one every couple of hours? Would that help more?"

"Sure," I said, "you can do that. It probably will help." It wasn't great for her health to take that many, but it was a moot point now.

After a long moment of silence she said, "Karis?"

"Yeah?"

"I don't think I'll make it to tomorrow."

My face crumpled, and I cried even harder. "I'm sorry. I don't want you to see me cry like this. I wish I could be stronger for you."

"It's okay, and I'm okay. I'm gonna be with my mom and Emma, so that's what you should think. I'm just sorry I have to leave you."

"It's okay. I have Zeke," I said with a sad smile. She smiled too. The rest of the day, we chatted, with me doing most of the talking because her throat hurt and she was drowsy from the pills. She fell asleep from time to time, but I remained at the window and kept talking, mostly to fill the silence. I didn't even get up to eat. I didn't want to miss a single moment we had left, even if it was just watching her sleep. She had another coughing fit, covering the towel in blood, and I saw how much pain she was in. "Julia, take another pill."

She could barely speak at that point but said, "But I just took one an hour ago."

"I know, but there's no point in holding back now, right?"

She looked at me and reached for the bottle. "Okay."

We sat in silence for a long time. When she fell asleep, my mind wandered until I looked over at her, alarmed because I couldn't see the rise and fall of the blanket covering her chest any longer. *Is she sleeping, or is she gone?*

"Julia?" She didn't stir, so I yelled again, "Julia!"

Her eyes fluttered open slightly. "Yeah?"

I exhaled. "Just checking."

She smiled at me and said, "I was talking to my mom and Emma. They told me it's almost time." She seemed happy about it, but I was devastated. "It feels like I'm going to fall asleep and never wake up. Is that okay, Karis? Will you be okay if I do that?"

Tears were pouring down my face. "Yes, I'll be okay. It's okay. You can go."

She lay back and closed her eyes. A few minutes later, she was breathing raggedly but managed to say, "Karis, can you sing to me?"

I didn't know if I could because I was crying so hard, but I had to try for her sake. I thought of an old hymn called "Farther Along" I'd once heard a Mennonite woman singing in a movie. The song had replayed repeatedly in my head, so I'd downloaded a Willie Nelson version and listened to it obsessively. It was really beautiful and seemed appropriate. I slowly started singing, my breath catching from time to time when a sob broke loose, and when I got to the last verses, I felt the song inhabit my soul. I wasn't very religious, but this song hit me in a raw place:

> "When we see Jesus coming in glory;
> When He comes from His home in the sky;
> Then we shall meet Him in that bright mansion.
> We'll understand it all by and by.
>
> Farther along we'll know more about it.
> Farther along we'll understand why;
> Cheer up, my brother, live in the sunshine;
> We'll understand it all by and by."

I finished the song with a slight smile and looked over at her. She wasn't moving, and her eyes were closed. I jumped off the sill, pulled up the window, and leaned forward. *Oh god.*

"Julia!" I screamed over and over, but she didn't move.

Zeke put his paws up on the sill and barked, but she still didn't move. My chest constricted, forcing my breath to come only in shallow spurts. I slid down the wall, sobbing, trying to catch my breath before another sob shuddered through me. Zeke lay down next to me and rested his chin on my foot. *What am I going to do now?* I told her I would be fine, but those words rang false even as I said them. I suddenly felt untethered and floundering with no anchor in sight. I was completely alone.

I slammed my fist into the wall behind me as my sobs took full control. My body felt as if it was slowly melting into a puddle. I sat under that window for another hour, letting grief have its way with me, crying until I fell asleep. When I woke up, it had grown dark, and my face felt swollen and numb. My nose was so stuffed that I had to breathe out of my mouth. I felt like a wilted flower in desperate need of watering. Zeke sat up next to me and licked my face. I wished he had the power to wipe away all my tears. I patted him and rose to look over at Julia.

I knew for sure then that she was gone. She hadn't moved a single inch since I'd started singing, and she was really pale. I took one last look at that apartment and her drawings still taped to the window all around her and said my goodbyes. I aimed my camera and took my last photo with the flash off. It was very dark, but I could see her outline, and that was all I needed. Slowly, I pulled the curtain over the window. I didn't want to be able to see into that window. There was nothing left for me over there.

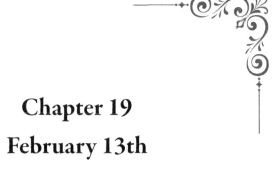

Chapter 19
February 13th

The next day, I did my best to keep busy. I picked up my phone to call my mom, but in shock, I realized my cell phone was dead. I grabbed my laptop and tried to boot it up, but my computer was dead too. I was completely disconnected from everything. My mom wouldn't know why I wasn't calling or answering since I hadn't told her about the power going out. I'd been too wrapped up in Julia to remember to call her back. I felt my pulse racing, and I bit my lip as I considered what to do. Panic rushed through me. *How am I going to do this without someone to talk to? I can't! I have to get out of here. But how?* I looked outside and began to shiver. I sat down at my desk and tried to calm down, hoping to clear my mind and think of some solution.

I put my hands on my knees and focused on Zeke's stuffed lamb, which was lying on the floor. After a minute, my breath returned to normal, and I stood up. But as my eyes left the lamb, they found the portable speaker with the charging dock on my shelf. My iPod and iPhone had the same type of plug. Maybe it would charge my phone too. I plugged my phone into the dock and waited several agonizing seconds until I saw the telltale Apple sign on the screen. I breathed a sigh of relief. I would have to use my phone sparingly because the speaker only had half its power left. There were only four D batteries in the combo pack, and the dock took two. I put the phone on speaker mode and quickly dialed my mom's number.

When she picked up, I quickly said, "Mom, it's me."

"Oh my god, Karis! What happened? I tried calling you all day yesterday, but you never picked up. It really scared me. I thought you were dead," she said, talking so fast I couldn't get a word in.

"I'm sorry. I didn't want to worry you, but our power went off. I don't know why. I heard a loud boom in the middle of the night, and the next morning, it was gone. My phone was dead, but I've been able to charge it with my portable speaker. The speaker has just about half its power left though, and I only have four batteries to use when that charge is gone, so we won't be able to talk as often."

"Oh no, Karis, this is bad! Do you have everything you need? What about water—without power, you may not have water. And food..."

I could tell she was panicking. "Mom, I'm fine. I filled the tubs in the building with water before it petered out. I should be okay for a while. It's just cold." I'd played down the whole food situation with her. There was no need to worry her more. I would figure something out.

She exhaled. "Oh good. That was smart. You'll just have to bundle up. How are you doing besides the power?"

"I'm okay, just trying to keep busy. Is there any news on the outbreak?"

"Um... not really."

"What aren't you telling me?"

"Nothing!"

"Mom," I said sternly.

"It's nothing." She sighed. "And I guess it doesn't really matter since you already lost power. But they've been discussing when they'll turn off electricity and gas. There've been fires, and it may not be safe to keep it on much longer. But it's just talk, speculation by the media. The government hasn't confirmed anything yet." She paused, and I thought about the fire in Greenpoint. "Oh wait. Without gas, you won't be able to cook!"

"I'll figure something out, Mom. Don't panic just yet."

She exhaled. "A new death count was released today. It's somewhere near two hundred thousand."

"In just two months, it's almost doubled? God."

"I know, honey. That's why I didn't want to tell you any of this. It'd be better if you just focused on your own problems right now. And you seem to have an abundance of those."

"You're probably right, but I want to know what's going on. I can't sit here completely disconnected from the rest of the world. What about that medication they were testing before? Anything new on that?"

"It's not working. They can't keep the virus from coming back. It just delays the inevitable."

Even though she'd been forthright with me, I didn't tell her about the girls or the men breaking into buildings. It would just make things worse for her. I was on my own, and I knew it. We said goodbye with a plan to talk briefly every other day, and I tried hard to shake off her ominous news. I switched my phone to airplane mode and turned down the brightness to conserve the battery. I gathered all the candles from the apartments then melted the ones with little wax left together in a pan to make one large candle. Remembering the tip from the apocalyptic movie, I grabbed my neighbor Isaac's big box of crayons to melt down into another candle, using a piece of waxed shoelace for a wick and one of my glasses as a container. I remembered that Kelly'd had a bag of Babybel cheese, the kind encased in wax, which I'd eaten weeks before. I ran up to the roof and rifled through the bags of trash until I found seven empty red wheels of wax. The smell of the trash and the many bags of Zeke's poop made me gag. I scooped everything back into the bags and ran downstairs. I repeated my melting method until I had one more decently sized candle. *For now, this should be enough.*

Later that night, I lit two candles and read a book by the flickering glow. But I found that I knew the words by heart, and it wasn't holding my attention. I looked out the window at Manhattan and sat upright. There were a few lights on in the city. I ran up to the roof and looked north and south. I could see some faint lights in Brooklyn, too, but all of Queens was dark. I felt ridiculously discriminated against. *Why just Queens?* I guessed that a transformer had blown the night I'd heard the explosion. I didn't know what a transformer was, but I knew from watching the news that it could cause an area to lose power. That must have been it. Feeling dejected, I went to bed.

Zeke started coughing the next day, a dry honking hack that terrified me. At first, I'd freaked out, thinking he'd somehow contracted the virus. But the chances of that were slim—it was more likely that the cold was too much for his aging lungs. He'd gotten coughs exactly like that in previous winters, but I couldn't afford for him to get sick. I had no antibiotics to cure him. The cold wasn't good for me either. My body ached and shivered, and my chest hurt from pulling in freezing air. We couldn't stay there much longer without heat, and I knew it.

I needed to find some way to make a fire without burning down the building. I looked at the defunct fireplace in my living room. The chimney was still on the roof and was hollow—my former roommate used to throw her cigarette butts into it. I crouched by the fireplace and ran my hand over the area where they'd clearly bricked up the opening. Since the building was so old, I guessed that they'd sealed it off because it hadn't met modern building regulations. *Is this too risky?* I pulled off a glove and used my finger to dig into the mortar, and a small piece crumbled under my fingernail. I grabbed the crowbar and used the flat edge to ram into the mortar over and over. Pieces crumbled as I scraped and pounded. Finally, I was able to pry one brick loose. The process became easier once I was able to put my hand on the back side of each brick to dislodge them. I piled the bricks up on the side so I could use them later.

When I had the square mouth open, I put my head in and peered up. I could see a beam of light from the sun, and my hopes soared. I used the bricks to form a low barrier between us and the fire. I sat back and inspected my work. *Not bad. But will it work?* I needed wood to test it. I took my screwdriver and hammer to the apartment below mine and disassembled Tom's coffee table and bookshelf. I figured the pile would give me enough wood for a few days. I hauled the wood back upstairs and placed some pieces on top of each other in a large metal roasting pan that I used for cooking my Thanksgiving turkey. I crumpled up a few pieces of paper from my old tax returns and placed them at the bottom.

I took a deep breath. *Here goes!* I lit the paper with my lighter and waited for the wood to catch. Zeke was sitting next to me, trying to garner some of my body heat. I wrapped both of us up in a blanket, and we watched while the wood slowly caught fire and began filling my living room with heat. I laughed as I pulled the blanket down, barely able to believe that it had worked. While it wasn't as warm as the radiators had been, it was enough to keep us warm if we sat right next to it. For the rest of the day, I went to each apartment and took apart all the wooden furniture, placing it next to the fireplace. I would have to conserve the wood as much as possible, but it would keep us warm until I could come up with an idea of how to get us out of there.

Chapter 20
February 17th

Zeke's cough was better by the next day. He lounged in front of the fire most of the day and slept under two down blankets with me at night. I kept up my workout routine and had been slowly adding to it for something more to do. My ankle was feeling stronger, and I went back to running the stairs with my ankle wrapped. My shoulder was no longer tender, and I'd stopped wearing the sling the day after Julia died. I could see remarkable changes in myself. I'd been in shape during my soccer days, but considering that I'd only focused on my flaws then, I couldn't imagine that I'd appreciated it enough. My arms and legs were toned, and my stomach was flat and slightly six pack-ish. And my shoulders! In soccer, we didn't work out our arms much, so the results were confined to the lower half. But since I'd been doing push-ups and working out with my ten-pound weights every day, man alive! My shoulders looked amazing. I'd always been slightly slope-shouldered, but now they were broad and alert, ready for anything. I felt powerful and invincible. I was beginning to think it was a first step into my new self, a violent shove into the person I hoped I was becoming. It was like wearing those panties. If I could make myself feel powerful physically, maybe I could make myself feel powerful mentally. At the very least, I had that.

I looked at myself in the mirror and took stock. My Norwegian-Mexican mix, which my dad jokingly called "Norwexican," had given me some nice features. I'd always looked at my face as a whole, not as a sum of individual parts. And because of that, I had invariably felt plain and unembellished, unlike other women. But as I perused my face, I noticed each feature independently of the others. The shape of my face reflected more of my Norwegian side, but I had the olive skin and dark hair and eyes of my Mexican side. *Not a bad mix,* I thought, admiring my face anew.

However, as I looked at myself as a whole again, head to toe, I clearly saw that my hair didn't fit this new mighty version of me. My hair had always been long and wavy, and I hadn't cut it since my breakup with Brian. It was much longer than usual and had grown past my shoulder blades, falling almost to the middle of my back. I'd been putting it in a bun most of the time to keep it out of my way, so I hadn't noticed how long it had grown. It was time to cut my hair to go along with my new body and mind.

I remembered that Kelly was a hairstylist, so I ran to her apartment in search of ideas. In her bedroom, I found a stack of magazines called *Hair's How.* I flipped through five of them, dismissing most cuts as not fierce enough before I found an image of Michelle Williams with super-short hair and longish bangs. It felt right and totally different than any style I'd ever had, mainly because I'd never had the courage to cut it that short. There was a step-by-step guide on how to cut the style, and I knew I wasn't going to find anything better.

I snatched a pair of Kelly's fancy scissors out of a black leather case by her bed and headed to the bathroom with the magazine. I pulled my hair into a low ponytail. I took a deep breath and exhaled, then cut off everything below the rubber band. I shook my head back and forth, and it felt like a hundred pounds of misery had been lifted, as if I'd chopped off bad juju. I threw a good fifteen inches of my hair into the trash. I wet my hair then checked the guide and sectioned it out to match the diagram on the page. I was ready to start cutting. I pulled each section through my middle- and forefinger and began cutting like the woman in the magazine. Each snip was like a step in the right direction, and I could feel myself emerging from a shroud of biting regret. When I was done, I put my hands on the sink and leaned forward to examine my work. *Who is this person?*

For the next few days, every time I caught my reflection in the mirror, I took a few moments to admire it. I was feeling stronger, with confidence that I'd never felt before tingling under my skin. I had an urge to read the end of the book about the bitter woman. I rushed to my bookshelf and spent the next hour reading the last pages. The woman ended up scrambling to find her long-lost family and friends in the last days of her life. They gathered around her deathbed while she used her last words to poetically list her regrets. I closed the book with determination. *That will not be me.*

I guarded my newfound spirit for the next two days, intentionally turning away from anything that would threaten its strength. There was no dwelling on failed relationships or enviously brooding about my married friends' happy kids. No ominous sounds outside or creaks in my building could make me crumble into a pile of anxiety. Walking away from those thoughts kept me grounded. Instead, I focused on ideas for how to make it to the border.

The bike in Tom's apartment wasn't a good or safe idea, but it was all I had. I'd dismissed it at the time because I didn't think I was in shape enough for that level of activity, but my workouts left me in pretty good shape, and I felt more assured that I could manage it, at least until I found a car with keys. But the bike needed to be my last resort, not my first. There were more cars on other streets that I hadn't checked.

Since I was feeling more confident, I decided to make another foray outside. I waited until just before sunset. While the low light would make it harder for me to see anyone lurking, it also meant they wouldn't be able to see *me* as easily. I brought a flashlight along with the box cutter and crowbar.

When I climbed down the fire escape on the east side of the building, my hands weren't shaking, and my breathing was even. I darted behind a car and looked around. Finding nothing, I rushed across the street and made my way to the next street over. As I rounded the corner, I spotted about ten cars along the block. Slowly, I made my way down, checking the doors, but I only found two I could get into. One was unlocked, and the other had a window opened enough for me to slide my arm in and unlock from the inside. Neither had keys, and I tried hotwiring, but again it didn't work. I wondered if I was doing it wrong or if the batteries were just dead from sitting on the street for so long. Without the internet, I couldn't watch the tutorial again.

I managed to check the next two streets but had no luck with keys or tapping the wires together. The last car on the third block was locked, but I could see a set of keys in the cup holder between the seats. My hopes soared. While I was nervous about smashing the window and drawing attention to myself, it was worth it. I grabbed my crowbar, held it like a baseball bat, and swung as hard as I could. The glass shattered loudly, a few pieces hitting my arms and face. I opened the door and slid into the driver's seat. I tried every key on the keychain, but none of them fit into the ignition. They looked more like apartment and mailbox keys than car keys.

The sun had fully set, and only a light glow illuminated my surroundings. As I dashed back toward my building with the intent of checking the streets on the other side, I heard a car engine close by that seemed as though it was heading in my direction. Not wanting to take any chances, I ducked into an alleyway across the street from my apartment. The car was coming closer, but I couldn't see any headlights. A few minutes later, I saw an SUV heading north along the main road. I pulled back into the alleyway until the engine faded away.

With my breath coming in shorter gasps, I decided to go back home. Over the next couple of days, I scoured the streets around my apartment but didn't venture past the park. There were too many hiding places for someone to lie in wait. My courage was weakening at the idea of going farther than I already had. I'd searched all the way to the bridge leading to Brooklyn on the south side of my apartment. On the north, I'd made it seven blocks. Past that was mostly industrial buildings where I would have been too out in the open. In total, I estimated that I'd checked at least twenty-five cars and come up empty. But I did find two granola bars, a half-eaten Snickers bar, and a switchblade.

On the fourth day, while trying to convince myself to check the streets past the park, I heard the tinkling of an ice cream truck. *That can't be right.* I walked over to the window and looked outside. I couldn't see it, but I could hear it, which led me to believe maybe it was in my head, but god, I hoped not. A few seconds later, the big white Mister Softee truck eased into my line of sight. It was going as slowly as an ice cream truck would if it were trying to lure customers out of their houses to buy a swirled soft serve with sprinkles. I couldn't believe what I was seeing. In an effort to clear the surreal image, I closed my eyes and shook my head. But when I opened them again, the truck was still there. It looked as if there was someone in the driver's seat, but all I could see from this angle were legs. The truck's tinkling and its slow progress on the deserted street were eerie in the silence.

I walked away from the window and thought for a minute. It just didn't make sense. I ran over to my dining room window and looked out again. The truck made a right and drove slowly toward the waterfront. I watched until it disappeared and the music faded away. I didn't know if it was real or not, and I didn't know which I wanted it to be. Neither option made me feel any better.

A minute later, a car alarm began wailing somewhere in my neighborhood, that annoying, repetitive *wah wah* alternating with a deeper buzzing that everyone living in a city was familiar with. *Great.* By the time I went to bed, it was still howling, and I'd failed to gather enough courage to head back outside. The next day, the alarm was still blaring on and off, *maybe.* It could just have been a residual scream in my head. It was driving me crazy, and I needed it to stop, but instead it seemed to be getting louder. I was having a hard time drowning it out even with my noise-cancelling headphones on.

All the progress I'd made was waning, and I knew I was standing on the edge of a mental breakdown. It was taking everything in me to not give in and let it happen. The car alarm continued wailing off and on, vibrating the walls of my ear canals and making it more difficult to tell if it was still sounding or not. *The car can't still have battery power left, can it?* And without my sound machine, I couldn't sleep with the alarm blaring. I remembered the combo pack of batteries, so I loaded two of the double A's into the sound machine and put it on the campfire setting. The pack had eight double-A batteries, and I hoped they would last as long as I would be there.

Zeke and I huddled under the blankets, and if I concentrated hard enough on the crackling fire sounds, I could convince myself I was in a warmer place. But the alarm still screamed during the day. I reread a couple of books that I'd only read once before. The alarm faded to the background until one glorious morning when it was gone for good.

But then I heard some banging that sounded like it was coming from inside the building. I couldn't be sure, so I needed to discuss it with Zeke.

"Zeke, what do you think, is that inside or out?" I said offhandedly, looking around and listening.

He looked at me and tilted his head. Another bang sounded. He looked toward the door then back at me. His eyes were still on the door when we heard another bang, which was loud enough to make me jump. He looked up at me and whined.

"That sounded close, but it could still be from outside," I said hopefully. He followed me over to the window to look around, putting his paws up on the sill. I didn't see anything on the street. There was another bang. "Where is that coming from?" I whispered.

I looked down at Zeke, and he blinked at me, pulled his paws away from the window, and went to lie on the couch. He'd lost interest. *Am I being paranoid?* I followed him to the couch. "That sound is outside, isn't it?"

He raised his head, and I could have sworn he nodded, his chin moving up and down. My eyes were wide with fear.

Did I imagine it? "Was that a yes?" I asked, testing him.

His nose came up, then he put his chin down between his paws.

That was another nod! I barked a short laugh. "You nodded. I can't believe you nodded!"

He sighed heavily as if annoyed.

"Hey, no need to have an attitude about it."

He snorted in return, and I realized how crazy I must have looked, sitting there and talking to my dog—not just talking, but interpreting what he was saying to me. And furthermore, I was sure I was right and knew what he was saying.

Did I jump off a cliff somewhere? I'd always had conversations with Zeke, but they'd been one sided. I suddenly felt certain he was communicating with me. I remembered laughing with my mom at this woman on a talk show who claimed to talk to animals. She'd seemed so certain of it that we'd thought she was crazy. *Does that make me crazy too?* I felt myself starting to panic about my sanity, so I decided it was best not to spend too much time analyzing it.

I needed a glass of wine to calm my nerves from the exchange. I went to the fridge but found only one glass left in the open bottle. I checked my stash, but in alarm, I realized it was my last bottle. *Crap,* I hadn't been paying attention to my stockpile of wine, only my food. I leaned back against the counter and sighed. There were still a few bottles of whiskey, but I really preferred the wine. *I'd better make the most of this last glass.* I poured it and went to sit with Zeke on the couch. But as I set the stemless glass down on the coffee table, it hit the edge of the remote control and rolled over, spilling all of the wine.

I gasped and screamed, "NO!" Because of my slanted building, the wine was slowly making its way across the table to the other side. Instinctively I ran over and put the glass under where it began to run off. After my glass was almost full again, I looked in. Little bits of lint and Zeke fur were floating around. *Dammit! How badly do I want this wine? Very badly.* I went to the kitchen, grabbed a sieve, and poured the wine through it a few times. I looked again. No fur. I knew it was gross, but I didn't care. I drank that wine as if it was liquid gold.

Zeke continued to communicate with me here and there with his various nods and facial expressions, convincing me I was right. He didn't seem interested in lengthy discussions but had no qualms about motioning for an extra scoop of food or a belly rub whenever he wanted one. I kept having bouts of uncertainty about some noise or glimpse I caught outside in my peripheral vision, which chipped away at my courage and kept me in my building.

I imagined more intruders, someone larger and more frightening than Charlie and Tony. Sometimes, when I saw trash or bottles of recycling that had spilled out of the bags on the street, my mind saw it as a dead animal. I would shake my head and squeeze my eyes shut, begging my mind to work properly. When I opened them, I could see what was really lying there. The hallucinations left me shaking and sweating as if they were symptoms of withdrawal from reality.

I didn't know how much longer I could take it. I clung to the concept of the new person I hoped I was becoming and used that as something to pull me back from my inner nightmares. My mantra had become "You can do this!" and I repeated it over and over when I heard noises. I took my mom's advice and put "You can do this!" and "You are strong!" and a variety of other self-affirming Post-It notes all over the house to reassure myself, but I wasn't sure if they were helping.

I had another vivid dream that night about finding a hidden door in Mr. Stanhope's apartment that had DUFRANE written across it in bold, black letters. The door opened into a long corridor that came out under the elevated seven train. An airplane was nosing into the street, and Zeke and I contemplated boarding it right when I woke up, feeling out of sorts, not able to reconcile that I was awake. I lay there, thinking back on my dream and about the other dream with the hole in the floor. I was going through doors and floors to find my freedom.

Something had to give. I had to get out of that building. I resolved to make my escape and revisited the bike idea. It had a box on the back for groceries. Zeke would have to ride in there. I told him about the plan, but he just looked at me, his eyebrows raised skeptically, and put his head down with a grunt. It did not seem like a resounding vote of confidence. *I can do this. I can do this. Someone, please tell me I can do this.* I heard nothing, not even Zeke.

Chapter 21
February 24th

T he next day, I made notes, mapping out a route in my big book of maps and generally feeling better about my plan. I didn't know if I would actually go through with it, but it gave me somewhere to direct my mental energy. My idea was to bike as far as I could go, checking cars for keys along the way. I was hoping I would get lucky and find one, but I couldn't count on that. I was also hoping I could find abandoned houses where we could sleep at night during our journey. I thought I could make it to the border in about a week. I was feeling pretty good about it until I talked to my mom.

"Karis, this is too dangerous! You can't ride a bike to the border! You'd be out in the open. Anyone could attack you."

"I know it's not ideal, Mom, but what other choice do I have? I can't sit here in my apartment anymore. I'm going stir crazy, emphasis on the crazy."

"I understand, but this is just too much. Let me talk to your dad and discuss it. Maybe we can come up with an alternative."

I sighed. "Fine, but I don't think there is one. The bike is the only option for transportation at this point unless I get lucky and find an unlocked car. I don't have much food left. And with no electricity, it's dangerous to live for long in these circumstances. Plus..."

I hesitated. I didn't want to worry her, and I should have cut the call short, but I was feeling emotional.

"Plus what?" she prompted.

"Mom, I don't know how much longer I can hang on. I think I'm hearing things that aren't there, maybe even seeing things. I don't know."

She paused to absorb my words. "Why didn't you tell me?"

"Because I didn't want to worry you, especially since you can't really do anything. I guess I was hoping I could handle this on my own. I don't think I can anymore. I have to get out of this apartment, Mom. I don't know what will happen if I don't." I sniffed as tears made their way off my lashes.

She sighed. "I get it. I'm not saying I'm disregarding this plan altogether, I'm just saying I want to see if we can think of a safer way. I'm sorry this is happening to you. Please tell me what's going on, you don't need to protect my feelings, okay?"

"Okay."

"I know we have to limit our phone calls, but if you're scared, just call me, day or night. I'll keep my phone with me at all times. We can do this together. You are not alone."

To my surprise, her words were helping me, and I felt stupid for not including her sooner. "Thanks. Talk to Dad, and we'll talk again in a couple of days."

"Okay. I love you."

"I love you too."

I hung up and sat on the couch. I spotted a Post-It note on the wall next to me. I leaned forward. It read, "Shake your money-maker." My eyebrows came together. *Why did I write that?* Then I remembered I'd had two glasses of whiskey the night before and used some of my precious battery power to play music. I vaguely recalled listening to my Ludacris album. I shook my head and laughed. The battery level on my speaker had dropped another bar. Damn, I needed to be more careful.

I went up to the roof with my binoculars for a while, thinking about what my mom said as I absentmindedly scanned the landscape for signs of life. I knew she didn't understand the urgency of my situation, not fully. But she was right, and saying it out loud made me realize just how dangerous the plan was. But it was just as dangerous to silently go crazy in my apartment. And furthermore, I was living on simple carbs and the small amount of protein I got from the acorns. I wasn't sure how long my body could subsist on that alone. It wasn't healthy.

And there was something else. My water supplies were dwindling. Only one bathtub full of water was left in apartment two. I'd been bathing only once a week with a washcloth in the sink to conserve, and I hadn't washed any clothes other than underwear in a month. I used a bucket to flush the toilet only once every other day. But it hadn't rained in weeks, and if I ran out of water, I would be dead. I knew I was trying to talk myself into the escape plan, but maybe I needed to. I was torn.

A few blocks over, I could see the top floors of an apartment building, and there was something in a couple of windows that I hadn't noticed before. I focused the binoculars on those windows and saw white paper taped up with words written in black ink. Walking over to the edge closest to that building, I focused the binoculars again. I could just make out what they said, and it was hopeful but also unnerving. One said WE ARE HERE. A few windows over, there were four pages up on the windows. DECEMBER 27, OWEN IS HERE, JANUARY 5, OWEN IS HERE, JANUARY 16, OWEN IS HERE, and JANUARY 29, OWEN IS NOT HERE.

The last note was written in dark red, and the word "not" was underlined. I pulled the binoculars away from my eyes and contemplated the notes. I didn't know what they meant, but that had been a few weeks ago. I made a mental note to keep checking to see if any others appeared. I scanned the terrain in the other direction until I saw the bridge. There were several cars parked in various spots along the two lanes, and two cars farther up that were blocking the roadway. Maybe one of those cars had keys. The bridge was far though, and it would be dangerous to go check. I pulled the binoculars down and went back downstairs. I poured myself an oversized whiskey in the hopes of taking my mind off those chilling notes and my limited options.

I puttered around the house, read another book, and organized my DVDs in alphabetical order. It was a fruitless activity, considering I couldn't even watch them, but it kept me busy. As I got to S, I heard a shout from the street below, then a few more. The shouting turned into scuffling. Zeke ran to the dining room window to look outside, and so did I. I pulled up the window and screen and leaned my head out to get a better view. I spotted a man running down the street with a large backpack on. Two men, one blond and the other with dark-brown hair, were yelling and chasing him. The backpack was slowing the man down, and they were gaining on him quickly. He made it all the way to my corner before they were on top of him.

They pulled his pack off, and he punched at them in an attempt to get it back, but he was outnumbered. The blond guy slammed his fist into the man's face repeatedly. The other guy kicked him in the stomach, and the man fell to the ground. My hand was over my mouth, so I didn't scream. Zeke began a low growl, so I led him to my bedroom and closed the door.

I peered down again and immediately noticed the bright-orange wristbands. They all had one. The two men were beating the man in earnest and egging each other on. I heard one of them say, "Get him! Don't let him up. I want another shot at him."

The other guy laughed, and it didn't seem to be out of a desire to get his supplies anymore. It was hard to watch, and I closed my eyes a few times. Finally, the dark-haired man pulled the other back and told him to stop. The man was unconscious and bloody. After searching his pockets for anything else of value they might want, they picked him up, threw him roughly onto my stoop, then ran off with their score.

I let Zeke out of the bedroom because he was scratching at the door. My shaky hands grabbed the binoculars, and we both went back over to the window to watch the man. He wasn't moving at all. *Oh god, is he dead?* I concentrated the binoculars on his chest, and eventually, I did notice a slight rise and fall. He was alive. *So now what? This guy could be a rapist or a killer. Or he might be a decent human being.* There was no way to know anymore. I could leave him out there, and eventually he would wake up and leave. Or someone sick or dangerous or both could come along. Leaving him out there could equal a death sentence. On the other hand, if I pulled him inside, I would be putting myself in unnecessary danger. I rubbed my forehead, trying to shake some solution loose. But the thought that kept repeating itself was that I couldn't leave him there in good conscience. Finally, I came up with a compromise: I would pull him inside and tie him up while he was still unconscious.

I went to my toolbox, pulled all of the tools out, and found a small bag of zip ties at the bottom. I grabbed the crowbar, went downstairs, and pried the wooden boards off the door. It took a huge amount of effort that left me sweating and aching. I almost gave up halfway through, but my conscience urged me on. I went to the first-floor apartment and looked out the window. Several minutes went by before I gathered my courage and deemed the coast clear. I opened the locked door, propped it open, then peered out the windowed outer door. I looked around for a few more seconds then down at the man. He was still there, unconscious. I watched for any sign of him waking, possibly hoping I would lose my nerve. But nothing happened on either front.

As fast as I could, I threw the door open and grabbed the man under his arms. I dragged him slowly into the building, grunting as I pulled, and quickly shut the locked door behind me. My heart was racing, but since I'd pulled him in and the door was locked again, I felt better. I took a second to catch my breath before I dragged him into Mr. Tablock's apartment. With as much remaining strength as I could muster, I pulled him up onto the low hospital bed that Mr. Tablock had set up in his living room. Sweat was dripping off my brow and neck, but my new muscles were serving me well. I reached for the zip ties and pulled one around each of his wrists and ankles, securing him to the bed. Once I was sure he was firm-ly bound, I took a look at him while catching my breath. He didn't look good. His left eye was swollen shut and starting to turn purple. He had scratches and cuts all over his face, not to mention a split lip.

I ran back to my apartment and grabbed alcohol, Band-Aids, and an Ace bandage. Zeke followed me back downstairs, curious about my activity. I swabbed the man's cuts and scrapes with alco-hol then put Neosporin and Band-Aids over them. I thought for sure it would wake him since some of the cuts were quite deep, and they had to hurt. But he didn't budge. I put butterfly bandages on the deeper cuts, pulling the skin together so they would heal prop-erly.

While Zeke sniffed our intruder, trying to determine if he was friend or foe, I pulled up his shirt to check his ribs. The men had kicked him a few times, and I was worried about broken ribs or a punctured lung. His breathing seemed even and unlabored, ruling out any lung issues, but his ribs were red and swollen. Ice would be best, but I didn't have any. As I wrapped the Ace bandage tightly around his body, lifting him up each time I went around, I heard a rattling noise coming from his jacket. Maybe the men had missed something. After clipping down the end of the bandage, I reached into his inner pocket and felt a small bottle. I pulled it out and sharply inhaled when I saw it was a prescription pill bottle. The hairs on my neck began to rise. As I turned the bottle around, the label told me the pills were amoxicillin. Immediately, I jumped back from the man.

My mind raced, and my heart was beating faster. *What have I done?* He was probably sick even though he had a wristband. He could have contracted the virus sometime after he'd been tested. *Why else would he have had these in his pocket?* I reached my trembling hand out and placed it lightly on his forehead. His skin was cool to the touch with no sign of a fever. I snatched my hand back and ran to Mr. Tablock's bathroom to wash my hands, arms, and face as a precaution. Under the sink, I found an unopened box of doctor's masks in the cabinet and slipped one over my head, down over my nose and mouth. I walked over to Mr. Tablock's office and sat down by his desk, thinking about what I should do. I couldn't let the guy stay if he was really sick. But I couldn't force him to leave either. He might have been too injured from the fight to survive.

My eyes popped open as an old memory slipped into my mind of my dad playing a prank on my mom, reversing the front door lock before he left for work. It took my mom ten minutes to realize what he'd done, her hand turning the knob over and over unsuccessfully and staring at the spot where the knob for the deadbolt had been replaced by a keyhole. Her face turned red as she dug her keys out of her purse and unlocked the door from the inside. She refused to talk to my dad for the rest of the day because he'd made her late for work with his antics. I had helped him switch the lock back that night, so I was pretty sure I could duplicate it to lock the guy in.

I walked over to the door and examined the two deadbolts. One was a standard lock, but the other was a large bronze Segal that someone had added later for additional security. The Segal would be a huge pain to switch, but the other one was similar to the lock I'd had back home. I would give him a couple days to heal then ask him to leave. It was a risk because he could refuse, and there wouldn't be much I could do about it. But I would have to cross that bridge when I came to it.

I rushed to the basement and found a screwdriver. Back at the door, I unscrewed the casing around the lock then wedged the screwdriver under the edge to pop it off. It had been painted over several times and didn't come off easily. Paint and dirt fell to the ground and mixed with the sweat that dripped off my face. It took me twenty frustrating minutes to get it right. I incorrectly inserted the lock into the hole several times before I finally lined up all the parts properly and was able to screw it back into place. I shut the door, and as I turned the deadbolt to the locked position, I heard the lock sliding into place. I turned the doorknob and pushed on the door, testing it. The door was firmly locked.

I walked back into the living room and noted that the man was still passed out. After washing my hands and face again, I went to Mr. Tablock's office with the mask over my face and hunted around for something to read while our guest slept. My eyes scanned a room filled with framed awards for journalism and pictures of a younger Mr. Tablock with colleagues. Pinned to a corkboard was a badge with *New York Times* printed on the front and "Stanford Tablock, Journalist" printed underneath. I never knew he wrote for the *New York Times*. The corkboard also held ticket stubs, articles that carried his byline torn from the newspaper, and pictures of him in foreign countries. Looking at all the remnants of a lived life, I realized I knew more about him from this collection of mementos than I did from all the years we'd lived in the same building. There was no evidence of a family, and I'd never seen anyone visiting him other than Regine. I guess he was a lonely soul too. I wondered if he was happy and whether it was possible to be lonely *and* happy. I wished I'd taken the time to ask him.

On the other side of his desk, I spotted a large stack of old *New York Times* issues, some going as far back as the sixties, but none from the last year. He must have stopped saving them when his health deteriorated. I grabbed a few and ran back up to my apartment to read, seeking any articles written by Mr. Tablock. Even though the stories were old, I learned some things. I'd never been much of a newspaper reader, so I considered it my New York history education. I read about everything from politics to culture and past events. I fell asleep while reading and woke up an hour later. The sun had set, so I lit a candle and made dinner for both Zeke and me.

While I ate my bland rice, I wondered who the injured man was and if anyone was looking for him. I imagined various reactions he might have when he woke up to find himself tied up. I would be freaked out if I woke up like that. After eating, I threw some of the rice in a Tupperware bowl as a peace offering. I grabbed two tortillas, a baggie of acorns, and a bottle of water then walked downstairs with Zeke in tow.

At Mr. Tablock's door, I pulled the mask up over my face again. When I walked into the living room, the man's eyes were partially open, and he was pulling at the restraints. He seemed confused and alarmed, but he hadn't seen me yet.

"Hi," I said simply, setting the food and water down on the coffee table. I took a few steps back. He didn't respond, but his eyes darted to mine, warily looking me up and down. I gave him a second to size me up before I held up my wrist and said, "I've got a wristband too."

He continued to look at me but said nothing.

"Don't worry, I'm not going to hurt you. But I'm all alone here, just me and my dog, so I have to be careful. Are you sick? You have a wristband, but I found antibiotics in your pocket." I raised my eyebrows, challenging him.

His eyes narrowed. He was shivering. *Was it from the cold or from a fever?* "No, I'm not sick. Lift up my right pants leg," he said, a British accent apparent in his deep voice.

I looked at him for a second, not wanting to move closer. *What if he's lying? But what would be the point in getting me sick too?* He hadn't felt hot when I touched him earlier. I readjusted my mask to make sure it was in its proper place and walked over to the bed. Gently I pulled up his pants leg and found a large gash that had been roughly stitched back together. The skin around it was pink but otherwise looked healthy.

"I sliced my leg a few weeks ago on a piece of broken wire sticking out in the basement of my building. I stitched it back together myself but didn't do the best job, as you can see. I found the antibiotics in the apartment below mine and figured it would be a good idea to stave off infection, you know?"

As I considered what he was telling me, my eyes must have shown my skepticism because he said, "I promise I'm not sick. It's just the cut. I swear."

I walked a few feet away from him and pulled off the mask. Narrowing my eyes, I watched him for a minute. He stared back at me in silence, letting me contemplate his trustworthiness. An uneasy tension flew back and forth during our mutual inspection. I heard a whine and looked down at Zeke sitting at my feet. He tilted his head, pulled his ears upward, and pawed at my leg. He walked over to the bed and sat down, looking at me, telling me that he trusted the man and didn't think he was going to hurt us. I didn't respond because that would look crazy in front of another human, but Zeke gave me reassurance.

Finally, I looked back at the man. "So here's what happened, I saw some men chasing you down the street. They caught you, beat you up, and stole your backpack. When they were gone, I pulled you inside, and here we are." I paused, hoping for a response, but none came. "I need to know more about you before I can take off the ties."

He nodded.

"First, why don't you tell me your name."

He looked at me for a second then sighed. "Oliver—Ollie—Wakelin. I'm from London, but I arrived here about two weeks before the quarantine hit."

"Why are you here?"

He eyed me again, taking his time to answer, and I wondered if he was coming up with a story. "I help my parents run the Wakelin Group. We own a string of hotels, restaurants, clubs, and spas across the UK. We've been looking to move into the American market. They sent me over here to start up our base operations. We don't have offices yet."

"Why didn't you get a flight out?"

"They weren't offering international flights at the time. The woman from the TSA told me they would at some point, so I decided to wait for that. But it never happened, and I got stuck here."

"Was there anyone sick in your building?"

"Not that I know of. I've been subletting an apartment from an old college friend. It was a brownstone. I had the top two floors, and there's only one other apartment on the bottom two. His mom owned the building and lived in that apartment, but she was already gone when I knocked on her door the day this happened."

"I see." I glanced down at my feet, thinking about his story. I looked back at him. "You being here is putting me in a tough position. You could be anyone. I have no idea what you might do, and like I said, I'm alone. But you are hurt, I can see that. You can stay until you're well enough to leave." I paused, apprehensive about what I was going to say next. "But I'm going to have to lock you in."

He started to protest, pulling himself up from the bed. But his swollen ribs quickly caused him to wince in pain, and he fell back.

I put my hand up. "Look, I put myself in danger pulling you in from the street. I didn't have to do that. I need to protect myself, and this is the only way I'll feel safe with you here. If you don't like it, there's the door." I swept my arm in the direction of the front door.

He glared at me for a few seconds, breathing heavily from the pain. Then Zeke came around to my side and sat down next to me, my only backup. Ollie's face softened slightly when he saw Zeke. He relented and said, "Yeah, I get it."

"Good. To be fair, there's a lock on your side too. You can keep me locked out if you want. I don't have much food left, but I fixed some rice for you. It's on the table. There are some tortillas and acorns too. That will have to take you through tomorrow. I'll check in after that." I reached into my front pocket then tossed his antibiotics onto the bed. "I'm going to cut one hand loose and put the scissors nearby. You should be able to cut yourself free. But I'm warning you, I'm trained in judo," I lied, "so don't get any ideas."

He raised his eyebrows but made no comment.

I walked over to the bed and cut the tie on his right wrist. Once his arm was free, his fingers closed around my wrist before I could move away. I tensed up, alarmed, and felt my pulse rise.

"Hey, thanks for pulling me inside and cleaning me up. You're right, you did put yourself in danger. Not everyone would have done that."

"Sure," I replied calmly. I looked down at my wrist with his fingers still wrapped around it.

"Sorry," he said, letting my arm go.

I leaned down and placed the scissors next to the bowl of rice, within arm's reach. My wrist was tingling in finger-shaped throbs. It was difficult to keep my movements natural and not show my anxiety. But my hand shook when I pulled it back up to my side.

He noticed the shaking and winced. "Sorry, I didn't mean to scare you. I'm not going to hurt you, for whatever that's worth."

I nodded in reply. "Take it slow on the water, I don't have much of that left either. I'll leave you now."

"I'm sure I'll be fine."

I looked around for Zeke and found him under the bed on the other side. Oliver was scratching his ears as much as he could with the tie restraining his wrist.

"Zeke, come on, let's go."

Reluctantly, Zeke followed me out the door. He must have been happy to have some other contact too. I turned the lock and listened outside the door. I heard the faint sounds of him moving off the bed. Feeling satisfied that he had been able to cut himself free, I walked back upstairs. Locking him in made me feel better about the situation. I didn't need any more complications.

Chapter 22
February 25th

I awoke early the next day to overcast clouds, and my hopes sky-rocketed. Maybe it would rain, and I could collect more water. Just in case, I ran to the roof and placed several large pots and bowls in various places. I put a large bucket from Barb's apartment on my fire escape.

I needed to call my mom and tell her about Oliver. I picked up my phone and saw that it still had a little juice left. I contemplated waiting until the next day for our scheduled call, but it was important that she know the man was in my building in case something happened. She wasn't going to like it. After a long, procrastinative cup of coffee, I picked up the phone.

"Hi. Anything new?" I asked, stalling.

"Not much. They released a new death count last night. Two hundred seventy thousand or thereabouts."

I closed my eyes. "Wow, that's just... I don't even know what to say. That's a lot. What about a cure? Have they come up with anything?"

"Not since the last time you asked, which was yesterday."

I chuckled. "Sorry, I'm anxious, I guess."

"I know, *mija*. Ask as much as you want."

"Something's happened. Please don't be mad."

I felt her apprehension through the phone. "Did you give me a reason to be mad?"

"Probably, but I had no choice. Yesterday, two men beat another man outside my apartment. They left him unconscious on my stoop. Now, this is the part you'll be mad at." I paused, reluctant to say the words. "I pulled him inside."

"Karis, are you crazy?"

"I know, Mom. I took a risk."

She let loose a string of rapid Spanish, which she only reverted to when really upset, that I didn't understand.

"Mom, English."

"Karis, that man could hurt you, or he could be sick! What were you thinking?" she translated.

"But I couldn't just leave him out there bleeding, could I? Would you have left him there? He's not sick. He has a wristband." I didn't tell her about the antibiotics. I believed he wasn't sick, but I wasn't sure my mom would.

She sighed and thought about it. "I honestly don't know, Karis."

"I don't think you would have left him out there either. I'm sorry to worry you, but I tied him up and locked him in. Remember that time Dad changed the locks on the front door?"

She groaned. "Ugh, I could have killed him!"

I chuckled at her still-fresh annoyance. "Well, I did that to the apartment he's in. I reversed the lock, so he can't get out to hurt me. I'm going to let him heal from the beating. His ribs are injured, and his face is swollen and cut. When he's better, I'll ask him to leave."

She paused, not expecting my solution. "Not so foolish then, are you? I guess your dad's prank served some purpose other than to amuse him. What if this man says he won't leave?"

"I've thought about that but haven't come up with an answer. I'll just have to wait and see what happens."

"I don't like this one bit, Karis. But I understand where your heart is, and I can't fault you for that."

"I need to trust my instincts right now. They're all I have left. But can you go online and look this guy up? His name is Oliver Wakelin, and he said his family owns a company in the UK called the Wakelin Group."

"Sure. Hold on."

I grabbed my binoculars and walked to my bedroom while she went to her computer. Because of the shape of the building, my bedroom window faced Mr. Tablock's apartment across a narrow middle section. I wondered if I could see into Ollie's room. Focusing the binoculars on that window, I was able to see half of the bed. I could just make out his back—he was lying on his side facing away from me, seemingly still asleep. I looked at my phone. The battery was deep in the red. I would have to be quick about this.

My mom came back on the line. "Okay, I have a picture of Oliver Wakelin. He's got light brown hair and blue eyes." She whistled. "He's handsome! Maybe he's single."

I rolled my eyes. "Mom, really? Come on."

"Hey, I'm a mom, I'm always looking out for you." I could tell she was smiling, and I was glad she wasn't angry with me anymore. "It says he's Executive Director of Operations for the Wakelin Group. He does a lot of charity work for the company. They've started an organization to fight hunger in the UK. He's never been married and seems close with his family. There are lots of pictures of them all together, and they look happy. That's good. Oh wait, here's a more recent article about an engagement. Darn."

"Does he have a scar in his eyebrow?" I'd noticed it when I was swabbing his cuts. I could tell it was old and not something from the fight.

"Hmm. Let me find a closer image." She paused. "Yes, here I see it, a diagonal white line that runs through the left eyebrow. Looks like he is who he says he is."

"Good. Can you find anything else on him? I just need to feel like he's trustworthy."

"Give me a second. I'm still looking."

I noticed movement in his window, so I looked again through the binoculars. He rolled over gingerly and tried to sit up. But immediately, he grabbed his ribs and lay back down. His head was bowed back, and his face was distorted in pain.

"This is interesting," my mom interrupted. "It's an article from the *Daily Star,* which is a tabloid, so who knows how reliable it is, but I'll read it to you. 'Hotel kingpin and resident playboy Oliver Wakelin stuns his family and the world today with a shocking decision to step down as Executive Director of Operations of the Wakelin Group. A source close to Mr. Wakelin confirmed he also called off his yearlong engagement to socialite Caroline Keaton. Their whirlwind romance has been the source of much gossip in recent weeks as their presence has been missed at several important events. The Wakelins and Ms. Keaton could not be reached for comment.' Hmm. What do you think?"

I pulled the binoculars down from my eyes. He clearly lied about what he was doing here. *What does this mean?* "I don't know, Mom. But I'm not gonna ask him."

"Aren't you even a little curious?" she pushed.

"No, I'm not. His personal life is none of my business. As long as he stays where he is and leaves me alone, I'll leave him alone," I said firmly, anxious to end the call.

She huffed. "Fine, but keep me updated. And be careful."

"I will, I promise. I'll start teaching Zeke to attack on command," I joked.

My mom laughed. "I can't even picture that. I'll let you go. Bye, sweetheart."

"Bye, Mom."

When I hung up, I plugged my phone back into the speaker to charge for a few minutes and looked in the window again. He was gone. I thought about him lying there, struggling to get off the bed with his injuries. I was conflicted. I wanted to help him but also needed to have my guard up. Not only could he hurt me, but he'd lied to me. I didn't trust him. Then another thought forced its way through: *what if he could help me make it to the border?* Getting across the country would be much safer if I had another person with me, but only if I trusted him. There were pros and cons to him being here. I made a list:

> **PROS:** Another person to talk to and help keep my mind in check.
> Having a man around is more security.
> Maybe he can help me make it to the border.
> **CONS:** He'll use up more of my meager supplies.
> I'll have to hide my conversations with Zeke.

I went back and underlined the most important pro and con, using up more of my supplies and helping me make it to the border. Those were the only two that really mattered. I assessed the situation and decided the pro far outweighed the con.

There wasn't much I could do about it immediately, so I went on with my day. During my workout, when I ran by his door, I stopped and listened a few times. Other than general apartment noises, I heard nothing else. I sighed, annoyed at myself. *What was I hoping to hear?* I shook my head and continued. Later that day, as I was starting to get uncomfortably restless, I started picking at a piece of loose yarn in the afghan my godmother made me as a farewell gift when I moved to New York. Instead of tying it back in, I began unraveling the blanket, trying to remember the pattern of loops and turns as I went. When the whole thing was a pile of maroon-and-yellow yarn on the ground, I stared at it, shocked that I thought I could learn how to knit that way. Slowly, I pulled the yarn through the various loops I created and knotted them when they didn't seem secure. I took several wrong turns and had to back-track, but four hours later, my blanket was put back together in some deformed Picasso-esque version of what it used to be. I held it up and smiled. It wasn't even close to being as pretty as it had been before. But I made it, and the messiness of it reminded me that I was putting myself back together too.

I'd been antsy since I pulled Oliver into my building, and I hadn't gotten much sleep the night before. I went to bed early after taking a Benadryl to help me sleep. In the middle of the night, Zeke woke me up, barking.

I bolted upright. "What's wrong, Zeke?"

He whined and looked toward the windows, cocking his head. He must have heard something outside. I got up and walked into the dining room. Without the noise from my sound machine, I could faintly hear someone yelling. I walked to the window and pulled it up. There was a ragged-looking man walking down my street. He had on several layers of dirty clothes and pulled a cart filled with his possessions behind him. He was coughing and stumbled a couple of times.

"Someone, help me. Please, I have nothing. My house burned down. Please, let me in. Someone, please." He doubled over and coughed violently.

My heart ached, but I knew I couldn't let him in. I wasn't sure if he was old or young, but the long, overgrown beard and shaggy hair made him look older in the moonlight. I watched for a minute as he walked slowly down the street and made his way toward the park. I walked back to my bedroom and sat on the bed, feeling guilty, but he was sick, and I'd already taken a risk by letting Oliver in. I went back to bed but had a hard time falling back asleep, the man drifting in and out of my consciousness.

The next morning, I looked around for the man while eating a breakfast burrito made of mashed acorns and coconut oil wrapped in a tortilla. I didn't see him anywhere, even with the binoculars. My phone ringing interrupted my search. It shocked me because I realized I hadn't changed it back to airplane mode. I needed to be better about that.

"Mom?"

"Hi. I did something that you may not like, but I had to."

"This sounds familiar," I said.

She laughed. "Last night, I looked up a contact number for the Wakelin Group and left my number for his parents. I said I had information about their son. His mom called me back this morning."

"Oh my god, I hadn't thought of that. What did she say?"

"She was worried about him, understandably. She hasn't talked to him since the electricity went out. She was very happy to hear he's okay. I didn't tell her about the fight. I just told her that my daughter is letting him stay in her building. She told me to tell you thank you."

"Did she tell you anything about him?"

"Yes, and this is even more interesting. His parents don't know why he left or called off the engagement. He just told them that he needed time to work some things out. No, she said, 'figure his life out,' but she didn't know what needed figuring out. He'd seemed perfectly happy up until two weeks before he left. He'd started skipping meetings and spent a lot of time on his computer. Then one day, he resigned and told them he was going to New York for a while and he'd call when he settled in. They asked questions, but he gave vague answers. The last time she talked to him was a few days before the power went out, but he didn't mention any plans to leave his apartment."

The term "figure his life out" left a sour taste in my mouth. I'd certainly heard that before. "Hmm. I don't know what to make of this. But I feel better now that you've talked to someone who actually knows him and can vouch that he's not a lunatic."

"Me too. She was really great and told me not to worry, that her son is a gem."

"Thanks for letting me know. I don't know what I'm going to do, but I'll let you know what I decide."

"By the way, you might be getting a storm in the next couple of days. Saw it on the news. Be careful."

I exhaled a sigh of relief. "Honestly, Mom, the storm is a godsend. I'm running low on water."

"Oh no. Do you have enough?"

"For now, yes. But I haven't bathed in over a week to conserve. Not even a sponge bath. I'll run out soon. I put buckets and pans out in case it rains."

"Good idea. Let me know if you are able to get more from the rain. But make sure you boil it before drinking. I need to know you're okay. You can't live without water."

"I know, Mom. I'll keep you updated."

I hung up the phone, slid it into airplane mode, and thought about what my mom just told me. I grabbed the binoculars and looked into the first-floor apartment. The bed was empty. I thought about yesterday and him struggling to get up. And since he was my only potential source of help, I gave in and decided to help him too. I fetched a bottle of Percocet from the bag of medicines I'd gathered from the apartments, a couple of candles, and more food and water, then ran downstairs. I pressed my ear against his door and waited. The floorboards creaked then something breakable crashed to the floor, followed by him cursing. I set the supplies on the ground in front of the door, unlocked it from my side, and knocked. Footsteps came toward me, so I quickly ran back up the stairs. The door opened when I got to the first landing.

"Hey, wait a minute," he called out. I stopped, feeling as if I'd been caught, and contemplated continuing on upstairs, but instead I turned around. He had his arm across his ribs, cradling his injuries. "You unlocked the door. This must mean you trust that I'm not going to hurt you."

"You could still try, but with those injuries, I think I could take you," I said defiantly.

He gave a short laugh. "Touché." He bent down and picked up the bottle of pills, holding his ribs. He looked at the bottle and then back up at me. "Thanks. This is really nice of you."

"You're welcome. Do you need anything else?"

He rubbed the stubble on his face, thinking about it. "I could bloody well do with a glass of whiskey to chase this down," he said with a smirk, shaking the bottle of pills.

I thought about the whiskey up in my apartment and knew I wasn't ready to share. We weren't there yet. But he laughed at my silence and said, "I'm kidding. You've done enough already, really."

I nodded. "Okay, see you later." I turned around to walk up the next flight. When I turned the corner on the stairs, I looked back down. He was still watching me. My stomach dropped, and my skin tingled as I ran up the last flights. *What is wrong with me?* I vowed to keep my hormones in check and keep it a platonic, mutually beneficial relationship.

I tried to keep my mind on other things the rest of the day without much success. I exercised longer than normal, sewed some patches onto my old favorite pair of jeans, and read a few more newspapers I'd brought up from Mr. Tablock's apartment, which I supposed I should start calling Oliver's apartment. But my thoughts kept turning back to Oliver, conjuring up story after story about what could have prompted his retreat from his life. By dinnertime, I'd come up with stories ranging from infidelity to attempted murder. Fed up with all my ridiculous conjecture, I took a shot of whiskey for courage and walked downstairs with the bottle of Woodbridge in one hand and two short glasses in the other.

I knocked on his door and felt my pulse racing. He answered the door, wearing what I could only assume were a pair of Mr. Tablock's sweatpants. He had a sweater in his hands that he hadn't pulled on yet. For a moment, I was stunned into silence by his flat, toned stomach and bare chest. The bruises on his ribs only added to it, in a strange way.

I snapped out of my trance when he said, "Hi."

I held up the whiskey. "I think I have that whiskey you ordered. Interested?"

His face melted in longing, and he groaned. "Oh, you're an angel. Do you want to come in?"

Zeke had already wandered through his door and was sitting on the couch with his stuffed penguin in his mouth. I thought I'd taught him better manners than that.

Zeke dropped the penguin and barked angrily at me, annoyed at my motherly concerns. I looked at him then quickly back up at Oliver. "Sure." But I hesitated in the doorway, rethinking my plan.

He put his hand over his heart. "I solemnly swear I will keep my hands to myself and will behave like an absolute gentleman. You can even zip tie me again if you want." He held his hands together in front of me, one of them still holding the sweater.

I struggled not to smile but lost the battle and laughed. "Sorry. Yes, I'll come in."

I walked over to the couch and set both glasses down while he threw the sweater on and wrapped a thick scarf around his neck. After I filled our glasses with whiskey, we both sat back and took a sip.

"Oh man, that's good. Where did you find this?" he asked.

"I had it before this happened. I've been saving it."

He looked at me but said nothing.

After a few uncomfortable minutes, I asked, "So what were you doing running down the street like that? Why did you even leave your apartment?"

He thought for a second, seemingly weighing what to tell me. "I was close to running out of food, and then we lost power. I decided it would be safer to leave. The guy whose apartment I'd been subletting had a car. I found the keys on the key rack by the front door." He paused and looked back at me.

A car! I'm sure he could see the thinly veiled excitement on my face.

"But honestly I have no idea what it even looks like. I know it's a Honda from the logo on the keys. I started trying them in any car that was a Honda. I didn't find it. He probably parked it in a garage somewhere rather than leave it out on the street since he was going to be away for months. Or his mom took it. Seems more likely."

My excitement quickly deflated. He was probably right. The chances of finding that car were slim. "Then those two guys saw you?"

"Yeah. I'd made my way through two blocks but had no luck with the keys. I saw them when I was about to turn down this street. I stopped, and I could tell that they saw me too. So I just ran, looking for somewhere to hide before they turned the corner. But everything was too out in the open. I heard them shouting at me, so I just kept running. I could have made it, I think, if I hadn't had my pack on. It slowed me down. I had stuffed it with bottles of water, whatever food I had left, and all the cash I had on hand. Looking back on it now, I know that was a dumb plan. I should have left all my supplies and brought the car back to my apartment to get my things if I found it."

I nodded and refilled his glass.

"Why didn't you get a flight out?" he asked after taking a sip.

"I had one, but they wouldn't let me bring Zeke. I couldn't leave him here alone, so I just stayed," I said with a shrug.

He nodded, seeming to understand my decision. "And how have you not gotten sick?"

I paused. It was a little embarrassing to tell him the truth, and I could gloss over it. But I wanted to be honest with him and myself, and I was starting to feel like I had nothing to be ashamed of. My dating history and the depression that followed were both a part of me, part of why I was a stronger person than I had been before. "I'd gone through some breakups and decided I was done dating. I guess I was a bit depressed by it all, so I've been mostly hanging out with Zeke lately. I have my own office where I work, so it was easy to stay away from people. But even if it did save me in a sense, I feel silly now that I wasted so much time on a bunch of jerks."

He looked away. "I know what you mean."

My brow furrowed at his comment, but I let it pass. We sat in silence, sipping our whiskey, but I was taking very small sips. I needed a clear head. I kept refilling his glass as we talked about mundane things. He got up to look outside, watching the wind blow the trees around and searching for signs of life.

When I heard the slow tap of rain on the window, I rushed to his side to look out. "Yes! It's raining." I paused and looked at him. "We need more water. I put some pots and buckets out, so hopefully, we'll have some more to add to the tubs. I've been charging my phone with a battery-powered dock, so I can still talk to my parents. My mom said we might get a storm. Sometime in the next couple of days. This must be the beginning."

He nodded, and we walked back to the couch. I could tell he was pretty drunk. He wobbled slightly before he sat down. It was my chance. "Oliver, can I ask you something?"

He looked back at me with heavy eyes. "Call me Ollie. Everyone calls me Ollie. Only one person calls me Oliver."

"Who's that?"

"Caroline," he spat, but he seemed to realize what he'd said and wanted to retract it.

I thought about the article my mom read to me about his engagement but decided not to push, and instead I came clean. "Ollie, I know you didn't come here to start up operations for your family's company. I had my mom look you up online. There was an article about you leaving the company recently."

He looked trapped, his eyes widening slightly. Then he exhaled and put his glass on the table. He sat silently, looking at his hands, probably trying to explain his deception. I gave him the space to do that, taking a sip and pretending to look at a painting on the wall.

Finally, he slumped back onto the couch, looking defeated. "It's a long story, not something I could've summed up in a few sentences when we talked about this before. What I told you was the truth as of two months before I came here. I was supposed to come to the US and start up the new offices. That was the plan all along. But then..." He paused, spreading his hands, looking for a way to explain.

"You don't have to talk about it if you don't want to. I just wanted you to know that I know."

He looked at me then, really looked at me. I held his stare.

"No, I should talk about it. I haven't told anyone, not my parents or friends. I didn't think they'd understand, it felt too... personal, something I needed to handle on my own. I only told one person, and that didn't go so well." He looked over at me, assessing my reaction.

I smiled slightly and raised my right eyebrow. "Consider me your confidante. I don't know any of those people."

He smiled thinly. "I had a girlfriend in college. Dana. She was from Pennsylvania but was doing a study-abroad program. She was so different from the women I'd dated before. Independent, bold, outspoken. We were completely in love, or at least it felt that way to me. I was just twenty-two years old. Dana got pregnant, and we both freaked out. Neither of us was ready to have a baby, I thought. When she told me, I didn't have the best reaction. I started talking about abortion and adoption. Our lives were just beginning, and a baby wasn't part of the plan right then. She was very quiet but nodded along with all my suggestions. I asked her if she wanted to keep it, but she just shook her head. We decided she'd have an abortion. I took her to the clinic, but she insisted on going in alone. I sat in the car for three hours. When she came out, she was crying and holding her stomach like she was in pain. She didn't want to talk about it, so I took her home, made her dinner, and stayed with her all night. We were graduating the next week, and I was worried about her. But after that first night, she seemed fine, as though she had pushed it all away."

"She was probably traumatized and didn't want to think about it."

"That's what I thought, too, so I let it be. We had been planning on going back to London. I was going to start working for my parents, and she was going to look for jobs. But the day after graduation, she said she couldn't go to London with me. I didn't understand, and she didn't really explain it properly. She said she loved me but was ready for something and somewhere else. She said that place and I reminded her constantly of what she'd done, and she needed to try to move past it. I was devastated. I argued with her, trying to convince her to stay or to let me go with her. But she refused. She moved back to Pennsylvania the next week. We kept in touch for a while, but I felt her pulling away. Eventually, we lost contact."

I understood. "It happens. Hard to stay in contact when you live that far away and have another life."

"Yeah, well. Five months ago, I was on Facebook, and you know how it gives suggestions for people you might know?"

"Yeah, of course," I said, anticipating what was coming.

"One of those suggestions was her, but with her married name. I clicked on her profile, and it showed she was married and had four kids. When I checked out her photos, there were several with younger children, and one with her son, who was much older. It was at his high school graduation. He looked to be about seventeen. Exactly how old our child would be."

"Oh my god! What did you do?" He had my rapt attention.

He shook his head. "I knew he was mine. His name was Caleb, Dana's father's name. But he had blue eyes, like mine. Dana had brown eyes, and from the photos, so did her husband. Caleb looked nothing like the other kids she had. I was shocked and furious, dumbfounded how anyone could do something like that. I sent her a friend request with a message, asking her about Caleb. Five days later, I received a reply that just said, 'I'm sorry. Please leave us alone.' No explanation. I tried to message her again, but she had blocked me. I couldn't view her Facebook page anymore either, or she took it down."

"Wow. I'm speechless. That must've been awful."

"I felt like I'd been punched in the gut. I immediately went to Caroline, my fiancée, and told her. You know what she said? 'He's all grown now, so what's the point?'"

"You're kidding me," I said incredulously.

He shook his head. "I couldn't believe it at first, but then I realized that's who she is. She didn't even know if she wanted kids, and she certainly didn't want any part of some other woman's child. She seemed relieved that Dana didn't want me in his life. Caroline can be quite cold and selfish, something I'd always brushed aside in the past. But after this, I was seeing her clearly for the first time. She was from a good family and sat on the boards for several charities. But it was all for show. She didn't care about any of those causes, not really. She only cared how it made her look to other people. She was with me for the same reasons. I can see that now. I called off the engagement. She didn't even seem to care. She just shrugged and said, 'Don't take too long coming back to me. I'll find someone else quickly.' I don't think she ever loved me, and I'm pretty sure I never really loved her either. My parents are close with hers, and they pushed us together for years. I think everyone breathed a sigh of relief when we finally got together. It was easy to go along with what everyone else wanted. But when I found out about Caleb, I started thinking about what I really wanted, and I realized I had no idea what that was. But I knew I wanted to find Caleb." He looked at me then, his eyes soft and worried.

"Of course you'd want to find him! But why didn't you tell your parents?"

"I don't know," he said, shaking his head. "My parents are amazing, but I'd just found out about him. I guess I wanted the chance to figure everything out first. I didn't know how he'd react. What if he wanted nothing to do with me? I couldn't put my parents through that."

"Did you contact him?"

"I tried, but I think Dana blocked me on his account too. His account was set to private, so all I could see was his profile photo and hometown. I researched her and Caleb online. There wasn't much—I couldn't find a phone number or address, but I knew from their Facebook pages that they lived in Brooklyn. I told my parents that I needed to find myself, so to speak, and resigned. Then I booked the next flight to New York. I called my friend to see if I could crash at his place, but he said he was gone for the next four months on sabbatical, and I could take his place while I was here. I didn't have Dana's address yet, just Brooklyn. For a week, I tried to find an address, but the closest I came was an old one in Cobble Hill. I went there, but the woman didn't know the previous tenants and didn't have an address for them. I hired a private investigator, and the day before the quarantine, he sent me their last known address in Park Slope. I went there immediately, but no one answered. I hung around for a few hours, got some coffee, came back, and tried again. But there was still no answer. So I left, thinking I'd come back the next day. But of course, that never happened."

I was literally sitting on the edge of my seat, listening. When he didn't continue, I said, "So you never got to see him?"

He shook his head and then leaned forward and put his head in his hands. He sat like that for a minute before pulling back up. He had tears in his eyes. "No, I never got to meet him. I never found out why Dana did this. When the Death List came out, I scoured it for two days before finding both their names on it."

"Oh my god, I'm so sorry," I said, my eyes wide and my hand on my chest.

He nodded, looked down, and continued to cry. I didn't know what to do or say. I reached out to pat him on the back but thought better of it and pulled it back. Instead, I just gave him the space to grieve.

Eventually, he let out a long breath and wiped his eyes. "Anyway, that's my story. That's why I'm here. To let my life completely fall apart." He gave a short laugh.

I nodded, feeling at odds with myself all of a sudden. I'd hoped to keep him at arm's length, to keep it all business, and to convince him to go with me to the border. But I couldn't do that because I felt genuinely sorry for the guy. "I understand. I do. I would have done the same thing."

He smiled with half of his mouth. "Thanks."

He yawned, and I could tell the story had drained him. I rose from the couch. "I'll let you get some sleep. It's getting late."

He nodded, looking down at his hands.

"Thanks for telling me. I'm sure it wasn't easy."

He looked up at me and stared. Then he lay back on the sofa. "I needed to talk about it, to get it out. It's been sitting in my gut like lead."

I nodded. "Well, get some rest."

"You too," he replied with a sad smile.

I smiled back—I couldn't help myself. The guy looked wrecked. I turned and walked out the door with Zeke. After closing the door, I leaned against it, trying to absorb Ollie's story. Then I felt Zeke paw my leg. I looked down, and he barked then turned around and walked up the stairs. He was anxious for his evening Happy Hips chew, which I'd been rationing out in small pieces, much to Zeke's chagrin. I followed him, feeling drained too. I had a hard time falling asleep. Before I finally drifted off, I realized the guy was getting under my skin. My mind circled around his story, his presence. I felt drawn to his pain, and I wondered if I should put some distance between us.

Chapter 23
February 27th

In the morning, I lay in bed, trying to make sense of my emotions surrounding Ollie and that incredible story. After sleeping on it, I realized it made me trust him more—it was a pretty personal story. But at the same time, he clearly didn't know what he wanted in life, which was a trigger for me. We could be friends. I could do that. I made a fire then ran Zeke up to the roof. While he peed, I emptied all the pans with a few inches of water into the largest pot. I boiled it, filled more bottles, then placed the pot back on the roof. It'd stopped raining, but hopefully the oncoming storm would give us more. After I fed Zeke, I made some corn cakes and fried them in a tablespoon of coconut oil. I grabbed my French press full of coffee and went downstairs with Zeke. I knocked, feeling anxious.

Ollie answered the door, seeming to be in better spirits than the night before. "Hi."

"Hi. I made some food and coffee. Want some?"

"Oh god, yes, thank you. I found some teabags in a drawer, but it doesn't have nearly enough kick."

He opened the door wider to let me in. We sat at the dining table, eating our food silently. He grunted about how good the cakes tasted a few times, and I felt pleased that I'd shared.

"I'd give anything for a lavender latte."

I made a face. "Lavender latte? That sounds weird."

He laughed. "I thought so, too, but the guy at the counter talked me into it. They're amazing. There's this place not far from here that makes the best one. Bean something."

"Are you talking about The Burly Bean?"

He snapped his fingers. "Yeah. You know it?"

"I do. Although after my last visit, I'd be embarrassed to go back. I kind of yelled at the girl behind the counter. Not my finest moment. In my defense, I hadn't had my coffee yet, and some guy almost ran me over because he wasn't looking where he was going." I paused. "Wait." I narrowed my eyes, and at the same time, Ollie narrowed his. We pointed at each other.

"That was you, wasn't it?" he asked.

"Oh my god, I can't believe this," I said, and we both chuckled. "It is a small community, and there aren't too many places to get a lavender latte in Long Island City. But still, that's crazy. Sorry, I was kind of a jerk."

"No, I should be the one apologizing. I was so consumed by an email I'd gotten from that private investigator that I wasn't paying attention. And I hate it when people walk while looking at their phone."

While we split the last corn cake, I told him about the man in the street from the other night.

He frowned when I told him I went back to bed. "You didn't do anything?"

"What was I supposed to do? He's sick. We can't let him in here."

He opened his mouth but immediately closed it and went back to eating.

I felt my face tense. "What?"

"Nothing, I just... you've helped me so much. I don't want to sound ungrateful."

"You can say it. What is it?"

He hesitated, weighing his words. "I know we can't let him in here, but you could have thrown him some food or a blanket or something."

I stopped drinking my coffee and looked at him sharply. "Ollie, I was half asleep. I'm supposed to come up with ideas at three in the morning? Besides, we need to conserve our resources. There's not much food left. That man is going to die, and we're gonna need the little food we have."

He looked pointedly at me. "We can get by. We can go gather more acorns or something. He's still a human being who's starving, whether he's sick or not. You could have given him something." He got up and went to the kitchen to clean his dishes, leaving me to watch his retreating back with my mouth hanging open.

I felt judged, and it irritated me. I wasn't a bad person—I'd dragged *him* in, after all. I followed him to the kitchen, and we wiped down our dishes with wet paper towels in silence. The whole time, I was rolling Ollie's words around in my head. I was getting angrier with each fork and cup I wiped. But by the time we were done and I was ready to go back upstairs, I asked myself who I was angry at. I realized I was mad at myself because on some level, I'd been thinking the same thing. The truth was, Ollie was right.

Before I opened the door, I turned to him. "You're right, I should have given him something. I wasn't thinking." I could have given him a few tortillas or even a pillow to sleep on.

He turned around and said, "Maybe we can still find him."

"I looked for him this morning but didn't see him. I'll keep looking. Why don't we gather a few things and have them ready in case we see him again?"

He gave me a triumphant smile.

And for some reason, it annoyed me. "I already said you were right. No need to gloat!"

He pursed his lips, stifling a laugh. "I'm not gloating, I promise."

We found a trash bag under the kitchen sink, and I took it upstairs. I added a couple of tortillas, a baggie of acorns, and a pillow. I wrapped the whole thing up in a thick wool blanket from Kirk's apartment then tied it at the top. I went on about my day, working out, reading, and making another batch of tortillas. The flour was running low—I only had enough for another batch or two. I could maybe make an acorn mash, but we would need to go out and get more.

By early evening, I was getting antsy, so I splurged and turned on my iPod. I lay on the carpet in the living room, put my earbuds in, and listened to a Linda Ronstadt album my mom and I loved when I was little. *Blue Bayou* always relaxed me. I was only halfway through the song when Zeke's worried face came into view above me. I pulled the buds out and immediately heard knocking on my front door. I ran over and found Ollie on the other side, breathlessly holding his ribs.

"That man from last night. I think he's outside."

I ran to grab the large blanket-covered bag and met Ollie in the hall. We ran to Barb's apartment and looked out the window.

"Where did you see him?" I asked.

"I didn't. I heard him. But he sounded pretty close."

We watched for several minutes, and I was about to tell him we would try again another time when I heard the man's raspy voice. "It's cold! I don't have anything. Please, can you give me some food?" I heard the cart's wobbly wheels to our left. We pulled up the screen and leaned out. There he was, walking toward us.

When he was at the next building, Ollie waved his arm. "Over here!"

The man looked up and hurried to our window, coughing a few times along the way. "Oh, bless you. I need to come in from the cold. Could I please come in?"

"I'm sorry, but we can't let you in—you could get us sick. But we have some supplies for you," Ollie replied. We both picked up the bag and squeezed it through the window. "Step back, and we'll drop it on the ground."

The man moved back a few feet, and we let the bag go. It landed with a thud.

The man looked up at us. "I'm Henry. Are you sure I can't come in? I could stay in an apartment no one's using."

Ollie and I shared a long look, and then I had an idea. "Henry, the front door is busted on the building right next to this one on Twenty-First Street. I think there are still some people in there, but most have left. I know that apartment 3B is unlocked. Why don't you go in there?"

Henry's eyes lit up as he smiled. "That should work. Thanks for the tip! And thank you for this stuff. If I need more, can I come back?"

Ollie looked at me as if it was my call to make. I looked at Henry and his sad, beat-down face then nodded. "Yes, come back when you need more. The cupboards have already been cleaned out in that apartment. I'm Karis, and this is Ollie."

Henry smiled at me. "Thank you. You are the first people to help since I made it over the bridge from Greenpoint. My house burned down in a fire, and I barely made it out with a few things. Do you have any cough medicine? My throat is killing me."

"Let me go look," I said.

Ollie and I went to Barb's bathroom and found some long-expired capsules of Nyquil that I'd been reluctant to give the girls. Ollie grabbed a plastic shopping bag, the pills, and a large bottle we filled with water. There was a small throw blanket on the couch, and we put that in the bag too. It was cold, and two blankets were better than one. Ollie leaned out and dropped the bag to the ground. The man peeked inside and looked relieved.

"God bless you two," he said, looking up at us with watery eyes.

We waved goodbye and told him to knock on Ollie's window when he ran out of supplies. After closing the window, I looked at Ollie. "You were right. I'm glad we did this."

He smiled. "Me too."

We walked back to the hall and said goodnight. I almost asked if he wanted to hang out, but I didn't think I was ready for that yet, no matter how much I'd like company. I wanted to be friends, but I admitted to myself that I found him attractive. It was best if we limited our time together. Instead, I went upstairs and wrote in my journal about everything that had happened that day, trying to make sense of it all. I was way out of my comfort zone, but it didn't feel so bad. I thought it might be pushing me further in the right direction. I went to bed, hoping I was right.

The next morning, I woke up late and took Zeke upstairs after lighting a fire in the fireplace. The sky was dark for morning, and it was starting to sprinkle. The minute the raindrops hit Zeke's fur, he squinted up at me.

"Come on, Zeke, you gotta go."

I dragged him around the roof, telling him we would stay out until he went. He finally relented and raised his leg on the side of the wall bordering the door. The clouds were an ominous gray and moving slowly. Rain sprinkled us as we hurried back through the door. On the other side, the rain tapped on the skylight in the stairwell. I rushed back to my apartment and made coffee with yesterday's grounds. I ran down to Ollie's door and knocked.

"Hey, it's raining. We should put more pans and bowls on the roof."

"Good idea. Let me put on my shoes."

We scoured the apartments for more pots, bowls and buckets, spraying them all down with Lysol. We ran them up to the roof, and by the time we were done, the roof was covered in containers. We walked downstairs and heard my phone ringing. I cursed, realizing that, again, I'd forgotten to put it on airplane mode. We rushed in, and I picked it up mid-ring.

"Hi, Mom," I said, breathless.

"Is it raining there?"

"Yeah, it's light though. Not too bad yet."

"Honey, they've just upgraded it to a superstorm. It merged with a tropical storm from the south. It's making its way up north along the east coast. It could bring up to fifteen or twenty inches of rain and wind gusts up to eighty miles an hour."

"Great, this is just what we need." I dropped onto the couch and rubbed my forehead. "I guess we need to tape up the windows. We were fine during Hurricane Sandy—we're in the C zone, above the flooding. We'll be okay, Mom."

She sighed. "Call me if it picks up. I'm worried about you."

"I will. Bye."

I filled Ollie in. He went back downstairs with a roll of masking tape we found in Kirk's apartment. I had a hard time locking all the windows since their latches didn't match up due to the building shifting. But I managed to force all of them in before using the tape to X out the windows in case the glass broke. By the time I was done, it was nearly one o'clock. I went upstairs and poured all the water from the containers into Kirk's tub and sinks. I replaced the containers and went back to my apartment to watch the storm.

Over the next few hours, the skies darkened even more, and the wind picked up significantly. Rain was coming down in sheets. I emptied the pans and buckets a few more times, filling three apartments' tubs and sinks. I boiled a large pot of water then filled more pitchers. Zeke and I watched through the window until I saw a large puddle of water in the street near the dog park. I grabbed my binoculars and looked again. The storm drain was covered in garbage and debris and apparently clogged. Water had started filling the street around it. I scouted around and found two more storm drains. Those two weren't as covered but would be soon. So much for not being in the flood zone. Without maintenance, the drains were no longer working, and the building could potentially flood. I ran downstairs and went to the basement. The floor was already covered in a light layer of water, and we still had hours of rain to come.

I knocked on Ollie's door then waited a minute before knocking again. I pressed my ear to the door but didn't hear any movement. I opened the door and called his name. No reply came, so I wandered in. The windows had been X'd out, but I didn't see Ollie. I found him in the bedroom, asleep on the bed. I nudged him and cleared my throat. He finally stirred, confusedly rubbing his eyes.

"Sorry to wake you, but I think you need to move out of this apartment."

He slowly pushed himself upright and shook his head. "I took one of those pain pills. Sorry I'm a little out of it. What did you say?"

"I think I was wrong about the flooding. The storm drains haven't been cleaned and are clogging up. It's already starting to flood, and the basement is taking in water. I don't think it's safe for you here on the first floor."

He stared back at me, obviously trying to make sense of what I was saying.

"Let's just gather up your clothes, and you can stay in Kirk's apartment, across from mine on the top floor."

"Okay," he said with glazed eyes.

"When did you take that pill?"

"Maybe an hour ago? My ribs were screaming after taping the windows."

He got up and wobbled but began stuffing some clothes into a bag. Once he had everything, we walked back upstairs with him pulling himself up to each level by grabbing the railing. I led him into Kirk's apartment. Kirk had spent an entire year fixing his place up, and it was beautiful. The floors had been redone, there was all-new cabinetry, and his bed was huge and super comfy. *He should be okay here.* I walked him to the bedroom and told him to lie down. He went willingly and collapsed onto the bed. I watched him for a minute until he started snoring softly.

I went back to my apartment and curled up on the couch next to the fire, watching the storm with Zeke. After another round of emptying the containers, all the tubs and sinks except mine were filled. I washed a load of clothes and hung them out to dry in my dining room. The thunder started an hour after that, causing fear to churn in my stomach. The streets were covered in a couple inches of water flowing like a shallow stream. I looked for the body of the woman who'd committed suicide and found her still there, her T-shirt moving slightly in the water. I'd been avoiding that window, and looking at her brought tears to my eyes. A knock on my door made me jump. Ollie was on the other side, looking confused and holding a candle.

He smiled crookedly. "I woke up in another apartment. What happened?"

I opened the door wider, welcoming him in. Even though I was trying to keep my distance, the storm scared me, and I badly needed a distraction. As we walked to the living room, I saw one of my Post-It notes in the hallway. As slyly as possible, I plucked it from the wall and crumpled it. I glanced over my shoulder, but Ollie didn't seem to have noticed—his attention was focused on the photographs on the walls. But maybe he was just being nice so I wasn't embarrassed. I grabbed a few more notes along the way, wondering how many others I needed to locate and destroy. We sat down on the couch, and I filled him in on the past few hours. He looked out the window, but the rain was so heavy that we couldn't see much more than a solid sheet of water. Ollie opened the window and pulled up the screen. The rain and thunder in the distance were so loud we had to yell to hear over them.

"It's filling up quickly. Look over there," he said, pointing to a gully across the street. The building across the street had water up to the second step of the stoop. "Was Hurricane Sandy like this?"

I shook my head. "No, Sandy was worse. I don't think it rained this much, but the wind was stronger. But the drains were cleared, and there were teams monitoring everything. Now, the drains are clogged from months of neglect, and there are all those bags of recycling on the streets. We're going to flood."

He closed and locked the latch then looked at me, alarmed. "Thanks for coming to get me. It's twice now that you've saved my arse."

"It's fine. We'll be okay. Water won't make it all the way up here, and we have enough water now to keep us going for longer than I thought. I filled all the tubs and sinks in the building. We should be good for a while."

He nodded absentmindedly.

"I'm worried about Henry. I'm just hoping he managed to get into that apartment I told him about and that someone else didn't find it first. There were a few apartments on the first floor that had broken doors, but that floor might flood. I looked outside but haven't seen him."

"Christ," he said, rubbing his forehead in concern.

"Do you want to call your parents? We have to conserve battery power, but a quick call should be okay."

He whipped his head toward me. "That would be lovely. Thanks. I haven't spoken to them since the power went off. I'm sure they're worried. I promise I'll keep it short."

I handed him my phone, thinking I should have told him my mom called his in case she mentioned it. But he'd already dialed and had the phone to his ear. I gave him some privacy and went to the kitchen with Zeke. I leaned against the counter. "What do you think, Zeke?"

He looked at me, whined, then turned his head toward Ollie and back at me. His ears went up, asking if we could keep Ollie.

I laughed. "I don't know if he wants to be kept. But I think you're right. He seems like an okay guy."

A second later, Ollie popped his head in. "Who were you talking to?"

"Oh, no one, just myself."

He looked at me funny. "My mom would like to talk to you, if that's okay."

"Sure."

He handed me the phone.

"Hello?"

"Hello, darling, thank god for you. Bless your heart for saving my Ollie. You have no idea how grateful we are. We've been so worried about him and didn't know if he was dead or alive." She sounded as if she had a stuffed nose, and I figured she'd been crying.

"I'm happy I could help. He can stay here until he figures out his next step."

"Yes, he's told me, and thank you for that too." She paused. "Do you mind if I ask you a few questions?"

"Um, sure, go ahead." I looked up to find Ollie watching me.

"How old are you, and where are you from?"

"I'm thirty-eight. I grew up in Northern California." I looked over at Ollie again, and he had a slightly surprised look on his face.

I wondered if it was because of my age since I looked quite a bit younger, or if he was surprised his mom had the audacity to ask me.

"Are you single?"

My cheeks warmed. I ventured a look back at Ollie, who seemed slightly embarrassed. "Yes, I am," I said reluctantly.

"Oh perfect, so is my Ollie. Maybe you two will hit it off," she said with a chuckle.

Are all mothers of single children this relentless?

"I'm sorry. I'm a domineering mother who can't stand to see her children lonely. Forget I said that. You sound trustworthy and lovely. I won't keep you any longer. Tell Ollie that I love him, and hopefully, we can chat again tomorrow."

"I will."

"Thanks again, dear. Talk to you soon."

"Okay, bye." I ended the call and looked at Ollie.

"Sorry about that. She's really worried about me," he said.

"I understand. My mom is, too, which is why you need to talk to her now," I said with an ironic smile.

"After that, I owe it to you."

I dialed my mom's number and told her that she could talk to Ollie. I handed him the phone.

He looked at me warily but said, "Hello?"

I hoped my mom wasn't bombarding him with questions about whether he was single, but all I could hear was "yes" and "no." Finally, he handed the phone back to me.

"Hi."

"I love him! He sounds so fancy and good looking."

"Yeah." I didn't say more because he was standing right there, but I wanted to know what good looking sounded like to her. I told her about the flooding and moving Ollie up to the sixth floor. She was worried but also felt better that he was across the hall in case something went wrong. I hung up and turned to him. "Well, it looks like both of our parents approve."

He grinned. "Yeah, I guess so." After a pause, he asked, "So how have you been spending your days?"

"Reading, working out, that kind of thing. But it's not easy, and I feel cabin fever settling in most days."

"I can imagine. It's been the same for me. Would you mind company?"

I paused, mentally testing the strength of my inner walls. Finding them secure, I said, "I would love company."

"By the way, what's with all the marks on the wall?" He pointed to my tick wall. "What are you counting?"

"Oh. Just keeping track of time passing, ya know?"

He nodded.

"I saw it while watching *The Shawshank Redemption* and thought it would help to keep time straight in my head. We are kind of like prisoners here," I said with a wry smile.

He gave a short laugh. "You're right about that. I found something in that apartment when I was looking for a lighter to light the candles. Be right back."

I watched him retreat, wondering what it could be. I'd scoured all the drawers and cupboards, but I guess I could have missed something. He came back and opened his palm, a baggie of popcorn kernels dropping from his fingertips.

"Oh my god! Popcorn! That's incredible."

"The baggie had fallen down behind the drawer. It's not much, but it should be enough for a bowl, don't you think?"

I excitedly made us popcorn, and the three of us snuggled up on the couch near the fire, noting the thunder rumbling in the distance. Zeke was happily tucked in between the two of us, Ollie and I feeding him pieces of popcorn here and there. Then I spotted my "shake your money maker" Post-It on the wall behind Ollie. I felt my face flush in embarrassment even though he hadn't noticed it—he would have said something. My fingers itched to snatch it off the wall. I didn't even hear the last thing he said because I was too busy concocting a plan to extract that note before he saw it. I absentmindedly nodded in response to whatever he'd said.

I noticed him wince when he tried to lean forward.

"Let me get you a pain pill."

He looked as if he might protest but then fell back on the couch with his eyes closed. I took that second to reach behind him and pull the note from the wall and quickly crumple it in my pocket. I exhaled and smiled at the absurdity of that note. I brought him the pills, and he took half of a Percocet, not wanting to be so out of it again. We both turned to look out the window to check the flooding progress.

"It's getting quite high now, isn't it?" he asked, looking over at me. In just a few hours, the water had climbed up another step of the stoop across the street.

"Yeah, this is about how high it was down by the water after Hurricane Sandy. And we're only halfway through this one." I became uncomfortably aware of how close our faces were and sat back down on the couch.

He looked at me for a second before following my lead. "We've never had anything like this in London. The Thames barrier burst once and flooded, but the water didn't come up much past the pavement. Should we go downstairs and see if it's made it inside?"

"That's a good idea. There was about an inch in the basement earlier. I'm sure it's higher now."

We walked downstairs with Zeke and candles to light the way and both felt relieved when we reached the first floor to find no sign of water. But when I opened the basement door, we immediately saw the water, which had risen to cover about a third of the steps. I looked over at Ollie, alarmed.

His eyes were wide, and his mouth gaped open. "Oh my god, I can't believe it's that high already. Should we go outside and try to clear a few storm drains?"

I opened the locked door and went to look out the window in the outer door. "No, it's not safe out there. It's halfway up my stoop."

"But shouldn't we at least try? We can't just do nothing. What if the whole building floods?" He was really worked up and seemed annoyed by my unruffled attitude.

I turned back to him. "Ollie, even if we did manage to unclog a couple, they'd just get clogged again with the flow of debris from the water. It would only help for a short time. The water's too high for us to go out there. It won't make it up to the fourth floor. We should go back upstairs. There's nothing we can do now." He seemed reluctant to go, but I brushed past him and walked up the stairs. After a few steps, I looked back.

He was still there, looking bewildered.

"You coming?" I asked, giving him what I hoped was a confident look.

He started at my question then shook his head. "Yeah." A loud bang outside drew our attention back toward the front doors. It sounded pretty close. More urgently, Ollie repeated, "Yeah" and hurried up the stairs behind me.

I heated up a few tortillas and brought out some more acorns. We sat on the couch and ate our lunch in silence for a few minutes.

He still appeared to be in shock over the flooding, so in an effort to take his mind off of it, I started talking. "I went to London once for work a few years back. We were trying to win over this big British client, so the whole team went to bat. I really liked it. I stayed at a small hotel on a side street, but it was so elegant. There were marble statues in the hallway and long, thick damask curtains in my room. I had afternoon tea at a restaurant that the concierge recommended around the corner, and I felt like I'd been dropped into the royal court. It was probably the best meal I had while I was there."

"Do you remember the name of the restaurant? I might know it."

I cocked my head and tried to conjure up the front of the place. "Roseville or Rosegarden? Something like that."

"Rosewyld?"

"Yes! That's it. It was in Knightsbridge near a clock shop."

Ollie started laughing. "That's one of my family's restaurants! My mom used to take us there when we were young for etiquette lessons."

"You're kidding me! The scones were incredible, and they were served with clotted cream and jam. I was in heaven!" My mouth started watering.

"Their pastries are amazing. My siblings and I used to sneak biscuits when my mom wasn't looking."

"What was it like growing up in London?"

He smiled. "I had a pretty idyllic childhood. Living in London, there's always something interesting to do. Much like here, I suppose. But my fondest memories are from our country house in Surrey. We'd go on the weekends when the weather was nice. My father and I would fish and hunt ducks. We always had dogs, and I got really involved with the animal shelters. I refused to allow my parents to buy the purebreds they'd always gotten before. They were exasperated with my insistence, but from that point on, they always got their dogs from the rescues I worked with. Is Zeke a rescue?"

"No, he's not. I wish he was though." Zeke lifted his head and glared at me. "I grew up with dogs too. We always had one or two running around. We had this one German shorthaired pointer named Maggie. One Halloween, she ate an entire pumpkin, including the seeds and stem, then promptly threw it up in the grass.

My mom was so angry. Then next spring, out pops a pumpkin plant that produced four pumpkins in the exact spot Maggie threw up. I remember my dad saying, 'Well I guess Maggie felt bad about eating that pumpkin. She's paying it forward!'" We laughed at the story and my poor mom's aggravation.

He seemed grateful for a distraction from the storm. After a pause, he asked, "So how did you get Zeke?"

"I was living with a boyfriend, but he didn't want a dog. He's more of a cat person. I begged and begged for over a year until finally I gave up. Then he got me Zeke for my birthday that year. I couldn't believe it. Zeke is amazing. I couldn't ask for a better dog," I said, glancing at my dog, trying to make up for the rescue comment. He looked at me with that goofy look on his face that told me he loved me too. "I always wished that I'd rescued a dog though. One day, I'll have a house with a big back yard and a bunch of dogs."

Ollie grinned. "Yeah, I feel the same way. It's been hard the past couple of years since I've been starting up different divisions of our company. I travel so much that it hasn't been possible. But moving into the American market was supposed to be the last of it. I'd been planning on buying a house and getting a dog or two. But as you can see, that plan has been thoroughly derailed," he said with an eyebrow arch. "I kind of want a pig too. There's a farm near Surrey where they have these pig races in the spring. My mom took us every year, and I always told her I was going to own a pig."

I laughed. "So now that you've quit your job, what are you going to do when this is all over? Do you think you'll go back to your parents' company?"

He scratched his chin and looked off into the distance. "You know, I'm not sure. I was good at what I did, and I liked working with my father. But I've realized lately that office jobs just aren't for me. My younger brother already took over my position."

"Oh, so there's no job to actually go back to?"

"Before I found out about Caleb, I'd been putting a proposal together. We work with several charities, but I wanted to start one of our own and hopefully head that up. I had an idea for an animal sanctuary that would also offer various after-school programs for underprivileged kids. Ideally, at some point, we'd have multiple locations."

"That sounds amazing. Zeke and I used to visit patients in the hospital. It was so rewarding to bring them even a small amount of happiness."

"That's exactly what I'm hoping to do. Fundraising and public outreach can be done remotely, so I wouldn't have to be in the office. I'll start it on my own if my father doesn't go for it. But I'm pretty sure I can convince him. He was really disappointed when I resigned. I think he'd do just about anything to keep me with the company."

"You'd go back to London?"

"I'm not sure about that. Honestly, I haven't been happy there in a long time. I'd convinced Caroline to spend weekends at our country estate. That's all she'd agree to. But now? I don't know. London doesn't fit me anymore, and I'm not sure it ever did. I guess I'll have to figure that out, but I'd love to live somewhere new," he replied with a smile. "I heard you tell my mom you're from California. What brought you to New York?" he asked.

"To be frank, I'm not quite sure," I said with a smirk and raised eyebrows. "My entire family are small-town sort of people. They still live in the Bay Area within an hour of one another. I'm kind of the black sheep in that way. I knew I wanted to try out a big city, so I saved a bunch of money and moved. I didn't have a job lined up. I didn't know anyone here. My family was against the move. They didn't understand my desire to move to a place as daunting as New York. When I think back, I can't believe I had the courage to do something like that. I really had to pound the pavement and take any job I could find for a while. But I'm glad I did it. For the most part, I've loved it here. Before all this happened, that is."

"That's impressive. To go against your family's wishes and move somewhere you know very little about... that takes guts." He smiled. "You're really self-reliant, aren't you?"

"I guess I've had to be. You can't make it in New York City without being able to take care of yourself, even if that means eating Top Ramen and working two jobs to scrape by. But I'm not sure I would have accepted help, anyway. I like doing things myself, and I wanted to see if I could make it on my own."

"In that way, you remind me of my mom. Don't get me wrong, we had maids and chefs, but my mom didn't rely on them like all my friends' parents did. We had chores every day. Granted, it was something simple like putting away our clothes or cleaning our rooms, but it still gave us a sense of personal responsibility. She'd send the chef home and make dinner every night. And we never had nannies. She did all the work herself. She grew up rather poor and had to fight for everything until she met my father. She's a force, to say the least."

"She sounds like someone I'd get along well with," I said, smiling.

"Oh, you'd love her. I guess she's why I've had such a hard time connecting with the women in my circle back home. Most of them expect to be waited on hand and foot because they always have been. I'm not knocking them for it, but for me, there's just no gumption there. You've got gumption written all over you. I like that."

My face warmed at the compliment, and I shifted a few inches back on the couch.

"What about now—if you make it out of here, I mean? If New York is livable again, will you come back?"

I took a second to think about it, looking out the window at the buildings. "I don't know. I want to say yes, but there's also a big part of me that's ready to move on. I feel like I've done what I wanted to do here. Who knows? Maybe I'll move somewhere completely different, like you."

He raised an eyebrow and smiled, stifling a yawn. I went to the bathroom, using some of the rainwater to flush the toilet. When I came back, he'd fallen asleep, his arms crossed on his chest and his head lolling to the side. I took a moment to really look at him. He was handsome even with the bruises and swelling. I inspected his strong jawline, his large but nicely shaped nose, and wide-set eyes framed by distinctive thick brows. Without thinking, I reached out and ran my finger along the scar in his eyebrow, silently wondering how he got it. Slowly, he opened his eyes, and I pulled my hand back quickly as though I'd been burned. I couldn't believe I'd done that. Clearly, my emotional wall was on a lunch break.

He didn't show any signs of noticing. He yawned. "The pill must have made me drowsy. Sorry." He pulled up his shirt and inspected his ribs. The swelling was down quite a bit—hopefully, they were just badly bruised and not broken or fractured.

"Do you want to go lie down?" I asked.

Before he could answer, a large crack of thunder broke through the air, closer than before. His head snapped toward the window, and he was clearly shaken by the sound. He looked out for a minute before turning back to me. "No, I'm awake now. For a second, I thought I saw a plane go by. I think my mind is playing tricks on me."

His words were oddly comforting. I wasn't the only one imagining things. I wanted to ask him if he'd seen or heard strange things, too, but I wavered, worried that he would think I was crazy. But then I heard Julia's words in my head: *don't let anyone else define who you are.* "I think that's been happening to me too. I've seen some things that I'm sure couldn't be real."

He turned his body toward me, his interest piqued. "Really? Like what?"

"I saw an ice cream truck driving down the street one day. It had the music on and everything. It also slowed down like it was trying to get people to come out of their apartments and buy a cone."

His eyes widened, and he laughed. "You're kidding me."

I shook my head. "I don't know if that was a figment of my imagination or if it really happened. It seemed too weird to be real."

"Not necessarily. I've seen some pretty odd things outside my building too. But you're right, maybe I made those all up in my head to combat the emptiness. I saw a garbage truck driving down my street, and I thought it might actually stop to pick up garbage. But it didn't. It just kept right on going. I also saw a whole family walking down the street, a man and a woman pushing a stroller. They seemed to just be out having an afternoon stroll. But I saw them from behind and couldn't see into the stroller. Who knows what was really in it."

"Oh, thank god!" I said, relieved, my hand on my chest. "I thought I might be going crazy."

He laughed again. "Maybe we both are."

"There are a few things that I know are real, such as some notes on a window in the distance, eerie notes about people being there and then not being there. I'll show them to you when the storm is over. And in the hallway, have you seen that hand on the window?"

"Yes! I almost asked you about it. It's a dead person, right?"

"I think so. It's been there for weeks. Just showed up one day. I think it's an old man."

"That's so sad but also creepy to have to see that hand all the time."

"I try not to look over there."

He paused, watching me. "I can see someone in the window on the top floor. Not very well, but someone on a bed, I think?"

My stomach dropped, and tears stung my eyes. I put my head down for a second, trying to compose myself. When I looked back at him, his brows had come together in worry. I opened my mouth then closed it, trying to figure out where to begin without completely falling apart.

"There were two young girls, Julia and Emma, who lived in that apartment. They died." My voice broke, and I swallowed, my throat suddenly feeling thick. "Their mom was sick, and when she died, it was just the three of us. We'd have long talks across the courtyard and watch movies together. We even had a snowball fight during that snowstorm. They were so cute. Julia, the older one, is on the bed in the window. I sang to her while she passed."

"Oh god, I'm so sorry. That must have been tough." He put a hand on my arm.

"Yeah, it was," I said, wiping away tears and pulling my arm away. "I took photos of them every day. Want to see?"

"I'd love that."

I walked over to grab my camera, wondering how it would feel to look at the photos, to see the girls again. I'd avoided my camera since Julia died, but part of me thought it would be a good thing. Our relationship helped me in so many ways, and I felt grateful to have had them at all. My mind wandered to the two men who broke in, but I instantly darted away from that thought. I didn't feel good about what I'd done even if my actions had kept the girls safe. I wasn't ready to tell him that yet. If he thought it was my fault, I didn't think I could take that kind of judgment. Not yet, anyway, especially since I would have agreed.

I brought my camera back to the couch, and we scrolled through the photos. I told him stories about each one. It was sad to look at them and trace the time we'd had together, but it also felt good to finally talk to someone about it. My emotions were still raw, but telling Ollie about the girls felt like slowly placing a bandage over that wound.

When we were done, we checked the progress of the storm again. It was dark and harder to see how the flooding was progressing, but I saw across the street that the short stoop was completely immersed. We ran downstairs and were shocked to see that the first floor held a light layer of water. Another crack of thunder pierced the air. We looked at each other uneasily and walked back upstairs. My living room windows were low to the floor and reached almost to the ceiling. We stood on the windowsill and watched the lightning attack Manhattan. It was beautiful and creepy at the same time. We stood, mesmerized by the light show, until we both grew tired. We said goodnight at the door, promising to leave our doors unlocked in case something happened. I walked back inside and called my mom.

She answered breathlessly, "Oh, good. I was starting to get worried. How's your building? Is it flooded?"

"It's starting to, yeah. The storm is in the city now. It should hit us sometime in the middle of the night. But we've got enough water to fill all the tubs and sinks, so that's good."

"Honey, call me if anything happens, even if it's the middle of the night. I'll probably be up all night worrying about you, anyway."

"Don't worry. I'll let you know if anything goes wrong. I'm tired, so I'm gonna go to bed. It'll all be over by morning."

"I know. It's just hard being so far from you. But I trust you, and I trust your instincts. I'll do my best to get some sleep. Call me first thing in the morning if I don't hear from you tonight, just to tell me you're okay."

"I will. Love you."

"Love you too. Goodnight, sweetheart."

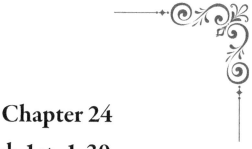

Chapter 24
March 1st, 1:30 a.m.

A loud boom crashed through the sky, jolting me upright in bed. The strike of lightning illuminated my entire room, and I saw Zeke's scared face at the end of my bed before he jumped frantically up into my arms. I held him and talked to him softly as several more claps struck around us. I lay back down and cuddled up next to Zeke, waiting for the storm to pass. We must have been in the thick of it. The wind was howling loudly, and it was freezing in my room.

I got up, wrapped the blanket around me, and walked over to the dining room window. The streets were fully flooded with branches and debris drifting by. I saw something large and white floating down the cross street by the dog park. *What is that?* It was so dark that I couldn't make it out. As it drifted closer to my apartment, lightning lit up the street, and I could clearly see that it was a woman's body. I gasped. It wasn't the woman from across the street. The body was wearing a long white nightgown, and it waved around her like a surrender. When she drifted past my apartment, I put my hand up to my mouth, my eyes wide as I watched her body being carried along to some unknown final resting place. My whole body shivered.

The lightning struck again, and I swore I saw her hand reach out to me for help. I blinked, and when my eyes opened again, her body was lifeless. Horror surged through me. *Did her house flood? Did she get caught in the current while trying to escape? Was she sick and already dead in the streets when the flood carried her body away? Was she real, or did I hallucinate again?* I went to the other window and saw that the suicide woman was also gone, pulled away by the water. I returned to my bedroom, shaken and morose.

I pulled on another thick sweater and lay awake for some time, listening to the storm and comforting Zeke, who stayed under the blankets. The image of the woman was burned onto my retinas, her ghostly figure refusing to disintegrate. Eventually, I fell back asleep, and I awoke in the morning to sunny skies. I put on a ratty old cardigan over my other sweaters and pulled a warm beanie onto my head. I lit a fire, and Zeke and I huddled around it until we warmed up. I went to the dining room and looked out the window. The water was at about first-floor level with garbage, leaves, and debris floating around like displaced survivors. I scanned the water, looking for more bodies, but I saw none. The only remnant of the dog park was the top of the short fence surrounding it. One tree in the park was split in half, the top dangling down into the water. I could only see the tops of some of the cars.

I pulled the tape off my windows before I called my mom and told her about the flooding. She was upset and asked me question after question, not even allowing me time to answer. Anxious to check the rest of the building, I cut in and told her I would call her later, once I had more information. After brushing my teeth and hair, I walked over to Ollie's and knocked.

"Hey," I said, rubbing my forearms for warmth.

He had on a bulky sweatshirt and sweatpants and was shuffling back and forth in an effort to generate heat.

"We should go downstairs and check the building," I said through chattering teeth.

"Yeah. Let me slip on my shoes."

A minute later, he came back, and we made our way downstairs. On the last flight, we saw that the first floor was flooded. The water came up to the third step of the stairs.

"I thought it would be worse than this," I said.

"Me, too, but maybe it's started to drain."

"Yeah, maybe. It could take a day or two, so you should just stay in Kirk's apartment." I looked back at him. "Want some coffee? I got the fire going."

"Absolutely!"

We ran back up the stairs, hoping the fire would warm us. I made us singed tortillas and weak coffee from three-day-old grounds while Ollie warmed up by the fire. After taking his last bite, he smiled at me, and my stomach flipped over. *What's going on here?* I looked away, and in an effort to get my feelings under control, I said, "I'm gonna go work out."

He looked at me questioningly. "How are you working out?"

"I've been running up and down the stairs then doing push-ups and sit-ups, that kind of thing."

"Impressive. I can tell you're in good shape."

I felt my face grow hot, and I knew I was blushing. *What is happening to me?* I didn't like it one bit. My stupid hormones were overriding my common sense to keep whatever we were doing a friendship.

Ollie interrupted my thoughts. "Would you mind if I joined you? I can't do everything you're doing because of my ribs, but I can run the stairs and maybe a few other things."

I hesitated. I had hoped to put more distance between us.

He must have sensed my trepidation because he said, "It's okay. I can work out on my own."

I felt bad, and I thought about what Julia would say. She would have reminded me that I wanted to be a different person, and part of that was being open and not running away from people. It scared me because I knew I was attracted to him, but I could keep that under control. *Couldn't I?*

"No, it's cool. You can join me. Meet me in the hall in ten minutes?"

He smiled. "Sounds good." He got up and took his dish to the sink, rinsing it off before putting it on the rack. As he walked out the door, he called out, "See you in ten!"

I waved to him and went to change. As I pulled on my leggings, I looked at the situation through Julia's eyes. She would have liked Ollie. She would have told me to go for it. But I knew I wasn't ready for that, and I didn't even know if he was attracted to me. I stopped pulling up my pants and laughed. There I was, thinking of all the ways to push him away in fear of getting involved with another man, when he'd just called off his engagement. How self-involved I'd become—it wasn't all about me. He had a say in it, too, and more than likely, he wasn't interested in getting involved either.

I looked at Zeke, who was on the bed, watching me. "Your mom is a nut."

His eyebrows went up, then he gave me a droll look before harrumphing, telling me it was something he already knew.

I shot him an annoyed look. After putting on a sweatshirt and tying my shoes, I walked to the hall. Ollie was already there, stretching his legs.

I joined him, and we stretched in silence for a minute before I said, "Ready?"

He nodded and followed me down the stairs. I went slowly, not wanting to overexert him, given his injuries. But after a minute, we both picked up the pace. About fifteen minutes in, we stopped on the top floor and stripped off our sweatshirts, sweat dripping off our faces. We ran up and down for another fifteen minutes, feeling like a unit. We stopped outside my apartment to take a breather before moving to my living room to start our other exercises. Between sets of curls, I told him about the woman floating by, which caused his eyebrows to arch in shock.

"I can't... I just..." He shook his head.

"Yeah, that's exactly how I feel."

I continued watching him, wondering what he was thinking. But he lightened the mood by making fun of me when we did our cool-down stretch. I'd always been inflexible and was never able to touch my toes even after all those years of soccer. We sat on the ground, feet to feet, reaching our arms toward our toes. Slowly, favoring his ribs, he reached around his feet and grabbed mine. I strained for a minute, trying to touch his hand, which was clasping my foot, but I failed by about three inches.

"I guess I'll be the one bending over backwards in this relationship," he said with a wink.

I smiled slowly and thought about his use of the word "relationship." He *was* starting to feel like a friend, someone I could count on, and god knew I needed that. He was different from the men I'd come across in NYC. His words rang truer than I was used to. Guys always seemed to have an ulterior motive, and I never felt as if I could take them at face value. Ollie seemed more genuine, playing no games or hiding hidden meanings. I would just have to keep my other desires in check.

After our workout, he went back to his apartment. I needed to bathe—I'd begun to smell my own body odor, so I reasoned that a bath was a necessary indulgence. I boiled four pots of water and threw them in the tub before adding two of cold water. I got in, sat back, and let the warm water penetrate my skin, feeling good about our time together. I felt strangely content. As I tilted my head back, letting the water rinse the shampoo out of my hair, I spotted a stray Post-It that had fallen on the shelf bordering the bathtub. I reached up and grabbed it. It read "Be safe. Be strong. Be happy." I didn't remember writing that one, but I laughed. *Yep, I am all of those right now*. I had goosebumps from the cold air, but I sat up and hugged my knees, savoring the new feeling.

Later that night, I boiled the last of my pasta and added olive oil and the dregs of a container of dry grated parmesan cheese. I tested it, and it wasn't half bad. I sat at the table and started eating my food, but it didn't feel right. I checked my iPod, and it still had a good charge, so I plugged it into my speaker and put on some music. I took a few bites, but something was missing. I went to the kitchen, poured myself a lukewarm whiskey, took a sip, and tried eating again. Nope, that didn't work. I reached for the salt and pepper and generously added both to the pasta. It helped, but I still felt off. I looked around and spotted Zeke on the ground near the hallway. He raised his head then looked toward the front door and back at me. He was right. I wanted company—wanted, not needed, and I found no reason not to indulge that craving. I got up and walked over to Ollie's apartment. He answered the door, looking frustrated, with a dishtowel in his hand.

"I was just wondering if you'd like to come have dinner with me. I made a pot of pasta. Not great, but not bad either. Have you eaten?"

"No, I was just choking down the concoction I made. Mashed acorns mixed with mustard doesn't taste good. Just a warning." He pulled a disgusted face, shaking his head. "Yours sounds better. Thanks for the invite."

He threw the towel on the counter, pulled the door shut behind him, and followed me over. I brought him a glass and pushed the whiskey toward him. After a few bites, he said, "This is good. You're much better at this than I am. I've actually eaten ketchup on crackers and mayonnaise sandwiches on stale hamburger buns."

I raised my brows and laughed. "I really like to cook. We were always on a strict budget when I was growing up. My mom could make a full meal for all of us on three bucks, and it always tasted great. She taught me everything."

He chuckled. "That's quite a talent. I can barely boil an egg. I never learned to cook properly, but in high school I had our cook teach me how to make beans on toast because my mom never let us have it. She was all about healthy organic foods, which I suppose was a good thing. But I just wanted canned Heinz beans on toasted white bread like my friends' chefs made us sometimes."

"Oh, I can do wonders with canned food," I said, wiggling my eyebrows at him. "Did you go to private school?"

"Yeah," he replied simply.

I waited for him to continue, but he seemed modest all of a sudden. I hoped he wasn't reluctant to talk about his posh upbringing because I'd just mentioned strict budgets. I was actually curious what that was like. I wasn't jealous because my education led me to a college degree from a good university. I thought about playing soccer in high school and college.

"Did you play sports?" I asked.

He grinned. "Yeah, I played rugby. I was pretty good too."

"Ah, so you were a popular jock. I hated those guys." I rolled my eyes and smirked.

He chuckled. "Yeah, playing rugby at my school automatically planted me into the popular group." He seemed more at ease talking about it since I'd made fun of him. "Our team was first place in our league, so we were like heroes at our school. When we won the championship, the school held a big celebration with the band touting our arrival. It was surreal, and I don't think I knew how to handle that type of adulation. My friends loved it, hamming it up when their names were announced. But I just felt uncomfortable and couldn't get any words out when the mic was passed to me. I froze. My teammate elbowed me in the ribs, urging me to say something. I opened my mouth, but nothing came out. It was the most embarrassing minute of my life. I ended up quickly passing the mic to another teammate, but I missed, and it landed on the ground and made a loud, piercing sound. Everyone put their hands over their ears, and I retreated to the refreshments table. No one mentioned it afterward, thankfully. I think they all felt bad for me. I miss rugby a lot, but my body just couldn't take it anymore. I blew out my knee in college, and it's never been the same since. But I still keep in touch with all my mates. We get together once a year, drink too much beer, and reminisce about our glory days." After a pause, he smiled. "I bet you were a cool kid too."

The way he was looking at me made my skin tingle all the way to my toes. I took a deep breath and shook the feeling off. "Oh god, no, not at all. I was a jock, too, not unpopular but not even close to popular. I played soccer ever since I can remember. But girl athletes weren't as cool as boy athletes at my school, if by 'cool' we mean 'popular and celebrated.' My first day of high school was a disaster. I'd spent the day before trying on different outfits and hairstyles to figure out what was cool enough for high school. But when my friends and I were walking to our lockers, we passed by a bench full of seniors from the football team. I got distracted and wound up walking right into a pole in front of everyone. They all laughed and pointed at me. Even my own friends. I had a huge bright-red lump on my forehead the whole day. It was so embarrassing. My school was really small, so by third period everyone was talking about it. Needless to say, I didn't make the best first impression."

He pursed his lips, trying not to laugh. Seeing the levity on his face made my lips twitch in response. I burst out laughing, and he followed.

"I'm sorry, I shouldn't be laughing. That's awful but really funny too," he said, trying to slow down his laughter.

When I was finally able to stop laughing myself, I said, "It's okay. You can laugh. It is funny, now that I think about it. I'm no longer traumatized."

"I'm assuming no cool cliques for you after that?"

"Nope. I tried to break in unsuccessfully. During the summers, we used to go to a nearby water park called Shadow Cliffs. There was a floating platform on the lake where all the cool kids hung out. You had to be a pretty good swimmer to make it out there. My best friend, Sarah, and I worked all summer, building up our swimming stamina to make it to that platform. One day we decided to try, and we swam as hard as we could until we made it to the platform. When we finally flopped onto the platform, we waited for the air of coolness to seep into our skin. We stayed for over an hour, but it never came. It was a huge disappointment to find out that merely making it to that platform didn't automatically make one cool. No one questioned our presence there, but they all treated us the same way they always had, neither rejecting nor accepting."

"I'm sure you were a cute kid," he said.

My cheeks grew warm, so I looked away and took another bite.

"Hey, what band is this? I really like it."

"It's Superdrag, one of my favorites. Luckily, I had backup batteries in my speakers."

"I love it." He listened to the song for several beats. "I have an idea. Those two thugs didn't find my iPod. It was in my back pocket. I have no idea how it survived, but it still works. Why don't we trade iPods? I can listen to your music, and you can listen to mine. What do you think? Might be a nice change. Mine still has a few bars of battery left. Does that dock charge your iPod?"

"Yeah, it does. And I have a couple more batteries if those die. That sounds fun, sure. We just have to be careful and keep an eye on the battery level if we need to charge them."

He ran to his apartment for his iPod. We exchanged and excitedly scrolled through each other's library, making comments on similar bands. Setting his iPod on my dining table, I suggested a game of backgammon while we had one last glass of whiskey. We cleared the dishes, and I brought a few candles over while he set up the game. We sat on opposite sides of the coffee table, him on the floor and me on the couch. We were almost eye to eye for a change. The atmosphere wasn't lost on me with the candles, the glasses of whiskey we clinked to start the game, the silence surrounding us, and that sexy grin he kept flashing. *Whoa, is this a good idea?* He rolled the dice to see who went first. *Would it be betraying who I am if I let go and let chemistry develop, if that's what's happening?*

He jarred me out of my self-indulgent postulating. "You gonna roll the dice?"

"Oh sorry," I responded while picking up the dice and throwing them. *Get over yourself, Karis, just go with it.* I gave a short laugh and looked up at him.

His face showed his confusion. "Why are you so happy? You rolled a four."

I looked down at the dice. "Hey, four's a good number."

I lifted my chin, daring him to defy me. He harrumphed and rolled the dice, starting the game. He won our first game, and I won the second, so we played a third to break the tie. We both sat back, happy with the game and the slight whiskey buzz. We sat in silence, finishing our drinks and looking at the lights in the apartments across the river. The air between us was charged with sexual tension. I felt it coming from him, too, and instead of running away from it, I let it wash over me. A half hour later, we heard a car start somewhere in the neighborhood, and we both went to the window to try to spot it. We heard the engine rev loudly, but the streets were empty. The sound faded, and we decided to call it a night.

At the door, Ollie turned and said, "Half of me wanted to go find that car and see if they'd take us with them, but it's too dangerous. We have no idea if they are sick or violent."

"I agree. Have you tried to find caravans or another car?"

"No, I'd pinned all my hopes on my friend's car. You?"

"I looked for a caravan constantly until the power went out. I even went outside a few times and searched the cars on the blocks surrounding my building. But none had keys. Do you think we can make it to the border another way?"

He scratched the scruff on his face. "I don't know. After what happened to me, I'm reluctant to be out in the open like that again. People have become savages."

My heart sank, but I knew he was right. "That's what I thought too." I yawned. "I'm beat."

"Me too. Goodnight, Karis," he replied, his eyes lingering on mine.

My body grew warm. "Goodnight, Ollie." My voice cracked on the last syllable.

But I didn't go inside, and neither did he. We stared at each other for a beat. We heard a short bark and pulled our eyes away from one another. I looked down to find Zeke staring at me.

"What?" I asked, not caring what Ollie thought of it.

He gave me a pointed look. Then he turned and walked into my apartment. *Man, even my dog can sense it.*

I looked back at Ollie, gave a slight wave, and turned to follow Zeke. I climbed into bed, pulling the comforter around me tightly. Zeke snuggled under the covers with me. Ollie and I were a good team, regardless of what else happened.

Chapter 25
March 2nd

*Z*eke's barking woke me up early in the morning. It was still dark outside. I walked to the living room window with my down blanket wrapped around me and looked out. The water was much lower but still carried debris. My breath caught when I saw something white floating down again. *Is it another body?* As it came closer, I saw that it wasn't just one body. It was two small bodies floating in tandem. When they neared my window, I gasped. It was Julia and Emma holding hands, their lifeless bodies being carried slowly away. Emma was wearing her frilly yellow dress, and Julia was in a white nightgown like the first woman. Their blond hair wafted around their little heads like halos. Tears poured down my face, and I cried out, my breath fogging up the window. Their eyes opened, and they stared at me as if they'd heard me. I could have sworn I heard Julia say, "Help us!"

Oh my god! I slapped my hands on the window and screamed their names. I shook my head. *Am I still asleep and dreaming? It can't be real.* I closed my eyes, my hands still braced on the cold window, and counted to ten. I took two deep breaths then opened my eyes again. They were farther down by the flower shop. I pulled up the window and grabbed the binoculars from the table. When I looked again, I saw clearly that it was a white trash bag with yellow drawstring handles. I dropped onto the couch and cried, my body shaking with each sob. Zeke jumped up, and I pulled the blanket around our bodies and over my head. We huddled together under the blanket while Zeke licked my tears. I wondered if I would ever get over the deaths of the girls. They'd become a part of the landscape of my life, a part I would always cherish and mourn. I fell asleep with Zeke on my lap, the blanket still covering us.

The sunlight shining brightly through the window nudged me awake a few hours later. I brought the blanket down and took a long deep breath, exhaling in a white puff. I started a fire and sat back down, waiting for the heat to warm the room. I needed to hear my mom's comforting voice. I rose and stretched my stiff muscles before dialing her number.

"Hi," I said sleepily.

"Has the flooding subsided?"

I looked outside. Only an inch or so remained. "Most of it. The sun is out. Hopefully, that'll help burn the last of it off."

"Honey, are you okay?"

"Yeah, I'm fine, just... had a bad dream. How's everything over there?"

"We're fine. Your dad hasn't been feeling well. He's a little run-down. I've been making him rest and making sure he eats properly. You know your dad. He'll go until dinner without eating if I don't remind him."

"Yeah, I know. It's nothing serious though, is it?"

"I don't think so. At first, I was worried he'd gotten the virus. But we had him tested again, and it's not that. He just works too hard and doesn't take care of himself. He has a check-up scheduled in two weeks, so we'll mention it to his doctor. By the way, there was a story on the news last night about a medication they are testing. It's supposed to be much stronger and bump up some immune cells called 'killer cells.' It sounds promising."

"That's good news! I really hope this one works out. What's the new death count?"

"They haven't released a new count yet. Something tells me they're dragging their feet. The last release was such a huge jump in numbers, people started to get frantic."

"You're probably right."

I hung up and pushed play on Ollie's iPod. I made a couple of corn cakes and ate while listening. He had good taste in music. Some of ours overlapped, but there were also some songs from bands I'd never heard. It was an eclectic mix, and I was enjoying that new way of getting to know someone. It was like looking into the darkest and lightest parts of a person, taking a musical journey through his soul. I heard a knock and went to let Ollie in. His face fell when he heard a haunting song on his iPod called "Brother" by a band I'd never heard of named Edward Sharpe and the Magnetic Zeros. I'd played it over and over again because it was so beautiful. "This song is amazing. I can't get it out of my head."

He brushed past me and hit the stop button on his iPod. I followed him and pressed the power off button on the speaker, curious about his sudden change in mood. I didn't say anything but watched him rub his forehead until he finally looked up at me.

"Sorry."

I pursed my lips and watched him look out the window. "Are you okay?"

He looked back at me, and his expression seemed angry and something else I couldn't place. "I'm fine."

I put my hands on my hips and studied him for a beat. "Are you going to tell me what you're so mad about?"

"I'm not mad. And no."

I flinched at his tone.

He paused then sighed. "It's not you. I promise. I just wanted some coffee."

I decided not to press him. "Sit down. I'll make you a corn cake."

He was quiet, staring off into the distance while I cooked. I could feel tension radiating off his body as he ate. When he was done, he rose to leave. I followed him out. At his door, I lingered, hoping he would tell me what was wrong. But he didn't. Instead, he opened his door and started to walk in.

"Knock if you need anything," I said.

He turned back and nodded at me then closed the door. Something about that song was bugging him. But I could only speculate and give him space. I contemplated asking him to join me for my workout a half hour later but thought better of it and worked out on my own. I spent most of the day listening to his iPod and braiding Zeke's huge, fluffy tail into small fishtail braids. When I was done, I wasted another hour undoing them and brushing out all the knots I'd created. Zeke watched patiently, licking my hand here and there. He didn't seem to mind. At five o'clock, I walked to the window. Purples, oranges, and reds filled the sky, reminding me of one of my favorite Klimt paintings. Zeke and I ran to the roof to watch. When I walked through the door, I found Ollie sitting on the ledge. He didn't notice us until Zeke ran over and put his nose into the hand that was dangling, urging Ollie to pet him. He jerked his head around, surprised not to be alone anymore.

I walked over and sat across from him on the ledge. "Hi."

His eyes flicked to mine. "Hi. Beautiful sunset, isn't it?"

"Yeah, so many colors. You been up here long?"

He turned his face back to the view. "A few hours."

I nodded and turned to take in the dazzling display. We sat in silence for a few minutes. I didn't want to intrude on his thoughts or make him feel like we needed chitchat to fill the silence. Out of the corner of my eye, I watched him. He seemed to be somewhere else.

Finally, he turned to me. "I'm sorry about earlier."

I kept my face toward the sunset. Its warmth felt luxurious on my skin. "It's okay."

I waited, hoping he would take the chance to spill his secrets. I heard him sniff.

"I had a brother named Phillip who died of leukemia when he was only five years old."

I turned to look at him then and felt myself leaning in.

"That song, the one you were listening to, it makes me think of him. It's kind of my song to him. And I just get sad. I didn't want to feel sad right then. But I did anyway, and I started thinking about Caleb. I got so mad at Dana. I kept thinking about this time we volunteered at a fundraiser. We'd spent the whole day with kids, and we talked about the children we'd have someday. I just can't believe she did this. I never got to meet my own son. And I..."

He was crying openly, his head down and his shoulders shaking. I scooted closer and put my arms around him. He rested his head sideways on my shoulder and continued crying, his whole body trembling. I rubbed his back, trying to comfort him as much as possible. Finally, he pulled back and wiped his red, swollen eyes.

When his tears finally stopped, I scooted back a little. "How old were you when your brother died?"

"I was just a year older than him. My first memory is of bringing his toys to the hospital and playing to try to cheer him up. He was so sick but very brave. He told knock-knock jokes to distract us whenever we got too overwhelmed by the machines and how sick he looked. He was so funny and kind. He never complained or cried. He just sat there and took whatever they gave him. He was my best friend. We were inseparable." He looked at me then, and I saw tears welling up in his eyes again. "My mom told me that when we were toddlers, she would find me sleeping in his crib, having climbed in there sometime in the middle of the night. A few days before he died, he pulled me aside and begged me to take care of Mom and Dad and his dog, Peanut. My parents were devastated when he died, but I did my best. I let my mom hold me and cry for hours. I don't think she's ever fully recovered. I still catch her in his old room, crying, occasionally," he said wistfully. "Why are *you* crying?"

I quickly put my hand to my face and felt the wetness there. I hadn't even noticed the tears. "Sorry, I don't know. It's just so sad." It made me think about the girls, and I wondered if I would still be crying over their deaths years in the future.

"I just needed some time to let the sadness run out of me. It hits me from time to time—a memory will spring up, and it'll consume me. But I'm feeling better now. I guess I needed to get that out. Thanks for letting me cry on your shoulder. Sorry I was so moody," he said with a sad smile.

"I understand."

"Do you have any brothers or sisters?"

"No, I'm an only child. My mom has a tilted uterus from a bike accident when she was sixteen. They told her she couldn't get pregnant, but I exist anyway. She calls me her miracle baby who refused to be denied existence." We both smiled. "But I had a cousin named Joaquina who was only a few years younger than me. Most of my cousins are much older, so the two of us really bonded at family gatherings. We were as close as siblings."

"Were?"

"She died in a car accident when she was fifteen. Her friend was driving, and they collided with a truck that ran a red light. The guy said he was late for dinner with his wife and didn't see the light. Her friend lived, but Quina didn't. It hit me really hard, but it was much harder on my aunt and uncle. She was an only child, too, and they never had more kids. I think they were too heartbroken. She was such a great person. Outgoing, funny, but with a really big heart.

Anytime we passed a homeless person, she'd go buy them food even if we were rushing to get somewhere. She pops into my head at the oddest times." I wiped a tear off my cheek.

"I'm sorry," he replied, touching my arm. "I think about Phillip all the time, and it's been over thirty years. Our HR manager told a knock-knock joke in a meeting once, and I burst into tears while everyone else laughed. So embarrassing." I heard the pain in his voice even though he was flippant about it. Then he shook his head. "Okay, enough of the sad stuff. What's your first memory?"

I thought about it for a minute before it came to me, a memory so strong and powerful that I was immediately filled with love. I smiled. "I think I must have been about four or five? We were at a family function, a birthday or something like that. It was late, way past my bedtime, but it was the weekend, so my mom was eager to enjoy her time with the family. I was getting really cranky and just wanted to be home. My mom was deep in a conversation with my aunt, so she picked me up and put me on her lap facing her. She put my head on her chest and her arms around me. I remember hearing her heart beating loudly in my ears. That's the first thing I remember, the soothing rhythm of my mom's heartbeat lulling me to sleep." The memory made me really happy, and although I didn't need proof, it reminded me how much my mom loved me. I looked over, and he was smiling at me. God, he was pretty. I felt my heartbeat quicken.

"That's a great story. You tell it very well too," he said, seemingly happy to have changed the subject to something more uplifting.

The sun had set, leaving only a light glow beyond the line of tall skyscrapers, so we went back downstairs. He came over and helped me make a pot of rice, and we chopped and sautéed some acorns to throw in for added flavor. We ate in comfortable silence, listening to his iPod. When we were done, I walked over to the tick wall and made the last tick for the third month and circled the batch.

Ollie watched me. "Three months, huh? Seems like longer."

"It does," I replied.

I thought about our conversations and how much they were helping me. I was more grounded and mentally in check. The other plus to him being there was that if I heard noises in the building, I assumed they were coming from Ollie and not an intruder. My paranoia was dwindling. I knew I'd been pulled back from the edge. *Maybe this is all gonna work out.* We played a few card games before calling it a night. My mind was clear for the first time in a long time, and I felt something like hope creep back in.

But the next morning, my mom called, and I could tell instantly that something was wrong. "Mom, what is it? Tell me." I heard a faint knock on my front door, and I hollered out a distracted, "Yeah, come in!"

"I didn't want to worry you." She paused and then said reluctantly, "Your father's had a heart attack. He's in the hospital. He went into surgery last night. He's stable now, and they are monitoring him. But they said everything went really well, and they were able to fix the blockage."

I could tell she'd been crying, and I felt tears pour down my face. I was in the doorway between the dining room and living room, and I placed my forehead on the frame. I couldn't say anything because I was crying too much. My mom was trying to reassure me, but it wouldn't seep in. It was one of my worst nightmares. Part of the guilt I'd felt when I moved to New York was the worry I had about my parents' health. I'd always assumed that one day I would have to move back and take care of them, but that was sort of off the table for the time being.

"Oh my god," I gasped. "I can't believe I'm not there. I should be there with him. I shouldn't be here. Why did I do this? I can't even sit by his bed and hold his hand." I sobbed uncontrollably.

"I know. I'm sorry you aren't here too. It'll be okay though. He's going to be fine." She tried.

"What if he's not? What if he dies, and I'm stuck here and never get to say goodbye!" I was almost hysterical.

"Karis, that's not going to happen," she said sternly. "The doctors say he should make a full recovery and will have to adjust his diet and exercise. That's all. I know it sounds bad, but he's going to be fine. We're going to be okay."

I tried hard to let her words penetrate my brain, but it wasn't working.

"I've gotta go. They are running more tests to make sure he doesn't get an infection. I'm sorry I had to tell you this, but I know you would be mad if I didn't," she confessed.

"I'm glad you did. Tell him I love him. Even if he can't hear you, just say it to him, please."

"I will. I love you, honey. Don't worry too much. We've got this under control. I'll call you later with an update."

"I love you too. Bye."

I hung up the phone and just stood there with my head on the frame and my hands gripping its edges, sobbing. Ollie cleared his throat. I looked up at him standing in the doorway to my dining room. He walked over and put his arms around me, returning the comfort I'd given him the day before. I fell into his arms and completely broke down, weeping on his shoulder. I didn't know how much he'd heard or if he even knew what was going on.

I sniffed into his shoulder. "My dad had a heart attack, and I'm not there."

"I'm so sorry," he said, his arms tightening around me.

I cried for another minute until I was finally able to calm down. My breathing evened out, but he continued to hold me, and I let him. It felt good in his arms, almost as if I was home. Absentmindedly, I wiped my face on his shirt before realizing what I was doing. We stood like that for several minutes before I began to pull away. But as I did, he tightened his arms, and our faces were close. I looked at him, and without thinking, I pulled him closer and kissed him. It was electric, my limbs tingling like they'd fallen asleep. Then all I could feel were his lips on mine. As the kiss deepened, I heard him groan. At least I thought it was him and not me. It was without a doubt the best kiss I'd ever experienced. My body was eagerly opening up to him just as my heart reluctantly had. The kiss went on for what seemed like hours but was probably only minutes, intensifying with each moment. Finally, he scooped me up and took me to the bedroom.

He slowly took off my clothes, unbuttoning my dress and pulling it down, kissing my stomach as he went. He continued to my breasts, kissing them through the mesh fabric of my bra. My body was tingling, and my breath was coming in gasps. I couldn't take it anymore, so I grabbed the bottom of his shirt and pulled it off. There was urgency to our movements, and I was glad he was feeling it too. I unzipped his pants and pulled them down while he removed my bra and underwear. When we were both naked, he eased down on top of me, and I wrapped my legs around him. He kissed my neck then moved back to my lips. I was writhing underneath him, urging him on. His movements started to mimic mine until we were both on the edge. I was so overcome that I didn't think. I just felt and moved.

Suddenly, he groaned, reached down, and entered me. My mind dissolved into thousands of little sparks. We were still, the intensity of sensation causing us to pause and revel in what was happening. We were clasped together in a soundless, airless room. Slowly that faded to the background as he began to move inside me. I matched his movements, going slowly. But soon it was too much for both of us, and our pace quickened until I felt a slow ache building in my lower back. I swam around in the sensation until it overcame my whole body in a final release. He yelled as he reached his climax too. He lay on top of me with his arms around me, spent and sweaty, kissing my face and lips.

Our breathing gradually returned to normal, and he rolled over, pulling me into his arms. We were both quiet, trying to take in what had just happened. It was an instance of complete mental and physical satiation, and I wished I had something else to compare it to, but that didn't exist anywhere in my memory. I fell asleep, happy for the first time in months.

I awoke a few hours later, still wrapped in Ollie's arms. I lay there, thinking about what had happened between us, and I was overcome, feeling large chunks of my emotional wall crumbling down—it terrified me. By force of habit and something close to panic, I mentally tried to pick the pieces up and force them back into that wall. For me, love resided in a deep, dark, impenetrable place, a hidden corner.

But I heard Julia telling me not to give up, to take what the world was offering me. I exhaled and let go. I couldn't keep those walls up forever, and I didn't want to. I wanted to let someone in, and for my own sake, I knew I had to. It was my opportunity to be brave and take what I wanted for once. I turned to look at him. He was watching me, studying my face. Slowly, he smiled, and like a contagious yawn, it made me smile too.

Chapter 26
March 5th

I'd been quickly checking in with my mom every few hours to monitor my dad's progress. He'd been in the hospital for three days, and they said he could go home the next day. I talked to him briefly the day before, even though he was out of it from the painkillers. I told him how much I loved him and that I was glad he was going to be okay. I made my mom put the doctor on the phone and give me all the details. After our talk, I began to believe he might actually be all right. The doctor said it was a minor heart attack, and the blockage was easily repaired. I had confidence in my mom to keep my dad in check by adjusting his diet and keeping him on an exercise plan. For the time being, we were out of the woods.

Ollie and I were in a euphoric state, in bed more often than not. Even though Kirk's apartment was admittedly much nicer than mine, Ollie moved in with me. The one time we slept over there, I woke up feeling like an intruder. My apartment was home to me, and I think Ollie felt the same way. Frequently, we had long talks about our lives before the quarantine and discussed what we hoped to do if we escaped and swapped stories about past relationships. He told me about his relationship with Dana before the pregnancy, which he described as the only time he'd felt real love. I told him the horror stories about dating in New York that had led to my decision to stop dating. I found it easier to share myself with him as time went by.

We continued working out and playing the games we'd found in Kelly's apartment. Ollie's ribs were healing, and his recovery from the beating was progressing well. We'd even ventured out once to check cars on a few streets past the park. But when we came back, his ribs swelled up, and we decided to wait a few more days before trying again.

My relationship with him brought out my nurturing side in a huge way. I hovered around him while he was changing, checking on his wounds and applying aloe or vitamin E oil so they didn't scar. He was obviously enjoying it, submitting to my caretaking with a pleased grin. I even made us rice pudding as a treat one night with coconut oil and sugar. We savored each bite, Ollie feigning ecstasy over the taste. It was nice having someone around to spoil.

We made another foray outside to gather more acorns and spent a day leaching out the tannins and roasting them. I had Ollie grind a large batch to make acorn flour. The next evening, we went up to the roof with my most recent experiment: ginger cookies made with coconut oil instead of eggs and an extra dash of molasses. I'd splurged, using some of our dwindling flour mixed with the acorn flour. They were really good, but I thought that was probably given the lack of flavor we'd had in our food lately. While we munched, I pulled out the binoculars and showed him the notes on the window.

"See the building with the red parapet right over there, just beyond the park?"

He looked for a second. "Yeah. I see the notes too." He studied them for a minute then pulled the binoculars down. "I think this guy probably died. Maybe that was a note for someone, warning them not to come back."

I shook my head. "I think the notes were a signal, letting some-one know he was still there until he had to leave."

"Hmm... could be. I guess you're more optimistic than I am." He raised an eyebrow.

"I wouldn't say I'm a naturally optimistic person."

"Really? Seems like it to me." He leaned over to brush a piece of hair off my face and tucked it behind my ear.

I smiled and considered the idea. It felt encouraging that maybe I had changed. Then I heard a light tapping, some coughing, then a distant voice saying, "Are you there? It's me, Henry."

Our eyes widened as we looked at each other happily. We ran down the stairs into Barb's apartment and leaned out the window. He had turned and was walking away looking dejected, pushing his rickety cart. I leaned out farther. "Henry! Up here!" I waved my arms at him.

He turned his cart around, smiled, then walked back. "Well hello! There you are."

It was good to see him safe and sound. "We were worried about you because of the flood. Are you okay?"

"Yeah. I was able to get into the building next door. The apart-ment you mentioned was empty, so I've been staying there. I scoured the apartments that were unlocked, but there wasn't much food left. I've run out. Can you spare some more?"

"Of course," Ollie said. "Give us a minute."

We both ran to our apartments and started loading up a large Ikea bag with some tortillas, bottles of water, and more medicine. I was so happy to see Henry alive that I put most of the cookies in a baggie and added those too.

Ollie looked dejected. "Hey, I thought those were for me!"

"I'll make you more!" I replied.

Back at the window, we leaned out, and Henry was doubled over, coughing into a beige towel. When he straightened, the towel had blood all over it. Our spirits deflated. He wasn't doing well.

"Sorry. That happens once in a while," he said when he saw our faces.

"How long have you been sick?" I asked. He had an orange wristband, so he'd clearly been infected fairly recently.

"I stayed here to take care of my wife. She wasn't sick but tested positive for the virus. A few weeks later, she got a fever. I took care of her until she died a month ago. I started having symptoms about that time."

"I'm so sorry," I said.

"Thanks. I'll be with her again soon." He smiled.

Ollie picked up the bag, held it out the window, then dropped it to the ground.

Henry struggled to pick it up in his weakened state, but he managed to heave it up into his cart. "Thanks. You guys are the best."

"We put some more medicine in there too." I paused. "Henry, there's a bottle of prescription pain killers in that bag. Use them near the end."

His eyes widened. "Oh, bless you. Thank you for helping me. I would have starved without the food you gave me, and now this. I don't know what to say."

"Just take care of yourself."

"I'll try." He smiled at us one last time before heading off with his cart. The sun was about to set, and he shouldn't stay out in the dark. We waved to him and closed the window. We walked back upstairs, relieved that he'd weathered the storm safely but also disheartened by his sickly appearance. We ate dinner in silence, thinking gloomy thoughts.

While we were washing the dishes, Ollie said, "It's so hard to see that firsthand. He's the only sick person I've come across. I saw people on the news, but it's not the same." He set the last dish in the rack and turned toward me. "You had to go through that with the girls. I can't even imagine." He shook his head sadly.

"It was hard." I couldn't think of any other way to describe it.

"Did you lose a lot of friends?"

I nodded. "When the Death List came out, most of my friends and co-workers were on it. I don't even know if it's really sunk in yet that they are all gone. My friend Lori, who lived a few blocks down, had a dog named Cody." I paused as tears filled my eyes. "We were close. We'd hang out at least once a week and walk each other's dogs when one of us had to work late. When I found her name, all I could think about was Cody, as if my mind was deliberately avoiding the reality of the situation and focusing on something easier to think about."

"I know what you mean. I found a few friends on there too. Not as many as you, I'm sure, but seeing their names was awful, and I kept thinking about their families instead of what they must have gone through as they died." He looked down for a second then pulled his head up. "It's nice that you had a friend in the neighborhood with a dog."

"It was the perfect situation. Zeke and Cody loved each other. On the rare days when Lori worked from home, she'd come get Zeke to play with Cody while she worked." Thinking about the two of them together brought a smile to my face. "Once, we took the dogs to a doggy swimming pool in Brooklyn, and... Oh my god!" My eyes popped open, and I looked at Ollie with a huge grin. "Oh my god!" I repeated, laughing.

He looked confused. "What?"

"I can't believe I didn't remember this sooner! Lori's ex-boyfriend, Dan, moved out of her apartment to the Upper East

Side when they broke up a little over a year ago. He had a car and kept getting parking tickets because of opposite-side parking every other day. We don't have that in Long Island City, so he asked Lori if he could keep the car here instead. He said she could use it whenever she wanted. That's how we took the dogs to the pool. What if it's still there?" My heartbeat raced at the possibility.

"But we don't have the keys."

"I have keys to Lori's apartment so I could walk Cody when she needed me to. We could go to her apartment and see if the car keys are there. They may not be. She could have driven herself to the hospital, or Dan could have gotten the car. But I found his name on the list, too, so that seems unlikely. We should at least go and check."

A smile lit up his face. "When do you want to go?"

I looked outside at the darkness that was creeping in. "Let's go tomorrow. I don't feel safe going at night. I hear things out there sometimes. Creepy things." I shuddered, thinking about going back out.

"Tomorrow, then."

I hugged him, feeling hopeful for the first time about a possible escape. As we slid into bed, that hope began to mingle with nerves. Going to Lori's would be much farther than I'd ventured in months. *What threats were lurking in the shadows? What will we find in Lori's apartment?* I had a hard time falling asleep, and listening to Ollie's steady breathing that turned into soft snoring was even worse. *Why isn't he as nervous as I am?* I finally fell into a dreamless, fitful sleep.

I awoke in the morning to the sound of a mourning dove, and its rhythmic cooing lulled me awake. I felt a weight on my ribs, so I opened one eye to see Zeke resting his chin on me, waiting for me to rise. He raised his eyebrows over his clear brown eyes, obviously trying to decide if he should take the flutter of my eyelid seriously or not. I opened my other eye and convinced him I was really awake. While he burrowed into the covers in excitement, I looked to my left, but the bed was empty. I checked my watch, and it read 11:22 a.m. I couldn't believe I'd slept that late. I climbed out of bed and found Ollie at the dining table, eating breakfast. A healthy fire was already burning in the fireplace. He turned and smiled then got up and fixed me a plate. I poured my coffee and joined him at the table.

"You slept late. I was getting worried about you. I took Zeke to the roof already."

"Thanks. I didn't fall asleep till really late. Nervous about today, I guess."

He nodded and went back to eating his rice. I wondered if he was nervous, too, especially after his beating—just watching it from my kitchen window had frightened me. We ate in silence then changed and brushed our teeth. I had on several layers of clothing and topped them with my short down jacket. We wore warm beanies and sunglasses to reduce the glare from the sun and pulled gloves onto our hands. I grabbed the empty backpack in case Lori had any supplies we could bring back. It seemed like we both wanted to get it over with. Before we left, I got down to Zeke's eye level and told him where we were going and that we would be back soon. He whined at me and shuffled his paws. I gave him one last kiss.

When we got to the front door, we looked outside for several minutes, scouting the terrain. We stepped out and listened for a few seconds but heard nothing other than birds singing and the wind blowing. Ollie grabbed my hand, and we darted to the doorway across the street. We looked around, waiting for someone to pop out and attack us, but nothing happened. I motioned to the park, and we crossed the next street, crouching down once we made it across so we wouldn't be seen from the street. The trees were bare, offering no coverage, but there were still overgrown shrubs near the ground that would help block any watchers. We cut through the park, and I pulled Ollie under an awning on the next corner.

We were both breathing heavily, our chests heaving. We stayed under the canopy for a few minutes, catching our breath and listening for people. I was a bundle of nerves, feeling too exposed. My head jerked toward every twig snapping and every bird taking flight—even the sound of my own breath made me edgy.

I leaned over and whispered, "Two more blocks that way." I pointed in the direction of the water. He looked down the street and nodded.

We darted out again and ran as fast as we could. The next block was all industrial warehouses that offered no protection. We rushed across an intersection and slipped into an alleyway between buildings. Catching our breath again, we waited and listened. Somewhere fairly close, we heard a noise that sounded like dragging, then some scrambling, followed by silence.

"It's only two buildings away across the street," I whispered.

He nodded. I looked out and didn't see anything, so I grabbed his hand, and we ran toward Lori's building. As we sprinted across the street, I kicked a metal can that was in the road. It made a loud clanking sound as it tumbled down the street before finally landing next to the wheel of a car. I winced at the noise. Lori's building had a large alcove at the front door, so we felt more protected as I pulled the keys out and unlocked the door. A powerful stench immediately assaulted us. We quickly shut the door and zipped our jackets over our noses. I wondered how many dead bodies were in the building. I really hoped we wouldn't find a dead Cody in the apartment. I didn't know if I could take that.

At Lori's front door, I fumbled with the ancient lock, having a hard time getting the key in with my gloves on. The smell dissipated slightly once we were inside, leading me to believe that Cody wasn't there. We looked in every room. I came out of Lori's bedroom at the same time Ollie emerged from the spare bedroom that Lori used for Airbnb guests.

"No Cody or anyone else?" I asked.

He shook his head then went to the kitchen to start our search for the keys. I looked on the key rack, but the only keys were mine and another set I didn't recognize. I rifled through the small table covered in framed family photos and knick-knacks near the door but came up empty. I turned to Ollie.

He threw up his hands. "They aren't here."

We looked through every drawer in the living room but found nothing. "Someone must have taken the car," I said, crestfallen.

We checked the cupboards and found a brand-new bottle of pasta sauce, a box of rigatoni, and an unopened bottle of red wine. We also took her full can of ground coffee, flour, cocoa powder, and sugar, piling it all into the backpack. There were four cups of Cody's dog food in a bag under the sink. I threw that in too—Zeke's food was running low. I'd been mixing it with rice to stretch it out as much as possible. A loud thump from floors above compelled us to look up. Someone was still living there. My skin prickled in fear. Ollie pulled the backpack on and tightened the straps. As we rushed back to the front door, I spotted something sticking out from under the table by the door. I reached down and felt the key fob for the car. I pulled it up and triumphantly showed the keys to Ollie.

"They fell under the table!" I said excitedly. "It's a dark-blue Kia Sportage, a small SUV. She usually parks it on this street or one of the three surrounding it. The street farther down is always packed, and you can never find parking. We can start on this street and work our way to the others." We heard another thump, and we both jumped.

"Let's get out of here," he said.

I took one last look at a photo on the table of Lori and Cody, and tears forced their way out. I wiped them away and pulled the photo out of the frame, sliding it into my back pocket before I walked out the door. Once outside, we walked to the middle of the street and scanned the parked cars. I didn't see any blue ones, so we walked farther. All of a sudden, three men appeared at the top of the street. One had a baseball bat in his hand, which he bounced against his other palm. I stopped, fear spreading through my body. We turned around to run in the other direction but halted in our tracks. Two more men were at the end of the street, both holding what looked like wooden boards with nails sticking out the ends.

Ollie's face was tense, his jaw muscles clenched tightly. I'm sure flashbacks were filling his mind. We both turned back to the three men at the top of the street. I looked around frantically, searching for a way out. I spotted the buildings on the left and had an idea.

As quietly as possible I whispered, "Ollie! See those two buildings on the left?"

His eyes moved to the left, and he whispered, "Yes."

"There's an alleyway between them where they keep the garbage cans."

The man with the bat interrupted me, yelling, "Don't make us wait! Just do what we ask, and you won't get hurt. Walk toward me slowly with your hands up. Don't try anything stupid. We saw you come out of that building. We just want the keys."

I was shaking, and my breath was coming in short gasps. I felt a trickle of sweat slide down my back. We both raised our hands.

I whispered out of the side of my mouth, "The alleyway has a few turns, and we'll have to go through a gate in a fence, but it lets out on the next street over. Maybe we can get ahead of them and run back to my building."

"Come on, ladies. We're not going to stand here all day. Walk toward me, *now!*" the man shouted.

"Start walking. On the count of three, follow me down the alleyway. I know where I'm going. I've cut through with Zeke and Cody a hundred times."

We slowly began walking toward the man. His hair was long and greasy, his clothes spotted with stains. He was wearing boots with spikes hammered into the toes. They all had on long-sleeved sweatshirts, so I couldn't see if they had wristbands. After ten steps, the alleyway came into my peripheral vision. I looked at the man, and he smiled and laughed.

"One," I whispered. "Two." We were almost there. I saw the narrow opening. "Three!"

We darted to the left, and I heard the man yell, "What the fuck! You guys are dead! Alex, Dom, go to the left and meet us on the next street. We'll follow them!"

Ollie and I were already halfway down the first leg of the alley when I heard feet slapping the pavement behind me. We hit the turn and made a right. I was hoping the men didn't know where the alley led. There were three garbage cans blocking the path up ahead. There would be no time to move them. When I got close, I launched and pulled my legs up as though I was jumping a hurdle. I barely cleared the cans and fell on the other side, my ankle pounding in pain. Ollie landed a few inches past me, and he reached down and pulled me up. After another ten feet, we reached the next turn and spun to the left. Before we turned, I looked back. The men were at the garbage cans, pushing them to the side. We had a little time.

When we got to the gate, Ollie pulled it open, and we rushed through. It had a U-latch, so I pulled it down and pushed the pin through, praying it would slow them down. We turned and kept running. I could see the exit up ahead and ran faster. I heard the men swearing at the gate. They could have opened it easily if they were familiar with U-latches, but it sounded as though they were climbing over instead. As we ran, I looked back and saw one man fall over the fence to the other side. We darted out the exit and looked to the end of the street. The other two men were standing there looking for us. They spotted us and sprinted in our direction. We dashed to the cross street and kept running toward Eleventh. We were on my street and just had to run two more blocks to my corner. We both turned to check their progress. The two men were only about twenty yards behind and gaining on us.

I felt my ankle getting weaker, but I pushed through it. All that time running up and down the stairs was paying off, I thought, as I felt a second wind coming on. As we neared Eleventh, I saw the edge of Henry's cart. *Oh my god, no!* I pointed at it, and Ollie saw it too. We looked at each other, worried. Henry peeked around the corner. Our eyes locked, then his eyes moved to the men chasing us. He looked back at us and waved his hand, indicating we should keep going. As we ran past him, we turned and saw that the other three men were now running behind the two on our tail. Once we passed Henry, he pushed his cart into the street, between the men and us.

"Henry, no!" I screamed.

I stopped running and turned around. Ollie grabbed my hand and tried to pull me forward, but I stood my ground and watched. Henry coughed loudly and yelled, "I'm sick. Someone please help me." He reached his hand out to the men and coughed some more. "Please can you help me?" He waved his bloody towel in front of them.

They stopped in their tracks and backed up a few steps, covering their mouths with their shirts. The man with the bat said something under his breath to the other men then pointed the bat in our direction. They backtracked toward the cross street and turned right. Henry looked back at us and raised his eyebrows, grinned, then waved his hands in a shooing motion.

I yelled, "Thanks, Henry!"

We turned and ran the last block to my apartment building on the corner. I was out of breath when we got to the stairs, and Ollie had to pull me up because my ankle finally gave up the fight. When we were back in my apartment, I lay on the couch while Ollie inspected my ankle. It was starting to swell again. He elevated my foot on a few pillows then rose to leave. "I'll be right back."

"Where are you going?" I asked, but he didn't respond.

He walked out the front door, leaving me gaping in his wake.

I waited ten minutes with Zeke standing in front of me, licking my hand and whining. I got up and hobbled to the kitchen, looking for Ollie. Finally, the front door opened, and he came into the kitchen. He frowned at me leaning on the counter, my foot pulled up off the floor.

I expected a scolding for walking around on my ankle, but he said, "I spotted them a few streets over. It looked like they were pounding on doors. But I think we're safe for now."

"I can't believe that just happened! And we didn't get to search for the car."

"We'll have to go look another day. I'm not going back out there. They're still looking for us. We really pissed them off. How's your ankle?"

"Numb," I said.

He picked me up and plopped me back down on the couch. I lifted my foot up onto Ollie's lap, and he examined it.

"How bad is it?" I asked.

"I can't tell. Let's wrap it up and get you some ibuprofen."

While he left my side to get supplies, I thought about how nice it was to let someone take care of me for a change. I'd always been the caregiver in my relationships, but I wasn't carrying the load for both of us—I was allowing him to carry it with me. I had never done that before.

My nerves were shot from our expedition outside, but I smiled anyway. My head dropped back onto the arm of the couch. I sighed and fell asleep.

Chapter 27
March 9th

For the next two days, I scoured the streets with the binoculars, searching for the car while my ankle healed. The good news was that it felt much better, and the swelling had gone down completely. The bad news was that the battery life was dwindling on my phone—only a quarter of the power was left. I hadn't played any music in days, and both our iPods had died. My mom and I decided to talk every three days instead of every other day, and I hoped that we would find the car before I called her again. I was up on the roof with the binoculars when the door opened and Ollie walked through, holding two glasses of whiskey.

"Any luck?" he asked.

"Well, there are two possibilities. There's a blue SUV over there, two blocks from Lori's building, and another right there." I pointed to the other side of the park. "I can't see that one very well, only the front end, but that could be it. Or it could be a sedan and not an SUV. It seems more likely she'd park it here than the other street. There's a police station on that street, and most of the parking is for them. I'm hoping it's the first one. That street is on an incline, and the car is at the top of the street. With the flooding we had, that car has a better chance of not being damaged. I think we're just gonna have to go check them out."

"I don't think your ankle will be up for it if we go tomorrow."

"It feels much better today," I replied.

The weather had been nicer and was slowly getting warmer. I was able to keep warm with just a thick chunky sweater over my knee-length dress.

Ollie came close to me, pulled the binoculars from my hand, and quickly kissed me. "I hope you don't mind—I called my mom just now and told her about the car. She was excited, to say the least. She wants us both out of here."

"Does she know about us?" I asked.

"No, my mom has a habit of running away with these types of things. I don't want to tell her until I know what this is." He paused. "Do *we* know what this is?"

I searched his face for an answer, but I didn't see one. I chose to be brave. "Well, for me, this is amazing. I feel lucky to have met you, even under these circumstances. I don't know where it's going, especially with everything else that's going on, but I'd like it to go somewhere. What about you?"

He leaned over and kissed me.

"Is that your answer?"

"No." He laughed. "Well, maybe it is. I feel the same way. I guess I haven't wanted to think about that part of it. This came out of nowhere for both of us. And maybe if we make it out of here, these feelings will go away. But I don't think they will."

"I don't think they will either," I said immediately. I didn't need to think about it. My heart was hammering in my chest, and it felt like I might explode with emotional excitement.

"But it's scary, you know?" he continued.

"I know. I remember after 9/11, I saw this article about how people felt compelled to connect with others, especially in a romantic way. That's been in the back of my mind. But even if that's what this is, I don't think it's a bad thing."

"I don't either. I guess all we can do is ride it out and see what happens. Just promise me you'll be honest about how you're feeling. Even if you think it'll hurt."

"Okay. Same goes for you," I said.

"How I'm feeling right now is I want to ravish you on this rooftop."

My face grew warm, and my body tingled. I let him lead me into the best use of my roof so far, which said a lot—I'd had some pretty awesome parties up there. He closed the gap between us and pushed me against the slope of the half wall surrounding the roof. Looking into my eyes, he kissed me and lowered his hand to pull up my dress and touch me through my underwear. I gasped and hugged him closer. I wrapped one leg around his waist, and I felt his hardness against me. He was kissing and licking every inch of me, and I encouraged him. I heard him unzip his pants and felt him slide inside me. The feeling was instant and overwhelming. Our rhythm gradually built until we climaxed together.

As I came down from my high, I kissed his neck and face, running my hands up his shirt and along his back. He tightened his arms around me and breathed deeply. I sensed a solid and consuming heaviness in him that I couldn't place. He clutched me tightly and breathed into my neck in an odd way. I didn't know how to respond. I pulled my head back and looked him in the eyes, trying to get a read on him. He put his forehead on mine and just stared at me.

"Are you all right?" I asked, worried.

"Yeah."

My eyebrows drew together. *What is he hiding?*

He kissed me deeply. I felt his emotions pouring into me—the air was suddenly thicker, embracing us like a cocoon. We remained that way until our heartbeats slowed to normal. Back downstairs, I made us a dinner of spaghetti and makeshift brownies from the extra flour and cocoa I'd found in Lori's apartment. I was feeling giddy from our romp on the roof and didn't want to talk about anything serious. An hour later, I was changing after taking a sponge bath when Ollie walked into the bedroom with a tight look on his face.

"What's wrong?" I asked, pulling my shirt over my head.

"Nothing's wrong. I just..." He paused and looked away. Then his eyes flicked back to mine. "I think I should go alone to check the cars."

"What? Why?"

"It's too dangerous. I can't put you in that danger. And your ankle isn't fully healed yet." I could tell he'd been thinking about it for a while.

"My ankle is fine. I worked out on it this morning. You aren't putting me in any danger." I started to get annoyed. "I'm putting myself in that situation."

"Karis, it's safer if you stay here. The other day with those men chasing us really scared me. What if they'd caught you? What if they'd hurt you?" His voice was slowly getting louder and more forceful.

"What about you? It's also safer if you stay here and let *me* go alone. I know the area better. And the car!"

"I can figure it out. Please, Karis, think about this. It's better if I go alone." His face turned red as he pled with me.

"Ollie, I'm not going to sit here worrying whether you're dead or alive. I'm going."

"We can't take that risk. We need to be smart about this. Just stay home!" The vehemence in his voice shocked me.

"You can't tell me what to do!" I replied, my heart pounding and my hands shaking in frustration.

He stopped, clearly having seen the logic in my statement. He looked at me with narrowed eyes, but I wouldn't back down. I could see his wheels turning, desperately searching for an argument to counter mine until he gave up and walked out.

I was shaken by our fight. But while I thought about our exchange, I got angrier as I argued my point silently in my head. *How dare he! I've worked so hard to get to this place. I've survived all these months on my own.* I finally felt confident in myself, and I wasn't going to let anyone take that away from me.

Over the next hour, we kept our distance, and I hoped he would come around, but I didn't see that happening. I was afraid he would sleep at Kirk's apartment, but he didn't. As I slid into bed, he walked in, looked at me, climbed in, and turned his back to me. I felt a wall of tension between us.

By morning, my anger had dwindled, and I was able to see that he'd been trying to do something good. I'd immediately assumed that he was trying to control me, but I knew that wasn't it—he was simply trying to protect me. I just needed to convince him that he didn't have to, that I could take care of myself.

I was in the kitchen when he came up behind me and placed his hands on my shoulders and his lips on the back of my head. "I'm sorry," he said. "I know it's your decision. I'm just scared. The thought of something happening to you is killing me."

My body relaxed, and I felt the tension between us melt away. "I'm sorry too. I know you were coming from a good place." I turned so we were face-to-face. "But, Ollie, I can take care of myself." I paused and took a deep breath. "Something else happened with the girls that I haven't told you about."

"What?" he asked.

"It's hard to talk about. And I'm worried about what you might think."

He looked at me for a second, waiting for me to continue. "So tell me now," he finally said.

My gaze veered to the side and out the window while I tried to find my words. A dog barked in the distance. "Two men broke into the girls' building. They tried mine first, but I had nailed boards over my door. They didn't get in, but I watched them get into another building across the way. I heard them attack someone, and when they walked out, they had blood on their hands and arms. They went for the girls' building next." I hesitated and looked back at him.

He'd knitted his eyebrows together and set his mouth in a tight line.

"You can cross over from my roof to theirs, and that's what I did. I went over there to protect them. I couldn't let them hurt those girls. I had my crowbar, and I hit one of them in the kneecap. I injured him pretty badly. The other one chased me. He pulled the crowbar out of my hands, and then I didn't have any weapons. But I poured some oil on the ground behind me to slow him down. He slipped when he was running after me..." I swallowed a few times, trying to get the words out. "He fell onto a broken rod that was sticking up in the stair railing. It killed him instantly, I think. Or I hope. I don't know."

"Oh my god! Did he hurt you?"

"We fought, he choked me, and I got a few bruises. But he *died*," I said, trying to convince him of the difference.

He looked at me oddly but didn't say anything.

"The other guy got really mad when he saw what he thought I did to his friend. Even though his knee was hurt, he chased me onto the roof. I ran over to the grocery store on the other side and jumped two flights down onto that roof."

"Karis, you could have killed yourself!"

"But I didn't. It was a risk I had to take. I was running on instinct, and I had to lead him away from the girls." I paused, waiting for an argument, but none came. "He ran after me, but he didn't know there was a gap between the buildings. He jumped off, but he didn't make it. He fell to the ground and died too." I watched Ollie's face, looking for signs of disappointment or repulsion. But all I saw was compassion, and I didn't know how to feel about that. I'd been unconsciously beating myself up for weeks.

He put his hands on my shoulders and looked me in the eyes. "You did what you had to do. You saved the girls. You can't feel bad about that."

"But, Ollie, those two men died because they were chasing me!"

"Right. Because *they* were *chasing* you. They chose to do that, and they paid for it. You did nothing wrong, Karis. You saved those girls." He lifted a finger and wiped away a tear I didn't know was there.

"But the girls died anyway," I said, letting myself cry freely.

"Yes, with dignity and with you by their side, not by the hands of some depraved men. They died with compassion and love. You did that for them."

His words were starting to sink in, and my tears slowed. I nodded in agreement. "I know you're right. I'm just having a hard time with it, I guess."

"I'm glad you told me."

I wiped away my tears and smiled at him. "Me too. Anyway, the point of my story is that I know I'm small, but I'm strong, and I'm fast. Don't underestimate me." I stared at him, unwilling to back down.

His brow furrowed. "Is that what I was doing?" He paused to think about it. "Maybe I was. I didn't mean to, I just... want to protect you."

"I know. But you can't, not always. I've been taking care of myself for a long time now, and I've survived this whole quarantine, just like you."

He took a long breath and pulled me into his arms. "You're right. I'm sorry. You'll come, we'll find the car, and we'll be fine. Both of us."

We stood like that for a few minutes, happy to be back in each other's arms again. I inhaled his scent and pulled him closer, trying to reassure him of my own strength. We made a plan to check the car by the police station first since it was slightly closer.

We waited until the sun went down, realizing that going out in the dark was a better idea no matter how much scarier it was. I leaned against the bathroom wall and propped my foot up on the toilet. I wrapped my ankle just in case. It felt pretty good, but we could easily run into those guys again. As I had that thought, fear raced up my spine, and my heartbeat fluttered. Still braced against the bathroom wall, I let my head fall back and took a few deep breaths. We had to do it. *I* had to do it—it was our only hope, and I wanted to be a part of it.

At seven o'clock, we dressed all in black and made our way downstairs with a small flashlight. We were both scared because of our last foray outside, but I looked at him and gathered courage.

Ollie slowly opened the door. We waited, straining to hear any signs of life. It was dead quiet. He looked back at me and jerked his head in the direction of outside, and I nodded back. He grabbed my hand, and we darted outside. We stopped at the corner and hid under the deli's awning, looking around to make sure no one was lying in wait. After a few seconds, we made our dash again and ran down the first block, scampering into the doorways of buildings intermittently to check our surroundings and make sure no one had seen us. We continued that way down to the next cross street then turned right onto the street where the first car was.

We were only a few cars away when the sound of glass breaking in the distance pierced the silence. Ollie grabbed my hand and pulled me into a narrow alleyway between two apartment buildings. We stared at each other and listened. Eventually we heard voices—two men and a woman, it seemed, not the men from before. That was a relief, but they were screaming profanities and coughing, which also wasn't good. They were clearly sick with the virus and coming closer to us.

I looked around to find some way to hide until they passed as I pulled my jacket up over my nose and mouth. Near the ground on the wall was a small opening for a vent to the underground garage. I looked at Ollie. He grabbed a large black trash bag that was dangling from the fence surrounding the building. I pointed to the opening to indicate that I was going to crawl in there. He nodded and pulled the bag around him and then crouched down under it on the ground. He looked like a bag of trash. I forced my body into the space, hunched over with my head on my knees. All those hours spent in the cramped hall window were paying off. I just hoped they couldn't see me.

I looked through the vent slats that led to the garage. It was dark, so I couldn't see much, but the moonlight was illuminating shapes all around. My eyes located a familiar silhouette on the ground next to a car. It looked like a person lying down, possibly hiding too. *Oh no, can they see me?* I watched for a few seconds, but the person wasn't moving at all. As my eyes adjusted to the dark interior, I began to understand what I was seeing, and I sucked in a gasp. Bloody wetness reflected the moonlight in dark shiny patches all over the face and arms, and I knew it was a decomposing body lying face up on the floor of the garage. Parts of the face looked like ground beef as if it'd been ripped away. I caught movement out of the corner of my eye—a rat was scurrying toward the body. *Oh god.* The rat reached the body and started eating its face, picking up where some other animal had left off or quite possibly finishing what it had started. I felt my stomach turn and forced myself to look away so I didn't throw up.

The voices were getting louder. I peeked to the side to try to get a glimpse. I could only see a sliver of the sidewalk, but I saw their legs as they walked by the alleyway. I held my breath as they passed right by us. I remained in the opening until their voices faded away. In my peripheral vision, I saw Ollie pull himself up and out of the bag. He reached down and grabbed my hand. I unfurled my body from the space and let out a long breath. Peeking around the wall of the alleyway, we could still see them far in the opposite direction of where we were headed. When the coast was clear, we dashed out of the alleyway and over to the car. I pressed the unlock button on the key fob a few times, but nothing happened. I looked at the bumper and saw that it was a Honda HR-V.

"This isn't it," I whispered.

We started running in the direction of the other car. I was mentally crossing my fingers that the other car was the one. I really didn't want to make the trek again. When we found the car, I pressed the key fob button again, and lights blinked on the door handles as they clicked into the unlocked position. We looked at each other, triumphant smiles plastered on our faces. We climbed in, and Ollie leaned over, touched my cheek with his fingers, and kissed me long and hard. If it hadn't been so dangerous, I would've been having a lot of fun just then. I put the key in and turned it. The engine coughed but didn't turn over all the way. Either months of sitting there uselessly had taken their toll on the battery or the flood had damaged the engine. I turned it a few more times, pressing the gas pedal to the floor. Finally, the engine turned over and sputtered to life. The gas gauge moved over to show that we had almost a full tank of gas. I drove the car with the lights off slowly and carefully back to my block. We parked right in front of my building and rushed in. Unless someone was monitoring the cars along my block, we were good.

After dinner, Zeke snuggled between Ollie and me on the couch, pushing his head into my hand and baring his belly for Ollie to scratch. He was getting audacious with his demands, assuming his requests for affection would always be granted. He wasn't wrong though. He looked up at me with heavy-lidded eyes and a pleased grin. Ollie and I were exhausted from the stress of finding the car and decided to wait until the next day to start planning our trip. While we turned in, I kept thinking about our escape. My last thought was a reassuring one. *This might work, and we'll make it to the border because there is no way I've waited all this time to find my partner just to die. I mean, fate somehow delivered a single, attractive, good man literally to my doorstep.* No matter what the circumstance, I had to salute that.

Chapter 28
March 17th

Over the next week, Ollie and I mapped out our route. We decided to go around the areas I'd marked as having been ambushed, which I'd read about back when I had internet. It added another day or so to our journey, but we both thought it was worth it. He agreed that we should try to find abandoned houses to sleep in along the way, and we hoped we could hide the car in garages so no one spotted us. The more we talked about it, the more excited we both got. Zeke was getting excited, too, running around while we planned and constantly bringing his stuffed lamb to each of us to throw for him. I called my mom and told her about the car.

She whooped loudly, causing me to pull the phone away from my ear. "Karis, this is amazing! I'm so glad we waited."

"Me too. Are you okay with vouching for Ollie when we make it to the border?"

"Of course! If he helps get my daughter back to me safely, he can have whatever he wants, including you!" she said with a chuckle.

"Well... Yeah, he's sort of already done that."

"Oh my god, really? This is so exciting!" she yelled.

"Mom, calm down. Don't go planning our wedding or anything. We don't know what this is yet."

"Sorry, but you won't be able to stop me from getting excited."

"Fine. How's Dad doing?"

"Much better. I took him to his checkup yesterday, and the doctor said everything looks good. His tests all came back normal. I got him to take a walk around the block with me this morning. He's still regaining his strength, so that's as far as he could go. But I think he's doing well."

"That's good to hear. When I spoke to him a few days ago, he seemed a little out of it."

"He was still taking painkillers then. He finished the bottle two days ago, so he has no excuse not to get out of the house and get some exercise." She chuckled. "He's doing great. Don't worry."

"We've mapped out a good route, but can you check the weather for these states over the next two weeks to make sure there's no bad weather coming? We'll be going through Pennsylvania, Ohio, Indiana, Michigan, and Illinois, and hopefully landing in Loveland, Iowa," I said.

"Sure, I'll check tonight and call you in the morning. By the way, the water and power are going to be turned off in three weeks. They made an announcement this morning that they aren't extending it. Not that it affects you much."

"Well, it's a good thing we're doing this now. We'll need power to pump gas along the way."

"Oh, I hadn't thought of that." She paused. "I'm excited but also nervous. This is a big chance you two are taking, but I feel better about it with him involved."

"Me too. I think we can do this. Any news on a cure?"

"No. They've been surprisingly quiet on that front. There was a new death count though. It's up to around three hundred fifty thousand."

"Honestly, I think I'm numb to it now. I know it's just going to keep going up."

"Me too. It's too hard to think about."

"I'm almost out of battery power, Mom. There's only two bars left. So I'll talk to you in the morning, but I probably won't call again after that until we leave."

"Okay. It'll be hard, but I understand. I'm so excited you have a man!"

I sighed in exasperation and ended the call.

Ollie and I decided to wait another week after my mom called the next morning with the weather report. There were a couple of storms predicted that were right in our path. We planned to take a northern route, as there had been far fewer ambushes reported along those roads. We knew that didn't mean we wouldn't come across them, but the fewer the better.

We spent a day going through the other apartments, looking for anything useful. Surprisingly, we found a gun in a metal box wedged behind a stack of sweaters high up on a shelf in Kirk's den. It wasn't loaded, but he had bullets in the box as well. The gun looked relatively new, so my guess was that he got it after a break-in he'd suffered about a year before. Kirk was a very mild-mannered guy, so I couldn't think of any other reason why he would have a gun, but it was a great asset to us now. Though I was out of practice, my dad had taught me to shoot cans off of a fencepost when I was younger, and Ollie had spent time hunting, so we at least had a rudimentary knowledge of how to work a gun.

Over the last few days, we made piles of supplies we wanted to bring with us. I used the last of the flour to make a small batch of tortillas. It yielded only five, and we had just one baggie full of acorns left. The pasta and sauce we found at Lori's were almost gone. We would be completely out of food by the time we left, so we were hoping to find some along the way. Ollie mentioned that we could eat Zeke's food if we had to, but I told him I didn't have much of that left either. We were taking all the painkillers and antibiotics I'd found—we didn't know what we might come across, and it was best to have our bases covered.

I went through my clothes and started packing a small bag full of my favorite things. When I packed my underwear, I came across the lace panties. I held them up, contemplating whether or not to throw them in the bag. I was reluctant to let them go—they'd been my crutch for a long time. But I knew that keeping them essentially would mean that I didn't have faith in myself, and that was the last thing I wanted. It was better to pin my hopes on the belief that past this point, I would no longer need them.

Ollie came into the room and gave me a sly smile. "Oh, those are nice. Are you bringing them?"

I shook my head. "No. I don't need them anymore."

I dropped them back in the drawer and turned to see a confused look on his face. I smirked and carried my bag into the dining room.

We went up to the roof with the binoculars. I showed him the cars on the bridge that were blocking the path. "See, that will make it harder. That's why I think we should try the tunnel first."

"That could be blocked with cars too," he said, lowering the binoculars.

"It could. It could also be damaged from the storm. But don't you think we should check it?"

"Yeah, it's a more direct path across Manhattan—if it's passable, that is. If we have to take the bridge, would we go across the city?"

"No, because if the Queens/Midtown tunnel is impassable, the Lincoln or Holland tunnels might not be good options either. I think we should take the FDR up to the George Washington Bridge and cross over to New Jersey that way."

He nodded. "I trust your judgment. You know the city better than I do."

We went back downstairs and looked at the map again, taking notes on alternate routes in case we encountered any obstructions. The night before our departure, we discussed timing. Our plan was to sleep for about four hours then pack the car and leave while it was still dark. We used the last of the battery power to call our parents one last time before going to bed. My mom cried, suddenly hit with the danger of what we were about to do and realizing she wouldn't hear from me until we made it somewhere to charge the phone again. I assured her that we would be very careful, and we had the gun if anything happened. After several rounds of "I love you," we hung up.

Zeke was snuggled in my lap, licking my arm while I stroked his fur with my other hand. I looked at Ollie, nerves bubbling in my stomach. "I'm scared."

"I am too," he replied. "But I'm not as scared as I was the first time I tried. I think we'll be okay. You can do this! You are strong!" he said, letting me know he did see the inspirational Post-It notes.

I felt my face get hot as I punched him in the shoulder and looked away. When I looked back, he was smiling at me, and my heart flipped over. We turned out the light and spent our last night making love and finally drifting off to sleep. At four o'clock, the alarm on my sound machine beeped us awake. After shutting it off, I looked at Ollie.

He appeared deep in thought, rubbing his eyes. "Are you ready for this?"

"Yep, as ready as I can be. Are you?" I felt a mixture of excitement and fear in my stomach.

"I don't know yet. I need coffee."

"You can do this!" I said with a laugh.

Even after coffee and half of our last tortilla, my stomach continued to scream for more food. We took all of our supplies down to the lobby, making several trips up and down the stairs. Back up in my apartment, I took one last look around. I was going to miss the place, and I really hoped someday I would make it back. I harnessed Zeke, and we all walked downstairs. I tied Zeke's leash to the radiator, and Ollie took the lead, poking his head out and looking around for a minute before signaling the coast was clear. As quietly as possible, we loaded the car with our meager supplies. I untethered Zeke, and we rushed into the car. With one last look at my building, Ollie started the car and slowly edged forward. Zeke was on my lap, looking from Ollie to me to outside, unsure of what was happening but clearly aware that it was something big.

We drove with the lights off, making our way down the cross street and onto the entrance ramp. When we got to the entrance of the tunnel, Ollie turned on the lights and crossed the tollbooth, where all the boom barriers were raised except one. At the entrance, the lights illuminated the tunnel about fifty feet in. We stopped and watched. Several cars were parked inside, but they weren't blocking our path. Drops of water dripped ominously from the ceiling of the tunnel.

"What do you think?" Ollie asked, looking at me.

"The water is not a good sign, but let's edge in a little ways and see what it looks like. We can always back out if we need to."

Ollie nodded and pulled his foot off the brake. The car moved forward, and we wound around the few cars still there. I wasn't sure how far we'd gone before Ollie stopped the car.

"Look," he said, pointing ahead.

I squinted until I saw that the road ahead was covered with a few feet of water. This wouldn't work. "Damn. I guess we go back and try the bridges."

Ollie put the car in reverse, and we both looked out the back window. After a minute, Ollie stopped the car. I looked at him, confused. His eyes were wide, and his mouth was slightly open. I looked out the back window and saw the silhouettes of three men standing at the entrance, backlit by the moon. One had long hair and was holding a bat.

"Do you think it's them?" Ollie asked.

I knew he was talking about the men from Lori's building. I shook my head. "I don't know. Just go, fast."

"What if they don't move?" Ollie asked.

I didn't have an answer. I just hoped they would. I looked out the window again. Gradually, Ollie pushed the gas, and the car backed out of the tunnel. I heard the men yelling but couldn't make out what they were saying over the sound of the car. We were only twenty feet from the entrance, but the men weren't moving.

"I think I need to stop!"

"No! They'll move. Just keep going!"

At the last second, the men dove out of the way, and Ollie quickly pulled a U-turn just past the entrance. He hit the gas again. I looked out the back, and the men came into view, waving the bat and screaming at us. My heart was hammering as we retraced our path and headed over to the bridge entrance a few blocks past my apartment. Zeke moved to the back seat, no doubt picking up my nervous energy and finding it unpleasant. We drove around the circular entrance and came upon our first cars. There were only two, and we easily got around them. We made it a third of the way across, reaching the two cars that were obstructing the road. Ollie put the car in park, and we pulled the doctor's masks we'd found in Mr. Tablock's apartment over our faces and slipped on gloves. When we opened the doors, Zeke sat up and whined.

"Stay," I said. "We'll be right back."

We walked over to the first car, a compact Nissan, and looked in. The car was empty. I opened the driver's side door and looked around but found no keys. I got out and shook my head at Ollie. I switched the car into neutral while Ollie positioned himself at the rear bumper, and we both pushed as hard as we could. The car began inching forward. Once we had it out of the way, we walked over to the other car, a large four-door sedan that would be much tougher to push. Ollie looked into the driver's side, and I looked into the passenger side. I screamed and jumped back. On the front passenger seat sat a dead woman, slumped over onto the door. Her head was sideways, resting on her arm. Her cheeks were sunken into her pale face. Her mouth and eyes were partially open, and I could almost hear her last gasp of breath from weeks or months ago. It was a scene straight out of a horror movie. Ollie came to my side and hugged me.

"I don't think we should try this one. It's too dangerous to expose ourselves," he whispered.

I kept staring into the car at her ghost, which refused to leave. "You're right. I don't want to get into that car." I was still breathing rapidly.

"Maybe we can just push the other car to the left instead."

I nodded against his shoulder, and we walked back over to the smaller car. We pushed the car forward as I tried to turn the wheel sharply to the left. Without power steering, I struggled to pull the wheel to the left, grunting with each turn. We managed to force the car to the left and back to the right around another car in the right lane. I kept my eyes averted when we walked past the car with the dead woman on our way back to ours.

We jumped back in, and Ollie pulled around the sedan. We drove the car slowly over the bridge, but no other cars blocked the way. We hung a right once we hit Sixtieth Street and saw the signs for the FDR. I looked into the buildings bordering the street. Some were covered in boards or curtains. Others were clear but with no signs of life. I saw a small boy looking out of one window on the second floor, but he snapped the curtain closed when he saw me watching him.

The city, always full of light and sound and life, was nearly empty, an abandoned shell of its former self. It made me sad to see it reduced like this, so I pulled out memories of me and my friends walking around the streets, laughing over long dinners at some of our favorite restaurants and people watching in the park. Ollie and I pulled onto the FDR and made our way to the upper level of the George Washington Bridge. All the boom barriers were down, blocking the entrance. Ollie revved the engine. The car lunged forward, and my head whipped back against the seat. When we got to the barrier, I closed my eyes and heard the crash as we plowed through the gate. My heart was pounding, but I was a little excited. Part of me had always wanted to do that. I looked at Ollie, smiling.

To my surprise, he was grinning too. "That was fun," he said before looking back to the road.

There were a few cars scattered throughout the bridge, but with the wider four lanes, none were completely blocking the road. I looked out at the water while we drove over, somehow expecting to see boats and barges trudging through. But the water was only marked by waves from the wind. When we were close to the bridge exit, we saw a large dark lump across the roadway.

"What is that?" I asked, squinting.

"I don't know. It looks like... oh my god."

When we got closer, the pile came into focus, and I sucked in a breath. A mound of bodies was strewn across the road as if a mass exodus had happened and they'd all been struck down mid-run. Ollie stopped the car in front of the row of bodies and looked at me.

"We're gonna have to drive over the bodies," he said quietly.

I turned my head, shaking it back and forth. "No, we can't. Ollie, we can't." I was starting to tremble at the thought.

"Karis, we have to. They're blocking the road, and we can't go out and move all of them. This is our only option."

I looked back at all the bodies, which included children, and swallowed a few times. I knew he was right, but man, I didn't want to do it. "Okay," I whispered.

He lifted his foot off the brake, and the car edged forward. I squeezed my eyes shut and put my head down—I couldn't watch. I felt bad that Ollie had to do it on his own, so I reached over and took his hand in mine. He was shaking too. When the tires hit the first body, Ollie had to push the gas to force the wheels up and over. I could have sworn I felt and heard the crunch of bones and the squishing of flesh as we drove over body after body. I kept my eyes shut while tears streamed down my face. I heard Ollie make a few noises low in his throat, and Zeke whined from the back seat.

Once we made it to the other side, Ollie said, "We're past it now. You can open your eyes."

My eyes popped open, and I saw a clear road ahead of us. I let out the breath I'd been holding. "Sorry."

His face was pale, and the look in his eyes was troubled. "It's okay."

The sun was shining brightly as we drove onto the Garden State Parkway. Our final destination was the checkpoint in Loveland, a town in western Iowa, with detours into Illinois and Michigan to avoid possible threats. We had calculated it would take us approximately three days and two nights, including stops to rest. From the Garden State Parkway, we made our way to I-80, which we would take for the majority of our trip. So far, we hadn't seen much evidence of other people, just a few trails of smoke from burning buildings in the distance and only one other car driving in the opposite direction. We were all minding our own business for now, and I was grateful for that.

We were about halfway across Pennsylvania when we stopped at a gas station to see if the pumps were working. Ollie put the nozzle in and squeezed the lever, and we heard the glorious sound of gas flowing into the tank. We looked at each other excitedly.

While Ollie filled the tank, I ran into the small store, clutching the gun. The place had already been ransacked, but I found a candy bar that had fallen behind the empty boxes. I ripped it in two and shoved my half into my mouth. I closed my eyes and groaned. I ate it slowly, savoring the chocolate, caramel, and peanuts. I grabbed an empty gas can from a high shelf then walked back outside. I threw Ollie his half of the candy bar and laughed at his excited yip when he saw what it was. With the binoculars, I staked out the terrain in the distance, looking for anything dangerous. After the tank was full and we'd filled the extra gas can, we hopped back in and continued on. I'd noticed some suspicious movement behind us and didn't want to stick around.

Five minutes after we made it back to the highway, we heard tires squealing and looked in our rearview mirrors. A small red car was back there.

Ollie looked at me. "What should we do?"

"Try to put some distance between us. They may be harmless, but it's better to be safe."

He pushed the gas harder, and the distance grew until we could no longer see the car. We drove for another two hours. I fell asleep, and when I woke up, Ollie had his eyes on the road, and Zeke was sleeping in the back. I yawned and checked the rearview mirror.

"Ollie! That car is back."

He looked into his mirror. "Dammit, I stopped checking a half hour ago. I thought we were in the clear."

"They aren't that far behind us. Speed up!"

We heard their tires squeal as they rounded a bend in the highway. Ollie put his foot on the gas, and I searched the map for some way to escape. We weren't far from Cleveland, but there was a national park coming up that might be a better bet to hide the car.

"In a mile, take Route 8. There's a bunch of roundabouts at the exit, so maybe they won't be able to see where we go. You're gonna get off right after we hit Route 8 on West Boston Mills Road. That'll take us into a park, and maybe we can find somewhere to hide." I looked in the mirror and noted that the distance between us had grown. *We might have a chance.*

Ollie didn't say anything but pushed the gas harder. He was gripping the steering wheel so tightly that his knuckles were white. We approached the exit, and he slowed slightly, but when he entered the roundabout, he accelerated. We flew around the corner and drove about a thousand feet before we entered another roundabout. It spit us out onto Route 8, and I saw the sign for the exit.

"There! Take that exit." I looked behind us and saw the red car entering the first roundabout. "They're following us! Oh my god, Ollie!"

He grunted and slammed on the gas, lurching the car forward. When he exited, there was a big sign pointing in the direction of Cuyahoga Valley National Park. We hit a long stretch, and eventually the red car came into view about half a mile behind. We entered a heavily wooded area then turned down a couple of side roads in hopes of losing our stalker. We found a dirt path, and Ollie turned onto it. The car bounced around on the uneven surface. The sun was bright, but the dense trees made it hard to see without turning on the headlights, which we were reluctant to do.

We came upon a row of houses surrounded by trees. I wasn't even sure if we were still in the park because we'd turned so many times that I couldn't find us on the map anymore. Ollie pulled the car into a space between the trees and turned it off. We sat silently, our hearts hammering in our ears while we looked around and listened for the car. In the distance, we heard an engine, but it could have been anyone. We waited for half an hour before we were certain the car wasn't lying in wait for us to emerge.

Ollie looked at me. "Are you okay?"

"A little freaked out but fine. Are you?"

"Yeah. We should just stay here tonight if one of those houses is empty. It's better if we drive during the day. Our headlights cutting through the dark could draw attention to us, possibly even from miles away if the terrain is flat."

"Good idea. After what just happened, I'm not keen on getting chased again, especially in the dark when we can't see as well."

"I'm gonna look in the front windows. You head around back and look too." We'd found some whistles in Kelly's apartment, so he handed me my whistle and said, "If anything happens, blow on this, and I'll come running. I'll do the same."

I nodded in reply, and we both exited the car, leaving Zeke watching us anxiously from inside. The wind rustling through the trees was so loud that it sounded like a waterfall. I made my way around the back of the houses with the whistle pursed between my lips. I needed to stand on my tiptoes to see into some of the windows. I could barely see into some of the higher ones.

The first house looked as though it'd been ransacked. Furniture was knocked over, and mirrors were smashed. In the kitchen, the cabinets and drawers were all pulled open. Someone had taken all of the supplies. There were no fences separating the houses, making it easy to pass quietly from one to the next. The second house had all of its curtains closed, which made me nervous. I didn't see any movement through the slight part in the drapes, but that didn't mean someone wasn't there.

The third house looked deserted. The rooms were empty, but clothes were strewn about and drawers were pulled open. One room's closet doors were thrown open, revealing only empty hangers. It appeared that the inhabitants had packed up in a hurry. I was on my tiptoes, looking into the kitchen window, when Ollie crept up behind me and put his hand on my shoulder. I jumped and almost screamed before I clamped a hand over my mouth. My heart was racing. He put his arms around me to help calm me down, but I could feel the smirk on his face that was resting on my forehead. I guessed scaring me was funny. *He and my dad will get along just fine.*

After a few seconds, he whispered in my ear, "The houses on the end are all locked, even the garages. But I could see inside most of the windows and didn't see anyone. They all look like they've been cleaned out. Empty cupboards and closets. Did you see anyone inside this one?"

"No, there's no one. Just some discarded clothes. I think this one will work. Look," I said, pointing to a cabinet with its door ajar. We could just make out the edge of a box of crackers.

We tried the back door then went around to try the front. They both were locked.

"I have the crowbar, but I don't want to bust the door. Then we can't lock it again when we sleep. That makes me nervous."

Ollie nodded and motioned to the garage door. A twig snapped somewhere to our left, and we both froze. A minute later, a deer meandered past the row of houses, darting into the woods when it saw us. We both exhaled and walked to the garage. Ollie reached down and turned the handle. The door rose easily. The garage held one car but had space for another. We went back to our car and pulled it in. After Ollie pulled the garage door closed and slid the lock down, we tried the door leading to the house, but it was locked. Ollie fiddled with the lock, hoping to jimmy it open. I grabbed the crowbar, shooed Ollie away and did as my dad had told me. The lock was really old and popped off easily. I looked triumphantly at Ollie, and he grinned back at me.

The three of us cautiously made our way through the house, Ollie leading the way with the gun drawn, me holding Zeke's leash tightly. After checking all the rooms, we felt secure that no one was there. We closed all the curtains and blinds then found candles to light our way. I plugged in my phone, hoping to call my mom once it was charged to let her know we were okay.

Our next order of business was to put fresh sheets on the bed we'd be sleeping in and spray everything with a disinfectant I'd found in a kitchen cabinet. While I was spraying everything, room to room, I noticed the family portraits on the walls. Looked as though the couple had two boys, maybe four and ten years old. In the younger boy's room, I ran my fingers over toy cars, basketballs, and a poster of the solar system. In the older boy's room, there was a photo of him with a blond girl about the same age. They sat next to one another on a low brick wall, laughing and holding a carved, toothy pumpkin. I thought about the girls and felt tears build up behind my eyes, but I pushed them back as I wandered back into the dining room.

I found Ollie passed out on a recliner in the living room and Zeke lying on the carpet nearby. The intensity of what we'd just experienced must have knocked both of them out. I put a load of laundry in the washing machine and took a long, hot shower, reveling in the warm water on my skin. I slipped on clean clothes while I was folding the load. It felt luxurious to have freshly washed clothes. Letting clothes hang dry like I'd been doing for the past three months always left them crisp on the skin. The clothes I put on were soft and warm from the dryer.

I fed Zeke while Ollie woke up then searched the kitchen for our dinner. I heard him let out a "Woohoo!" so I walked over to see what he'd found. His head was buried in the freezer.

"Oh my god, look at all this! I'm in heaven. I love junk food," he said as he pulled out frozen pizzas, burritos, chicken nuggets, tater tots, and potpies. "The freezer is still stocked."

"Ollie, we can't eat all of this tonight," I warned, even though my mouth watered looking at all the food. My stomach grumbled, loudly protesting my words.

He popped his head out and gave me a sour look. "Maybe you can't, but I can. I'm a man, and men eat," he said with a stern look, puffing up his chest and flexing his muscles for effect. "Come on! My mom never let us eat this kind of food, but my friend Leo always had a full pantry. We'd pig out all the time. I felt like I was cheating on my mom, but I didn't care. Please indulge me?"

I laughed because I couldn't resist his boyish happiness. "You're right. Let's eat all of it! Why not? We haven't had any real food in months, so we might as well take advantage of it. And we can take anything we don't finish with us," I said, throwing up my hands.

I unpacked the food and turned on the oven. I searched the fridge for something to drink to accompany all the junk food. After moving around a few condiments, I found something amazing. "Oh my god!"

Ollie heard me, and immediately, his worried face appeared around the corner. "What?"

"Oh nothing, just found something. I'll tell you later," I said with a sly grin.

He looked at me for a second. "What are you up to?"

"Nothing. I promise!"

He moved back into the living room, but I heard him mumbling something under his breath. I was busy heating everything up when I realized Ollie wasn't helping. *Typical guy,* I thought. I walked to the living room to give him a hard time but stopped, stunned by what I saw. He had lit the gas fireplace, laid out a large blanket in front of it, and was busy lighting a collection of mismatched candles all around the blanket. He looked up and smiled.

"What's all this?" I asked.

"I thought we could use a little romance."

I knew there was a huge grin on my face—I wasn't used to that from men. I walked over to him, pulled him into my arms, and gave him a long kiss. "Thank you."

"You're welcome," he said.

In the dining room, I found two beautiful serving platters, probably the couple's wedding china, and piled all the heated food onto them. I found champagne flutes and added them to the tray with everything else. The sight of all the frozen junk food on such nice china was incongruous but seemed appropriate somehow.

When Ollie saw the heaping platters, he pointed to the cans on the tray and asked, "What's that?"

I held up a can, and in my best Vanna White impersonation, I said, "My all-time favorite soda in the world. This is what I found that made me so happy. Whenever I had to go to the dentist, my mom would take me around the corner to a small convenience store afterward. It was the only place we knew of that sold it. She'd buy us two Fanta Red Cream sodas as a reward. Probably not the best thing to have after just having your teeth cleaned, but it's delicious!" I poured the fizzy soda into the champagne flutes slowly.

"Red Cream Soda? So what, it's like cherry or strawberry flavored?" he asked, the skepticism clear on his face.

"That's the best part. It's not either of those. It actually tastes like the color red. I can't explain it. You just have to try it." I handed him a glass and clinked mine with his. "Cheers."

We each took a sip, and I was filled with a longing for my mom and those twice-a-year afternoons, sitting across from each other, savoring the taste and feeling as though we were breaking the rules. I looked over to see his reaction. He seemed to be swishing it around his mouth like wine.

"So?" I asked after he'd swallowed.

"You're right. It tastes like red! It's great. I've never had anything like it."

I grinned back at him.

We picnicked in front of the fire, feeding each other pieces of food here and there. We finished off by sharing a Magnum ice cream bar I found hidden behind a large Tupperware container of what looked like frozen chicken broth. Maybe the mom had been hiding this last solitary bar from the rest of the family for her own personal pleasure. My stomach hurt from eating so much food after months of eating so little, but I couldn't stop. As Ollie was wiping chocolate off my chin, I couldn't help but think back to the picnic I was supposed to have had with Brian. There had always been an element of ambiguity between us that made it feel as if we were out of focus somehow. That relationship never felt right. The one with Ollie did—it was sharp and present.

We stayed up for a while longer, lounging in front of the fire, both overly stuffed from our junk-food binge. I grabbed my phone, which was fully charged, and tried to call my mom. But the call failed.

"Ollie, look, we have no signal." I showed him the phone.

He took a look. "We're in a forest, surrounded by huge trees. Maybe we aren't in an area that gets service? Or the trees are blocking it?"

"Maybe. Hopefully we'll get some bars tomorrow. I just hope the towers are still working without maintenance. I don't want my mom to worry."

Before we went to bed, Ollie peeked out all of the windows, checking everything outside. We managed to sleep deeply and soundly in the unfamiliar environment. In the morning, we ate a quick breakfast and filled a bag with additional supplies we could use from the house. We were anxious to set out and make up lost time from our frantic detour the day before, and we'd slept later than we'd intended. I found Ollie in the garage, plowing through a box of old tools and tarps.

"What are you doing?" I asked.

"We should check to see if there's any gas in this car. We can siphon it if we can find some kind of tubing."

"Good idea," I said, joining the search. I looked in all the rooms, and Ollie finished checking the garage, but we came up empty.

Then he snapped his fingers. "Follow me."

I trailed him back to the kitchen sink, and he pulled out the sprayer to reveal the clear plastic tubing attaching the sprayer to the pipes. We cut it from its attachments and walked back to the garage. When we got to the car, Ollie handed me the tubing.

I looked at him, confused. "Why are you handing it to me?"

"Uh, I don't know. How do you siphon gas out of a tank?"

"Ask it nicely?" I said, stealing my dad's joke.

Ollie chuckled. "Cute. But do you know how to do it?"

"I don't think so," I said. And then I had a thought. "Wait, maybe I do." I told him about growing up in a falling-down house. "Our ancient wall heater broke one winter and had to be removed. So my dad went out and bought heaters for our bedrooms. They required a siphoning pump to get the kerosene into the heater. But one night when it was really cold, the pump got a hole in it and wouldn't work. My dad showed me how to use part of the tubing from the pump to suck the kerosene through and let gravity do the rest. This probably works the same way." I put one end of the tube into the gas tank then handed him the other end.

He looked at it skeptically but reluctantly took it. His masculinity may have taken a hit by not knowing how to siphon when I might.

"I'll keep watching, and once I see gas coming through, I'll say 'stop.' You'll need to pinch the end so you don't get it in your mouth, then quickly put the other end in the gas can and release the pinch. It should just start flowing into the can if there's anything in there."

We'd already emptied the gas can we'd filled in Pennsylvania into our tank and found another empty gas can in the trunk of the car in the garage. We were hoping there would be enough gas to fill both cans. Dubiously, he put the tube in his mouth and started sucking. At first, we saw nothing, so I told him to move closer to the tank—maybe the tube wasn't reaching what was left in there. He moved closer and started sucking again, and after a few seconds, I saw yellowish liquid pulling through the tube. It was about four inches from his mouth when I yelled, "stop!" He quickly pinched the top and pulled the tube from his mouth. He placed the tube into the gas can I was holding, and we heard the gas hitting the bottom of the can.

He wore a big, triumphant smile. "Bloody hell! That worked!"

Zeke came around the front of the car and dropped a bright-blue ball at my feet.

"Where'd you find this?" I asked, picking up the ball.

His nose motioned to the other side of the car.

While Ollie continued to fill the cans, I bounced the ball against the garage door for Zeke to catch. His nails clacked loudly on the cement floor as he repeatedly ran after the ball. After a few minutes, we had filled one gas can, and the smaller one we'd pulled from the trunk was about half full. Ollie placed the cans in the back of the car and slammed the door shut, signaling the end of the ball game. The added gas would certainly be a big help. We felt exultant and ready to set off for the day. I told Zeke he could keep the ball and threw it in the bag with his other toys. After loading up the car, we jumped in and looked at each other. There was fear there but also hope. Ollie smiled at me, and we eased out of the garage.

Chapter 29
March 28th

We hit our first detour five hours later. There had been several ambushes reported along the Michigan/Indiana border, so we drove around that section, going north into Michigan via Route 127 then catching Highway 12 west and back down Interstate 94 to link up with I-80 again. After another five hours of driving, we took a break near the Illinois border to stretch. We found a secluded spot near a bank of trees to sit under and eat our lunch. I kept my binoculars nearby and frequently checked the landscape as we ate. Zeke ran around for a few minutes until I gave him his last Happy Hips chew to gnaw on. We poured the rest of the gas cans into the tank. It was three-quarters full and should take us through the day, but we would need to find another gas station before we set out again the next day.

Back in the car, I kept checking my phone, but I wasn't getting more than one bar. I tried making a call when that solitary bar showed up, but it failed. At one point, two bars appeared, and I quickly called my mom. The phone rang once, then the call dropped. I swore and slapped my hand on the seat in frustration.

We were four miles away from Highway 55, which would take us down to our second detour, when I spotted something in the distance through the binoculars. The landscape was flat, so I could see quite a ways ahead of me. Something sparkled slightly, but it was just one flicker. *How seriously should I take this?* "There's something up ahead. You should pull over."

He looked over at me. "Are you sure?"

"No, I'm not, so we should check it out," I said pointedly.

"You're right," he conceded as he pulled over.

We got out, climbed onto the roof of the car, and lay on our stomachs. I looked through the binoculars for a few seconds, but I didn't see anything. Maybe it was just a hubcap, or maybe I was hallucinating again. Then I saw the same flicker I saw before, a sharp, bright reflection off of something metal. I navigated the binoculars to that section and focused them. It was hard to see, and I couldn't tell how far away it was, but there was definitely something there, lying across the roadway. I handed the binoculars to Ollie.

"You see that big bank of shrubs on the right? Look slightly to the left of those."

After a few seconds, he made a deep noise in his throat. "I see it. It looks like it may be one of those spike strips police use to stop cars during a high-speed chase. Good catch." We climbed down and got back into the car. Ollie pulled out the map and studied it. "Okay, here's something. A mile or two back, there's a route we can take that will link up with 55 about twenty miles down. I think that's our only option without going completely out of our way." He pointed at the route on the map.

I nodded. "Let's do it."

Ollie turned the car around, and we circled back until we found the route marker we hadn't seen when we passed it the first time. It was covered in dried mud, and I got out to scrape it away—whoever was setting up that trap probably covered the sign too. We made a right and headed down into Illinois with me checking the binoculars more diligently than before. Looking through them while moving was making me queasy, but it was important, so I continued, taking gulps of water intermittently. The sky was overcast, and it looked like it might rain. I had the binoculars focused on the upcoming roadway when the first drops hit the roof of the car. It was light at first, but the wind quickly picked up, and the rain pounded the hood of the car so loudly that I couldn't hear Ollie when he yelled to me.

"What?" I hollered over the roar.

"I think we should pull over. The wind is blowing us all over the road."

He was right. I felt the car being pulled around. Then it started hailing like I'd never seen before. I almost expected the windshield to crack. It only lasted a minute before it stopped, and we were left with nothing but a gale force wind. I looked all over to find somewhere we could take shelter, but all I saw were fields. Finally, through the binoculars, I saw an overpass in the distance.

I pointed. "Up ahead, maybe we can take cover in that overpass."

He nodded and pushed the gas pedal to the floor. We approached the overpass, and Ollie pulled the car up right next to the giant cement block in the middle of the road. He turned the car off, and we listened to the disturbing sounds of wind and debris flying around.

"Jesus, what is this?" Ollie said, reaching for my hand.

I could feel him shaking next to me. I was about to reply when a low siren sounded in the distance. "That sounds like a tornado warning. This is tornado country. My mom warned us about this." My heart pounded, and I gripped the door handle so tightly that my fingers ached.

"Are we safe here?" he asked nervously.

"I don't know. I've never been in a tornado. But this seems like our safest option."

A tricycle came barreling along, crashed into the overpass, then cartwheeled past our car. Our front window was covered in leaves and grass, making it harder to see what was going on outside. Ollie turned on the wipers to clear the window. A small car flipped down the road up ahead and then was dragged into a field. Zeke was cowering and whining so I pulled him onto my lap and whispered that we were okay. Our car shook violently a few times, and I squeezed my eyes shut, hoping we weren't about to be lifted from our hiding spot and thrown into the tornado.

About ten minutes later, the commotion died down, and the sirens stopped. We decided to venture outside, and once we opened the door, we were amazed at the scene. The sky was bright blue with hazy red filtering in. There was debris littering the ground everywhere. We cleaned the windows off before hopping in and continuing.

We hit the exchange over to 55 shortly after. We found a few gas stations, but they were all empty. After another two hours of driving, our tank was getting low, and I was starting to worry that we wouldn't find one. All of a sudden, I felt the car slow down.

"Jesus, look at that," Ollie said.

I looked out the front window. A tractor trailer had slammed into an electrical pole, taking it down across the road in both directions and leaving electrical wires dangling all around. The truck's contents had spilled out all over the road. Boxes and packing peanuts were blowing around in the breeze. "Do you think the tornado did that?"

"Probably." I hit the door with my fist. "Dammit! This is just what we need."

"We're gonna have to find another way." He put the car into reverse.

"Can't we just go around it?"

"With those wires, I don't think it's a good idea. Plus, the road drops down into a ditch on the other side of the shoulder. We can't risk the car getting stuck."

We'd had a long day of driving and were exhausted by the past two drama-filled days. I was reluctant to find another detour, especially since the sun was going down, but he was right. While Ollie turned the car around, I checked the map. "If we can find our way to Route 9, we might be able to go around and link back up with I-74."

I instructed Ollie to get off on the next exit and turn left. I followed our progress on the map. It had seemed simple enough. But my map was at least ten years old and didn't show half of the side streets. The street we were on was the only one I could find, but I couldn't tell if we were going north or south. I tried Google Maps on my phone but still didn't have a signal. The tornado could have damaged the cell towers. My phone battery was also dwindling. I told Ollie to turn a few times, but after another half hour, we were completely lost. The sun had set, and I couldn't find us on the map—the surrounding streets were nowhere to be found.

I threw the map down. "Ollie, what are we going to do? We could be in Indiana for all I know."

"Yeah, this isn't good. I don't like that we're driving with the headlights on. Maybe we should find a place to hide and sleep in the car tonight."

I chewed on my lip, not liking that idea, but not disagreeing either. We kept driving slowly, trying to find somewhere to hide. Eventually, we saw a cluster of trees and thought that was the best we were going to find in the dark. Ollie pulled off the road and drove through the rocky field until we were shielded from view. By the time he turned off the car, the dashboard clock said it was eight o'clock. We ate some snacks, fed Zeke, and decided to take shifts so one of us was awake at all times. I took the first shift, too wired with anxiety about sleeping in the car to fall asleep. Ollie climbed into the back seat and huddled under a blanket we'd been wise enough to bring. He balled his coat up for a pillow. Zeke nudged the edge of the quilt I'd draped around my body, and I lifted it, allowing him to climb onto my lap under the blanket.

The wind whistling just outside made sitting in pitch darkness even more creepy. The moon only illuminated vague shapes. At one point, I became convinced that a black blob in the distance was a person coming for us. I watched the shape for a long time before I was able to talk myself into believing it was a bush. Every noise outside made me jump. My cuticles were shredded by the time Ollie took over several hours later. What was left of winter came on full force at night. I shivered under the blanket with Zeke.

In the morning, Ollie woke me up early, just as the sun was rising. After letting Zeke out to go to the bathroom, I hopped into the driver's seat and strapped in. I turned the key, and the engine chugged heavily, struggling to turn over. But it wouldn't start. My heart sank. The gas gauge was past the red line. I kept trying to turn the engine over, but it was no use. There wasn't enough gas, and we'd already used our cans. I slammed my hands against the steering wheel, cursing as tears of frustration slid down my cheeks. Ollie's hands were over his face, and he grunted his own irritation.

"I guess we've got to go on foot and find some gas," he said, looking at our barren surroundings.

"What are the chances we'll find a gas station out here?"

"Not very good. But maybe we can find a car and siphon its gas."

We took the gun, the crowbar, and the tube along with the larger of the two gas cans. I leashed Zeke, and he jumped out of the car. Since I still couldn't find us on the map, we chose a direction to walk after Ollie looked through the binoculars and saw buildings off in the distance.

We alternated between jogging and walking to conserve our energy. We'd both only had bites of a granola bar as breakfast, and I could feel my temples start to throb. I wasn't sure how long we had walked, but I guessed by the sun that it had been around an hour. We came across an industrial building and passed countless silos. We found no cars and, luckily, no other people.

I was just about to give up and suggest we head back when Ollie yelped, "I think I see a parking lot with some cars!" He lowered the binoculars and grinned.

"Let me see!" I grabbed the binoculars from his hands.

After focusing them, I saw a car lot next to a row of buildings. I lowered the binoculars, and we smiled at each other. Bolstered by the possibility, we broke into a run. It was farther than we had thought, and by the time we reached it, we were both out of breath. But our workouts had done their job. My muscles were tingling and energized. There were about twelve cars in the lot, and some of their gas tank doors were already popped open. We tried a few of those first, but they seemed to be empty. Someone else must have had the same idea. We moved on to the other cars, popping the gas tank doors open with the crowbar. After working our way through the remaining cars, we had about two-thirds of the can full.

Ollie leaned over and pulled me into a hug. We resumed our jog back to the car, going a bit slower than before. Zeke was panting heavily, and I didn't want to overwork him. It took longer than expected. The sun was directly overhead when I spotted the car. I escalated into a sprint. Ollie jogged up behind us and began pouring the gas into the tank. I hoped it would be enough.

Back on the road, I checked the map every time we passed a road with a marker. I still couldn't figure out where we were, so I began widening my search on the map. I finally found us when we passed a sign that said we were in a town called Ellsworth. We'd gone in the wrong direction and somehow passed Route 9 in the dark without realizing it. I-74 wasn't far, so we headed in that direction. By the time we hit the junction that would reconnect us to the main highway, the sun had dipped in the sky. It was already four o'clock—we'd lost half a day of driving. We kept going, stopping along the way when we saw an ancient gas station. There was a small amount of gas in the solitary pump. Every little bit would help.

We were almost back up to I-80 and around our last detour when dusk started to creep in. It was straight-up farmland, and the houses were few and far between, so we took a chance and drove up the next long driveway we came to. The house at the end was out in the open with no coverage from the main road, but we didn't know how far it would be to the next one. The house had a garage, and the windows were clear, so we hoped it was empty. I let Zeke come with us as we walked around the house, peering into the windows. The back ones had curtains closed over them.

As we walked back to the front, Ollie said, "What do you think? Should we try it?"

"Sure. Do you have the gun?"

He pulled it out of the back of his pants and clicked off the safety as we came upon a side door. We pulled on our masks and gloves before he put his hand on the knob and looked at me. "On the count of three."

He counted to three and turned the knob. The door opened slowly, and we walked into a small laundry room. There was an odd smell, but Ollie went to the next door and opened it anyway. The minute the door opened, we were assailed by a strong rancid odor. My hands flew up to my face, dropping Zeke's leash as I gagged.

"Oh god," I said. "Close it. We can't go in there."

Ollie started pulling the door shut, but Zeke barked and dashed into the house. "Zeke! Come!" I yelled.

He kept going and didn't acknowledge my command. I rushed past Ollie, but he grabbed my arm. "Karis, you can't go in there!"

"I have to get Zeke! Let me go!" I wrenched my arm free and ran into the house.

"Damn it," Ollie muttered as he followed me.

I called to Zeke, but he didn't come. We walked down a hallway and found four rooms. Two were small bedrooms with the doors open. We peered in and found them empty. The third was an empty bathroom. The fourth door was closed. Ollie pulled out the gun and placed his finger on the trigger.

He turned the knob, and the door creaked open. We moved into the room in tandem and stopped abruptly. My body tensed, and I held my breath. On the king-sized bed were three bodies, a man, a woman, and a teenage boy, lying next to one another. They must have been there for a long time because their skin was gray and sunken, revealing their skeletons. Flies buzzed around them, and the stench was so strong I almost threw up. I ran out of the room, trying to breathe. Ollie followed me, closing the door tightly behind him. I put my hands on my knees and took several deep breaths, trying to slow my heartbeat and not vomit on the floor. Ollie rubbed my back, but I heard him gag too. Once I felt steadier, I walked into the hallway, calling for Zeke. We finally found him in a den on the other side of the living room. He had a small orange tabby cornered behind a desk. The poor thing was scrawny, its ribs fully visible. Zeke whined and pawed at it, making it hiss. I found the end of Zeke's leash and pulled him away while Ollie bent down and picked up the cat.

"Hey there, little fella. You must be hungry," he said, scratching the cat between the ears. It was so starved for attention that it pushed its head farther into Ollie's hand. He squinted at the tag on its collar, which also carried a small bell. "It says 'Lily.' Must be a girl."

"We have to take her with us. We can't leave her here."

Zeke whined and looked at me. He agreed—he'd always wanted a cat.

"Let's see if there's any food," Ollie said, walking back toward the kitchen.

The cat was weak and didn't fight in Ollie's arms. It almost seemed to be in a trance. In the kitchen, we found an empty bag of cat food lying on its side. Lily must have pulled it out of the open cabinet. There were several other empty bags of chips and crackers lying around. We opened the cupboards and eventually found a full bag up high in a cabinet above the microwave. I found Lily's cat dish and empty water bowl next to the side door and took them with us back outside. Ollie set Lily down while I rinsed the dishes out, poured food, then turned on the faucet and filled the water bowl. Lily ate ravenously. I sat on the ground next to her, stroking her bony back until she finished her meal. Ollie went to the garage and brought back a cat carrier he found on a shelf. I picked Lily up and cuddled her next to my chest while she purred. Zeke licked her ears, and she didn't seem to mind that time. Ollie opened the carrier, and we placed Lily inside. She lay down willingly. Zeke jumped into the back seat and lay down next to her.

"Well, Zeke, I think you have a cat."

Over my shoulder, Ollie said, "I think you're right."

We smiled at each other. The little creature had survived months in that house, and even though the three bodies on the bed were horrifying, rescuing Lily was worth it. It also reassured me that I'd made the right decision with Zeke—that could have been him. We hopped back into the car, neither of us discussing what we'd seen. It was too gruesome. We took off our gloves and rubbed hand sanitizer over our arms and faces. We drove back to the main road. The sun was starting to set, and I was anxious to get inside.

We saw several paths up to potential houses but kept going because they were too exposed. We found one farther along that was surrounded by a bank of trees. We parked the car and repeated our routine, peeking into windows and casing the place. It was two stories so we could only check the bottom floor, but it seemed empty. After a thorough check, we decided it was a good place to rest, and Ollie pulled the car into the barn to hide it. After searching the place and finding it empty, we brought Zeke and Lily inside. I set Lily up in a bedroom on the ground floor with food, water, and a makeshift litter box, which I made by shredding some newspaper in a baking dish from the kitchen.

When the sun went down, I flicked the switch for the kitchen light, but nothing happened. I walked around flipping switches until I noticed the clock on the cable box was not lit up.

"Ollie, there's no power."

"Damn. Maybe the tornado took down the nearby power poles."

I was glad that we'd taken extra food from the house in Ohio. We ate a dinner of day-old French fries and pizza rolls then cut the night short and turned in so we could get an early start. We were both quiet that night. The combination of our journey to find gas, the dead bodies, and the tornado was taking a toll on us. After checking on Lily, we went upstairs. The stairwell was filled with family photos spanning many years with one photo at the top of an older couple surrounded by generations of kids. It must have been their home. The minute we lay down on the squeaky old bed, Ollie reached for me, and we made love, taking comfort in each other. It almost erased what we'd been through and the potential danger that lay ahead.

A few hours later, we were awakened by Zeke's low growl.

I sat up, immediately alert. "What is it, buddy?"

He stared at me, then at Ollie, then back at me. His eyes darted outside, and his eyebrows came together pointedly, telling me he'd heard something suspicious.

I looked at Ollie. "We should look outside and see if anything's there." We both got out of bed and crept over to the windows, peering out. I didn't see anything. *Maybe it was the wind?* I looked back at Zeke, who was staring at me intently, and it almost looked as though he was shaking his head. He thought I was wrong—it wasn't the wind. I believed him but didn't know what to do. We went around the house, peeking out all the windows, surveying our surroundings, and checking all the doors and windows. We found nothing.

I glanced back at Zeke. "Sorry, buddy. I'm sure you're right, but we don't see anything out there."

He looked at me for a second longer then turned in a huff and walked back to the room, where he cuddled up on a rug. We all went back to sleep, but my uneasiness didn't go away.

In the morning, I awoke to find myself alone. Maybe Ollie was putting together some kind of breakfast for me, I thought happily. I slowly rose and went to the bathroom before heading downstairs. The weather was nice—it looked like a good day for driving, and I hoped we would make it to the checkpoint before nightfall. Halfway down the stairs, the dining room came into view, and fear slid up my spine. I froze on the bottom step, not sure what I was seeing. Ollie was tied to a chair, his mouth taped shut. His eyes bored into mine, frantically trying to warn me. I could faintly hear Zeke barking somewhere in the distance. He must have been in one of the back rooms. I hoped he was okay. I must have been in shock because everything was moving in slow motion, and my limbs suddenly seemed confused and unsure.

In a matter of seconds, I was seized from the front by huge arms that pinned mine to my body. The force of the ambush threw me into the stairwell wall. The side of my face slammed into it, and my cheek exploded with pain. The man steadied me and pulled me up straight, laughing viciously at my pained face. He was about a foot taller than me, but I was still standing on the last step so I was almost nose-to-nose with him. He smelled of dirt and sweat. His face was filthy, and his rancid breath was making my stomach turn. Ollie was trying to scream through the tape and banging the chair around to get free. The man smiled at me. He was missing a few teeth, and the ones that remained were yellow. I was sure he could feel me shaking.

"Well, aren't you a pretty one," he said with a sneer. "I'm sorry to do this to you, darlin', but I need a car. And it just so happens you two have one out there in that barn. I just need you to tell me where the keys are."

"How did you know we were here?" I asked through clenched teeth.

"I didn't at first. I was planning on sleeping in that barn for the night when I saw the car. So I staked out the place and saw you two. I wasn't expecting a sexy little thing like you. Maybe we'll have some fun of our own later. I don't want to hurt you, but I will. Now don't make me ask you again. Where are the keys, sweetheart?"

I looked over at Ollie, my eyes wide with fear. I didn't know what to do.

"Don't look at him. Look at me. I'm the one you need to deal with now."

My eyes snapped back to the man, and I was face-to-face with his nose again. Instantly, I was assailed by a vivid memory. I heard the voice of my college soccer coach, a ruthless drill sergeant who didn't believe in "can't," as though it was happening in that moment. When she'd learned of my fear of head balls, she was determined to fix it. Every day after practice, we sat across from one another with our legs bent, feet to feet.

"Karis, this part of your head is the thickest part of your skull," she said, placing her fingers on my forehead about an inch above my eyebrows, running them up to my hairline then knocking the area with her knuckles. "See? You can hit many things as hard as you want with this area, and you'll be fine. I've broken a man's nose by headbutting him, and you're scared of a little soccer ball?"

She'd made me feel so stupid about my fear that I was willing to try anything. She pulled the ball up and slammed it into my forehead. I had braced my neck, but my head still snapped back painfully.

She sighed. "You aren't doing it right. You can't just tense your neck—you have to tense your shoulders and arms too. You need to meet this ball with your entire upper body. Can you do that?"

"Yes," I'd said resolutely, refusing to let her down. I tensed my entire body just in case. She slammed the ball into my forehead, and I barely moved. She looked at me with a big grin. My breathing quickened, and a huge smile lit up my face. It had worked—I'd hit a head ball.

"There you go! Now we just have to do that fifty more times."

I was brought back to the present by the man yelling at me to tell him where the keys were, his spit spraying all over my face. I flinched and pulled my face back from his. Anger began slithering through my limbs. My body was poised for a fight, every muscle tightening and jumping to attention, my hands clenching into hard fists. But that was just half of me. The other half was still scared shitless. Unfortunately, I didn't have the luxury of fear. I had no choice. I had to fight.

"You spit on all women like that?" I asked in a low, hard voice I didn't recognize.

He sneered. "You got a smart mouth, you know that?"

"Yep. Wanna see what the rest of me can do?" I replied with a calmness I didn't feel.

His eyebrows came together, and his eyes narrowed. He glanced down to check that my arms were still confined by his. I pulled my head back as far as it would go and slammed it into the man's nose as hard as I could. I heard a crack, and his arms immediately released me. I saw stars and stumbled back a little before my vision cleared. He was screaming and grabbing at his nose, and then I saw his orange wristband. *Oh, thank god!* I looked over at Ollie, and he jerked his head toward the floor off to the side. I saw the edge of his bag lying behind another chair. Finding the gun inside, I pointed it at the man, who was still screaming in pain.

"Stay where you are. Don't move!" I yelled, the gun shaking violently in my hand.

With my other trembling hand, I reached for a pair of scissors from a nearby utensil caddy then worked on the twine the man had used to tie Ollie up. After a few tries, I managed to break through the ties holding his hands together. He pulled the tape off his mouth, took the scissors from my hands, and cut himself completely free of the chair. He jumped up, and without a word, he yanked the man into the chair and tied him to it. The man was moaning about how much pain he was in and how we couldn't leave him there tied up. His nose was already starting to swell and turn purple. Blood flowed out of his nostrils. *I really got him good!* Once he was tied up, I found Zeke in a laundry room near the back of the house. He darted out and ran up to the bound man, barking furiously. I guess he had a few words for the guy.

We gathered our things as quickly as possible. I just wanted to get the hell out of there. We packed the car and grabbed some granola bars in lieu of breakfast.

Then I asked, "What do we do about him? We can't leave him here like this. He's right. He'll die."

"I honestly don't care. He hurt you!" he replied, sounding angry.

"Ollie, come on. We aren't killers. We can't leave him tied up," I said, imploring him to remember his humanity.

Ollie sighed, rubbed his forehead, then looked back at me. "We'll untie his hands and keep the gun on him. That's all we can do. Don't ask me to let him go after what he did."

"That's fair. I'll go get Zeke and Lily into the car and pull it around. When I honk, the car will be right outside, ready to go."

"Okay, I'll wait for the honk." He leaned over and kissed me quickly, his left hand gently touching the place where my cheek had hit the wall. He seemed reluctant to let go. I gave him a smile and then pulled away.

I pointed the gun at the man while Ollie walked over and cut his hands free.

The man's hands immediately went to his nose. "Ah god, you crazy bitch! I wasn't going to hurt you! I just wanted your car! You're gonna pay for this. I'll break more than just your nose."

He continued to curse me, but I handed the gun to Ollie. I opened the door to the room where Lily was and found her waiting for me expectantly. She seemed much more alert, meowing loudly before I picked her up. I set her up in her carrier on the back seat again, steered Zeke to the back, and jumped into the driver's seat. I eased the car out of the barn and pulled up right outside the front door. I honked twice. A few seconds later, Ollie ran out of the house and jumped into the passenger side. I hit the gas and took off before he even had his door closed. My heart was pounding, and I was shaking with adrenaline.

"Are you all right?" he asked, obviously worried. "Your cheek is going to bruise. It's already getting puffy."

Quickly, I checked my face in the rearview mirror and saw the red swollen patch below and just to the right of my eye. I touched it gently, and it immediately stung.

"Yeah, I figured. I'm fine. I saw stars when I hit him, but my head feels okay, I think." I rubbed my forehead to check. "It's a little sore. Are you okay?"

"I'm fine. He came at me from behind when I came out of the stairway. He pinned me down, but I almost had him. I was so close to the bag with the gun when he pulled a knife out and put it to my throat. He kept saying that if I didn't keep quiet, he was going to go upstairs and cut you in two, so I did what he said." He looked at me, a cloud darkening his features. "He'd just finished tying me up when we heard the bedroom door open upstairs."

I felt nauseated at the thought of a knife on Ollie's throat. I quickly pulled over, opened the door, and threw up all over the road. After a few more heaves, my stomach was empty. I didn't even notice him rubbing my back. I shot him a glance over my shoulder and thanked him. He handed me a bottle of water, and I rinsed my mouth before taking a huge gulp.

Ollie's eyebrows came together. "Are you sure you're all right? You could have a concussion."

"My head feels fine. Must be the adrenaline or something. I felt sick the minute he grabbed me. I almost threw up all over him. Maybe I should have," I said with a short laugh.

The worry eased off his face. "That was a pretty badass head-butt." He raised one eyebrow and gave me an impressed smirk.

I grinned back at him. "My soccer training came in handy."

"It was probably him that Zeke heard last night," he said, looking over at my dog. I could see Zeke in the rearview mirror. He looked at Ollie, and if ever a dog could say "I told you so" with a look, that dog could.

"Do you mind driving? I need to get my nerves under control," I said.

"Sure, slide over. I'll go around."

After several minutes, I felt better. I resumed my binocular danger watch, inviting Zeke onto my lap. I leaned into his furry neck and whispered, "Good job, buddy." He licked my face in return. I looked at the map to check our progress. I thought we were near a town called Wenona and should only have about five and a half hours of driving left at most. I glanced at the fuel level. We were close to empty again.

"We should keep an eye out for gas stations and cars. There's not much left, but I think we'll be near the checkpoint before sundown." I looked at him and smiled at this happy thought.

We continued on until I spotted a store not too far away with a car parked in front. "What do you think? It's just one car, and it could belong to someone still in the store."

Ollie glanced at the fuel gauge. "I think we need to risk it. Everything is so spaced out here. Who knows when we'll find a gas station or another car?"

"Okay, but we should go in from the side," I replied, looking through the binoculars. "The front has huge windows, but the side of the building has none. Can't see the back from here."

When we approached, we veered off into the field of grass next to the store and eased up to the side of the small structure. Ollie parked the car right up against the building. Tall corn fields bordered the rear of the store. We left Zeke and Lily in the car, got out, and made our way around to the back. Narrow floor-to-ceiling windows spanned every few feet. I stayed at the edge while Ollie sidled up to the first window and peeked inside. Over his shoulder, he gave me a thumbs-up. He rushed to the spot between the next two windows. As I was about to cross the first window, I saw a hand reaching to grab something off a shelf inside the store through the second window.

"Ollie!" I whispered as loudly as I could. He must have seen it, too, because he flattened his body against the wall between the two windows. The figure was moving closer to the window closest to me, but he had his back to me. I took the opportunity and dove to the ground in between two rows of corn. Wedging myself between the stalks, I pushed up to my elbows and looked at the windows. A man holding a shotgun was peering out of the window right next to Ollie. *Oh my god, did he see me?* If the window hadn't been separating them, the gun would have been right next to Ollie's temple. My heart raced.

The man scanned the area before moving on to the front of the store. I motioned to Ollie that the coast was clear. We both sprinted to the car and jumped in. We were on a slight incline, so Ollie released the parking brake and put the car in neutral. Slowly, it moved forward, and we silently made our way back the way we had come through the grass. When we made it to the road, Ollie started the car, and we took off.

"That was close," I said.

Ollie grabbed my hand in his and kissed it to reassure me, but I could feel his hand shaking. We kept driving until we finally saw a gas station in a small town called Ogelsby. The gas needle was rapidly nearing the red line. We parked in back and crept around the front of the small convenience store. It had big windows in the front but none anywhere else. The store appeared to be empty.

"I'm gonna go see if there's a restroom," I whispered.

"Wait. I'll come with you."

Ollie tucked the gun into his waistband then walked the short distance to the store with me. The front door was shattered, and I walked through the open frame carefully. Glass crunched under my feet as I made my way to the back of the shop. At the last aisle as I was about to reach the open bathroom door, I glanced down the row and screamed. Ollie came running, the gun drawn. He followed my eyes and gasped. A man with a shotgun in his hands was lying on the floor, one leg propped up on a shelf at a sharp angle, the other splayed out before him. He wasn't moving, but his dark eyes were open. We walked slowly toward him.

"He's dead. Look at his forehead," Ollie said.

There was a gaping hole in his forehead, and dark-red blood was dried around it and splattered on his face. His vacant eyes watched us, and I half expected him to say something. He had an orange wristband. I closed my eyes.

"I'm gonna go use the bathroom," I said, turning away from the horrific scene.

I wandered over to the bathroom and tried closing the door. But the lock was busted, so I squatted and peed with the door open. The dirty mirror across from the toilet had a message in dark red—I really hoped it was lipstick—that read "Welcome to Hell." I shuddered and finished as quickly as possible. Ollie was outside the bathroom, waiting for me, his eyes still scanning the area around the entrance.

"Keep an eye on the front," he said before walking into the bathroom.

I waited until he was done. We walked around the store, searching for anything of value. I found two cans of cat food and slipped them in my pocket for Lily. The shelves were sparse, but I grabbed a box of Ritz crackers and a jar of peanut butter. The next aisle had some toys and dolls on the shelves. I took a stuffed cow for Zeke. As I walked to the refrigerators in the back, I spotted a pink rhinestone-encrusted plastic tiara. A jumble of emotions rushed up from my chest. *It looks so much like Emma's.* I picked it up as tears ran down my face. I rubbed the tiny crystals with my thumbs, conjuring images of her dancing around in all her costumes. Ollie found me hunched over the shelf, trying to stop the flood of tears.

"Hey, are you okay? What is it?"

I held the tiara out to him. "Emma had one just like this."

He drew me close and let me cry for a minute.

I pulled back and wiped my eyes. "I'm okay now."

He put his arm around me and squeezed. We walked to the refrigerated case, and I grabbed a few warm bottles of water.

I heard Ollie say, "You've got to be kidding me!"

I pulled my head out of the refrigerator and looked at him. He was holding up a bottle of beer. "They have Boddingtons! I haven't had it in months."

He pulled a six-pack out, unable to keep the grin off his face. We went back to the car, and I opened a can of food for Lily. She gobbled it up quickly then spent several minutes cleaning her face and paws. We drove around and tried a few of the pumps, but the levers clicked up and down with no resistance. The fourth had some gas. We were both relieved to hear it flowing into our deprived tank, but it puttered out after only a minute. Ollie squeezed it over and over, trying to force out every last drop. We were able to get a bit more out of the last two, but that only yielded three-quarters of a tank.

I checked the map. "I think we're only about four hundred miles from Loveland. It'll be close, but maybe we can make it."

"We'll keep looking for stations."

After tossing the drinks into the back, we hopped in and drove for two more hours before passing a state park and approaching a bridge spanning a river. The scenery was beautiful and made me nostalgic for the camping trips my dad and I used to take. Zeke was sitting on my lap, the wind flowing through his fur. He looked at me, and I could tell he was happy.

Just as we exited the bridge, the car lurched, and Ollie had to struggle to maintain control. The tires squealed loudly. Zeke and I were thrown against the door. I used my body to shield him and ended up cracking my head on the window. Pain erupted from my temple. The car continued to swerve for several more seconds before it stopped in the dirt just off the road.

"Holy crap, what was that!" Ollie yelled.

I tried to catch my breath. "I have no idea, but it doesn't seem good."

We opened our doors and walked around the car. On the passenger front side, our tire was flat, and we found a large puncture. Ollie smacked the car and cursed. When he looked at me, he frowned and touched my forehead.

"Are you all right? Looks like you're gonna have another knot there."

"I'm okay. It's just a bump."

"We need to change the tire, but I don't like the idea of doing that out in the open like this."

"We'll just have to work fast. There's no other option."

Ollie cranked the car up on the jack. A few of the nuts were practically stuck, and it took both of our strength and the better part of an hour to get the tire off. We took turns scouting the area. Luckily, the spare was in good shape. When we were done, we stood back and admired our work.

"I've never changed a tire before. I'm kind of proud of us," I said.

"I never have either." Ollie smirked and patted his own back.

We got back on the road and quickly approached the I-80 junction. We were back on track. I kept checking the binoculars, but nothing jumped out at me. We were anxious to get to the checkpoint before the sun went down, so we didn't stop for lunch. Instead, I made peanut-butter sandwiches and fed Ollie bits of sandwich and Ritz crackers as he drove. At the last bite, he licked my fingers to get all the crumbs and peanut butter off, or so he said, but I felt it all the way to the tips of my toes. When he was done, he smiled at me mischievously. I smacked him on the arm in mock indignation.

About an hour later, we crossed another bridge that took us over the Mississippi River and into Iowa. We were in the home stretch, and I was actually enjoying the last leg of our journey. On every side were gorgeous landscapes and blue skies with fluffy white clouds. A half hour later, we saw a blue van driving in the opposite direction. We waited anxiously for them to turn around and chase us as the red Honda had, but they continued on, and we breathed a sigh of relief. We didn't need more drama.

The interstate took us through a small suburban area, and we passed a long stretch of houses that were burned to the ground. I watched, my mouth agape, as row after row of singed ruins flew by my window. It went on for about a mile, the wreckage of people's lives reduced to nothing but dust. The jagged, irregular forms of the houses reminded me of the erratic New York City skyline instead of a suburban housing development. The burned area finally ended, and we looked at each other, unable to put words to what we were feeling. A few miles past the skeletal graveyard of homes, we stopped at some more gas stations, but they were all empty. We weren't far from the checkpoint, but the gas needle was rapidly approaching the red zone.

I checked the map. "We should start seeing something within the next half hour. Do you think we have enough gas?"

He glanced at the gauge. "I don't know. We're pushing it. I guess we just have to keep going and see what happens. We'll walk the last few miles if we have to."

My stomach was a mass of nerves and excitement. Zeke must have felt our eagerness because he sat up and was watching the scenery go by, shuffling his feet on my thighs. I pulled out the binoculars and searched north to south. I didn't see anything, and it felt like we should've already been there. *Did they take down the checkpoint? Could we not cross here anymore?* I looked at the gauge—it was rooted heavily in red. We were running on fumes. I-80 turned into I-680, which would take us directly into Loveland and to the checkpoint, I hoped. As we rounded a corner on the route and approached the deserted town of Loveland, we saw it. It had been hidden by a line of low, tree-covered hills. A seemingly endless, heavily reinforced metal fence spanned up and down in both directions. As we got closer, military trucks and men with guns lining the checkpoint came into focus. The setting sun stretched their shadows along the ground ominously.

I pulled down the binoculars and looked at Ollie. "This is it."

"This is it," he repeated.

Chapter 30
March 30th

When we were about a hundred feet in front of the fence, the men trained their guns on us, and a man with a megaphone told us to stop and exit the vehicle. They were all wearing full military gear and masks. Ollie stopped the car and pulled the brake. Zeke looked at me and whined. We took one last look at one another and exited the car. The man with the megaphone put on his HAZMAT mask and walked toward us, another man trailing behind with his gun drawn. I thought about the posts I'd read about people being shot by the military, and I started to shake. We both stopped, and Ollie grabbed my hand. When they reached us, the man with the gun kept it pointed at us, which made me even more nervous. The other man pulled out an electronic device. He walked toward us and asked to see our wristbands. Ollie dropped my hand, and we both stretched our arms out toward the man.

He scanned our wristbands, and they both got a loud beep. He took a long look at us. "I'm Sergeant McClellan. Where did you folks come from? We haven't had any survivors in over a week," he said in a Southern accent.

Ollie spoke up. "We came from New York City. We've been driving for four days."

"You sure are lucky to have made it here," he said. "Go ahead and grab anything you need from the car. This is the last you'll be seeing of it for the time being."

The tension slid off my body when I sensed we would be welcomed. We grabbed our bags and Zeke's food then pulled Lily's carrier out of the back. We walked back over to Sergeant McClellan, and he led us to the fence. We were ushered through and greeted on the other side by a man in a CDC suit and mask. He led us to a series of tents.

He walked to one and pulled the curtain back. "A doctor will be along shortly to take your blood samples. Do you need anything? Food or water?"

We both shook our heads. "We're okay, but thanks," I replied.

He nodded and walked out.

A few minutes later, a CDC doctor with long red hair and kind eyes came in to take our blood. "Hi. I'm Dr. Cross, but you can call me Debbie. What are your full names?" she asked as she wrote on a blue pad.

"I'm Oliver Wakelin. This is Karis Hylen, our cat, Lily, and our dog, Zeke." Zeke and I both looked at him at "our dog." He looked sheepish. "Sorry."

I smiled at him. "It's okay."

"This test will take longer than before because we've learned more about the virus in the past month. We'll need to check more extensively," Debbie told us.

She pulled out her supplies, took two vials of blood from each of us, then left with a wave of her hand. Lily was meowing in protest at being left in the carrier, but we had to keep her there. We lay down on a cot in the room and fell asleep. An hour later, three doctors with masks on woke us up, asking us to get up.

As we rose off the cot, Ollie asked, "What's wrong?"

One of them answered, "There are abnormalities in Ms. Hylen's blood work, and we need to take her for further testing."

"What? Wait, that can't be right. I was already tested, and I haven't been exposed," I said. Then my mind flashed to Charlie and the house with the dead bodies. My limbs began to shake, and I swallowed a few times. Panic crept in. Maybe, like Henry's wife, I was infected but not showing any signs yet.

Ollie reached for my hand, but one of the other doctors stopped him. "Sir, we'll need you to step back and let us do our jobs."

"Can I go with her? Look at her. She's scared! If she's infected, so am I."

I was crying, worried that I'd been infected and had gotten Ollie sick too.

"Sir, your test came back negative. I'm sorry, but we can't allow more people into the facility than is necessary. You'll have to stay here. It shouldn't take long. We'll have her back soon."

They flanked me, each taking an arm as they led me away. I looked back at him, fear snaking up from my gut. "Oh my god, Ollie!"

Zeke was barking at the doctors and lunging for me, but Ollie had him on his leash. His eyes were narrowed in anger. He looked so helpless that it broke my heart. We walked for a few minutes before I was led to a low, wide building encased in a white tent. Inside, there were machines with tubes making electronic beeping noises, refrigerators, and hospital beds. *What have they been doing in here?* My fears were escalating rapidly, and I could hear my heartbeat hammering erratically in my ears. They took more blood and hooked me up to an EKG. Another woman took my temperature, recording ninety-nine-point-five. *This isn't good. Could I really have been infected?* I started to feel clammy and hot. My altercation with Charlie happened over a month before. *Can it take that long to show up? Could it have been inside me all along, lying dormant, waiting for the opportunity to attack? Had it finally made its way to the sur- face now to ravage my body? But if that's true, why isn't Ollie sick?* I was worried about Zeke too. I knew he was upset about seeing me being led away. Ollie would try to calm him down, but there was no one to calm me down.

Next, they placed a swab in my mouth to take a DNA sample. I asked the woman what they found, but she said they weren't sure yet. They needed to see the results of everything they were doing before they could determine what was going on. I was asked to breathe into a device as hard as I could. Then they checked all my vitals, including my reflexes, which seemed to be in good shape. Lastly, they asked me to provide a urine sample, and I trudged to the bathroom. Inside, I was shaking, my mind spinning out the worst possible outcome. While I washed my hands, I noticed the poster on the bathroom wall. This building must have been a gym because the sign had a fit woman running on a treadmill, a delight- ed smile on her face as she looked out a window. The tagline read "Every day is full of new possibilities. Find yours!" Despite my anx- iety, I had to laugh—*what a way to bookend this crazy experience.* I emerged to find Debbie standing outside the bathroom. She smiled at me, probably trying to ease my concern.

"Thanks," she said as I handed her the sample. "Sorry about all this. We just don't know what's going on with your blood work."

"What did they find that's confusing?"

She looked around and then leaned in toward me. Her voice lowered, she said, "You have a slightly elevated temperature, which isn't too troubling as many things could cause that. But you also have highly elevated levels of a hormone called HCG that we've found elevated in people testing positive for the virus. However, you don't seem to have any of the other elevated levels that they had. We want to check every possibility for the elevated hormone, so we can't clear you just yet. Between you and me, I don't think you have it. But your abnormalities are causing quite a stir in here. We haven't seen anything like this since we set up camp here, so everyone is being cautious about it."

"Thanks for telling me. No one would tell me anything." I felt a little better.

She put her gloved hand on my arm. "Look, I know this is scary, and I'm sorry it's all so hush-hush—this is just how the CDC operates. Information is always confidential until we know it's innocuous," she said with a wink. "I'll take you back to your tent now."

"Thanks."

We walked together back to the tent, and Ollie and Zeke ran toward me. Zeke jumped all over me while Ollie pulled me into a hug. We sat down on the cot, and Ollie wanted to know everything. I told him what they did to me and what Debbie had said.

"Hmm, that's weird," he said. His brows were furrowed, and he looked as worried as I felt.

"Tell me about it. I don't know what to think. It's just scary."

"I know," he said, putting his arm around me. "If you have it, then I'm sure the test is wrong, and I have it too. So we're in it together, okay?"

I felt a rush of love fill my heart as I smiled at him. "Okay."

Zeke was in my lap, licking my face, happy to have me back. Ollie told me Lily had finally calmed down and had been sleeping for the past half hour. We waited in the tent for another hour, and they brought us sandwiches, chips, and water. I fed Lily more canned food and gave her some water. While I poured kibble into a paper bowl for Zeke, Debbie came in with another CDC doctor. She was smiling—*that's a good sign, right?* I also noticed they weren't wearing their masks anymore. I started to get excited but tried to tamp it down. Something wasn't right. *I shouldn't get ahead of myself. That was the most thorough physical I've ever had, and they could have found something else.* Ollie and I sat down, and the doctors perched on chairs opposite the cot.

The male doctor spoke first. "I'm Dr. Gonderman. We know you're worried, so we came as soon as possible to discuss your test results with you."

"Am I sick?" I asked anxiously.

Dr. Gonderman smiled. "No, you aren't."

Ollie and I both sighed in relief. "So what's going on, then? Why are my results abnormal?"

"Well, we were really concerned when we saw an elevated hormone level. From what we've learned in the past month, that's a good indicator of this virus. But the rest of your results came back negative, which was confusing."

I guess Debbie hadn't let on that she'd already told me. I looked at her.

She smiled and looked away.

"So we've run more tests and checked everything we could to be certain that you aren't infected, and in the process, we found something else."

Oh god, do I have cancer? Meningitis? Or maybe something no one's ever heard of before? Am I creating a new disease here? He was taking his time, so finally I asked, "What is it? Just tell me."

He smiled. "You're pregnant."

Wait, what? Did I hear that right? It's been less than a month since Ollie and I started having sex. Can that be right? I was thirty-eight years old, and I knew it wasn't impossible, but it wasn't that easy at my age either.

I looked at Ollie, who was stunned. We were both in a state of shock. Dumbfounded, we looked back at the doctor, hoping he could give us all the answers.

"About two to three weeks, I'd say," Dr. Gonderman said. They both stood. "We'll give you two a few minutes to digest this."

We watched them leave then turned to one another. I laughed nervously. "Oh my god. I can't believe this."

"Yeah, I mean I guess it's possible. We haven't used any protection."

I was trying to gauge his feelings, but his face showed only shock, revealing nothing about how he really felt. I couldn't tell if it was good or bad news for him. Even if Ollie and I didn't work out, for me, it was an incredible gift, something I had ruled out at that point in my life.

I knew I would be crushed if it wasn't the same for him, but I would understand. I was just some woman he'd met a month before, who had gone through a horrible situation with him. I wasn't spectacular in any way except for the circumstances I'd found myself in and how I'd responded. But then I realized that it did make me kind of remarkable, and so did a lot of other things.

He laughed, and I looked over at him. He had a huge smile on his face. "I don't know what to say. But this is good, right?" He fidgeted nervously.

It hit me that he was just as worried about my reaction as I was about his. I smiled. "Yes, this is very good. But at some point, we should probably go on a real date."

He laughed and pulled me into a hug, squeezing me tightly. "At least one, I'd say."

Tears were sliding down my face, but for once, they signified happiness instead of pain. We were excitedly discussing what to do next and how our parents would feel when the curtain parted and the two doctors walked back in. They could see our excitement and smiled.

"Congratulations!" Debbie said.

"Thanks!" we replied in unison.

Dr. Gonderman continued, "Now that that's out of the way, we wanted to tell you that because of your test results and your pregnancy, you're providing us with more clues about the virus. Over the last month, our research uncovered what a large role hormones play in the infection. We then concentrated on that angle but still hadn't focused primarily on HCG.

"It's a hormone that's produced by cells that form the placenta, but everyone has it in their body naturally, men and women alike. There are many reasons for high or low levels, but when you're pregnant, your HCG level doubles every forty-eight to seventy-two hours. The same levels are found in infected patients who are not pregnant. Other hormones become elevated as well as a result of the virus progressing, which is why we didn't single it out as a particularly impressive clue. But HCG is the first that elevates, which is interesting. Considering that, it seems likely that it's related to what we've found in your test results."

I nodded.

"You are the only person we've tested this extensively who has an elevated HCG level but isn't infected. Our theory at this point is that the virus somehow takes on the same characteristics of a placenta, continuously feeding the body the virus, which results in the elevated levels we're seeing and making it almost impossible to treat. This is actually a big breakthrough for us. Your coming here has helped us immensely in our understanding of how the virus works. And in turn, that may help us find a cure or vaccine."

"Really? That's amazing. I'm glad we braved the trip, then!" I laughed.

The doctors smiled. "We are too," Debbie said. "I'm sure you're both tired. Would you like to call someone? We can start setting up the verification-of-host process so you can go home."

"Yes, that'd be great. Thanks."

"Someone will be in shortly to escort you to our offices."

They both left, and Ollie and I looked at each other. I couldn't believe what we'd just heard. My mind was still swirling around the pregnancy and the incredible news that we might have inadvertently helped find a cure. I felt giddy.

A man with a clipboard came in and escorted us to the main office, which happened to be a hijacked post office. We filled out some paperwork with all of our information, including our host contacts. He then sat down with us to go over everything and call my family.

"May I please speak with Marin or Randy Hylen? Yes, ma'am, I'm with the CDC, and I have your daughter here with me."

I heard my mom's excited hoots through the phone. The poor man was trying to get a word in, but she could really talk when she got excited.

"Ma'am, I just need to verify that you are willing to host both her and Oliver Wakelin at the address of 2103 Honey Lane and that you are the homeowner." He paused. "Thank you very much. I'll pass you to your daughter now."

He handed me the phone. "Mom, I'm okay. We're both okay. We made it! Zeke made it too! And we have a cat!"

"Oh my god, Karis, I'm so happy right now. You're safe! My baby is safe! When can you come home?" I could tell she was crying, and I heard my dad in the background asking questions.

"I don't know yet. I think they're going to start arranging that now. But most likely not until tomorrow. We'll probably have to stay here tonight."

"I can't wait to see you and meet this handsome man of yours!"

"He can't wait to meet you too," I said, looking over at Ollie as he laughed. "I want to give Ollie a chance to call his parents and let them know he's safe. I'll call you once we know what the plan is."

"Get a good night's sleep. I love you!"

"Love you too!"

I handed Ollie the phone and listened to him tell his parents we'd made it safely and would call them when he knew what our plans were.

In some unspoken promise, we'd both decided not to tell our parents about the pregnancy. It was too new, and I, for one, wanted the two of us to relish it for a bit before we spread the good news around. It was pitch black outside, and we were both tired. The man with the clipboard came back and told us they had a room for us at a nearby hotel that was being used to house all the CDC and military staff. A flight to Sacramento had been arranged for the next morning. My parents had retired to a large house about an hour south of Lake Tahoe. It was beautiful with orchards and a creek running through the property. I couldn't wait to get there.

Once in the hotel, Ollie pulled his six-pack of Boddingtons out of his bag and popped one open.

"Brought those with you from the car?" I asked.

"You're damn right I did." He smiled then took a swig and groaned loudly.

I called my mom to give her the flight details and let Lily out of her carrier to roam around. While Ollie called his mom back, I took a long shower, enjoying the warm water on my skin. The shower door opened, and I turned around. Ollie walked in, naked and beautiful. I couldn't keep my eyes off him as he stepped forward and wrapped his arms around me. Without a word, he kissed my neck and face. I ran my hands down his back and wrapped one leg around him, pushing myself into him. He groaned and lifted me up so I could wrap the other leg around his waist. We were both worked up and didn't want to wait. He entered me and thrust gently. The feeling was pure ecstasy, but soon I wanted more, and it seemed like he was touching me more gently than before. Maybe he thought he should because of the baby.

I tried to urge him on. "Harder," I whispered into his ear. He immediately picked up the pace. Within seconds, I was thrown over the edge, and he soon followed. We were both exhausted and fell into bed completely naked.

He placed his hand on my stomach and kissed my shoulder. "I can't believe there's a baby in there. Our baby."

"Me neither. Just a month ago, I didn't even know you."

During that time when people were dying and violence was the norm, the thought of new life was encouraging. I knew it would be another roller-coaster ride, and I was strapped in, already enjoying the rush. For once, I wasn't focusing on the possibility of getting crushed. I was just there in the moment.

Ollie turned out the light, and we drifted off to sleep. It was the first time in months we could sleep without one ear open to the dangers beyond.

Chapter 31
March 31st

The next morning, we tidied the room, made the bed, and packed our bags. I checked my face, and the swelling under my eye had gone down some, but the apple of my cheek bore a nice purplish-blue bruise. I sighed, knowing it would upset my mom.

Ollie's parents had booked the first flight into Sacramento arriving the next morning, anxious to see their son. Ollie brushed his teeth while I played with Zeke. I hopped on and off the bed while he chased me, barking happily. He clamped down on my pants leg, trying to pull me off the bed by tugging and growling like the dangerous animal he was not. I was lying on the bed, laughing and telling Zeke he wasn't so tough, when I noticed Ollie watching us with his toothbrush hanging out of the side of his mouth. I couldn't read his expression.

"Hi," I said tentatively. He was looking at me so seriously that I was instantly worried. "What is it?" I rolled onto my stomach to get a better look at him.

He stared at me. "I love you."

And there they were, the words I'd waited my whole life to hear from a man I loved. "I love you too."

We both smiled, and he walked toward me while I jumped up. On my knees, I met him halfway. He pulled the toothbrush from his mouth and kissed me quickly.

I was a firm believer that whenever one saw something beautiful or felt something strongly, the first time was always the best. One could see it or feel it over and over again, but it would never fully live up to that first time. I kept expecting a diminished feeling for Ollie to hit me, but it hadn't. My love for Ollie was instinct. It was something I felt but also something I knew—I felt a natural pull every time I was near him.

At ten o'clock sharp, a man who introduced himself simply as Shane came in a military Jeep to take us to the airport. A second Jeep pulled up behind Shane, and Debbie hopped out. She was smiling and out of breath as she walked toward us. "I'm glad I caught you before you left."

"Is everything all right?" Ollie asked.

"Yes. Everything is great. I have some exciting news that I wanted to share with you. We've been working throughout the night. After we understood the placental properties of the virus, we began attacking the problem from an entirely different angle. The results we've produced in this short amount of time are really promising. I won't bore you with all the details, but I think we are on our way to creating a vaccine. It would not be a cure, so we can't treat already-infected patients, but if our theories prove correct, we might be able to vaccinate the uninfected and stop the spread."

"Oh my god, that's so great! Thanks for letting us know. How long until you know for sure?" I asked.

"At least a few months. Once we have a working vaccine, it'll need to be tested more thoroughly before it can be distributed to the masses. We're still in the very early stages, but we're optimistic."

Shane cleared his throat and looked at his watch.

"I'll let you guys get going. Have a safe flight, and I'll try to keep you updated."

We waved as she ran back to her Jeep. Ollie and I hugged each other. We'd both seen firsthand what the virus could do, but I had mixed emotions. I was overjoyed that we were on the way to beating the virus, but my thoughts also turned to all the people the vaccine would be too late to help.

We piled our bags into the back of the Jeep and hopped in. I held Lily's carrier on my lap. Zeke must have sensed that Ollie was there to stay because he camped out on Ollie's lap for a change. At the deserted airport, we were escorted to the terminal then led down the jetway onto a mid-sized plane. At the entrance, Shane said, "Goodbye and good luck."

There were only three other people on the plane, so we could sit anywhere we wanted. We chose first class, but I wasn't used to the huge comfy seats with more legroom than I would ever need. Ollie groaned as he stretched out. He was accustomed to it, I assumed. Zeke lounged in the seat beside us, and I put Lily's carrier on the ground near my feet.

The minute the engines started, Zeke sat up and whined at me, and Lily began meowing loudly. I grabbed Zeke's calming drops and forced both him and Lily to take a few. After a few minutes, he lay back down and rested his chin on his paws. I sat back and dozed for a while. An hour later, a flight attendant brought us drinks and snacks.

While we munched, I brought up the pregnancy. "Do you want to wait until your parents arrive so we can tell them together?"

Ollie thought for a moment. "Yeah, we'd better. If my mom thought she was second to know, she'd throw a fit." He smirked.

"We'll wait, then."

"They're going to want to know what our plan is, where we'll live, where we'll work, all that. What do you think?"

I shook my head. "I don't know. I honestly hadn't even considered this as a possibility at this point in my life."

"Look, I know all this came out of nowhere for us." He paused. "Do you not want to have the baby?"

Stunned, I looked back at him then realized he was worried about making the same mistake he'd made with Dana. "No! Of course I want to have the baby. I just don't have any kind of plan for a baby in my head. I stopped thinking about this area of my life a while ago. I feel... unprepared."

"So let's take this one step at a time. Where do you want to live?"

I looked at my lap and paused. Up until recently, I'd thought I would live in New York for the foreseeable future. *Since that isn't an option right now, where do I want to live?* With the baby coming, California or London would be ideal, so we could be close to family. I came to a decision. "I want to have the baby in California, near my family. My parents aren't going to have any other grandkids. I know they are going to want to be a part of it. What do you want?"

He nodded. "Well, I'm sure my parents want to be around for it too. But I understand what you're saying. My parents can come and visit as much as they want. And once the baby is old enough, we can take trips to London to see the rest of my family. I want to be with you, wherever that is."

"Are you sure? Is your mom going to be mad about that?"

"I don't think my mom can be mad about anything right now. She's just happy I'm alive, and once she hears the news, she'll be overjoyed. Don't worry about it. They have enough money and time on their hands to visit often. My dad and I can work from anywhere. I'll convince him to go forward with my charity proposal. We can start by setting up one location in California, and we'll go from there. The only part of working there that I disliked was going into an office dressed in a suit every day. This solves both those problems."

"If you say so." I smirked. "I'll let you tell them, then."

"Oh great, thanks," he replied. "Well, that was the biggest decision we had to make. Is there anything else we need to figure out now?"

I'd been concerned that he would want to live in London. Without that worry, I felt a huge relief and figured everything else could be worked out along the way. "No. I think that's enough for today." I leaned over to kiss him.

I took out my digital camera and started scrolling through the images. Stopping at the photos of the girls, I ran my fingers over their tiny smiling faces. I felt a beautiful sadness tug at my heart as a tear slid down my cheek.

Ollie squeezed my hand, and I looked up at him. "What if the vaccine works and they stop the virus?" he asked quietly. "At some point, they'll get the rest of the country up and running again. Would you want to go back to New York?"

I furrowed my brow and glanced down. "I don't know. I'm not sure if it's the right place for me anymore."

Do I want to go back? It was a hard question to ask myself because that apartment and that city had both given and taken so much. I'd learned who I was in that place, but it had also broken me, turning me into someone I never wanted to be again. I'd allowed all the things that kept darting from my grasp to define me. That apartment was a shrine to the person I used to be. It was both a prison and a sanctuary.

I thought back on my time with the girls and with Ollie and Zeke in that apartment. It was riddled with both good times and bad. I'd been waiting for my life to begin there, and it did even as the world crumbled around me.

I kept coming back to my conversations with Julia, the ones where we bared our souls and admitted our insecurities and fears. I knew she would have been happy for what I had gained and who I'd become. I'd learned to trust my instincts and go after what I wanted without hesitating. Most importantly, I wasn't afraid to be honest with myself anymore. It had taken a horrible catastrophe to get me there, but I had become who I'd always hoped to be, never wishing, never wanting, and never waiting.

Acknowledgments

Writing this book has been an amazing adventure born from a crazy dream during a snowstorm. It never would have materialized if not for my best friend, Debbie Kriger, saying, "You have to write this!" Thank you for your unrelenting support, for reading my book chapter by chapter, and for giving feedback every step of the way. You've changed the course of this story so many times with your helpful notes and suggestions. Quite honestly, this book wouldn't exist without you. You have made my life better in infinite ways, and I'm thankful every day that our dogs brought us together.

To my mom, you've shown me how to be a strong, confident woman. You have always believed in me, even when I didn't believe in myself. And I guess now I have to concede the point: You were right. I am a writer. To my dad, for being the best, most positive male role model, for teaching me to enjoy the outdoors, and for giving me the skills I'd need to survive an actual apocalypse. You've both supported all my wild ideas over the years, and it's been the one thing that has pushed me out of my box and helped me find my happiness.

I am eternally grateful to Stephanie Durso Mullin, who began writing her debut novel soon after I did. Sitting across from you at coffee shops, each tapping away on our laptops and sharing ideas, sentences, words, and dreams, has been one of the highlights of this process. Your feedback on every detail of my book has made me a better writer. Thank you for listening to me cry over every setback and celebrating each win with me. I couldn't ask for a better writing partner.

To my agent, Lisa Grubka, thank you for taking a chance on me and for your tireless edits. I've learned so much about the industry and writing from all your helpful advice.

To Jessica Battaglia, my childhood friend-turned-biochemist, when I messaged you asking to create a virus with very specific properties, your response was, "Ooh, interesting!" I knew I could count on you to help and to support my endeavors as you have throughout my life. Thank you so much for taking the time to research and create an amazing virus for me. It became a jumping-off point to build my pandemic setting. For that and so many other reasons, I am grateful for your friendship.

To everyone at Red Adept Publishing who have helped me every step of the way, thank you for your advice and encouragement. Special thanks to Sara Gardiner and Kate Birdsall, my amazing editors. Your notes and changes were more helpful than you'll ever know. I am so thankful for your patience and steadfast efforts. To Lynn McNamee, thank you for giving my book a home and supporting my work.

To the Murray Dog Park crew, you know who you are, thank you for always having my back, for reading very early versions, for pushing me to keep going, and for being the best support system I could have ever asked for. Thank you for being awesome dog parents who've helped me become one myself. Thank you most of all for being my tribe.

And finally, to my beloved Zeke. You've changed my life in so many ways. You taught me how to love unconditionally and brought so many amazing people into my life just because no one could resist you. I am thankful every day that you came into my life. I miss you every day, buddy.

About the Author

Nicole Mabry spends her days at NBCUniversal as the Senior Manager of Photography Post Production. Her nights are reserved for writing novels. At the age of seven, she read The Boxcar Children, sparking a passion for reading and writing early on. Nicole grew up in the Bay Area in Northern California and went to college at UCLA for Art History. During a vacation, she fell in love with New York City and has lived in Queens for the past sixteen years. On weekends, you can find her with a camera in hand and her dog, Jackson, by her side. Nicole is an animal lover and horror movie junkie.

Read more at www.nicolemabry.net.

About the Publisher

Dear Reader,

We hope you enjoyed this book. Please consider leaving a review on your favorite book site.

Visit https://RedAdeptPublishing.com to see our entire catalogue.

Don't forget to subscribe to our monthly newsletter to be notified of future releases and special sales.